MARIA FRANKLAND

The Man Behind Closed Doors

The Other Side of Domestic Bliss

AUTONOMY
PRESS

*This book is dedicated to those men and women
who have suffered at the hands of a partner
who is supposed to have loved and cherished them.*

*To join Maria Frankland's 'keep in touch' list,
and receive a free collection of short stories,
visit www.autonomypress.co.uk*

Prologue

Dogs are good at keeping secrets. That's because they can't talk. I used to get told off for talking all the time. Now I'm told off for not talking. People keep asking questions. About what I saw. What I heard. How I am feeling. I don't want to talk anymore. I wish they would all leave me alone.

The girls at school have stopped trying to play with me and be my friend. That's because I don't have my mummy and daddy. I'm different from them. But I have my dog. She's my best friend. I can talk to her just by thinking things, so I am able to tell her everything.

Chapter One

H is fingers probe her wrist and he gulps bile, retching with the stench of blood hanging in the heat of the June night. "My wife's been stabbed!" Paul slithers down the front of the cooker next to where Michelle is slumped on the tiled floor, amidst blood-splattered cupboards.

"In the chest. I don't know." He's gabbling into his phone. "Michelle Jackson. Yes, there's a pulse. No bubbles from her mouth. The knife's stuck." Reaching up, Paul drags a towel from the worktop, bringing a shower of cutlery down. He wraps the towel around the impaled knife, his chest thumping. She goes limp. He feels for a pulse again, his blood-soaked hands smearing against her wrist. "Paul Jackson. Summerfield Holiday Park, Filey. I don't know!" He hauls himself back up and glances out of the window. "There's a silver Ford Focus outside."

He strokes the hand on which Michelle wears her rings, then lets it flop back to the floor. *This isn't happening.* He glances back at the lounge. "No, nothing's been taken … Emily, stay in there. Close the door. Daddy'll be there soon." Avoiding the seeping blood, he rises and lurches towards Emily's bedroom door along the hallway, broken glass crunching under his feet. "Yes, I'm still here. It's my little girl. Six years old. No, I don't know what she's seen."

"Daddy!"

"I'll be there in a minute."

Paul peers around Emily's door. He decides not to go in, covered in her mother's blood. The room is in semi-darkness so hopefully she can't see it. She peers at him above the pillow she is clutching to her chest. "It's alright, it's going to be alright, Daddy's here. Mummy's going to be fine. The ambulance people will be here any minute. Emily?"

She says nothing. Probably in shock.

He wants to go to her, comfort her but to cover her in blood isn't the best course of action. "What happened?" He tries to disguise the urgency in his voice towards his daughter. "Tell me."

She is trembling. He should go back to the kitchen but can't bear to. What if Michelle has died? She didn't look good. No, he's best staying with Emily. He can pretend for a moment that his wife isn't half dead a few feet away.

"Come here girl." Carla, their Spaniel, slinks from under the bed and cowers at Paul's feet. "They're coming!" He pulls back the hallway curtain in response to the shrieking sirens, before darting back to his wife. Michelle has slid further to the floor, her hair fanned around her. He kneels at her side.

"Mr Jackson?" Within moments, two paramedics stand at the cottage doorway into the kitchen. "If you could move aside for us please." They approach Michelle and squat either side of her. "Mrs Jackson, I'm Joel, a paramedic for the ambulance service, and this is my colleague, Marvin. We're here to help you. Can you hear me?" His gaze flicks from Michelle's ashen face to Paul's. "What's happened here?"

"I found her." His own voice sounds alien to him. "Emily, stay in your room." He notices the door twitching along the hallway. "I'll be back in a minute." The red-haired paramedic pulls items from his bag and cuts Michelle's blouse open with scissors.

2

"*You found her?*"

"I don't know what happened, we had a row, I left her to calm down, and then I came back … this is how I found her!"

Paul leans against the door, watching as they inspect the protruding knife. Becoming faint, he crouches against the wall. He has never seen as much blood in his life. The voices of people gathering outside swim around him.

"We need to stem this bleeding then we can move her." Marvin tugs a radio from his belt and Paul notices how freckly his face is. "I'll let control know what we're dealing with. This should be left in situ." Marvin points to the knife.

Paul follows Joel's diverted glance back to the door where two police officers now stand, one male, one female. "Mr Jackson?" The man crosses the threshold towards where Paul slumps. "I'm DC Calvert and this is my colleague, PC Bradshaw". The weight of his hand rests on Paul's shoulder. "I need to take a few details from you."

"I need to be with Michelle. How can I leave her after what…"?

"Let the paramedics do their job. She's in good hands." He frowns at one of them. "Remember this is a crime scene." He gestures towards the medical equipment littered around them. "Make sure the weapon is bagged, as soon as you're able to."

Calvert glances towards the door where another police officer has appeared out of the darkness outside. "Put the cordon round," he commands of his colleague.

"Sir."

"And when you've done that," Calvert continues. "Don't touch anything. I want you to radio through. We need the forensics down here. Tell them we're dealing with an aggravated assault with a weapon."

"Sir."

"My daughter!" Paul gestures towards the bedroom. "She's in there.

I can't leave her – she's only six." He looks in turn at them all. "She was asleep." He's aware of their possible judgements of him, yet their expressions are not giving anything away. "I should never have left her!"

"PC Bradshaw will take care of your daughter whilst we talk to you." Calvert nods to his colleague.

"What's her name?"

Paul is marginally reassured at the voice of the female officer with a blonde ponytail poking out from under her hat. "Emily." Paul sees her now, she's opened her bedroom door and stands, shivering in her pyjamas. He wants to scoop her up and make it all better. "Will it take long … your questions, I mean? I need to see to my daughter and go to the hospital with my wife." The female police officer walks towards Emily and Paul feels anxiety rising in him like vomit.

Calvert turns to him. "An officer will go with your wife. I'm going to read you your rights and then we'll head to the station. We can record your interview and then depending on the outcome of that, we'll have you straight to the hospital. I'll drive you myself."

"Are you arresting me?"

"Yes. Paul Jackson, I'm arresting you on suspicion of attempted murder. You do not have to say anything, but it may harm your defence if you do not mention when questioned, something which you may later rely on in court." His voice is robotic. This is something he's clearly said countless times before. "Anything you do say may be given in evidence. Can I have your mobile phone please?" His tone becomes more *conversational.* "You'll get it back after the investigation has been conducted."

"Attempted murder? But…" Paul's attention is averted to the paramedics as they manoeuvre Michelle from the floor to the stretcher. He cannot tear his gaze from her face, and he wonders if he will ever see her again.

Chapter Two

P aul grips the table, his knuckles whitening.

"The data is Monday, June the eleventh, and the time is twelve twenty am. My name is DC Joseph Calvert, interviewing officer and I am conducting this interview with my colleague DC Alan Whitaker. For the benefit of the tape can you both confirm your presence?" He nods to Paul first.

"Paul Alan Jackson." This is surreal. Paul can't believe where he is. Any moment he will wake up to find Emily and his dog bounding into the bedroom and he will be telling Michelle about the awful dream he's had.

Calvert nods to his colleague.

"DC Alan Whittaker."

"DC Whittaker will be taking notes and assisting with the interview." Calvert turns towards Paul. "Can you confirm you do not wish to have a solicitor present?"

"No, I don't." Paul clears his throat. "I want to get this over with and be with my wife." Glancing around the confining green walls, he ignores the nagging voice that says of course *you need a solicitor, you idiot.* His work colleague, John, who *is* a solicitor, is going to kill him. Part of him has decided he doesn't want anyone to know of his predicament; this is coupled with the certainty that he can sort it out himself.

"I thought Mummy was coming. When will she be here?"

He followed Emily's gaze towards the path they had reached the beach by. Families basked contentedly behind windbreakers, chatting, sharing a picnic or having a snooze. Others played cricket or flew a kite. His was the only 'family' with no woman present. He ached to his core yet, couldn't be sure if it was Michelle he was missing or the idea of her.

"She might come soon." Paul reached forward and tickled Emily's ribs. "Come on. Race you down to the water. I'm off to paddle."

Another hour passed. The sandwiches were eaten. The tea and squash were drunk. They gathered up their beach gear and hauled themselves up the steep slope, back towards the holiday park. "Carry me Daddy."

"You must be joking. I've got all this to carry!" Paul then paused at the ice cream van to give in to Emily's next lot of pleading. He noticed his wife, sitting alone, nursing a glass of wine in the beer garden at the end of the road in which they were staying. Something inside him sank when he saw the expression on her face.

"Mummy!" Emily shot towards her, throwing herself beside her mother on the bench. "You should see my sandcastle. Daddy's taken a picture."

Paul dropped their stuff at the side of the table and glanced around the empty beer garden. "Where were you?" He hoped he was keeping the irritation out of his voice. "I thought you were going to join us?"

"Sounds like you've been fine without me." She fastened her dark hair into a bun.

Paul detected an antagonistic undercurrent in her voice, however, he couldn't read the expression in her eyes as she was wearing sunglasses. "Are you going to buy me and Emily a drink? I don't think I'll have enough money on me." Resentment stole over him. He was *always* having to ask her for money. This had been fine in the beginning. Both their salaries were paid into a joint account. Michelle was frugal, sensible and things got paid on time. Paul had always been renowned for being useless where finances were concerned. At first, he'd thought it was quite romantic to have all their resources pooled. But he'd soon got fed up when she questioned every penny he spent. She'd gone ballistic when he had suggested opening a solo account for his salary to be paid into. It wasn't worth the hassle of the arguments so he went along with her demands. *Anything for a quiet life.*

"You can go to the bar then. I'll have another one." She smiled at her daughter's ice-cream stained face as she rummaged in her bag and pulled out a tissue. "Look at the state of you!"

"How many have you had Michelle?" This was a dangerous question, he knew that. Once she started drinking, she couldn't stop. He stared at her blue painted toenails as he waited for an answer.

"Only the one." She adjusted the parasol over them all. "Another won't hurt. Stop nagging at me, will you!"

Paul rose from the table and wandered over the grass, vowing to buy her a *small* wine, mixed with plenty of ice and soda water.

It was relatively quiet apart from the sound of distant seagulls. "What are we going to do for the rest of the day?" Paul asked as they sipped their drinks. "We could have a drive out somewhere."

"Can't be bothered." Michelle screwed her mouth up. "I'm OK here. Pack it in Em."

Paul glanced towards Emily who was blowing bubbles into her drink using her straw. "But we're supposed to be on holiday. Emily's bored. We can't stay here all day." He tried to keep his voice steady but was inwardly seething. *Couldn't they do anything without her getting sozzled? When was she going to put Emily first?*

"Why not?" She shrugged then added a flourish of her arm. We can do what we want. Like you said, we're on holiday." Her voice was cheery. "I'll have some of that sun cream."

9

He watched as she slathered it onto her freckled shoulders before gesturing to him to rub it in on the back of her neck. "Can you give me some more money then?" This could go either way. She would be glad to be rid of them or might start a row. "We'll get out of your hair for a couple more hours." He tapped Carla's head. "Carla will keep you company, won't you girl?"

"Where are you off to?" Michelle's bracelets jangled as she reached into her bag.

"To the amusements." He smiled as Emily's head jerked up in excitement. "We'll pick something up on the way back. Do you fancy a steak later? After we've put Emily to bed?"

"Could do, I suppose." She slid the bank card across the table. "In fact, that sounds lovely." She smiled at the bar man as he removed her old glass from the table.

"I don't know the PIN." He took his wallet from his pocket and inserted the card. "You changed it, *remember?*"

"Two, three, zero, nine. Our wedding day." She smiled. "You won't be ages, will you?" Her eyes narrowed and her smile vanished.

"I'll try not to be." He jumped to his feet, nearly hitting his head on the parasol and laughing as the dog jumped up too.

"You can't come Carla." Emily patted her head. "Dogs aren't allowed on rides. You stay with Mummy."

"Well don't leave me on my own all day." Michelle drained her glass.

Paul hoped she would not drink much more as he kissed the top of her head.

You're choosing to be left on your own so stop giving me grief, he wanted to say but thought better of it. Inside himself, he swung between humour and irritation that she had the cheek to demand of them not to be long. Surely she didn't expect them to stop there and watch her get slaughtered.

Emily fiddled with the radio stations as they approached the sea front. "Why didn't Mummy want to come?"

"She's a bit tired. We can still enjoy ourselves, can't we?"

"I wish Mummy was like Imogen's mummy."

"Don't say that Emily. You only ever have one mum." Michelle would go mad if Emily ever said anything like that in front of her. "Blimey it's packed. It's going to take ages to park."

Paul tried not to notice couples and families everywhere he looked. Outwardly they may have appeared happy and united but who knew what went on behind the scenes? To outside eyes, he and Michelle probably looked like a perfectly happy couple too.

"Can we go on the water chute, Daddy?" They watched as the logs sprayed sparkling water into the afternoon sunshine. Emily grabbed his hand, attempting to steer him in the required direction.

"Go on then," he grinned, coercing himself to cheer up as he clasped her hand. After the ride, they continued to wander around. Paul tried to ignore the heavy dragging in his belly. He supposed it was better than the angry knives that often lived inside him. Michelle's drinking and mood swings were gnawing away at their family. To be parted from her made him anxious, yet he dreaded returning too.

He 'raced' on the bikes with Emily inside an amusement arcade whilst the flashing lights, disco music and whoops of enjoyment tried to press his mood into a sunnier one. But he could not shake Michelle from his thoughts. Would she still be in a decent mood? How much would she have had to drink? He had been looking forward yet dreading this holiday in equal measures. It was a chance to relax but an opportunity for her to drink more.

He and Emily traipsed around the supermarket, slinging in steak, potatoes and pepper sauce. In the wine and beers aisle, he paused, but thought better of buying any. It had only been a few days since she had last 'lost it' with him.

Scanning the faces of other shoppers, he yearned for their triviality as they went about their lives. To return home and flop in front of the TV, or go for a stroll. Not having to justify every move or respond to jealous allegations.

Calvert leans forward across the table whilst his colleague starts a new sheet of interview paper. "When you returned to your holiday cottage," he asks, "had your wife returned by then?"

"Yes. It was late. I'd stopped off with Emily on the way back as she needed some tea and I knew it would be a while before her mother and I would be eating. At first I thought Michelle was still out but then I realised she was sleeping."

"In the bedroom?"

"Yes."

"And at what time was this? Your return to the cottage?"

"Around eighty thirty pm." Paul glances up at the clock. It's only a few hours ago yet it's like an eternity.

Calvert runs his finger down a sheet of paper. "You arrived back two hours and twenty minutes before you made the three nines call to the police?"

"Yes, that sounds about right." Paul is too exhausted to work this out clearly. He must stay focused. He hopes he's saying the right things.

"What happened in that time? The two hours and twenty minutes."

Paul hesitates. "Michelle was groggy and grumpy; she always is when she's had a drink earlier in the day."

"How do you know this?"

What a stupid question. "I've been with her for ten years. I know when she's in a bad mood. She shouted at me for not waking her earlier."

"Then what happened?"

"At her request, we sent Emily to bed and I was chopping salad up for dinner." Paul rubs at his eyes. They are burning with exhaustion.

"In the kitchen?"

Another stupid question. What planet is this man on? Perhaps I should tell him I usually chop salad next to the toilet. "Yes. Michelle came through after she had woken up. She was upset I had been out with Emily for the day *and* the evening."

"What do you mean, upset? How did you know?"

"She was complaining she was sick of always being on her own and she thought I didn't love her anymore."

"What exactly did she say?" Calvert asks.

"I'm not sure … Something like *I can't believe you've left me all day, like you do at home, we're supposed to be on holiday.* Then she said I didn't love her. "

"And is she right in this fear?"

"What fear?" Paul wonders what he's on about. *Has he listened to a word of what he's said?*

"That you don't love her?"

"No of course not, we were only married last September. We're having problems, granted, but it doesn't mean I don't love her."

"Quite." Calvert's face relaxes into a ghost of a smile. "Do you 'leave' her on her own often?"

Paul isn't sure what he's driving at and wonders for a minute if he should have contacted John. He'll ring him in the morning if things aren't resolved. "Not at all, I told you how it was today. We weren't leaving her out, she had a choice."

"Did you remind her of this?"

"I didn't have the chance. Like I said, she was in a foul mood, and she had started throwing things at me." Paul stares at the table, fixated on his clasped hands. He hates admitting to all this.

"Like what?"

"Silly things." He hopes his face isn't as red as it feels. What a man he must sound like. That's if they believe him. "The salt pot, a shoe, a can of hairspray."

"And did you retaliate?"

"No, I was trying to calm her down. Emily was fast asleep. I'd checked on her and didn't want her woken up by us rowing." This is hard to admit to. Paul feels like more of a failure.

"Are these rows a regular thing?"

"It's up and down." Paul sighs. No one could possibly understand the unpredictability of his situation. Anything could set her off.

"So, you had objects raining across the kitchen at you. What did you do?"

"Left the chopping. Tried to get away from her. But then she grabbed the knife."

"And?"

"She held it towards her chest saying if I didn't love her, she may as well not be here anymore. I've heard it millions of times. I never thought she meant it!" As he says the words, Paul senses how far-fetched the whole thing must sound. Not to mention how insane his wife comes across. He imagines she's been doing a good performance in the hospital if she's come around. Blaming him. Making him out to be some kind of wife beater. He hates her right now.

"And all this was going on with your little daughter in the property?"

"She was asleep."

"What happened next?"

"I told her I was off for a walk. Give her chance to calm down."

"You left your daughter with her in that frame of mind?"

"Michelle loves Emily." Paul throws his hands upwards as he speaks. "And like I said, she was fast asleep. And I thought she'd stay that way if I took myself out of the picture for a bit."

"Where did you go?"

"I had a pint in the pub we'd been in earlier."

"And what time was this?" Calvert looks at his watch.

"I don't know. Around ten pm?" God, what he'd give to be back there. He should have carried on drinking. Any other bloke would have done. What a bloody idiot he's been. He should have stayed away.

"Can anyone confirm this? Who did you speak to?"

"Just the bar staff."

"Right, can you give a description?"

"A man and a woman. I don't know … the man was about my age, maybe a bit younger, I can't remember to be honest, I didn't take much notice. The woman had red hair."

"Right, she shouldn't be too hard to track down. Anyone else?"

"No. It was empty, like it had been when we were in earlier. There were loads of people sat outside though. Another man asked me about the racing results, but I can't remember what he looked like." *Why am I having to recall this?* The banality hits Paul. This is not important compared to what is going on at the hospital. "I need to know how Michelle is doing. Will this take much…" He jumps in response to an abrupt knock followed by a PC peering around the side of the interview room door.

"DC Calvert, there's a telephone call for you. I think it's important."

"Is it about Michelle?" Paul senses it is, by the way the constable is avoiding his eye. "I need to know. Please tell me."

"It *is* the hospital," the constable looks at him. "But they haven't told me anything."

"I, DC Calvert am leaving the room for a few moments. Interview paused at twelve fifty five am." Calvert is on his feet and presses a button on the recorder before brushing past his colleague. "I'll be right back when I've found out what's going on."

It is the longest five minutes Paul has experienced. Ignoring the presence of the other police officer, he sits motionless, staring at the graffiti carved into the table, willing her to be alright. He could never have imagined things would escalate to this.

"Paul," Calvert's voice slices into his thoughts. "I'm afraid it's not good news. Michelle is in theatre."

"And?" Paul's voice croaks. *She can't be dead. She can't be!* He closes his eyes as though he might shut out the words he's unable to hear. "She's still alive, isn't she?"

"Yes."

Paul drops his head into his hands. "I thought you were going to say…"

He slips back into the chair opposite him. "She's lost a lot of blood. They're transfusing her but the internal injury is apparently causing problems. It sounds like you need to be prepared for the worst."

"Oh my God!" Paul sits bolt upright. If he's at her side, he might be able to make a difference. She's the only one who can change the situation he's in. She can't die. "I need to be there!"

"Paul," Calvert says, contempt apparent in his face. "You're under arrest. I'm afraid you're going nowhere."

"I didn't do anything. I didn't mean for this to happen." He wipes away his torrent of tears with the back of his hand. "I would never have hurt her. Never."

There's not a hint of emotion in Calvert's face as he says, "are you really sure you don't want a solicitor?

Chapter Three

Paul heaves himself into a seated position on the thin mattress as the officer places a tray of 'breakfast' beside him. Every part of him aches from thirty six hours in this police station. The aroma of cheap margarine makes his insides churn. The nausea combined with exhaustion is like a hangover.

"Is there any news on my wife?" Paul is gratified for the respite that fitful sleep has provided for a couple of hours, but reality thunders back down on him. He struggles to assemble his jumbled thoughts. *How the hell has all this happened?*

"Not yet. You'll be the first to know if we hear anything." The words ricochet around the concrete walls of the cell like a bullet.

"What about my daughter? Within his blue paper suit, the heat is already stifling. "When can I leave?" He needs to get to them both. Fast.

"Concentrate on your breakfast. You should try and eat something." The officer walks towards the door, keys jangling. "We'll be loading the court van shortly. You'll know more soon."

As the door clangs, an image of Michelle, bleeding on the floor, swims into his mind. She had appeared close to death, though he senses she *is* still alive. He's been charged with attempted murder.

All hope of making sure Emily is alright and him getting to Michelle's bedside is gone. He's so exhausted he can barely think straight. Every hour he has spent in custody has felt like a day. They think he's hurt her. He's been going through what happened that day, that night, in his mind but it's all become a blur. From the time of getting back to the holiday cottage with Emily, he can't recall anything clearly and is worried that his mind is playing tricks somehow.

One day, they will reflect on their 'holiday' with a judder, but they will put it behind them. Today everything will be alright. He will make sure it is.

"We've got a few minutes before you're on." Paul could weep with relief as his colleague, John Gibbs, a criminal law solicitor, appears in the cell below the court. "We need to talk. Quickly." He rests a hand on Paul's shoulder. "You're not on your own out there mate; I've brought Alana with me. Your friend is here too. Nick, is it? And your brother. Your mother-in law has been and gone. She has your daughter, well, not here obviously, she's left her in school."

"Thank God. They apparently put her with foster parents to start with on the first night." Paul closes his eyes. "But you shouldn't have brought Alana."

John sits beside Paul. "She wouldn't let me abandon her at the office. She hasn't stopped talking about you." A smile tugs at the corners of his mouth. "Here, I've brought you some clothes to wear. Your mother-in-law, Susan, is it, brought them on her way back to the hospital."

"Do you know if Emily's alright?" Paul accepts the small bundle of clothing, glad he's going to be able to discard the police station 'clothes.'

"I think so. Susan didn't say. But she's her grandma. She'll be taking good care of her. She's mainly concerned as to whether Michelle is going to pull through."

"What a fucking mess!" Paul swings his body around to face John.

"You must know I didn't do it." He can't control himself. His shoulders shake as he breaks into fresh sobs. John's is the first 'friendly' face he has seen since being brought in two nights earlier. "I can't believe this is happening!"

"We're going to get you out of here." John squeezes Paul's shoulder. "Trust me."

"You'll be able to sort bail?" He can't believe he's crying again. Like that's going to change anything. "With a charge like this?"

"I'll do all I can." John thrusts a hanky into Paul's hand. "You know I will."

"I'm glad they were able to contact you. None of it seems real."

"I know. Whatever's happened. You should have called me straightaway. I've been going through your interview transcript and there's a few holes in it. We'll sort it though."

"What if she dies? Oh my God!" It's as though actuality keeps batting him around the head. "What an utter nightmare!" He drops his head into his hands. "It should never have happened! Why the hell did it have to happen?"

"I know. I know Paul."

"I need to see Emily!" Paul sits upright. "What she must be going through!"

"One thing at a time. She's alright, like I said."

"I *need* to know how Michelle's doing. Nobody's telling me a thing! She could be dead for all I know! *She could be dead!*"

"Like I said. Bail first." John speaks in a firm voice, his hand not leaving Paul's shoulder the whole time. "Then we'll contact the hospital. I know it's easier said than done but you *must* stay calm. You would have heard if there'd been any change."

"I can't stand it," Paul's head is still burrowed in his hands.

"Come on, mate." John claps his back as he hauls himself up. "For now, let's concentrate on getting you bail."

Paul's eyes link with Alana's as he stands in the dock. She stares at him for a few seconds than looks away. She's impeccably turned out, as usual, making Paul more aware of his own dishevelment. Nick sits beside her, and nods towards him. David, his brother, offers a weak smile which is difficult to read.

"For the benefit of the court, please state your full name." The courtroom collapses into a hush. Sunlight glitters through the ornate roof, reminding Paul of normality still progressing beyond these walls.

"Paul Alan Jackson." His face flames beneath the glare of the overhead lighting.

"Your address?" The eyes of the entire courtroom dart back and forth, as though watching a tennis match between Paul and the court clerk.

"Forty two Bracken Bank, Osbaldwick, York." His words quiver as they leave him.

"What is your occupation?"

"Legal Executive."

"Paul Alan Jackson," The clerk reads from a sheet. "You are charged that on Monday the eleventh of June, at Summerfield Holiday Park, in Filey, you attempted to murder your wife, Michelle Marie Jackson. The purpose of this hearing is not to enter a plea in relation to this matter, but to decide when and where this will take place. It is also an opportunity to process any application for bail."

"Is there an application for bail?" The voice of the magistrate conveys no emotion.

"Your honour, there is." John addresses the magistrate. "My name is John Gibbs from Brown, Gibbs and Jackson. I am acting today for Paul Jackson." He clears his throat. "I put before you the case for bail, based on the fact that Mr Jackson is of good, sound character, has an untarnished record and is unlikely to commit any act which might be construed as perverting the course of justice. He would be willing to reside at the aforementioned address, and to surrender his passport.

"I would have to contest that." A woman from the prosecution desk speaks.

"Go on."

"Mrs Jackson is currently in intensive care." Her voice sounds scratchy, as though she's a heavy smoker. "Given the severity of the situation and indeed the charge, Mr Jackson may try to pervert the course of justice by encouraging a change of story to protect his own interests."

Paul's heckles rise. *What does she know?*

"Whilst I accept what my colleague asserts about the defendant's unblemished record, the prosecution has decided, whilst this investigation proceeds, that to grant bail presents risk to Mrs Jackson, the couple's daughter and to the defendant himself."

"Give me a moment." The magistrate flicks through several papers before beckoning the lady from the prosecution desk towards him, then John. After seeing John 'in action' throughout their work, Paul thinks how surreal it is that he is now on his feet, defending *him.* He tries to decipher the words from his body language and facial expressions, but it is impossible. It seems like a personable exchange but are they going to let him return to Michelle and Emily? It is the longest 'moment' of his life. "I am inclined to agree with the concerns of the prosecution," the magistrate eventually announces, looking straight at Paul, whose head throbs. "I'm going to have to refuse bail. The risk of interference with potential witnesses is too great. And due to the seriousness of the charge, this matter will have to be referred to the crown court to adjourn the matter for a plea and trial preparation hearing."

"I'll pass it forward for mention." The court clerk looks towards the magistrate.

The magistrate looks at Paul whose legs are crumpling. "Paul

Jackson. You are to be remanded into custody of a category B establishment, until such time that your trial can be heard. Your solicitor will be made aware when the crown court have listed it." He then nods towards the guards.

"All rise," commands the clerk.

Chapter Four

The phone had flashed on the table. "Are you going to answer that?" Nick asked. "It's your 'stalker' again. I don't know how you cope mate."

There was no way Paul was taking the call in front of Nick. He would have a field day. "She'll ring again. She always does, if it's important anyway." He shuffled on the wooden bench, shifting his feet on the tacky carpet. All around them, glasses and conversation tinkled pleasantly, reminding him of a world he used to inhabit. Once, the aroma of steak which drifted from the pub kitchen would have tempted him. He might have enjoyed the luxury of lingering over another pint with Nick. He tried to think of how he could change the subject.

"I'd switch it off if I were you." Nick pushed the phone towards him.

"Nah, it's not worth it." He glanced up at the window. In the distance the town hall clock informed him he was half an hour late.

"Paul." Nick swigged his beer. "You've not been yourself for a while mate. Is everything alright? With your psycho wife, I mean?"

"I'm fine. Honest." Paul fiddled with a beer mat, knowing he needed to leave the pub and get his arse home. He should never have come. He wasn't exactly enjoying himself. "It's, you know, stuff."

"What do you mean, stuff?" Nick's eyes never left Paul's face. "Come on? How long have you known me? I'm not gonna go telling anyone,

23

am I? Out with it."

"Ah, you know. A few problems with Michelle. We'll work it out. We'll be fine." He drummed his fingertips against his glass, wishing he had kept his phone out of sight. He could handle it. So far, he had. He avoided Nick's eye. He felt like a right prat.

"You've only been married five minutes! What the hell's wrong?" He did the calculation on his hand. "Five months. You should be shagging each other's brains out! Perhaps you should have stayed as you were. Mind you, she was just as schitzo then, if you ask me. Although I *did* think being married might sort her out a bit."

"Anyway, change the bloody subject." Paul took a swig of his bitter. "Are you watching the footy tonight?"

"Once upon a time you'd have watched it with me."

"I know," Paul sighed, "but I'm a married man now aren't I?" He knew how feeble he sounded.

"*A married man.* So what! Jacqui's fine about me watching footy with a couple of pints. She's glad to be rid of me."

"I'll stay and watch it next time." Paul dropped his phone into his pocket and stood up. "I'd better be off."

"Stay and have another! Go on! It's been weeks since we've had a beer. I'll get them in again." Paul felt a stab of envy as he watched Nick tug a stuffed wallet from his top pocket. "Sod *her*. Be a man and show her who's boss!"

"I can't. Drag me here after work another time though." Paul forced a grin, wishing he could say this with true conviction. "And I'll remember to bring some cash next time."

"Do you know, I can't remember the last time we played golf," Nick continued. "It's about time I gave you another pasting! You're going to have to sort that bloody wife of yours."

"I know. I'll give you a bell." Paul drained the last of his pint.

"Paul. You know where I am. There's always a sofa at mine if she does your head in too much. I won't say anything, I promise."

"I know. Thanks mate. But it's all under control."

Letting out a laboured breath, he exchanged the cosy pub for the slap of the evening air. Normally, he welcomed this time of year. However, he felt as bleak as the winter nights he had hoped were being left behind.

It had not seemed possible, but things at home had gone downhill even more in the months since the wedding. There was no way he could discuss it with Nick or anyone else for that matter. He *could* handle it. But he was fed up. Nick was right. They'd not been married long at all.

Paul traipsed towards the bus shelter. A bus was due but he had no inclination to rush for it. Each day was like a lottery of possible scenarios that might await him. He ferreted around in his jacket for his wallet, from which the image of Michelle and Emily beamed at him.

"I'm home. Everyone alright?" Paul loaded joviality into his voice as he pushed the back door open into the kitchen. The heat of the house, combined with the scent of fresh laundry, blasted onto his face.

"Daddy!" Emily burst into the kitchen and launched herself at him. He wrapped his arms around her, briefly enjoying her warmth. Carla, their Spaniel, vaulted at him, from behind her.

"What a welcome!" He laughed.

"You decided to join us, did you?" Michelle, stood in the doorway, arms folded.

Paul searched her face, looking for a hint of something he could encourage. He lowered Emily to the floor. "I'm sorry I'm a little late. I had a quick pint after work." There was no point in denying it.

"A pint? Didn't you want to come home? I miss you all day, you know."

"Of course I did." He glanced at a painting Emily thrust in front of him. "Brilliant, ask Mummy to stick it on the fridge." He picked up a pile of letters from the kitchen table. "I'd missed a bus and I fancied a pint while I had a look at the paper. Michelle, why are you opening letters addressed to me?"

"What, on your own? You never go to the pub on your own." She ignored the question about the letters. "You weren't with a woman, were you?"

"Don't be daft. If you must know, I was with Nick." He stuffed a letter back into its envelope and picked up another one, not wanting to see her reaction. In the beginning she had liked Nick but over the last couple of years, she had grown jealous of their friendship. Of *any* of his friendships.

"Nick this. Nick that. You're supposed to be married to me, yet you leave me out *all* the time." Stamping towards the clothes airer, she yanked clothes from it. "Maybe *I'd* like to have been invited out for a drink."

"Go and play in your room." Ruffling Emily's hair, he sent her towards the door with a gentle push. "Take Carla with you."

Emily looked from her father to her mother. Her eyes emitted a look that caused Paul a pang of guilt. "Yes Daddy."

"You ought to move in with him and have done with it." Michelle folded a towel into quarters and slammed it onto the kitchen table. "It must have been prearranged. Couldn't you have checked with me first? My mum would have babysat."

"Give it a rest Michelle." Paul glanced up from his letter as he recalled the freedom Jacqui afforded Nick. "It was a drink; I shouldn't have to check with you. I'm a grown man."

"Where did you get your money from? I only gave you a fiver this morning."

"Nick bought me a pint." He replaced the letter beside the pile of laundry. "It's no big deal."

"It is when you don't roll in till this time." Her voice was acidic as she undid the catch on the clothes airer, allowing it to collapse with a crash to the wooden floor. "It's not fair you know. You swan in here when you want to. Em thinks the sun shines out of your backside. It's *me* looking after her whilst *you're* in the pub. We're supposed to be a family."

"I'd do *anything* not to row with you." Plunging his hands into his pockets, he started towards the door. He'd been hungry but his appetite had waned along with hopes of a normal evening.

"Do you know something? I don't believe you've been with Nick." She came towards him. "Show me your phone."

"For God's sake, Michelle. Why?"

"So I can check. Put my mind at rest."

"No, I won't. I don't look at your phone." He reached for the kitchen door handle. "If you don't trust me, it's your problem." She lunged at the pocket he was guarding with his other hand. She grasped his arm. Her nails bore into it. "Ow! You're hurting me!"

"Give me the phone!" Her nails dug further into his skin, forcing his hand away from his pocket, leaving the phone free to be plucked. Seemingly satisfied with her 'gain,' she retreated into the living room. Paul followed, rubbing his stinging arm.

"I don't know what you think you're going to find," he said. "You're wasting your time. I've nothing to hide. I can't believe you're acting like this."

Michelle said nothing as she propped herself against the fireplace and inspected the messages and calls. "I bet you've deleted what you don't want me to see anyway." After several minutes she tossed the phone towards him. "You've had seven missed calls!"

"Have I?" Trying to sound nonchalant, he sank onto a chair.

"You know you have. Don't play dumb!" She stepped towards him.

"I've been ringing all evening. Why didn't you answer?"

"It must have been on silent." He shrank back from her. "I was in a meeting earlier today and didn't switch it back."

"Swear on Emily's life that you don't want someone else."

"I'm telling the truth but don't ever ask me to swear on my daughter's life." He tried to keep the exasperation out of his voice.

Paul strode out of the lounge, his wife's elevated voice echoing through his mind. Glancing up the stairs, dismay pooled in his chest as his noticed Emily crouched on the landing, peering through the bannister.

Chapter Five

Paul leans heavily against the metal backrest. He is travelling backwards in the prison van, which increases his sense of disorientation. The stark metal container in which he is incarcerated makes him claustrophobic. The doctor once advised Michelle to breathe in through her nose and out through her mouth when affected by panic attacks. Recalling this advice, he tries it himself.

The sickly rumble in his belly suggests it must be around lunchtime. It is ages since he has eaten. He has refused all offerings at the police station. To accept food is like a resignation of his situation. He wonders if Emily is at school, carrying on with any semblance of normality. He recalls the last time he picked her up.

"Daddy!" Emily had smiled at Paul. "Why're you here?"

"I've left work early." He was always grateful for the chance to meet her from school.

"Shall we finish the decorating tomorrow?" Paul hooked his arm around Michelle as they headed towards the gates. "Since I'm not working, we should do something."

"Don't you worry," she winked at him as she tightened her grip on Carla's lead. "We will definitely 'do' something. I have plans for you. But I want us to finish the lounge first."

"Can I help Mummy?"

"Course you can. You can be the tidier-upper." Michelle ruffled Emily's hair.

"I guess three of us will be faster." Paul drew Michelle closer as they walked towards home. He squeezed Emily's hand. "Well this is nice." He hoped things stayed this way. "We might be able to squeeze in a film and a takeaway if we're a three-man team."

"Silly Daddy! Mummy and me are girls."

"You tell him Em," Michelle shrugged out of Paul's arm and slipped behind them both to take hold of Emily's hand.

"One, two, and three…" Paul laughed as he and Michelle swung Emily into the air. "Look what we've started."

"Hello Mrs Fawcett." Paul called to their neighbour as they turned up their garden path. She hastily retreated from where she had been clipping her hedge and slammed the gate.

"What's wrong with her?" Paul let go of Emily's hand as he fumbled for his keys. "She's got a face like a bag of spanners."

Michelle laughed. "Ah, take no notice. It's probably her age. Let's put the kettle on."

Emily soon grew bored of collecting wallpaper trimmings and disappeared to her room with the dog in pursuit. "I knew she wouldn't last long." Paul kissed the tip of Michelle's nose as he brushed past her at the bottom of the ladder. "They're soon bored at that age. I'm looking forward to having some couch potato time later. Especially if joined by a beautiful lady."

"Where are you going to find one of those?" Michelle passed him a cloth. "Should I be worried?"

"I don't think I will have to search far. We might also be joined by a small lady and a dog though."

He tugged off his jumper before ascending the step ladder to hang the next strip of wallpaper. "What are you smiling at?" He threw his jumper down to Michelle. "You're gorgeous when you smile, you know."

"Just admiring the view." Her smile became a frown as Paul's phone rang from beneath a pile of wallpaper cuttings. "Who's that?"

"How should I know? I'm up a ladder." The length of the wallpaper he was holding fell against the wall.

She peered at the phone. "It's bloody Nick. What does he want?"

"I don't know. Well answer it for me then. Tell him I'll ring him back." He smoothed the wallpaper down.

"Hello? No, he's not available at the moment. No. He won't be able to ring you back today. He's busy."

Paul stayed quiet. He recognised her expression only too well. "Shall we have another cuppa?" He cursed himself for leaving his phone on.

"No."

"What do you fancy to eat tonight?"

"Dunno." The next ten minutes were excruciating. She pasted. He hung. Apart from the slop of the paste onto the paper, the grinding of the scissors and the echo of whatever DVD Emily was watching upstairs, the lounge was silent. He prayed she would snap out of it.

"I'll mix more paste." Paul was startled as Michelle spoke. While she was out of the room, he switched the radio on, grateful for the hum of Radio Two to break the silence. After listening for a few moments, he remembered Nick so grabbed his phone and fired off a text. *Busy mate, will ring you tomorrow.*

"Who are *you* texting?"

Paul jumped as Michelle re-entered the room with the paste. "Only Nick. C'mon Michelle. Don't be like this. We've been doing great these last couple of days."

"I'm fine. I'll change my clothes and sort Emily some tea."

"Alright. Give me a smile then." Mildly reassured as she reciprocated, he carried on with his work.

It was approaching seven when Paul rose up to his six foot, from pasting down the final piece of wallpaper. "My back's killing! I'll go and read to Emily."

"Well don't be all night." Michelle stuffed wallpaper trimmings into a plastic bag. "I've already bathed her."

"Aww. I'd have done that. I'll have to read her an extra story instead."

"I wish you'd make as much effort with me as you do with Emily." Michelle's expression darkened as she tucked her hair behind her ear.

The countryside rushes past the darkened window, making Paul momentarily thankful he can see out. Trees, sky, birds, fields, blue motorway signs. It could be an ordinary journey. *When will he see all this again?* To give him a clue where he is going, he tries to read the signs backwards. All he knows is that he's on the M1, heading South. Or maybe to hell.

Chapter Six

Michelle balanced on the ladder as she re-hung the curtains. "You've been ages," she said.

"You know what she's like. She wouldn't let me go. I was exactly the same at her age." Whilst upstairs, Paul had allowed himself to be immersed for a moment in a memory of himself at five years old, twiddling with his mother's necklace as she read to him. He shut her and his father from his thoughts usually, it was too painful to reminisce. He'd never dealt properly with their sudden death when he was a teenager. He'd somehow closed down about it.

"I've ordered us a Chinese." Michelle descended the ladder.

"Cool." He brightened, anticipating an evening curled up with his wife on the sofa. "I'll tidy up." He looked around. "It looks great in here. We can sit down soon and admire it."

As Michelle went to answer the doorbell, he set about moving the furniture back.

"That smells good." He clasped his arms behind his head, stretching as he entered the kitchen. "I'm starving … how much of that wine have you had?" He watched as she drained her glass and something plummeted inside him. *Couldn't she last five minutes without drinking bloody wine?*

"Only a bit. I thought we could warm this up later." She pushed the food containers to the back of the worktop as she gave him a flirtatious glance.

"What do you mean, '*warm* it up.' It's hot already isn't it?" He removed a lid from one of the containers.

"I thought I could take you to bed for a bit first." She moved towards him whilst flicking her hair behind her shoulders. "Emily's sleeping now."

Paul put his arms around her. "I'm knackered Michelle. I haven't stopped all day. I'll have to give you an IOU this time. I want something to eat and to chill out on the sofa with you."

"Ah come on. You're always giving me the brush off." She pouted. "It's not as if you have to be up for work tomorrow."

"That's true. I could make it up to you in the morning then." He had solved it, he was sure. "Is it a date?" She stiffened in his arms and anxiety prickled at him in a way he wished his sex drive would again. But the months of constant rows were having an effect and if he was honest, although he loved her, he wasn't sure he fancied her anymore. They were calm today but things had a habit of suddenly deteriorating.

"What's wrong Paul? Why are you always rejecting me? Don't you fancy me anymore?"

"I do, honestly." Maybe he could try and switch it on. "Look, we'll go upstairs, I'm sure you can get me going ... that sounded wrong, I didn't mean ..."

"You might as well tell me to fuck off." She stepped back. "What's up with you?"

"No, look, it's not like that..."

Before he could avert it, food rained down the sides of his head, burning his face. He clenched his fists whilst trying to suppress his temper. He was close to thumping her, or a wall, if she was lucky.

"You ... no!" He ducked as she removed the lid of the other carton to fling at him. Yellow curry sauce, mixed with sweet n sour, dripped

34

down the wall. He strode towards her, anger masking the burning pain.

She backed away and made towards the door.

"Come back here." One way or another, she would regret this.

"If you don't want me, I'll find someone who does." She stormed through the hallway and slammed out of the house. Still wrestling with the urge to punch something, he squatted down against a cupboard as he tried to steady his breathing. Within a few minutes, he had composed himself slightly and considered how a pleasant day could have gone so wrong.

Emily appeared in the kitchen doorway, with an expression of bewilderment. "Daddy, why's Mummy shouting?" Her hands rested on her hips, in the same way her mother often stood. "What's all this mess?" Carla, who had followed her into the kitchen, made straight for the splattered food. Paul shooed her away with his foot.

"Just a bit of an accident." He tried to force normality into his voice. "I'm going to clean up. But first I'm going to tuck you back in." He tugged a towel from the laundry pile to clean sauce from his neck and chest. "I'll be right behind you; I don't want to get food on you."

"Love you Daddy." She whispered in the darkness. "And Mummy."

"Love you too. And so does Mummy." His voice cracked. "Go back to sleep."

The stench of sauces walloped him as he neared the foot of the stairs. He was reluctant to tackle the mess. *Why should he?* Then, realising it was likely to infuriate Michelle further if he didn't; he decided to sort it.

The steam of the water curled towards him, bathing his face as he watched the bucket fill. The mess had splattered into every corner, invading the kitchen like a disease. The smell as he dabbed at it was nauseating; Chinese curry and sweet 'n' sour combined with the lemon cleaning solution he had added. It all slimed against the cloth.

As the wall and floor became cleaner, his self-disgust grew, what on earth was he doing, cleaning this up? *What a man you are!* Shame snaked around him.

A shower made him feel more human. He watched the orange and yellow sauces disappearing down the plug hole, suspecting from the silence that Emily must have fallen back to sleep. He kept picturing her, wide awake, listening to them fight. As time was progressing, he was becoming further out of his depth in his relationship. Pacifying Michelle whilst attempting to maintain some semblance of normality for Emily was enough to grind anyone down. Not to mention having to give his all to a demanding job. And now she could be doing anything. She had always been good at chatting men up in bars. Something lurched within his belly as he contemplated this.

Raking a comb through his hair, he studied his expression. Lines were appearing in the corners of his eyes. Soon he would overtake his brother in their 'contest' of *who looks the oldest!* Before returning downstairs, he peered around Emily's door. Her arms were draped around her bear.

Glancing up at the clock, concern washed over him. 11:35. *Where the hell was she?* She shouldn't be out on her own at this time. Perhaps she would have calmed down. He cursed himself for caring after the way she had behaved.

"What do *you* want?"

"Where are you?" Pressing the phone to his ear, he kicked the lounge door shut as he raised his voice so she could hear him above the din of the dance music.

"I'm having a great time."

"Michelle, come home."

"Perhaps I should do this more often."

"Do what?"

36

"Go clubbing."

"Michelle. No. We can sort this out."

"Maybe I won't come back till tomorrow."

"You're being stupid. Tell me where you are, I'll phone a taxi for you."

"No chance." The musical beat quickened, emulating his racing thoughts.

"Who're you with?" Jealousy stabbed him as he heard a male voice in close proximity to her.

"Wouldn't you like to know?" Then the line went quiet. He redialled her number. "Hi, this is Michelle. Please leave a message after the tone."

"It's me... I'm sorry... I didn't mean to upset you." It was becoming commonplace, him apologising for her tantrums. "Come home... make sure you ring a taxi... I'll wait up." He threw himself back into the armchair. "You're a wimp," he said to himself as he dug his fingers into his temples. "An absolute wimp." After lots of pacing, he settled down with a bottle of beer.

A key in the door heralded her return. He glanced groggily at the clock. 4:24 am.

"Where the *hell* have *you* been?" He propped himself up on his elbows as he squinted at her. "Look at the state of you." Paul's attention was averted to the dog, who had been sleeping beside the sofa but was now slinking out of the room like an insect. Immediately Paul imagined that in her drunken state, Michelle had let some man take advantage of her.

"Going out tonight has made me realise what I'm missing." She knocked her leg on the coffee table as she wobbled towards him. "I'm wasting my life with *you*." The words slurred out of her.

"Go to bed Michelle." His voice was quiet, masking his rising surge of fury. "Sober yourself up. You're a disgrace."

"I've been given *three* phone numbers." She held up the same number of fingers. "See, *I've* still got it, even if *you* don't want me."

Michelle towered above him, wagging her fingers in front of his face. He could feel the waft of air generated by it as she continued ranting. He recoiled with the force of her hand as it connected with his face. Michelle then sunk to her knees, sobbing. His anger gave way to bewilderment. She was behaving like a mental case.

"It's all your fault. You make me act like this." She clenched her fists in her lap. "You don't do it for me. Not in bed anyway. You're rubbish. You don't get a proper erection. And you hate me, don't you?"

Her words stung like her slap. "Please go to bed." He leaned back against the cushions. "I've had enough ..."

"I wish we'd never met." She sobbed like a grieving widow. "We should split up."

"Michelle. Go to bed. Please."

She lurched towards the door. He listened as she stumbled up the stairs, clattering around for a while, before spending several minutes retching into the toilet. Normally he would go and see if she was all right and hold her hair out of the way. This time he lay, gaping into the gloom of the living room, hardly daring to breathe until he heard the creaking of the bed, reassuring him there would be at least a few hours of respite.

Chapter Seven

Not knowing how long fresh air will be robbed from him, Paul inhales deeply as he is escorted from the van into the prison's holding area. The grey-stone building looks like a gothic castle from a Bram Stoker nightmare. As he glances towards the normality of blue sky, he catches sight of the razor wire topping the enclosure wall. In silence, he is led by the officer who he tries to keep in step with; his wrist stings from the handcuffs he has spent the last two hours wearing.

It is hours since he has received an update about Michelle's condition, and he doesn't know with any certainty how Emily is coping. He watches another officer stride in front of him. He'll be clocking off soon, driving home to his wife, eating steak and chips for dinner, reading to his kids. Paul would do anything to swap places with him.

Two more prison officers perch behind a counter in an airless room. The man who has been leading him slides a form onto the counter with his free hand. "Paul Alan Jackson." His voice bears no trace of either warmth or disgust – at least he's civil.

The female desk officer scrutinises the paperwork then looks at Paul. He can't read her expression but is sure it is one of aversion.

"Any property?" She glances towards the officer who is releasing the handcuffs. Paul notices how pale his own arm looks next to the other man's sun-weathered arm.

"Just this." A polythene bag containing Paul's keys and wallet is pushed across the counter. A wave of misery sweeps over him as he observes the photograph of Michelle and Emily smiling out of his wallet.

"Right we'll book you in. Sign here." A form is thrust towards him.

Paul shudders as he contemplates the inmates he is going to be mixing with.

"Right, Jackson," the desk officer rises from his position. "You'll spend tonight in the induction wing. There's a few more things to take care of first."

"The induction wing?" Paul can't be arsed with all this. He just wants to be alone with his thoughts.

"All 'first nighters' have a night there. To transition you in. But first, I want you to walk through the scanner, and into the shower room where you'll undress." He gestures towards a cubicle shrouded by a yellow curtain. "I'll be through in a moment to do a search before you shower."

"A search?"

"Yes. It won't take long."

With each article of clothing he removes, another scrap of dignity falls away. Fear claws at his chest as the prison officer reappears, his hands gloved.

"Surely you don't have to..."

"It will just take a moment. I'm afraid it's procedure for everyone. If you could drop yourself down into a squat for me."

Fear mingles with fury, making the hairs on the back of his neck stand up. Scrunching his eyes, he braces himself to accept the inevitable.

Having showered, he is clad in his prison 'uniform.' The shirt flaps from his slim frame and the jeans are too short. He follows an officer as they progress through several sets of doors.

"Paul Jackson?" A woman peers at him over the top of her glasses as he is finally brought to a desk in front of another set of double doors. She's dressed the same as her male colleagues. "I need to go through a few things with you. Firstly, you're on remand. You don't have to work, but you will be paid an extra two pounds twenty a day, on top of your weekly two pounds and fifty pence, if you do."

"I don't know." Trepidation at having to work alongside the other inmates creeps over him. Maybe he should keep himself to himself.

"The time will pass quicker for you."

"Right, I'll work."

"Or you could do education. There's computer skills, literacy or numeracy." She folds her arms as she awaits a response, flashing her wedding and engagement rings. The sight of the rings brings Michelle back to the forefront of his mind. Not that she has moved far from it.

"I'll work." The smell in here is making him feel sick, it's a mixture of sweat, tobacco and cabbage, the unpleasantness exacerbated further by the heat.

"You have an hour's exercise outside every morning at eight, and an hour's association at six each evening." Her voice is robotic, she's clearly repeated this information many times. "You'll be banged up from seven." She pushes her glasses from her face so they rest on her hair, tightly scraped into a bun.

"What's association?"

"You can play pool, watch TV, mix with the others and make phone calls; that kind of thing."

"I can make phone calls? Can I make some now?"

"You'll need to wait until the next canteen order goes in on Saturday." She pulls out a form and a leaflet from under the desk. "Then you can put in for a phone card. Your order will come in the Saturday after."

41

"I've to wait nearly two weeks until I can ring anyone?"

"Only if we've verified all your numbers. You're allowed five." She points to the corresponding information printed on the leaflet. "We'll ring and check them, they must be landlines." She looks again at his paperwork. "You work in law, don't you? You must be familiar with how it all works?"

"As a legal executive." That life is a million miles away now. "In conveyancing. I've had nothing to do with criminal law." Pausing for a moment, he wonders about this woman. Perhaps she will help him. It's worth a try. "I'm anxious to know about my wife's condition, she's in hospital in Leeds. I haven't heard since I was at the police station this morning. And my daughter. She's been taken to my mother-in-law. Would you be able to find out for me how they both are? I won't rest till I know. Please?"

He is sure the officer's face softens. "If any messages come in for you, they'll be passed on as soon as possible. Your solicitor can ring you too." She twists her ring round and round. "As long as it's during working hours, we'll find you." She slides the leaflet until it touches his fingertips. "This gives you details of all the rules and routines. If you've any more questions, ask one of the officers during association. You're in time for dinner. For tonight, you're on the induction wing so it will be brought to you. From tomorrow, you'll join the others. If you'd like to go with my colleague, he'll walk you to your cell."

Paul follows the jangling officer along a quiet corridor towards a door that's ajar within the green-bricked wall. A tray of food has been left on the table of the cell. Well food of a sort. It's a kind of cold pie accompanied by a pile of what looks like vegetables and an apple. He takes in the white brick walls. Table. Chair. Bed. Cupboard. All are bolted to the floor. Behind a dividing wall is a toilet and sink. If an officer looks through the viewing panel in his door, they will be able to see him on the toilet. Great. He's not going to be able to crap in peace.

"You'll be in a single cell for tonight. We'll double you up in the next day or two when you're allocated your permanent cell."

"I think I'd rather be on my own," Paul contemplates the possibility of who else might be lurking on the wing he will be moved to.

"You don't get to choose." The officer's voice is flat, cold. "I'll leave you to settle in."

"Settle in? Thanks." Paul mutters into the draught caused by the heavy door as it clangs shut. He stares miserably at the tray. Images of Emily and Michelle will not leave him. Dropping his head into his hands, he weeps with a ferocity he never imagined existed. This is really not happening.

Chapter Eight

Standing in a line of similarly dressed inmates, Paul could be hallucinating. This is like something from a crime drama. There is no way he is standing here, queuing alongside God-knows-who, in for God-knows-what. He's spent the whole night and the following day barely moving, laid on the bed, thinking. Mulling over how the hell he's going to deal with this. Sometimes dozing off. It's been an endless twenty four hours, spent with officers opening the observation flap on his door every thirty minutes. Probably checking he's not trying to do himself in.

"I'd give the peas a miss," the inmate in front mutters, appraising Paul from head to foot as he speaks.

"Why?" Paul clutches his tray, feeling anything but hungry but knowing he must eat something if he is going to survive until his trial.

"You're new in here right?" His greasy dark hair is combed over his forehead. It is hard to see any areas of tattoo-free flesh on his arms.

He is, Paul decides, what he had always imagined an inmate to look like. "Yeah?"

"The lads behind the servery." The inmate rolls his eyes towards them. "They sometimes mess with the food."

"Mess with?"

"You're pretty safe with sandwiches, burgers, meat, you know, that kind of thing ... solid stuff. But peas, custard, stay well clear unless

44

you want to swallow someone else's snot, or worse. What you in for?"

"I'd rather not talk about it." Paul tries to quell the rising bile at the back of his throat. "I'm still trying to get my head round everything." He needs to go over what happened that night. It's a blur, he can't remember. It's as though he's blacked it out.

"We'll read all about it in the papers over the next couple of days." He shrugs. "Welcome to Wonderland anyway. I'm Tommo. Come and see me if you need anything. You look like a first timer."

"Paul. And thanks." Balancing his tray in the crook of his arm, he accepts the handshake.

An officer is waiting for him at the end of the line, after Paul has taken a pasty and an apple from the servery. He passes Paul a plastic knife and fork.

"Is that all you're having?" He looks down at the tray.

"I'm not hungry. Where do I eat?"

"In your cell. If you want to follow me." The officer strides towards a steel staircase.

Paul follows, up a flight of steps, along a landing. The prison is as he imagined it. Yellow steel: as far as the eye can see; banging, shouting and an ambience of unspent testosterone. He's seen images of this sort of place many times on the news.

They arrive on the first landing. Paul shudders as he notices the overhead steel mesh, presumably there to prevent suicides from second or third floor landings. The floor vibrates underfoot as he continues to follow the officer. He catches sight of the signs outside other cells. *Robinson; 60310 5 years. Metcalfe; 52798 9 years. Lambert; 31542; life;* then he sees his sign: *Little; 6 years; Jackson; 78465 RP.* It might as well say *RIP.*

"That means remand prisoner," explains the officer. "It'll be changed after sentencing."

"I won't be sentenced. I shouldn't be here in the first place." Paul tries to stop his voice from rising as he notices a man in the cell staring at him from where he sits at the table. "I didn't do what I'm accused of."

"If I had a pound for every time I heard that." The officer's laughing at him. "Let me introduce you to your new cellmate, Paul Jackson, Stephen Little. I'll leave you two to become acquainted. Oh, while I think on." He sweeps his gaze over them. "Do you both want a TV organising? It's fifty pence a week off your allowance. Each."

"Please." Stephen answers quickly without looking at Paul. "How soon can we have it? That alright with you mate?"

"Yep."

"Within a day or two." The officer replies to Stephen then looks at Paul. "Association's at six. We'll come and unlock you both when it's time. You can choose whether you want to come out for an hour. Or you can stay here. It's up to you. You'll be unlocked regardless."

"Thanks." He takes a bite of his apple as the lock clicks in the cell door. "How are you doing mate?" He looks at Stephen. He looks OK. Not a tattoo in sight.

"Er, yeah. Alright I suppose. Considering. What you in for?"

Paul steels himself to answer the question he knows is going to keep coming up. "My wife's been stabbed. They think I did it."

"And did you?"

"No."

"Well that's good enough for me." Stephen holds out his hand. "Good to meet you. I wondered how long I'd be on me own."

"Paul. Likewise. Albeit it's a shame we're not in different circumstances. How about you?"

"I killed three people. I was steaming. I was the driver."

"Shit." He's sharing a space with a man who's killed three people. Yet he seems pretty respectable. *What a nightmare!* The cell reeks of cleaning fluid. Still it's better than the stench on the landing. Paul slides his tray onto the table opposite Stephen although he has no idea how he is going to swallow his food or keep it down. He tries to banish unwanted images of men excreting bodily fluids. *Welcome to wonderland.* The earlier words he heard echo through his mind.

Chapter Nine

Emily's voice rang out far too loudly. "Why are you sleeping here Daddy?"

"Quiet Emily." Paul hissed. "The last thing we want is to wake your mother." As Emily shrank back from him, he realised he'd been too harsh. He yawned as he sat up. "Sorry Emily. Daddy's just tired."

"Can I open the curtains?" She tiptoed towards the window, her exuberance somewhat curtailed.

Paul rubbed his eyes then closed them again at the memory of the previous evening. *God, what was today going to bring?*

"Can you make me some breakfast Daddy?" She flung the door of the living room open as she spoke.

"Emily," he snapped. "You're going to have to keep your voice down." He felt wretched keeping her quiet but desperately did not want to encounter Michelle yet. Especially when she'd be in a hungover state. Hopefully she had hit the toilet when being sick. He wouldn't be able to manage cleaning that.

"Ugh." Emily's nose wrinkled as she trailed behind her father into the kitchen. "It smells in here." Clearly, Paul could have done a more efficient job of cleaning the takeaway debris the night before. The smell turned his already churning gut some more.

"Eat your breakfast in the living room." He pointed towards the door.

"Won't Mummy go mad with me?" A worried look crossed her face.

"She won't know. Keep the noise down." He patted the top of her dark head as he presented her with a bowl of cereal. "She's in bed. If you stay quiet, we'll go to the park."

"Can Mummy come too?"

"We'll see."

Paul left her eating and crept upstairs to wash and dress. A search amongst the ironing pile yielded some jeans and a hoody, which he pulled on silently, not giving a toss how creased they were. Since he had married he had lost at least an inch around his waist. People kept commenting on it. There was no way, however, he was venturing into his bedroom to find a belt.

Tiptoeing around Emily's bedroom, he innately knew which bits of floor squeaked and which drawer to open slowly because it scraped. Then, knowing the boiler would make a whistling, blowing noise given the chance, he ran the cold tap, which was a shock as he splashed it on his face. He was taking no chances of waking Michelle up yet. The longer she slept, the more amenable she would be upon awakening. He couldn't take her crap today. That much he knew.

Upon hearing the rattling of her lead, Carla rose dutifully from the spot on the landing where she had spent the remainder of the night.

"Hurry up Em," he urged, hearing a creak overhead as she dragged her coat on. "We need to go now if we're off to the park."

"But what about my hair Daddy and I haven't brushed my teeth?"

"Never mind all that. We'll sort it later."

Hearing the bedroom door open, he grabbed his leather jacket, and they sped out of the door. It was not until they had gone beyond the cul-de-sac in which they lived, that he could breathe. Emily smiled up at him. "We've forgotten bread for the ducks Daddy."

"We'll feed them next time." He tugged an exuberant Carla back towards him. "For God's sake, heel. We can't go back now."

The walk, he hoped, would clear his head, and as they entered the park gates he let Carla off her lead, to run with Emily. They distracted each other, giving him space to gulp in the cleansing morning air. With each step he took, his fists unknotted slightly. But his thoughts were more muddled. The more he tried to find a way forward, the more trapped he became. It was like living in some sort of labyrinth with only darkness at its centre.

Thinking back to the time when he had lost his parents, he remembered how he had tried to visualise the time when his own family would be a reality. This was awful; certainly not what he had envisaged. Far from it.

Emily hooted in excitement as she encountered one of her school friends. She had *both* her parents there, looking united and content. A weariness descended as he scrutinised the man that was overwhelming. *I bet you weren't wearing your supper last night.*

He yearned to be like him. To have his normality. He was going to have to regain some control. Whatever it took. He yearned to hear a voice so he took out his mobile and rang Nick.

"Alright mate. Sorry I couldn't speak to you yesterday."

"It's a good job it wasn't important."

Paul wished he hadn't rung him. There was enough crap at home without his mate giving him it too. "I've apologised."

"I was going to suggest going to the gym. I've got a guest pass. But can you get a pass *out?* That is the question."

"Don't be like that. I'm my own man. I'm just at the park with Emily."

"What was she doing answering your phone then?"

"I was wallpapering."

"You wanna watch her mate. I can't believe how rude she was on the phone."

"Leave it Nick." Paul looked over at Emily who was pushing her friend on the swing. "Emily stand back."

"She has you well under the thumb mate."

"What because I'm at the park?"

"It's *everything*." There was a chill in Nick's voice. "Watch yourself."

"Yeah. Well. Give me a ring next time you go. I'll see what I can do."

"I'll email you a permission form first for her to sign."

"See you soon." Paul sat on a bench and decided to call Alana.

"Fancy hearing from you on a Saturday."

"I had a bit of trouble at home last night. I'm in the park."

"Shall I meet you?"

Longing tugged in his belly. He fought to override it. "Nah. I'm with Emily. Just wanted to hear a friendly voice."

"Glad to be of service. What's happened?"

"Oh, you know. Some throwing of food. A bit of staying out all night." Paul sighed. "Nothing I can't handle."

"You don't deserve it." She sounded as though she had lowered her voice. "You know what I think of her. And you."

"Where's Lee?"

"Mr Exciting? Oh he's fixing something upstairs." She giggled. "I'd have much more fun at the park with you and…"

"Sorry Alana. Go to go. Michelle's ringing." He pressed the button that swapped calls from Alana to Michelle.

"It's me," she announced. "I'm sorry. I don't want to lose you."

Chapter Ten

Michelle tugged Paul's dressing gown more tightly around herself as she sipped her coffee. "I *am* sorry, you know. Do you have to look at me like that?" It was an expression she had come to recognise; disgust mixed with pity and perhaps fear. There was no love in his eyes anymore. She banged her cup down on the kitchen table. "I know I look a mess but don't make me feel any worse." She had glanced at her reflection after crawling out of bed. Her hair was Medusa-like and last night's make-up had slid down her face. That which she hadn't cried off. She had the hangover from hell and the coffee wasn't doing her any favours. Its heat slid downwards, giving her heartburn. One wrong move and she'd be puking again.

Emily trotted in behind Paul. As soon as she noticed her parents, her expression changed and she retreated into the hallway, catching Carla's collar as she went. For a moment, Michelle considered calling her back and challenging her. Why was Emily being like this? What had Paul said to her? She was becoming insecure about her own daughter to the point of being jealous of their little father and daughter unit, which made her hate herself more. She was *always* excluded. When she was on her own with Emily, she would constantly ask for her father. It was as though she could not compete with him.

"You said a lot of nasty things Michelle." Paul strode towards the kettle. "You don't know how awful you are when you're drunk. You lose all control of yourself." He wrenched the kettle from its base. "And we were fine yesterday. I don't understand."

Michelle wished he would hug her and the thought made her want to cry more as she imagined being cosseted in his scent and warmth. They had not slept in the same bed for several nights lately. It was her fault; she was driving him away with her insecurity, her drinking and subsequent temper. She was in a vicious circle but had no idea how to break it. It was as though she was sucked inside her own self and couldn't escape.

"I can't remember." In fact, trying to remember was making her head buzz. "Like you said, I was drunk."

"You shouldn't have been out in the first place." He cursed out loud as he overfilled the kettle and water spurted up into his face. "Not like that."

"Are you begrudging me a night out now? It's fine for you to go out though?" He wasn't to know she had spent much of it, apart from about an hour, sat alone in the park, drinking wine straight from the bottle. The alcohol had anaesthetised her from the chilly night air and the hours had ticked by whilst she mused over her torment. He was going to leave her, she was sure. They all did eventually. Even her own father. She'd had years of being belittled by him. It had been him and her brother on one side and her and her mother on the other. Her brother had been vile. The years of being bullied had taken their toll. And there'd been no let up at school either. She'd been a pretty teenager with lots of the lads after her so all the other girls had hated her.

"No, of course not. I think we should go out *together*." He dropped the kettle onto its base and flicked the switch. "If you can stay off the booze. We can't go on like this Michelle. I think we need some counselling or something."

"I know. I'll do whatever it takes. I do love you."

"Have you eaten?"

"I couldn't eat a thing." She stared at him. He was being civil with her but hadn't reciprocated when she'd said she loved him and was avoiding looking at her directly. But he cared if she'd eaten. Although ashamed, something brightened within her. She had been an absolute cow. It was somewhat hazy but she could remember some of it. Shit. She had slapped him. She glanced at his face, checking for bruising. It looked a bit red but that was all. If he could put up with her like this then it meant he loved her. *Didn't it?* "We were happier before, weren't we Paul?" She wrapped her fingers tightly around her mug, slightly more relaxed. "When it was me and you. Before Emily came along? We had some good laughs."

"We're happy now Emily *has* come along." Paul faced her now. "You need to trust me and to stop giving in to these damn awful moods."

"I wouldn't be in them if I came first with you. *I* should be top of your list. In front of Emily, your job, everything, especially that bloody secretary of yours. Anyway, one day Emily will grow up and you will be left with me again." *If you haven't abandoned me by then, her* inner voice was whispering to her. She was going to drive him away. She could see it on his face.

"For God's sake Michelle. She's six years old and you're talking about her leaving home." Paul slammed his cup on the draining board. "You must be the least maternal person I know. What's the matter with you?"

Michelle sat silently as he stormed from the kitchen. Normally she would have retorted but continued to sit in the now silent room, sick and lonely as she heard the echo upstairs of her husband talking to their daughter. She could go up there and join in but was too ill and they wouldn't want her to. She was on the outside of her own family like she had always been on the outside of everything.

Her hangover intensified as the morning wore on. She spent it sprawled on the sofa, in front of the television, still wrapped in Paul's dressing gown.

"I'm going out for a while," announced Paul as he scanned the room. "If I can find the car keys, that is. I'll take Emily. Give you a bit of space. I could do with some, I know that much."

Michelle lifted her head from the cushion. "I hate being left on my own, you know I do. Where are you going? Can't it wait till I'm a bit better and can come with you?"

"I'm off to see our David for an hour. It's been ages since I've seen him." He swiped at the car keys, having located them.

"What's brought this on?" Their rows had escalated the last few times in front of Paul's brother. "It's a bit sudden. When did you plan this?" Perhaps David would take advantage of Michelle not being around. He could give Paul his opinion and make him consider leaving her. Paul listened to David. He didn't like her which made him a threat. And he had room for Paul to stay with him. She was jealous again of this relationship he had that she couldn't be part of and wished she had siblings too. *God, she hated feeling like this!*

"Michelle, I'm taking Emily to visit her uncle. Nothing sinister."

"And you're going to leave me here?" Tears stabbed at her eyes and she fervently wished he would wrap his arms around her. Was it possible to be this lonely when they had been married for such a short time?

"I won't be long." Shuffling towards her, he took hold of her hand.

"Can't I have a hug?" she whispered, trying to catch his gaze. "You're distant from me. You never hug me anymore. I can't stand it."

"I'm not distant. You're hungover." Still he crouched further down and Michelle was able to bask in five seconds of his warmth. But his body was stiff and she sensed he couldn't wait to let her go. She remembered she hadn't yet brushed her teeth and was conscious of her breath, soured from being sick and stale alcohol.

"Why are you wearing aftershave if you're only off to see your brother?" She caught a whiff of the Calvin Klein aftershave he normally reserved for nights out.

"Oh for God sake! I've had a shave. Do I challenge you about wearing perfume or make-up?"

"No, but then you don't care about me, do you?" She knew she sounded like a petulant child but had gone beyond caring. Tears were rolling down her cheeks. She hoped it was the hangover making her this low.

"Of course I do."

"So why don't you *ever* ask me to come with you?" She didn't know why she was saying this. Like she *really* wanted to dress and go to David's where she always felt unwelcome. He was civil enough, but his smile never reached his eyes with Michelle.

"You're hardly in a fit state. Stay here and sort yourself out."

"I don't believe that's where you're going." She searched Paul's face for a hint of guilt.

"That's your problem. Look, I can't do this. Enjoy the peace."

The familiar fury rose in her like an uninvited guest. "What if I don't want you to go? I don't want to be here on my own." At that moment, she despised herself.

"I'm an adult. I don't need your permission to go anywhere Michelle."

He sounded different, *what had got into him?* She'd noticed that more lately; once he would have tried to talk her around, but now, he'd argue back. "I think you're off to see Alana." She rammed her fist into a cushion without realising she had. "I don't think I'd blame you. But I can't take it anymore."

"You're talking rubbish." He rose and backed towards the door. "I'll see you later. Emily," he called. "Come on."

"You'll only be an hour, won't you? Promise?"

"I'll be as long as I want."

Michelle wept as the engine of their Ford Focus ebbed into the distance. Darkness weighed on her; yet she was powerless to alter it. Paul was slipping away. Emily was the only reason he was still around, she was sure. Her conscience nagged her for being jealous of her daughter but she could not help it. They had been all right until she had come along and taken the attention. Michelle could still recall how everybody's focus, including Paul's, had been all on *the baby.* She might as well have not existed, apart from being there to have all life literally sucked from her. She'd been exhausted and unable to stop crying. Her boobs had half killed her and she didn't have that same 'whatever it was' that others displayed towards Emily. At times she had hated her. The sound of her crying became like a pneumatic drill. One day the health visitor had frog-marched her to the GP. The anti-depressants had helped. But Emily now looked at her with the same expression in her eyes as Paul.

Michelle wished she could stop imagining Paul with another woman. Alana, no doubt. Kissing her, having sex with her, having secret outings with *her* daughter. Had she not been feeling so ill, she would have cycled up to David's to check for his car. Her miserable thoughts were cut into by her ringing mobile phone. She snatched it up, quickly checking the display and instantaneously sinking a little.

"Hi Mum. What do you want?"

"What do you mean? *What do I want!* What's up with you?"

"Nothing. It's Paul." Michelle's voice wobbled as she said his name out loud.

"Oh Michelle. You've not been arguing again, have you?"

"Yes." Michelle was choking back tears. It was her mother's warm and sympathetic tone. Right now, the fact she was being nice to her was not helpful.

"What about this time?"

"I went out and was late back. And now he's gone to his brother's house with Emily."

"Well that hardly sounds like grounds for divorce." Her mother's voice lost its anxious edge. "You'll be fine."

"I don't think he loves me anymore Mum." Michelle pushed her hair off her face. "You should see how he looks at me."

"All marriages go through peaks and troughs." Her mother's voice was gentle and Michelle yearned for her to be there, giving her a hug. "Of course he loves you. You need to make more effort."

"We're never on our own." Michelle wished she could be talking to her mum about something normal. "He cares about his stupid secretary more than me."

"Ah, now that's not true. You'll drive him away if you're going to be accusing him of going off with other women."

"I don't need you to start going on at me. I feel bad enough as it is."

"Well you'll know what 'bad' is if you go wrecking your marriage with your jealousy, love. Take it from someone who knows. Have you any idea how hard life is as a single parent?"

Michelle felt something twist inside her. "I should. You've told me often enough."

"Look. I'll take Emily for the weekend. As soon as you want. You and Paul go away. It'll do you the world of good."

"Thanks." Michelle sniffed. "That's if he wants to." After the phone call, Michelle wrenched herself from the sofa and headed upstairs to the bathroom.

For a moment she wasn't sure if she was going to be sick again. She gripped the basin and gulped in deep breaths as she shivered in the cool air. As the nausea subsided, she filled a glass of water and took a few sips. She caught sight of herself again in the mirrored cabinet and scraped her fingers through her unkempt hair. She looked awful. Red eyes, blotchy skin and utterly miserable. She could hardly remember what it was like to smile. Her reflection stared back at her. *Ugly! Ugly! Ugly!*

She threw open one side of the cabinet and rummaged within it for the one thing that would make her feel better, spilling other items onto the floor as she searched. Taking out a razor blade, she sat back onto the toilet lid. She twisted it gently, this way and that, between her thumb and forefinger. Its trapezium shape reflected at her as it glinted around the tiled walls in the early afternoon sunlight.

A familiar calm stole over her. Paul would be devastated but it might make him realise what he was doing to her. If he noticed. He hardly saw her undressed anymore.

She hitched up the dressing gown, ready to attack where there was plenty of untouched flesh. Wounds of previous years had faded to silvery lines. With the anticipation of a child ready to imprint its footprints onto an untouched field of snow, Michelle sliced into the top of her leg. Feeling a slight sting, she pressed the sides of the cut to squeeze the blood out faster, knowing she might let out her internal pain with it. She cut again, about a centimetre away, then again and again, marvelling at the ribbons of blood, oozing from her wounds separately, before merging as one.

The power she had over them made her smile through her tears. She hadn't realised she was crying and gratitude washed over her that she had found a way to release her torment again. It was the same release she had granted herself previously but had managed to resist for ten years. The face of her former psychotherapist swam into her mind and she imagined his disappointment.

With each new incision, her anger and frustration diminished. That was soon replaced with more tears. As she dabbed at her wounds, she realised she could not stop the bleeding. Nor could she stop her tears. She dabbed at them, mingling salt water and blood upon her face. They dripped onto her legs, making them sting more or were they smarting anyway? Either way, it felt good. Running a hand along the top of her forearm, her palm slid over the ridges of bumps. These were the cuts that over the years, hadn't healed as well as those on her legs. She paused as she held the tip of the razor over the area. Everyone would notice it here. *No, not this time,* she returned to her leg, adding two more incisions before rinsing the razor blade under the tap and replacing it in the cabinet.

She found herself a bandage, then balanced her leg on the loo to methodically wrap it around her cuts. She pulled it taut, feeling comfort as the tightness strangled her leg.

More composed and feeling freer than she had felt in years, she realised that in the last hour she'd not once thought about Paul and Emily. Often losing sight of who *she* was, as a person, she was fed up of succumbing to the roles in her life that usually managed to swallow her up. At this moment she was Michelle again.

Chapter Eleven

Paul tugged a mug from the cupboard. The house was silent. Sometimes it was difficult to believe it was occupied by a family that should be laughing, chatting and playing music, easy in each other's company... "Michelle!" He jumped as his wife slinked into the room. "You're looking better."

"I got some sleep and a shower. I can honestly say I'm never touching wine again."

"Yeah, yeah." Paul forced a laugh. "How many times have you said that?"

"It's good you're laughing." Michelle smiled at him. "You seem in a better mood than you did earlier."

"I told you. We needed a bit of space."

"I am sorry about last night you know. I really am." Paul could see from her expression that she meant it. Perhaps they had a decent evening ahead of them. She went on. "I've been speaking to my mum. She's offered to have Emily for the weekend. We can have some time to ourselves."

"You've been talking to your mum? About us? Again?"

"I haven't been slagging you off. She rang and could tell I was upset."

"Great."

"You don't want to go away with me then? I think we should."

He didn't. Not now. She'd probably use it as another excuse to get drunk anyway. "Look we'll talk about it later."

"It's alright." She strode towards the kitchen door. "I'll tell her you're not bothered. I know when I'm not wanted." The door banged behind her.

It was not possible for him to duck out of the way as moments later, she burst back through the door, flinging his phone at him. It collided squarely with his nose. Damn! His phone! He'd left it in his jacket pocket.

"You've rung your girlfriend!" she cried.

"What are you on about?" His nose throbbed as he raised his hand to it. It was bleeding.

"Your call log. You can't deny you called Alana. Nine, fifty-six. For five minutes. Why are you speaking to her on a weekend? What were you talking to her about?"

"To let her know I'd be back in work on Monday, you know, after I threw the sickie to do the decorating."

"I bet you'd take *her* away for a weekend, wouldn't you?"

"No Michelle. I wouldn't." From within, a strength was rising that he'd forgotten he had. "You've no business looking at my phone."

"I'm going out," Michelle announced after spending over an hour upstairs. Paul had assumed she was having another lie down and had been harbouring hopes she would wake in an improved mood.

"Mummy, you look pretty. Where are you going? Can we come?" Paul and Emily's attention was deflected from the TV to where Michelle hovered in the doorway. Her dark hair hung down her back and she peered at them from behind her heavy eyelashes.

"Not again! You never said you were going out. In fact, you said you were never drinking again. Who're you going with?" Paul wasn't sure if he felt annoyed or glad of imminent peace.

"Never you mind! Why should I tell you? You're the secretive one with your bloody secretary." She swung around and slammed out of the house. As he watched her wobble along the driveway in her towering heels, he was half relieved and half jealous but accepted he was powerless. All he could do was hope she refrained from drinking too much.

After Emily had gone to bed, he slouched on the sofa, and seemed to spend hours gazing out through the un-curtained window at the shadows that threatened to overcome him. Usually he liked an evening on his own, but tonight the stillness gnawed at him, his earlier fleeting strength had departed.

Three-and-a-half hours later, he awoke stiffly in the same position on the sofa. It was well after midnight. Misery stole over him along with the realisation that he had no idea where she was or who she was with. Her phone was switched off. Under all that bravado, she exuded vulnerability and he could not help but be worried. It was necessary to concede she was putting herself at risk by what she had been wearing. Or not wearing, more to the point.

Carla followed dutifully behind as he ascended the stairs and checked on Emily. She deserves a happy family, he thought. She deserves better than this!

It was difficult to pinpoint exactly when it had soured between them. By marrying her, he had hoped some of the trust and happiness could be recaptured. It had been perfect between them in the beginning. But from around eight months into their relationship, he had been constantly chasing to get that time back.

The wedding actually seemed to have provided a catalyst for a speedier deterioration of their relationship. He'd known what he was taking on. She believed all men were like her father who had gone backwards and forwards between her mother and another woman for years, until he had finally left. Michelle had tried ringing to see him; he'd arrange to pick her up or meet her and then wouldn't arrive. She'd had a poor relationship with her brother as well, who had bullied her.

Wandering into the room he had shared with her for the last year, he scanned his eyes around the debris which had been left. Clothes littered the floor. She must have tried on several outfits. Lidless cosmetics were strewn across the dressing table. Picking up a discarded bottle of wine, he was pleased there was enough left for a glass for him. It might settle him down. The room reeked of perfume. Cheap, musky perfume. Why she wore it, he had no idea, instead of the bottle of Estee Lauder he had given her the previous Christmas. The cellophane from the box had not been unwrapped.

At the time, she'd casually informed him that her boyfriend prior to him, Ed, had bought her the same perfume. Paul often felt he was being punished for his mistakes too. He'd apparently given Michelle the run-around, often disappearing for days and messing around with other women. She had become ill to the point that she had taken an overdose. And here Paul was now, able to empathise with Ed. Since they'd married, he was seeing her true colours.

Returning downstairs, he drained the wine bottle and tried to distract himself with the TV. All he could do was wait and watch the shadows. Hope she returned home safely. Rock-like, he sat, anxiety mounting for another three hours.

Carla curled up beside him, nestling her head knowingly in his lap. As he stroked her, she absorbed some of his tension as she stared up at him with wise eyes. *Everything will be alright,* she seemed to be saying as she fought to keep her tawny eyes open. Finally, influenced by her peaceful breathing and her soft, relaxed body, Paul fell asleep with her.

"Daddy!" Emily bounded into the room. "Why didn't you sleep in bed?"

Paul shot into a sitting position. Confusion was quickly replaced by a sickening, dead sensation. Michelle hadn't been home all night. His tongue was bitter in his mouth.

"Can I have some breakfast please?" Emily tugged at his arm.

Paul absently replied to her cheerful chatter as he automatically fulfilled her requirements in the kitchen. "Yes Emily, really, maybe, we'll see." She seemed satisfied with his vacant replies. He would have to ring the local hospitals, the police.

There were no friends, as far as he knew, that she was close enough to stay the night with; apart from a friendship she had mentioned with a woman at work, though he could not recall her name.

Dragging himself back to the living room, he steeled himself to ring her mother.

"Susan. I'm sorry to bother you. Have you seen Michelle?"

"No. Why? Isn't she at home?" Her voice sounded groggy with sleep.

"Well I wouldn't be ringing you asking if she was, would I?"

"Alright Paul. There's no need to be like that. Where is she then? When did she go out?"

"Last night."

"She's been out all night! Have you two been rowing again?"

"Look." Paul sighed. "I know you probably mean well but…"

"What if somethings happened to her?" Susan's voice rose up an octave.

Paul regretted ringing her. She'd be round at the house if he wasn't careful. "Look Susan. I'll find her and I'll tell her to give you a ring when she turns up."

And then he cut her off, in mid flow of whatever she was saying.

For the next call he had to make; he tried to recall what she had been wearing.

The police would need a picture of her. He grabbed at their wedding one on the centre of the mantelpiece. He turned it face down.

The click of the door made him jump. She staggered into the living room, looking as though she had not slept for a week.

"Where have you been? I was about to report you missing."

"Leave me alone. Don't pretend you care. I'm off to bed!"

"What?" He stared at her incredulously. "Without a word of explanation! Do you bloody realise what you've put me through? I've been awake all night!"

"But it's alright for you to go out to ring your secretary?"

Anger took hold of him. He grabbed the wedding photo again and smashed it on the floor.

"You arsehole!" She stared, open-mouthed into his face, panting as they squared up to each other in front of the mantle piece.

"Michelle, I can't cope with you anymore. I don't know if I want to be with you." He watched her fists curling up by her sides.

She turned her face away from his, rendering him completely off guard for what happened next. He could not have prevented the glob of spit which was sprayed directly into his face.

"You should be ashamed of yourself!" His hand leapt to his cheek.

He held his breath until he could be certain her footsteps were on the stairs, then dashed to the kitchen to scrub his face. The thought of it languishing, unwashed on his skin with dregs of it in his hair was making him want to throw up. He wanted a shower but was not going upstairs until she was asleep.

"Mummy's up early," observed Emily, nonchalantly spooning coco-pops into her mouth as she sat at the table watching Hannah Montana. Paul splashed water into his face and hair, wishing he could rinse away some of the shame along with the toxic saliva.

"She's going back to bed for a little while." He rubbed his head with a tea towel, grateful she was unaware of what was going on.

Chapter Twelve

U nable to open her eyes and bear the light, Michelle slid the phone towards herself from her bedside table. She could hear the muffled voices of Paul and Emily drifting up the stairs. 12:55 pm. At least she had slept all morning. Her head was thick with the wine she had drunk before she had passed out on *her workmate's* sofa. *Never again.* She couldn't remember what they'd been talking about, but the sting of her eyes reminded her she had been crying. Again.

Paul's tone sounded different, as though he was on the phone. She strained to hear who he might be talking to but couldn't make out his words. Then he laughed. He was probably on the phone to that *bloody Alana.* The bane of her life. What she would do to make her disappear. Mostly, Michelle managed to keep her out of her own life and had recently only been subjected to her at the wedding when the silly cow had tried to dance with Paul.

Oh, and at their housewarming party, the year before. She had looked forward to it with every fibre of her being, but now tried to banish it when the memory came bubbling up. Here, as she lay in her hungover state, she could not shake it away.

Even in August, they had known they were taking a gamble, having an outdoor party. Michelle had kept a close eye on the weather forecast in the preceding days and had borrowed a couple of gazebos just in case. She spent the previous night decorating the garden with fairy lights, candles and had prepared a playlist of carefully chosen songs.

Paul had done the shopping for the barbecue, so the shed was full of alcohol, although they had told guests to bring a bottle, something to sit on and a contribution to the barbecue. Paul hadn't been as bothered about the party, but she had put that down to him 'being a man' and not wanting the 'hassle.'

She'd had various 'run ins' in previous months with his friends and family and was determined to show everyone how happy she and Paul were and for them to accept her. She could no longer bear living on the outskirts. And if she was to be honest, it would be good to put Alana in her place. As the saying goes, *keep your friends close and your enemies closer.*

She'd searched all over for a dress. The first one she'd bought, Paul had described as 'frumpy.' *I bet he wouldn't say something like that to Alana*, she thought. She settled on something not unlike what Alana would wear. Short, sexy, asymmetric, summery – perfect. And once she'd had a spray tan and the hairdresser had arranged her long dark hair in tumbling curls, she knew she looked the part. And yet she'd spent the best part of the night stood in the kitchen, frying onions. In between running around, waiting on everyone and having to make polite conversation with people she'd never met, who clearly didn't like her. By ten o clock, she'd barely seen Paul. David had been at his side as he presided over the barbecue. Socialising. Enjoying himself.

The barbecue had finished. Michelle scanned the garden, looking for Paul, desperately wanting him to wrap his arms around her and show the world how they belonged together. Instead she found him, sat in the garden chair swing her mother had given them as a housewarming present, swinging as he chatted to Alana. Michelle went back inside, poured a large glass of wine and decided she wouldn't allow herself to be side-lined in this way.

"Great party," one of the neighbours commented as she passed.

"Er, yeah." Carol, her neighbour was stood alone and looked like she would welcome company, but Michelle had a more pressing item on her mind. Like separating Paul and Alana. Though she was furious, she attempted to swallow the emotion as though it was a glob of chewing gum. If only it was that easy.

"Hi gorgeous man." She stood beside Paul and reached for his hand. His fingers didn't curl around hers as they usually would. In fact, his hand stiffened. Alana looked the other way.

"Would you mind giving us a few minutes Alana." Michelle stood firm. "Paul and I have barely seen each other this evening. Perhaps you could go and find your husband." She spoke with a bravery she was struggling to emulate.

"Actually Michelle. Paul and I were in the middle of a conversation. I..."

"I'm not asking you. I'm telling you."

Alana quickly stood up and strode away without looking back.

"Michelle, that was rude. There was no need for that."

"There was every need. Who the hell does she think she is? And you?" Michelle took a huge swig from her glass. "What the hell are you playing at? It's supposed to be *our* party."

"She was right though Michelle. We *were* in the middle of a conversation." Paul stared into his pint glass. "And it was important."

"More important than me?"

"Grow up Michelle. For God's sake. I'm off to the loo."

"You mean you're off to find *her*." Michelle watched as he retreated and slumped onto the swing in the spot from where he had emerged. Hot tears prodded the back of her eyes as she avoided making any eye contact with people. She drank the remainder of the wine in her glass then made her way back towards the kitchen for a refill. She forced a smile at a heated conversation that was taking place between her mum and Paul's brother.

"Michelle will tell you how it was," Susan affirmed. "There's no way you will be able to argue with what she has to say."

"Later Mum. There's something I must do." She would give it a few minutes and then it would be time to catch them in the act. If that was the case, she had to know. She stole a glance around the congregated people in her lounge. No sign. She tried the handle of the downstairs loo and was surprised to find it open. She pulled the front door ajar and peered around the cul-de-sac. Still no sign. *They must be upstairs.*

Michelle inadvertently bunched her fists and with a heavy pulsating sensation in her chest, she gingerly ascended the staircase. She could hear muffled voices coming from within one of the rooms. *Her bedroom.* Resisting the urge to burst in, she stood and listened for a moment. The tones of Paul and Alana were indistinguishable, clearly they were making great efforts to keep their voices low. Hardly daring to breathe, she continued to listen.

Finally, Alana's voice resounded with clarity. "Without that, it all falls apart." Paul's deep, guarded lilt followed but Michelle couldn't make it out. *Without what? What falls apart?* She asked herself. What were they talking about? What were they doing in her bedroom? Finally, she could bear it no more and stormed in.

"What's going on?" She stood in the doorway, observing them sat side-by-side on the bed. They jumped apart.

"Looks like I caught you in time," she continued, moving towards them. "You didn't have the chance to get your knickers off, did you? Get out of my bedroom. NOW." Alana rose to her feet and marched past without looking at her. Paul remained where he was, his mouth set in a straight, hard line.

"How could you?" Michelle snapped. "After all we've been through."

"You need help. Do you know that?

"You and *her* in *our* bedroom!" Michelle fought the temptation to hit him. There were too many people around. "What do you expect me to think? And what did she mean, *without that, it all falls apart?* Without *what?*"

"Leave me alone." Paul stared at her with cold eyes. "I mean it."

A sob caught in Michelle's throat as she flounced out of the bedroom. If he wouldn't tell her, she would go and find Alana. But a glance around at the remaining party guests confirmed Alana had gone. As had many of the others. "Right party over," she shouted, yanking the plug from the speaker out of the wall. "Everybody leave. Now!"

"Michelle! What the…"

"I'll ring you tomorrow mum. Just make them all go." She hollered into the garden, "the party's over!" before striding back towards the foot of the stairs as tears took over. Paul barged past her on the landing. "I'm going to stay at my brother's. I will be back tomorrow."

"No! Please, I…"

"Leave it Michelle!"

She sat on the side of the bed for a few moments, listening to voices, slams of doors and car engines. She had never been more alone. She kicked off her shoes and tugged off her bracelet and earrings. What a disaster. She had looked forward to this party so much. And she still hadn't found out what they'd been discussing.

As the house quietened, she noticed a box on her pillow. With tears in her eyes, she picked it up and untied the ribbon. Inside was a beautiful engagement ring. Under the box was a torn piece of paper. She smoothed it out, one of her tears dripping onto the page and smudging the thick, black ink. One word. The *thing* they must have been talking about. *TRUST.* She snatched it up, screwed it into a ball and threw it at the bin.

Chapter Thirteen

A voice jolts Paul into the present.

"How long you in for mate?" A hefty inmate with rolled up sleeves leans on a pool cue. Paul feels like a specimen under his microscope. Having nearly opted to spend the entire evening in his cell, he has been lured out by the urge to be near others, whatever sort they might be. Stephen is fast asleep in there, so being abandoned with his own thoughts tonight feels like torture.

"I'm on remand," Paul replies. "How about you?"

"Five years." The balls clink. "ABH," he adds, as though an afterthought.

Paul decides not to request further information. *I'll keep on the right side of you.*

"What you been remanded for?" Another man with slicked back hair and sunken cheeks calls from the table beside them. The smooth skin around his eyes suggests he is barely out of his teens, though his teeth tell a different story.

Paul pauses, recalling what he has been told in the dinner queue. His story is bound to make the papers. He will probably do himself no favours by lying. It's best coming from him. Not that he gives a toss what anyone here thinks.

"My wife stabbed herself. I've been blamed for it. I didn't do it though."

"Yeah, yeah!" The two men laugh as they exchange glances. "You won't be the first man who's done their missus in. Not on this wing."

Paul does not return the question to the man with the sunken face. There is something about him. Paul doesn't want to know what he is in prison for. He senses he is being watched and glances up to meet the stony stare of a huge man who cracks his knuckles. Paul looks away quickly.

"You alright? You're fairly new on this wing, aren't you?" an officer curls his head around the cell door.

"I suppose."

"Just making sure. I'll leave you both to it then." He nods towards Stephen, who's laid on his bed, staring at the ceiling.

"Can I have something to read?" Paul is pacing up and down the cell. He hasn't a clue how he'll manage another night's sleep in this hellhole.

"What do you think it is? A library? You can order papers and magazines with your canteen on a Saturday."

"What if I want a drink?" Paul picks up a plastic beaker.

"Plenty of water in the tap." He gestures towards the sink. "You can order some juice with your canteen. And if you can have a kettle sent in, then we'll fit it with a sealed plug."

"But I'm not allowed to make phone calls yet, nor do I have any money to order anything." Paul steps back and sits on the edge of the skinny mattress. "What am I supposed to do? Aren't you people supposed to be helping me with all this?"

"Easy mate." Stephen sits up and looks at him, frowning.

"No one will be *helping* you if you're displaying that sort of attitude Jackson." The officer, or screw as he's heard them called, leans against the cell door. "But you can work you know, you'll receive a bit of money then, has anyone told you? You can receive cheques sent in

73

from the outside as well. Obviously, they have to clear before they can be added to your canteen."

"So this is it for a couple of weeks?" Paul gazes at the concrete floor, trying to contemplate how he's going to survive.

"Am afraid so. You might be able to borrow some books from the prison library. Or maybe one of the other inmates'll take pity on you." He looks at Stephen then. "It's a 'you scratch my back' situation in here."

"Right. Thanks."

"It's OK." His expression softens slightly. "The first couple of weeks are the worst. It'll get better once you become familiar with the routines." As the echo of the door shutting resounds in Paul's ears, he trembles at the thought of *familiarity* in here and it becoming ingrained in his routine. He needs to distract himself. Take himself out of here, in his mind anyway. Laying down on his own bed, he thinks of Emily then of Nick and remembers their recent gym trip.

It was one of those upmarket gyms where membership costs a fortune. Paul recalls striding beside Nick, as they made their way past the indoor tennis courts. It was as though he was entering another world - one inhabited by happy, normal people in happy, normal marriages with happy, normal wives. He shed his clothes in the changing room, like he was peeling off the skin that contained him. For the time being, he could be happy and normal too.

All morning Paul crackled with unspent anxiety and anger. Some of it was emitted on the treadmill and a bit more was released as he wrestled with the weights. Swimming up and down the pool helped him to think a little clearer. He needed a plan of how to deal with Michelle. For all their sakes as well as for them as a couple. He could not go on any longer like this. As he sat in the jacuzzi beside Nick, he felt human again. But the prospect of returning home was causing him to regret how he had chosen to spend his morning. *Had it been worth it?*

"Are you going to tell me what's going on, or what?" Nick pressed the button to reactivate the jacuzzi. "You've barely said two words since we arrived. Is it *her* again?"

"Nothing to tell, honest."

"I've noticed your arm, and your nose." Nick nodded towards Paul. "C'mon, I'm not daft. You've not been yourself for a while. What's going on?"

"Nowt. Look, I can handle it." He extended his arms across the tiled ledge behind them as the chlorinated bubbles popped into his face, making his eyes sting. He absently watched as the swimmers in the adjacent pool swam up and down, down and up.

"You want to leave her, you know. She's going to drag you down to where she is."

"Nick leave it. I'm having a break from it all."

"Maybe I should have a chat with her." Nick's face hardened.

"Stay out of it." Paul's stress levels rose with his voice. "I'm not involved in rows you have with *your* missus, am I?"

"My missus isn't a psycho."

They sat in silence for a couple of minutes. Paul's thoughts were whirring like a washing machine. He wished he could switch them off.

"Right, that's me." Nick hauled himself out of the bubbles. "I'm off for a shower. Are you stopping here?"

Paul restarted the bubbles. "I'll have five more minutes in here then have a blast in the steam room, I think."

"I'll meet you in the bar." Nick rubbed at his head with a towel. "I'll give the missus a bell and let her know we're having a pint before we head back."

Paul watched him retreat along the poolside. From his head to his toes, he ached, nothing to do with the weights he had lifted, but the constant contemplation of the mood Michelle might be in when he returned home. Without meaning to, he envied his friend for the comfortable simplicity he had in his life. *I'll give the missus a bell and let her know we're having a pint.* Jacqui, Nick's wife was a pleasant woman, who always made him and Emily welcome.

It had become necessary to refrain from involving Michelle in his friendship with Nick and Jacqui due to her hostility towards them and Nick hated Michelle right back. She would latch onto each snippet of conversation, only to blast it back at Paul later when they were alone again. She hated hearing about the past, about days which did not include her.

Jacqui and Nick had not invited them out as a couple since a few weeks after his and Michelle's wedding. Jacqui had made a throwaway remark about Paul's ex-girlfriend. Noticing the expression on Michelle's face, Paul had wanted to crawl under the table. Michelle had wound herself towards a jealous crescendo before eventually storming out of the house and into the night, forcing Paul to go after her.

Being in company of any description had been curtailed. It was a risk. Something would always be said that could be misconstrued. Or one of their friends or a friend's partner might happen to be physically attractive. It became easier to turn invitations down. Until eventually, they dried up completely. *Why had he married her? Idiot.*

The bubbles subsided, signalling the jacuzzi was entering its rest period.

Paul plodded across the tiled floor and into the steam room. He sank onto the bench, grateful for the anonymity which the steam provided. If only his gloom would mingle and evaporate with it. He was oblivious to the heat as he sat, drowning in his thoughts, knowing he would soon have to leave here, then return home to face the music.

As he pulled up outside his house, he checked his phone, having been absent for nearly four hours.

Seventeen missed calls! As he yanked the handbrake on, he studied the exterior of their house, stalling for time. He wanted to restart the engine and go. Anywhere but here. His hands gripped the steering wheel vehemently; the veins in them looked as though they might explode. *She was going to kill him.* If only he could enter their home, plant a kiss on her forehead and flop out in the armchair with the Sunday papers. *No way.*

All was quiet. "Hello," he called, his voice hesitant in the quiet hallway.

"Daddy, I've been playing with Phoebe and Sam and they have a big trampoline in the garden, and ..."

"Go to your room Emily. Tell him later." Michelle didn't look at her.

"There's no need to send her to her room." Paul opposed her in the hallway. "Why are you sending her to her room?"

"Where've you been? Bedroom Emily. Now please."

"To the gym." His voice shook, though it had a defiant edge as he watched Emily disappear up the stairs.

"*The gym!* Who with? *Alana?*"

"*Alana!* Of course not." Tugging off his jacket, he hung it on the peg. "Don't be ridiculous."

"Do you think it's acceptable," she folded her arms, "to bugger off and leave us all day like we don't exist?"

"I needed some time to myself." He unzipped his holdall and took out his wet towel. "I work hard all week, Michelle, and things haven't been too good lately, have they?"

"So do I. I work hard too. And I know it's been shit but I don't go off all day, do I?"

"Look Michelle. I'm sorry I've upset you. I'm back now. Let's not do this. We have the rest of the day. *What am I apologising for?* I've done nothing wrong!"

"Yes you have. You've ignored all my calls. What if something had been urgent?"

"I'm sorry. My phone was in the locker. I didn't hear..."

"Well, I've been thinking. I think you should leave."

Paul, ignoring her, headed towards the kitchen to stuff his wet things in the washing machine.

Michelle launched herself in front of him, obstructing his path. "Go back to your girlfriend."

"What are you on about?"

"I want you out of my house." Her face was nudged right up to his. "I mean it."

"It's *our* house!" The front door was still wide open, allowing the prying eyes from the house opposite a front row seat.

"You don't want me? You don't carry on living here." Her voice cranked up a notch. "Go on, pack your stuff."

"Don't be daft. I'm going nowhere."

"I'll ring the police."

"And tell them what?" He was starting to panic a bit. He had expected ructions but nothing like this. With his foot, he shoved the door closed before returning to face her. He resisted the urge to slap some sense into her.

Her chin jutted out, defiantly. "I can tell them anything I want. They've a duty to protect us, especially with Emily in the house."

"Protect you from what? From me? *You'd do that?*" In astonishment, he gaped at her. He raised his arm to scratch his face and she flinched. "Yes, of course you would. I don't know what's got into you. You nutter!" Backing away from her, he advanced towards the kitchen but she grabbed at his jacket.

"I said I want you out!"

"Oh yeah, and where am I supposed to go? And do you think I'd leave Emily with *you?*"

"I don't care, I want you OUT!" As she shouted the final word, she lunged at him, making straight for the hand which held his set of keys.

"Get off!" he yelled as she dug her nails into his hand. It was taking every effort to keep hold of them. He was unsure what was smarting more, her entrenched nails in the back of his hand or the keys which remained locked within his grasp.

"Give me them," her voice was thick with rage, as she clasped hold of one of the keys and twisted it across his fingers.

Letting go, she lunged for the landline telephone. "I'm going to ring them you know."

"And tell them what?" Despite the situation, amusement bubbled up within him. "Please arrest my husband because he went to the gym?"

For a moment, a wave of calm seemed to stop her in her tracks and normality crossed her face. Paul was momentarily reassured. Until she smashed herself in the face with the telephone receiver.

"No! Stop it! Michelle! Please!" Grabbing her arm in mid-flight, he managed to wrestle the self-imposed weapon out of her hand before she tore from the hallway, into the lounge.

"Daddy, what's happened?" cried Emily behind him. "Mummy's face is bleeding!" Paul's chest thudded with guilt as he peered over his shoulder to see Emily creeping down the stairs.

"She's just had an accident," he picked her up when she reached the bottom. "It'll all be OK." He then lowered her to the tiled floor as he stood for a few minutes trying to compose himself. He couldn't believe it. He hoped Michelle stayed where she was. It was a miracle he'd not flattened her.

"Why's there a police car Daddy?" Both turned to the window where blue light intermittently reflected through the hallway window. A police radio sounded in conjunction with Michelle's sudden desolate sobbing from the lounge.

"Oscar winning performance darling, keep it up!" He shouted at the closed lounge door. "Oh for God's sake!" He rammed his fist down into the bannister, not feeling the pain. "She's rung them. I don't believe it! She's gone and rung them!" He rose and lunged towards the door, nearly knocking Emily over in the process. Before they had chance to ring the bell, he swung the door open.

"Paul Jackson?" enquired one of the two officers, both men. "There's been a report of an assault. Can we come in?"

Paul held the door ajar, with a nod of his head as he faced them in the hallway, locking his eyes with one of them. No way were they carting him off. Not when he had done nothing wrong. He noticed them staring at his curled-up fists, bloodied from where he had punched the banister. He uncurled them and tried to focus on his breathing. *Calm, mate, calm*, he told himself. "The only assault in this house, pal, is the one she's done to herself. Go to your room Emily." She turned and ran upstairs. "No, all the way to your room please," he added as he noticed her huddled form beside the banister. The adrenaline drained from him as he prepared to face the severity of his predicament.

"Your wife claims you've assaulted her." The older officer spoke, his entire expression showing distaste towards Paul.

"I haven't." His voice was steady. "I would never hurt my wife. She's lying."

Michelle appeared in the lounge doorway, blood trickling from the self-inflicted injuries to her forehead, nose and top lip, tears streaming down her face. *Well done you!* Paul congratulated her silently. *You look every inch the battered wife.*

"Thanks for coming quickly," she sobbed. "I know you're busy, but I didn't know what else to do."

"You're a liar," Paul spoke through gritted teeth. "She really is. I haven't laid a finger on her."

The older officer nodded towards his colleague. "Take her back in there and I will talk to our friend here in the kitchen. Is it this door here?"

Paul felt the officer's hand on his shoulder as he allowed himself to be led into the kitchen. All the while, he could hear Michelle's weeping from the other room. *How did they ever get to this?*

Once in the kitchen the officer spoke into his radio. "I require another unit to 42 Bracken Bank, Osbaldwick." After a few crackles and beeps, a voice acknowledged his request. "I will need an officer to take a statement alongside PC Taylor from the complainant and we may need to make provision for a child in the house."

The full burden of the circumstances pressed down onto Paul as he contemplated what this meant for Emily. He could ensure the police took her to David's but her presence in the house through all this would mean her school would be informed. And social services. *Oh God ... what had they done?* "I honestly haven't laid a finger on my wife," his voice cracked, all hints of any sarcasm gone as he faced the officer.

"You'll have the opportunity to tell us your side of things, but we will have to do that at the station. Paul Jackson. I'm arresting you on suspicion of occasioning a Section 18 assault. You do not have to say anything, but it may harm your defence if you do not mention when questioned, something which you may later rely on in court. Anything you do say may be given in evidence."

By now a third officer was in their home and had entered the kitchen. "If you could just face the sink, Paul and place your wrists together behind your back." He jumped as the cold metal was snapped onto him. He had never been handcuffed in his life.

Flanked by both policemen, he was led out of his door and marched down the path, in full view of several neighbouring onlookers. Paul bowed his head. He knew exactly what they would all be thinking and wanted to shout out, protesting his innocence. *It's her,* he wanted to tell them all. But what would be the point? In situations like this, it was a woman's world.

"Stand there. Someone'll be along to process you shortly."

Paul obediently positioned himself next to the tall desk. Everything was green. Sweat dripped from his armpit and slid down the side of his body under his loose-fitting tee shirt. Clearly the custody 'suite,' as he had heard it being described, was being baked from the outside in. A stench of stale sweat hung in the air. It was like being in hell. He couldn't believe he was here.

"Right Jackson, this way." A hostile looking man held a nearby door ajar. "We're putting you in a cell for a while."

"*A cell! But* I didn't bloody do anything to my wife. She did it to herself. You can't put me in there!"

"Remove your shoes please. And your belt. And any jewellery, including your watch."

"Why?"

"Why do you think?" He outstretched his hands to receive the requested items.

"I'm hardly going to hang myself in there. It's my missus who's more likely to do herself in."

"Just a precaution." His voice was brisk and business-like. "It's the same for everyone."

"How long are you locking me up for?"

"It all depends on the Crown Prosecution Service. His eyes wandered towards the clock. At the moment you're under arrest. They'll decide whether you'll be charged after we've interviewed you."

"And when will that be?"

"Not too long hopefully. We'll be liaising with the officers that are taking your wife's statement and we'll take it from there. It's busy tonight so you might as well make yourself comfortable. I'm not sure how quick it will be."

"*Make myself comfortable?* Are you having a laugh? I can't believe it."

The heavy door clunked shut behind him. Paul flopped onto the thin mattress.

Another metallic thump, coupled with the rattling of keys, signalled to him he was truly incarcerated. Closing his eyes, he tried to shut out the barren, grey room. Perhaps he preferred the green. It wouldn't be long until they released him, surely. He stretched out on the 'bed' and hoped Michelle would tell the truth.

Chapter Fourteen

Michelle jumped at the knock at the door. *Who could it be?* It was after midnight. The police had been and gone hours ago. She'd had a phone call to say Paul had been released and was going to spend the night at his brothers. She had been forced to admit the truth about what had happened. It was going to go too far otherwise. He would have been bailed to stay away from her. His job would have been in jeopardy and social services would have been called in. Her common sense had prevailed. But what was done was done and she knew she had hammered another large nail in the coffin of their marriage.

A bottle of wine had numbed her self-inflicted facial injuries, but it would take more than wine to deal with her internal pain. She had no idea why she acted the way she did sometimes. It just happened. Another knock on the door jolted her out of her thoughts. If it had been Paul, he would have let himself in. She hadn't put the bolt across. Though maybe she should have done. She jumped again. Whoever it was wasn't knocking, rather thumping on the door.

"C'mon. I know you're in there."

"Who is it?" She could make out a male silhouette in the darkness. She had switched the porch light off but now wished she hadn't. It wasn't Paul. She shouldn't have called out. But as well as being curious as to the identity of the post-midnight caller, she was anxious not to have Emily woken up.

"Open the door, you stupid bitch." The thumping continued.

Nick! It was Nick. She recognised the voice, although muffled. *Oh God. This was all she needed.* Once upon a time, Nick had fancied her. She'd had a drunken fumble with him in a club and he'd pursued her for a few weeks afterwards. It was before she'd ever met Paul and she hadn't been interested. There was something about the bitterness inside him and a condescending attitude towards women that reminded her of her father. She hadn't been able to believe it when he reappeared as Paul's best mate, years later. And he never tried to make much of a secret of his hatred for her. *Jealousy*, she thought.

"What the hell do you want?" She called out in the hallway.

"To talk to you. Now. I've a few things to say."

Against her better judgement, Michelle attached the chain and gingerly opened the door to the chain's two-inch allowance. She stared at his face, rigid with dislike and immediately caught the fumes of whatever he had been drinking.

"You stupid cow." He shoved the door. "What do you think I'm going to do? Just open it. I mean it."

"No chance. What do you think I am, stupid?"

"You don't want to know what I think of you. Let's say, there's not much I wouldn't do to make you disappear."

"Why?" Michelle's anger was in danger of becoming tears. "What the hell have I done to you? Why are you here?" Michelle tensed the muscles in her leg to stop them trembling. "Has Paul sent you?"

"You'll be lucky if he ever comes anywhere near you again after tonight. What's wrong with you?" He booted the door.

"Fuck off Nick. It has nothing to do with you." Her voice was a hiss in an effort not to wake Emily. "Keep your nose out of our business."

"He's been at my house. In bits. So it *is* my business. And I'm not going to stand by any longer and allow you to do this. You're gonna get what's coming to you."

"What do you mean? Does he know you're here?"

His bony fingers grasped at the door. "Take this chain off."

"No chance. You're not stepping foot into my house."

"*Your house!* You work in a school for God's sake. Make the most of the time you have left here. You're a charity case. Leeching off other people."

Tears sprang to Michelle's eyes. *Why was he so cruel?* What had Paul been saying to him about her?

"I think you're a nutter," he continued. His voice rose again after she had managed to peel the grip of his fingers from the door, to close it on him. "You should be sectioned. I'm gonna do everything in my power to bring you down."

She tried to keep the shake out of her voice. "Please leave me alone. Things are bad enough."

"Aaargh, poor little Michelle. What's the matter? Won't your little hubby do what you tell him to?" His sneering voice became louder. "I'm not going to stop chipping away at him until he leaves you. With a bit of luck that will be now."

"It's none of your business Nick. Go away." Although she was fighting back tears, she had a surge of energy. "Do one! Or I will ring the police."

"Do it. You schizophrenic."

"Right that's it." Michelle reached for her phone from the hallway table, pressed nine three times and held it to her ear. "Yes, police please. There's a man outside my house. He's been trying to break in and he's threatening me."

"Schitzo. Fucking schitzo." He carried on shouting as she tried to listen to what the operator was saying.

"Can you hear him?" She was relieved when they affirmed they could and he would be taken into custody on their arrival, if he was still there.

"Yes. He's a friend of my husband's. I will give you his address." She became calmer. More in control. She would take a knife to him if he got in.

"Just you wait. You'd better be looking over your shoulder. You wait."

She wondered if the neighbours could hear him. She might need witnesses. "Can you hear him now? Yes, I will stay on the line." *Surely Paul would stick up for her, after this?*

"The police are on their way." She shouted through the letterbox. "Hopefully they'll have you for drink driving as well."

She stood against the hallway wall, listening to the fading away of his footsteps. Hopefully, Emily had stayed asleep. She picked up the telephone again, intending to contact Paul but then thought better of it and decided to check on Emily instead. The police were coming. And after they had gone, there would be only one way to numb the pain.

Chapter Fifteen

Paul taps his feet as he watches the clock devouring the hour. 6:40 pm. 'Association time' is sacred. Not that he particularly wants to spend it conversing with other inmates or playing pool, but he's consoled by being able to linger on the outskirts of human interaction. Stephen's not bad but there's only so much conversation to be had with the same person, night after night.

His nails rap against the coveted phone card which he has traded with another prisoner for some legal advice. Without it, there would be over a week to wait until he could contact anyone. *"C'mon!"* 6:45 pm. Finally, he reaches the front of the queue and dials David's number, the only number 'verified' so far by the prison.

"It's me. You don't know how good it is to hear you mate." He chokes on his words as he hears his brother's voice.

"Thank God you've rung. What the hell happened? Is there any word on Michelle?"

"No, not yet. You'll probably hear before I do." Paul leans against the wall as if this may prevent him from drowning in misery. "I didn't do it. You do know that, don't you?"

"But who the hell did if it wasn't you?"

"We were arguing and I stormed out." Paul grips the phone. "I was only away for half an hour or so. I found her when I got back ... I can't bloody believe it."

"Are you coping in there bro?"

"Just about. I haven't a lot of choice, have I? It doesn't seem real." Hearing David's voice makes things momentarily normal, but things are never going to be 'normal' for him again. Even if she miraculously pulls through.

"I can't imagine what it must be like. We're trying to keep in touch with the hospital but they're being cagey."

"I can't believe they're pinning it all on me."

"From what I've been hearing from Nick, you've been putting up with far more than a lot of people could."

"That's not going to keep me out of prison though, is it?"

"You should have talked to me Paul. *Why didn't you?* Why have you been going through it all on your own?"

"Ah, you know … I thought I could handle it."

"You know I'll do everything in my power to help you, don't you? No matter what it takes, or costs. Whatever's happened and whatever you have or haven't done, I'm here for you."

"I know. Thanks. But I need you to believe I haven't done anything."

"Hurry up, will you!" A voice demands behind him.

Paul ignores it. "You do believe me, don't…"

Paul swings around to face the owner of the fist that has thumped the end call button. "What the-?" He stops short. Towering over Paul's six-foot frame is a man with a face as brutal as his fist.

Paul retreats to his cell and tries to read a book from the prison library. Stephen's asleep. Lucky sod. Days of nothingness yawn in front. Tomorrow is Monday, when he should be at work. In his normal life. What he wouldn't give to be back there. He allows his thoughts to recollect the last day he spent there and Alana's face creeps into his mind.

"Morning Alana. How are you doing?" Paul had dumped his bag on the desk as though it were a sack of potatoes.

"Better than you by the look of it. Are you OK?"

"Fine. A bit knackered." He pulled files from his bag that he would have worked on at home if he'd had the chance.

"It's more than that." Her perfume wafted in the air as she glided towards him. "You look done in."

"Do you want a coffee?"

"Don't change the subject." She clasped her papers closer against her chest. "Is it Michelle? Have you two been rowing *again*?"

"Kind of." He had confided in Alana several weeks previously but kept regretting it. From then on, Alana was constantly checking in with him.

"That looks like more than a row." She looked at his arm.

"My own fault … I was late home and I'd ignored her calls." Paul perched on the edge of his desk. "I guess she thinks I have something to hide."

Alana came towards him, took hold of his arm and inspected the nail wounds. "That looks sore." Her touch was gentle.

"It's fine." Paul pulled his arm away, berating himself for wearing a shirt with short sleeves. "I'll go and make that coffee."

With trembling hands, he tried to transfer a spoon of coffee from the jar to the cup.

She emerged in the doorway. "Blimey. You're a bag of nerves!" She passed him the milk. "You sure you don't want to talk?"

"I'm fine. I need to plod on with some work. Hold my calls will you? No matter who it is."

"You should leave her you know."

"I don't want to talk about it." He didn't want to meet her eye.

Slopping coffee, he sank into his office chair. Waiting for his PC to fire up, he tried to concentrate. E-mails would be a sensible place to start. A couple of personal messages nestled amongst the work ones.

A reminder about golf! Paul thought how he would like to spend the day on the golf course with Nick, however, it wasn't worth the hassle he would have, before and after from Michelle? Especially after last night. *If your possessive wife can't spare you for a day – I will bloody well come and drag you away from her.*

Hey bro! It was good to see you the other day! David had messaged him too. He had only seen him a couple of times since the wedding. *I'm coming over at the weekend.* Gone were the days when he could make sure he saw him every week. His last remaining family member and Michelle was jealous of him. *How could a woman be jealous of time spent with his brother?* He thought again of Nick's wife and how she would encourage him to be 'out of her way,' then she could crack on with her own thing too.

He now gave out his work e-mail address as a contact. He and Michelle had been using a joint email address. It seemed a nice thing when they were keeping in touch with everyone about wedding preparations, but it meant that she could delete messages without him knowing he had ever received them.

He'd told them to stop texting him too – that made her suspicious. One text could ruin an entire evening. Nowadays, when he remembered, he would turn his phone off when he was at home.

Paul slid a notepad across the desk. Perhaps if he made a list, it might help him do something useful. After scribbling a few things down, he remembered a call he needed to make. As he waited for an answer, the words *'Keep calm and carry on'* bellowed from the back of his office door. An overused slogan that had become his mantra.

"Oh hello. Is that the agent handling the sale of Seven Sycamore Court? I'm ringing to request a document so we can progress to completion? Yes, I'll hold."

Paul's brow relaxed as his gaze fell upon a drawing from Emily. *Me and my daddy.* Her face smiled out from a photo, next to it. He had to sort things. For her sake. For all their sakes.

"Yes thanks, if you could email it to me. No. That's all for now. I'll be in touch." Putting the phone down, he picked up his pen and crossed the first item off his list.

His mobile phone sprang into life. Michelle. He couldn't be bothered with her at that moment. It rang again. He switched it into silent mode. In his chair, he wheeled himself to his filing cabinet. Opening a file, he attempted to read its contents then picked up his dictaphone. "Alana," he mumbled into it. "Can you type a letter to Mr Brookes of Brookes, Lawson and Smeaton? Date it last Friday. *Dear James. I am writing regarding the exchange of contracts in the matter of Spalding Farm.* Alana, can you look up the rest of the address on the database?"

Paul glanced at the clock. It was nine thirty and he was worn out; as though he had worked a complete day already. Sighing, he pressed the record button on his dictaphone and continued.

"There's a few call-backs from the answer-phone." Alana marched into his office and thrust a handful of paper at him. "And a certain person keeps ringing. I've told her you're busy but to say she isn't happy is an understatement." She flicked her hair over one shoulder. "You should sort it. She's clogging up the switchboard."

He began flicking through his messages. "I'll give her a call later. I'm no letting *her* hold me to ransom."

RING ME ordered the text message, flashing on the desk.

"I'll leave you to it then." Alana rolled her eyes as he picked his phone up. She retreated towards the door.

Knowing he would be unable to achieve anything until he had pacified Michelle, he dialled their landline number. It was answered before the first ring.

"It's me."

"Paul. Why are you ignoring me again? I can't take it. We need to sort this out."

Paul stayed quiet as she ranted. Holding the phone away from his ear, he could still hear her clearly.

"Ring me when you've calmed down," he said at last, ending the call, empowered. This became anxiety as he considered how upset she was likely to be. Perhaps he should ring her. No, sod it. It was time to fight fire with fire.

"Fancy some fresh air? We could grab some lunch?" Paul had returned his calls and e-mails and was glad of the distraction when Alana poked her head around his door. *What harm could a bit of lunch do?*

"Yep." he peeled his jacket from his chair. "A break from here is what I could do with. I haven't much cash on me though." He felt like an idiot. "I've left my bank card with Michelle. I'm not sure if I'll have enough on me for lunch for both of us." *Hell, how embarrassing.*

"My treat this time," she replied. "Lee was paid a bonus this month."

"It's a relief to be outside for a bit," Paul exhaled as they settled on a bench overlooking the museum gardens. "The walls start to close in on you."

"Try working in admin." Alana passed him a sandwich. "At least you spend time in court and go out doing valuations and things. I'm stuck in there all the time!"

"Ta." He tore off the wrapper. "I'm ready for this. My treat next time."

Basking in the early spring sun, Paul and Alana sat in silence.

"What's going on at home now then?" She clicked open her pop.

"Nowt much."

"It doesn't seem like nothing to me. You're not on your own with this, you know. Maybe I can help you."

"I doubt it. It's fine." He wrenched the top of his crisp packet apart. "Let's talk about you for once. How's Lee doing?"

"Oh, same as ever." Paul thought a bored expression crossed her face. "We're like we always were. An old pair of slippers." She looked down at her hands. "Not a right lot to talk about."

"Do you argue?" *Is such desolation normal after marriage, was what he wanted to ask?*

"When you've been with someone as long as I've been with Lee; you kind of run out of things to row about." She fiddled with the corner of her sandwich wrapper. "The fire goes, after a while."

"Michelle and I definitely have fire." He brushed a crumb from the side of her face. "It's just always me who gets burned."

"She's lucky to have you. If I…"

"I know. But we'd better change the subject. Oh no!"

"What's up?"

Paul felt the sickening thud in his belly as he observed the parked car through the gates of the gardens. Yes, it was their Ford Focus. He was not close enough to distinctly pick out the features of his wife but could certainly imagine her expression. "It's her." He wrestled with the option of going over but quickly decided that would make things worse. Especially in front of Alana. No, he thought. I'll ring her this afternoon. Let her *hopefully* calm down first.

"So what. You're not doing anything wrong." Alana too, stared at the car. "I thought she'd be less jealous now you're married."

"It's fine." She was going to go mental. He'd better think, quickly, of some reason why they could possibly be sat outside eating lunch.

"Shall I have a word with her?" offered Alana.

"Er, best not. She'll not be friendly."

"Do I look like I care? I'm *your* friend, not *hers*." Alana rose to her feet, smoothing down the folds in her skirt. She glanced in the direction of the car. "God Paul. You could do much better than this."

Chapter Sixteen

Paul sits upright in the gloom of his prison cell. The thin bed creaks as he shivers. Unfolding the blanket at the bottom of the bed, he tugs it towards his chin, scuffing it against his skin as he remembers where he is. For a second, he wonders what time it is. His eyes leap to the overhead barred window, searching for signs of dawn. Then he realises he no longer cares about time. It makes no difference.

He shrinks back onto the lump masquerading as a pillow, then realises silent tears are sliding down the sides of his head, into his ears, into his hair. Trembling with the force of them, he takes care to ensure he stays silent, not wanting to draw attention to his state of mind or wake Stephen up. *Men don't cry, do they?* But this is all threatening to break him. The guilt and despair are too much to live with.

Stephen has already warned him if he is ever judged to be a 'suicide risk,' he will be taken to *'healthcare;'* a wing apparently so dire, everybody does all they can to avoid ending up there. Although he cannot imagine anywhere could be worse than *here*.

Closing his eyes, he wills sleep to rescue him. Instead, he goes over what might have happened to Michelle a million times. He keeps trying to recall the actual night but it's as though something in his mind is blocking it out. He's heard about *blackouts* and worries what his brain might be concealing from him. *He hadn't had that much to drink, had he?*

He should have foreseen the decline in her mental health long before. But he hadn't, and he knows he has failed them all. He tried but clearly not hard enough. He recalls the conversation when she agreed to see someone.

His phone had shrilled in the darkness as he lay on the sofa in Nick's lounge. She had locked him out for being late home from work.

"Hello," he had whispered.

"It's me. I'm sorry. I'm so sorry." Michelle was crying. "I don't know what's got into me lately. I don't want to lose you."

"Well you've a funny way of showing it!" He sat up as he spoke. "You're acting like you hate me!" His voice inadvertently escalated. "Why else would you lock me out? *And* threaten to have me arrested? *Again!*"

"I know. I'm sorry. I haven't been thinking straight. I think I need some tablets or something." She took a deep breath. "I'm not right Paul. I'm not myself. Please don't leave me!"

Paul rubbed his eyes, now able to make out the shadowy shapes of the living room furniture. "You have to learn to bloody trust me. And you must sort your temper out. I hate to see you like this!"

"Will you come to the doctors with me? Will you help me?"

"Of course I will."

"Will you come home? Now, I mean? I need you here!"

"I can't. I can't wake Nick up at this time. I'll be over first thing in the morning. I'm on his sofa."

"Are you sure you're not with someone else?"

He sighed into the silence. "I'm not going to answer that."

Without giving her the opportunity to change her mind, that same day, he made her an appointment with the doctor. He sat, sandwiched between Michelle and Emily in a waiting room as crammed as a bar during the World Cup. After twenty minutes, Michelle rose from her seat and stomped around. The agitation buzzed from her like electricity from a pylon.

"How long's it going to be? My appointment should have been ages ago!"

"Try and read a magazine or something. Relax, for God' sake." He passed her a copy of *Hello*, which she flicked through, before slamming it onto the table. Several people peered curiously at her across the confined room.

Another fifteen minutes elapsed until Michelle stormed out of the surgery. "Call this a service?" she blustered at the startled receptionist, the waft of her departure causing papers on the reception desk to flutter.

Paul and Emily tore after her. "Just a bit longer," he pleaded. He was unable to contemplate the consequences if they continued as they had been doing. "I'm sure the doctor will be able to give you something. Let's wait a little longer."

"No. I'll come back next week while you're at work. Which is what I should've done in the first place. I'm perfectly capable of bringing myself to an appointment."

"I need to have a word with you Paul." His heart lurches with the abrupt voice. He realises he must have fallen back asleep. Stephen stirs and turns over in the other bed. The vision of the prison chaplain framed in the cell doorway can be likened to answering the doorbell to find a policeman standing there. If he was at home. But for once, the dreadful realisation of his location isn't the first thing that hits him upon awakening. What they're going to tell him is.

"What time is it?" Maybe he can deter the inevitable if he keeps him talking.

"A little after three." The chaplain sits beside Paul on his bed.

"I already know what you're going to tell me." Paul feels sick. "It's Michelle, isn't it?"

"I'm afraid so. We took the call about an hour ago. I'm sorry to have to tell you she passed away shortly after midnight."

Paul sits motionless as the words swim through his brain, gulping down the rising vomit. She's died. He nods slowly. "My daughter. Has anyone ..."

"I'm afraid I can't answer that, but I imagine it will be the morning when she's told. Is she with family?"

"Her gran. Oh my God. Isn't there any way I can be the one who tells her? She should hear this from me."

"I don't think that's possible. But I will see what I can do to organise a phone call, then at least you can comfort her a bit."

"I can't believe she's gone." Paul's whisper is a ghost in the silence of the night. Yet he is strangely calm. Part of him expected to be hysterical. Michelle is gone. *Forever.* What does he feel? Anger she's given in? Sadness? Relief? Fear about the fact he's now on a *murder* charge? No. Nothing. Numb. Absolutely nothing. "Will I be allowed to go to the funeral?" An image of being handcuffed to an officer in front of family and friends emerges in his mind. Then, he's angry at himself. She's barely cold and he's thinking of her funeral.

"Given the circumstances," the chaplain places a hand on Paul's shoulder, "that probably won't be an option. But we can have a service here in the prison chapel. Light a candle and say a few words for her. Say a prayer."

"A prayer." Paul snorts. "What good's that going to do? *A bloody prayer.* I'm totally screwed."

"You're allowed to be angry." the chaplain squeezes his shoulder. "It's a natural response at a time like this."

"Angry?" Paul is surprised at the shaking within his own voice. "I'm more than angry, let me tell you! At least she's out of it but she's left me to face all this. It was all her fault."

"Easy mate." Stephen's voice sounds into the darkness.

"She didn't choose to die." The chaplain's voice is gentle. "I'm sure she fought for life as hard as she could."

"She chose to stab herself, though didn't she? What sort of a mother slices at her own arms and sticks a knife in her own chest when things are rough?"

"Shut up dickhead!" Another inmate's voice echoes along the landing.

"We don't know what happened yet." The chaplain's voice echoes in the stillness. "But you need to keep your voice down. You're waking everybody up."

"Look, I need to be on my own. Get my head around things. She could have told them I didn't do it. But she can't now, which changes everything. I have a bit of thinking to do."

"Of course." The chaplain rises to his feet. "We'll be keeping an eye on you. And I'll be back in the morning to see how you're doing. It'll probably take some time to sink in."

"You alright pal?" The other bed creaks as Stephen sits up. "Silly question, I know."

"She's dead." As Paul says the words out loud, he doesn't yet believe them. "I expected this. Everyone thinks I did it anyway."

The clunk of the cell door sounds louder in the dead of the night.

"You wanna talk mate?"

"Nah. Thanks. I need to think this one through."

Paul sinks back onto his pillows. His mind chatters so loudly, he wonders if anyone can hear it. *She's dead. She's bloody dead. And he's on a murder charge.* He drinks a glass of water, trying to quell the sickness. He'll think about that later. He wants to think about her.

Hear her voice. Pretend she's alive and none of this is real.

"I'm missing you. I can't wait to see you tomorrow." He was surprised to hear from her the night before the wedding. He was sitting in Nick's kitchen, glass of whisky in one hand, mobile phone in the other. "I thought I'd give you a quick call to say hello."

"I thought you'd be busy. Your nails. Your friends."

"I've only had a couple round. They've gone now. Are you missing me too?"

"Er, of course! How's Emily? Has she gone off to sleep yet or is she too excited?"

"Why do you always have to make it about *Emily*? Surely tomorrow is about me and you."

Surprised by this, he replied, "it's about us *all* surely? You're both going to look beautiful."

"Would you be marrying me if it wasn't for Emily?"

"What on earth do you mean Michelle? You're going to be my wife tomorrow. We're going to be a proper family. Not that we aren't already. Stop being daft." *Don't let us be arguing the night before our wedding*, he thought, holding his glass out to Nick for a top up. He ducked as David entered the room and tried to lunge at his phone. "What are you up to? Has your mum gone to bed yet? I imagine she's had a few to drink by now."

"Yeah, she's gone up. I'm on my own. Just poured a glass of wine." She paused for a moment. "Do you promise you'll turn up tomorrow? I need to know."

"Where's this coming from? Of course I will. We've been through this."

"I couldn't bear it if you didn't. It would kill me." He could hear the wobble in her voice and had a twinge of guilt, yet this was overshadowed by irritation. If she couldn't manage to allow herself to be happy and positive on the eve of their wedding day, what hope would there be when problems cropped up in the future?

He stopped himself from sighing down the phone and attempted his cheerful voice. "We'll both be there. It'll be great. Stop worrying and just enjoy your last night of freedom." He frowned as his brother performed cut throat gestures. "Right, I'm gonna push off. David and Nick are waiting."

"They've heard every word you've said to me? Well thanks a lot."

"Look, I'm off. I'll see you tomorrow. Get some sleep."

"I'll try." She sounded far away.

"Good night." All was quiet in the kitchen for a few moments.

"Our kid, are you sure you know what you're doing?" David slopped a bit more whiskey into his glass.

"Of course he doesn't. How could he? Marrying *her!*" Nick pulled his chair closer, so he faced Paul. "You've fourteen hours to come to your senses. After that, you're done for!"

"I can't back out now." Without warning, Alana's face swam into his mind. Swiftly followed by Emily's. "We've a daughter, and – "

"So?" David took a swig from his glass. "I have a spare room."

"And I've got a sofa," Nick added. "As you well know. It's not too late to reconsider. People will understand."

Paul shook his head. "I know you mean well. But give it a rest. I don't need this. Oh God." His eyes dart to the screen of his phone.

I hope you're at your brothers and not having a last fling somewhere. Please turn up tomorrow. x

"Are you sure you don't want to talk mate?" Stephen's voice slices into the silence of the cell. With tears leaking from his eyes again, he realises every time he thinks about Michelle, the memory is sullied with her insecurity and unhappiness. He would give anything to go back to before their argument in the holiday cottage. *Anything.*

Chapter Seventeen

*S*tabbed Wife Loses Fight for Life

Police have confirmed a woman involved in a domestic incident at Summerfield Holiday Park, at Filey, died last night.

She has been named as thirty-six-year-old Michelle Jackson. Her husband, Paul Jackson was remanded into custody after appearing in court on Wednesday.

Police were called to their holiday home at around 10:15pm on Monday where Mrs Jackson was found with extensive stab wounds to her chest. A weapon was recovered at the scene and Mr Jackson was subsequently arrested.

Their six-year-old daughter, who cannot be named for legal reasons, is being cared for by family and is currently being questioned by specially trained officers.

The family, from Osbaldwick, North Yorkshire, were on the second night of their family break. Floral tributes and messages of condolence continue to be left, both at the family's home in Osbaldwick, and outside the cottage where the tragedy happened. Enquiries are continuing.

"She's dead." Alana tosses the newspaper towards Lee. "Shit."

The silence of the room dangles over them as she watches him skim the article, squinting in the evening sun flooding through the window.

"Pull that curtain across, would you?"

Alana wonders whether Paul has been made aware of her death yet. The whole situation is haunting her and she's missing *him* too. Their calls, their texts, his presence at work. *It wasn't supposed to be like this.* Michelle had never known her good fortune. She had it all. Everything Alana wanted. Maybe now ….

Lee folds the newspaper into quarters, shaking his head. "She was a nasty piece of work. Spoke to me like shit on a couple of occasions. It goes to show you, doesn't it?"

"Show you what?" Alana stares at him.

"What people can be capable –"

"Shut up Lee, will you?"

"He's been *charged* with it, hasn't he?" The newspaper crackles as he stuffs it down the cushion of his chair. "And they're not looking for anyone else. *Are they?*"

"Reaching forward, she grapples for her glass of wine. "God do I need this."

Lee aims the remote at the TV and looks at Alana in a way she doesn't like. "Let's see if it's on the news as well."

"Paul's told John that Michelle turned the knife on *herself.*" Alana swallows a mouthful of wine; it slides comfortingly down her throat. "She'd a history of self-harm; she did it before she met Paul."

"You know a fair bit about it, don't you?" He's staring at her again. *That look!*

"I told you ages ago they were having problems. God only knows why he didn't split with her."

"And then what. *Come running to you?* You'd have liked that, wouldn't you? Nice virile man who isn't firing blanks."

"Don't start Lee." The familiar rage is stirring inside her. At every opportunity he reminds her of it.

"It'll all come out." Lee is like a dog with a bone. "A person wouldn't do that to themselves."

"Do what?"

"Shove a knife in their own chest."

"It depends on their state of mind." Alana picks up the wine bottle from the table beside her. "Paul's been living through hell. Michelle's been heading downhill for a while." She enjoys the satisfying glug of liquid as it spills into her glass. "Paul was way too good for her."

"I might've known you'd be on *his* side!" Lee flicks through the channels. "Michelle knew it too, *didn't she?*"

"Knew what?"

"That time she came around here, carrying on. She wouldn't have done, if she hadn't of suspected something." He leans over and grabs the wine bottle from Alana's side.

"I know what she's put him through. Stop doing that will you!" Lee's channel hopping is as irritating as him. "Leave something on!"

Alana wishes he would just leave her to think. She needs to straighten her head out. *Michelle is dead. Paul is in prison.* For a moment she wonders about Emily too. *Poor Paul.* She would never have imagined things would turn out like this although she has sensed his misery on many occasions. The last time was when he had arrived at work after Michelle had had him locked up.

"She had you *arrested*!" Alana had nearly choked on her sandwich as they ate lunch. "You're the last person in the world I would expect to *ever* be arrested!"

"Nearly five hours in a cell." Avoiding eye contact, he furiously picked blades of the grass they sprawled upon. "It was horrendous. I never want to see the inside of one of those places again." Dropping the handful of grass, he looked at her. "They spoke to me like I was scum. I suppose they would, thinking me capable of beating my wife up."

"What happens now?" Alana resisted the urge to put an arm around his shoulder and gently rested her hand on his arm instead.

"Nothing. Thank God. Apparently, they were talking injunctions and court hearings to Michelle. She backed down. She admitted she'd caused her own injuries. She'll have panicked."

"She ought to be sectioned." Alana placed the remainder of her sandwich in its wrapper. "Look, sorry Paul, I know she's your wife, but her behaviour's getting worse. What the hell are you going to do? You can't stay with her." *You should be with me,* she screamed inside. *We'd be perfect!*

"I'm trying to get her to see someone." Alana watched his lips as he took a huge breath in, then let a jagged one out. "I know she's hiding in there somewhere, she's beneath layers of hate and jealousy."

"Well I think you're amazing." Alana squeezed his arm. "Don't ever forget that. But I wonder how you can leave Emily alone with her. I wouldn't. *Is she safe?*"

"Michelle would never harm her. It's *me* she's angry with."

"Where's it come from though? She's got worse since you were married." She waited for Paul to suggest their friendship as a reason. At least it would give her an 'in.'

"It's to do with past relationships. Men running out on her, even her dad." He sipped at his coke. "She's been made to feel pretty worthless over the years. I guess she wants me to feel as horrendous as she does."

"Us being friends doesn't help does it?" Alana decided to come out with it. "Lee's jealous too. I'm not giving up our friendship though!" Her hand brushed Paul's as she gestured towards him.

"Yeah. Umm."

"She's bloody lucky to have you." Alana thought he looked uncomfortable. Clearly, he fancied her too. "Most men would have walked out ages ago."

The muscle in his jaw pumped as he spoke. "I can't. She's my wife.

My own family is all I've ever wanted. And besides..." His voice trailed off for a moment. "There's no court in the land that would give me custody of Emily." Something darkened in his eyes. "Michelle keeps threatening to boot me out and stop me seeing Emily. I have to make it work with her."

"Paul. You've had enough grief in your life, losing your parents like you did. What do you think they'd say about you living like this?"

"Been confiding in you a lot then, has he?" Lee rests the remote on the arm of his chair.

"We're work colleagues."

"Not his marriage guidance counsellor. Or his shrink."

"I'm his friend." She cradles her wine. They stare at each other for a few moments. "Stop looking at me like *that?*"

"To be honest Alana, I'm sick of talking about it now. We both know what we know." He reaches for the remote and snaps the TV off. "Don't you think we've enough shit of our own?"

At least he could give his wife a daughter. Misery courses through Alana. Not that Michelle deserved one. Not like me. *But now I've no chance.*

Chapter Eighteen

Overcome by melancholy, Paul tries to distract himself with the portable TV he and Stephen are being charged fifty pence a day for. He has been in this nightmare for five weeks and has only had the TV for a week. There are only so many news bulletins, soap operas and game shows that can be watched before your head starts to go batty. The headline jolts his attention back into life.

*The funeral has taken place today of thirty-six—year-old, Michelle Jackson. H*er white coffin is carried into church. Susan walks behind it, closely followed by Michelle's younger brother and sister-in-law. *He has made it to her funeral. Hypocrite.* When she was alive, he didn't give her the time of day.

"Oh my God. This is us. Stephen. Are you watching?"

Stephen looks up from the table where he is playing cards. By himself. Paul couldn't be bothered. Patience. "Shit. Is it your missus?"

"Yup." Paul recognises one or two women she worked with. Their next door neighbours are there. And even the police. "There doesn't seem to be as many there as I would have thought." Hopefully there are more inside. He's sure David will be there somewhere. Michelle was a solitary person. Maybe things could have been different if she'd had more friends and family support. She was so damaged. More regret steals over him. What's done is done but God! *If he could only go back.*

The focus returns to the news reporter. *Mrs Jackson, a mother of one, became a victim of a stabbing at her holiday home five weeks ago.* Shots of the entrance to the holiday park appear on the screen, followed by the cottage. The cordons have been removed and it looks as uniform as the others. Surely no one would want to stay in it now though? His mind drifts back to that evening. It's a complete haze.

So far, the motive for her killing has not been established. Her husband, Paul Jackson, has been remanded into custody until August 6th when his next hearing will take place. Mrs Jackson was laid to rest at St Joseph's Church, close to the home she shared with her husband and young daughter. It has only been nine months since she was married there.

As the reporter speaks, their home is flashed onto the screen, a carpet of flowers hides their garden wall. He's amazed by this. She didn't mix with many people. The news has spread out there; it's probably down to domestic violence campaigners. *They don't know the half of it.* A picture of Michelle is shown now. It was taken by her mother the previous Christmas. Paul recognises the top she is wearing. He bought it for her.

"Not a bad looking bird, was she?" Stephen is watching the news bulletin as intently as Paul. "It's not had as much news coverage as my shit though." The camera shows one final shot of her coffin finally disappearing behind the church door.

The familiar tears which come easily, slide down his face again. The vision of that lily-bedecked coffin, containing the woman he had once expected to spend the rest of his life with, will haunt him forever. *And he could have prevented it all.*

"Paul, I've managed to organise a phone call for you." The gentle voice of the chaplain is a welcome interruption to Paul who has fallen into a fitful sleep in front of the TV. Stephen's still playing cards.

"What phone call?"

"Your brother is on the phone. You can take it in my office. Emily is with him."

Paul makes the short walk, following the chaplain from his cell and down the two flights of stairs. News has obviously spread amongst the other inmates. One or two nod at him, others look away and one, Mick, he thinks his name is, pats his arm as he passes. He was the first one who showed him any solidarity in here, back in the line for his first prison meal.

"Hey buddy. It's good to hear your voice."

The heat rushes to Paul's eyes at David's words.

"I've booked a visit to come in a fortnight. With Susan too. Nick's booked a visit this week sometime."

"Susan's going to come, is she? I wasn't sure."

"When I asked her, she said she needed answers."

Paul tries to still the tremble in his voice. "Is she alright? Susan, I mean."

"Well you know. No parent expects their own child to die ahead of them. I think Emily is a welcome distraction though."

"That's good." Paul sinks onto a chair the chaplain has slid towards him. A couple of visits will give him something to hang onto.

"We can talk properly then without being cut off. I can't bloody believe it, any of it. I didn't think she'd - ... I thought she'd make it. *I did.* You must be gutted mate. What are you going to do?"

"I don't know." Paul wants to talk to him about it but knows Emily might be in earshot. "How's Emily coping?"

"She won't talk mate. Not at all. She hasn't said a word since that night. So when I call her in and put her on, don't expect anything."

Paul closes his eyes as he pictures his normally chatty, outgoing little girl. *"She hasn't said a word?"*

"The specialist she's seen has said it's not surprising at this stage. But listen, whatever has happened, you will both get through it. Things aren't going to stay like this,"

"What do you mean, whatever's happened?" Paul detects a note of something in David's voice he's not sure of. "You don't think I did it, do you?"

"Paul. We'll talk when I see you. Emily's here. I'll pass you over."

"David, I need to talk to you… I can't have you thinking…" He stops as he hears what sounds like his daughter breathing. The heat rushes to his eyes again. "Hello Emily. Daddy's here."

Silence.

"It would be lovely to hear your voice Em." This is torture. He should be there.

Still silence.

"You have Carla with you haven't you?" He again realises he would have endured anything at that moment, to turn time back and undo it all.

Nothing.

"Have you been told about Mummy?" Saying her 'name' out loud makes him feel more dreadful. She doesn't reply again.

"Emily, are you alright?" Still she says nothing. Paul wonders if she is crying. "Can you remember that night? Or were you sleeping?"

"Paul." The gentle voice of the chaplain sounds behind him. "I'm afraid you can't ask questions like that." Paul feels his hand on his shoulder. "I will end the call if you keep going down that road."

"OK … Emily, the angels are looking after Mummy now, but she loved you, and …" he chokes back the sob sticking in his throat. "Daddy loves you too." He pauses for a response that doesn't come. He has to know what she saw or heard.

"Paul." David's voice returns to him. "She's not right at the moment. Perhaps she needs more time. She's having a few days off school."

"I wish she'd have spoken to me." Paul is more devastated than when the call began. "They finally let me talk to her, and …"

"I know but she has a hell of a lot to cope with. She's only six."

"I know how old my own bloody daughter is! Has she really not said anything to *anyone*? About what she might have heard or seen that night, I mean?" Paul speaks quickly, avoiding the eye of the chaplain.

"Paul," his voice is stern. "I'm afraid you'll have to end the call."

"But I've hardly been on." Paul needs to know. It will make all the difference.

"Say goodbye Paul."

"David, I'll see you soon. You'll definitely come, won't you?"

"Of course."

"Give her a hug from me, won't you?"

"I'll try." David lowers his voice. "She's not letting anyone near her." He lowers his voice further. "But like I say, Susan's keeping a close eye on her. And I'm going to as well."

"Thanks. Let me know if she starts to talk."

"Paul." The chaplain reaches for the phone. "Now."

"I have to go mate."

"I'll see you next week then. You keep your chin up."

Chapter Nineteen

A chink of optimism nudges through Paul's desolation like a spring shoot. Today, Nick is going to visit him. Paul's name has been read out as he queued to escape for morning exercise.

Few opt for it as it means waking an hour earlier. But his sleep is erratic anyway. This isn't helped by the frequent checks they still do on him through the night to make sure he hasn't 'done himself in.' The constant disturbance is annoying Stephen too. This morning Paul's been awake since five, tortured again by that final day. He can't shake Michelle's face from his mind. But as he tries to recall that night, it's all a blur. Like his subconscious has blocked out the pain. So, he can either lie in his cell, gazing at brick walls or enjoy some fresh air on his face and see daylight.

Each time he comes out, he is reminded he has built the 'exercise' session into something it is not. The prison yard is barren. Nothing to do but think. Nothing to see apart from walls and seething barbed wire. No reason for hope. Apart from Nick's visit ... he would have been amused a few weeks ago to have thought the prospect of seeing his friend would have such a monumental effect on his state of mind.

Paul waits in the inmates' holding area. There is a cheery ambience, as one by one, prisoners are summoned by surname, before being given the table number where their visitors are waiting. They literally skip towards their loved ones who are either at the table or in the queue for a drink. This is what keeps everyone strong.

Each time one of the officers enters the room, they are set upon by several pairs of eyes. *Is it me yet?* The mood diminishes as the waiting room empties. Paul has heard from other inmates about the despair when a visitor doesn't show up or perhaps isn't let in. Maybe they haven't brought enough ID, or they have forgotten their visiting order. Or perhaps they've arrived late or can't remember their visit reference number.

Time is ambling by. Three become two. Paul and the last remaining inmate survey each other. They sit for another five minutes. Paul's spirits soar as the officer re-enters the room. *Dobbs 37801.* Then sink again. *Surely Nick wouldn't let him down?*

"Jackson?" A voice jerks Paul from his misery. "Table three."

Paul stops himself from running towards Nick who rises from his seat when he sees him. "I thought you weren't coming." Outstretching his hand to Nick, he is surprised to be enveloped in a bear hug.

"No contact." A voice barks from behind him. "Sit in the yellow seat Jackson and remain seated at all times."

"Bloody hell," Nick looks around. "I can't believe you're here. It would have been easier to enter Buckingham Palace. I've been scanned, searched, sniffed, I've been in four different waiting areas, and they've photographed me, taken my fingerprints ..."

"What?" Paul feels guilty. "No wonder I've been waiting so long. When did you arrive?"

"They take visitors through in dribs and drabs. I'd say about an hour and a half. It's like waiting to be hung, drawn and quartered. It must be awful for the wives who are here all the time." Nick glances up and down the room.

The chairs are all fastened to one another and the floor, with tables fixed in the middle. Partners and kids occupy some of the red plastic seats. Paul follows Nick's gaze to where it rests at the children's play section. "At least they have that. It must be boring for the young uns."

"Who'd bring their kids in here?" Emily's face fills Paul's mind. "There's some right types in this room."

"Have any of them said much about what they're in for?" Nick, again, looks all around him, an expression of disgust evident.

"I don't ask, and I don't want to know either. Luckily my cell mate is OK. He's in for manslaughter – driving when off his face but he regrets it. Nice bloke really."

"What the hell are you doing amongst these people?"

Paul stares at the floor. "It's a bloody nightmare." Cheerful voices echo around them. It could be a Saturday morning in a café.

"Do the others know what *you're* in for?"

"Yeah. It's been in the news, hasn't it? Nothing stays secret."

"What happened mate? One minute, you're on holiday … the next, well, the phone's ringing…" Paul is uncomfortable as Nick stares into his eyes.

"I didn't do it. I don't know what happened. I'm convinced she stabbed herself." Paul's voice shakes as he tries to read Nick's expression.

"Stabbed herself? How? *Is it even possible?*"

Paul tries to blink away the image of her blood-soaked hair fanned on the kitchen floor as she had lain dying. "I wish I knew what had been going through her mind. I might have been able to help her." For a moment, he reconsiders the plausibility of whether she could have inflicted her own injury as he recalls the knife lodged, deep within her chest. "Part of me hates her for what she's done. I know she was ill but she's deprived Emily of a mother and landed me in here in the process. I'm trying not to be angry with her but it's hard."

"I don't see how or why she could have done this to *herself*." Paul thinks Nick looks uncomfortable. He's shifting around in his seat and avoiding eye contact.

"I've told you. She used to cut herself when she was young. And she was doing it again."

"There's a difference between cutting yourself and shoving a knife into your own chest. There must have been someone else involved."

"How could there have been? We were on holiday."

"I, more than anyone, know what was going on between you." Nick's jaw hardens. "You knew my thoughts on her – the way she was with you. If you snapped, it would be understandable, you know. She'd have driven a saint …"

"*Cheers mate.*" Paul's fears are confirmed. They're all suspecting him. If this is coming from his friends and family, what chance will he have with the court? "I didn't kill her. I don't care what any of you think. It wasn't me." There is a sudden hush all around them and Paul realises he's raised his voice too much. He wants to tell them all to do one, to stop looking at him.

"Easy mate. I'll buy us a drink." Nick reaches for the little stack of pound coins on the table between them. "Do you want some chocolate or anything with your brew?"

"No, I couldn't eat a thing. A coffee will be fine."

As he watches Nick queue at the kitchen area, he doesn't know whether to feel better or worse for seeing him. He's wearing new jeans and trainers. Paul looks down at his own prison clothes. He'll have to contact John, quick. Go over his defence a bit. The prospect of being found guilty is real.

"There you go buddy." Nick places the cup in front of him. "All I was saying there is that we all make mistakes." He clicks the lid off his coffee and takes a sip. "What's done is done and we have to support you through it."

"Keep the lid on the cup please."

Paul nods towards the balding, overweight prison guard. "Sorry mate, I'm new in here and this is *his* first visit."

"One thing Jackson... I'm not your mate. Remember that."

"They're friendly souls, aren't they?" Nick leans back in his seat and clasps his hands behind his head. "Anyway ...I know you didn't tell me much about what was going on between you and your mental wife but I'm not stupid Paul." He rakes his fingers through his floppy, dark fringe and pauses for a few moments as though he's choosing his words. "She was making your life a misery mate. I'm sorry. I don't buy that she did it to herself. I know she was some kind of schitzo, but..."

"Well if you don't *buy it,* who else will?" Paul can't believe what Nick's saying. *He thinks he did it.*

"Are you sure you haven't blanked the whole thing out? The mind can do strange things when something awful has happened."

"For God's sake. *You* don't know about her self-harming history. It'll all come out."

"She's stitched you up good and proper this time. I don't know how you stand it in here. I wouldn't last five minutes." His eyes scan upwards. "Blimey, they've enough cameras. No one could get away with anything."

"For drugs, I guess." Paul watches as Nick counts them. "Or to stop people getting it on." Amusement stirs as he watches an officer pull a man and woman apart two tables down. The scantily clad woman, sits back in her seat, looking flushed and slightly sheepish, under her heavy make-up. He realises he's smiled and allowed himself to feel something other than desperate misery. His thoughts quickly sober themselves though. "Have you seen anything of Emily?"

"Ah mate." Nick looks straight at him. "She's not herself but then I guess she wouldn't be. She won't talk at all, according to Michelle's mum."

"So she hasn't said *anything* about that night? Hopefully she stayed asleep until I went into her room."

"Not a thing as far as I know. About what happened *or* anything else. *Poor thing.* Was she there the whole time?" Paul notices Nick's avoiding his eye.

"*I* wasn't there the whole time." Paul struggles to keep his voice steady. "I've already told you I didn't do it. Whatever happened that night, there's a good chance Emily saw or heard something. I need to try speaking to her face to face."

"I've already asked John about that." Nick scrunches up his paper cup. "You'd be allowed to see her, but it would have to be in here. And it would apparently have to be supervised. She was going to be called as a witness but obviously won't be if there's no chance of her speaking."

"A witness! She's six years' old."

"I know, but she's one of the few who might know what happened."

"I'm not having her in here, I've already said. Not amongst this lot. No way." Paul's eyes dart in all directions. "Besides, I need to talk to her on my own."

"I don't think they'll let you yet." Nick rips his KitKat open. "Do you want some?"

"No ta. My appetite's shot."

"You need to put a bit of timber back on. Keep your strength up. You look really pale as well."

"I won't tell you about how some of them supposedly tamper with food, for a laugh, apparently. I'll let you eat your chocolate."

"Oh bloody hell. You're joking, right?"

"I told you, it's awful." Paul shakes his head. "But one way or another, I'll make that court believe me. I have to."

Nick stays quiet.

"Time, ladies and gentlemen, please." The bald-headed officer parades up and down the central aisle like a peacock.

"Anyone would think we were in the Black Horse." Nick's eyes flick up to the clock. "I've only seen you for about twenty minutes. What a joke. I've been in this place nearly two hours. I'm gonna complain on my way out."

"No point," Paul shrugs his shoulders slightly. "You're no-one to them … and we're even less."

"If you could be making your way to the exit please," the same voice bellows out. "No contact, you've already been warned." Paul feels the rap on his shoulder from the officer as Nick pulls himself back from his brief hug.

"Keep your chin up pal. I'll be back." Paul hasn't seen Nick look this miserable since his mother's funeral. "Hopefully I'll be allowed in quicker next time."

"Thanks for coming. I'll send another visiting order out. Keep trying with Emily for me, won't you?"

"Course I will. I'd better go." Nick shrugs away from the hand an officer is trying to place on his shoulder. "Catch you soon." Paul watches his retreating figure and fights the familiar heat behind his eyes as he gives him a parting wave at the exit. Nick's fingerprint is checked on a machine and then he's gone. Paul rises from his chair.

"Remain seated until you're told. And pick that rubbish up."

Paul doesn't look up to see who the authoritative voice is originating from. He fears he will tell him where to go.

"Tables one to ten, make your way back to the holding cell."

Paul trudges back the way he came.

"Jackson, you stand over there please. We need to do a search."

"A search. What do you mean, a search?"

"Physical contact. Unnecessary studying of CCTV cameras…."

"What?"

"We'll be with you in a minute. If you'd like to step in there and put your clothes in this basket."

All fight, if any is left, seeps out of Paul as he accepts the basket and moves into the cubicle as directed, bracing himself for the inevitable.

Chapter Twenty

P aul rubs his eyes as a box of cereal, a banana and carton of juice is dumped onto the table beside him. "Eight o'clock Jackson... Little. Here's your breakfast packs. And there's a paper here for you Jackson. Room service, eh? You don't know how lucky you are!"

"Sarcastic pillock." He smiles as Stephen's voice sounds from the other bed. "Fancy a game of cards over breakfast mate."

"Nah. Maybe later. Can't be arsed pal. I just want to read the paper." On a Sunday, it usually keeps him going for a bit. By the time he's read through it, it will be exercise time. He has nearly survived into August.

The sun blinks through what masquerades as a window in the top corner of the cell. As he glances at the front page, he wonders if Emily's talked today. He notices the date on the paper. July 29th. How could he have forgotten her birthday? Gloom creeps over him.

Her gran will be making a fuss of her but hell - he should be there. He can't believe he hasn't sorted a card out. Discarding the newspaper, he flops back onto his bed. Bollocks.

"Time for exercise gentlemen. Nice day for it."

Stephen jumps up from his bed and heads towards the door. "You coming mate?"

"I'm stopping here."

"Suit yourself." The hatch slams behind the voice of the screw.

For the rest of the day, Paul remains slumped on his bed, absorbing rubbish on the TV as he thinks about Emily. Reliving walks in the park, trips to the swimming pool, her last birthday party. Stephen doesn't come back. He's got a visit. And he's having education. He likes to keep himself out of the cell. Paul is glad they're amicable, knowing he could have been padded up with anybody.

When night finally comes back around, he sleeps fitfully, having not exerted any energy the previous day.

"Jackson?" Paul squints in the darkness as the hatch in his door is yanked open. Stephen's bed creaks as he turns over with a sigh. "Raise your arm. Good. That's fine. Go back to sleep." Hourly checking of his 'well-being' has been reduced to two hourly at least.

"Will you just leave me alone?" Staring into the void of the night, he contemplates how much longer he can survive without physically cracking up. Finally, the darkness permits him some peace, allowing him to fall into a shallow, restless sleep.

"Daddy!" Emily races towards him, folding her arms around his neck and planting a kiss firstly on his forehead, then on his cheek. "I've missed you. I'm seven now, you know!"

"I know. I didn't forget!"

Holding her at arm's length, he gazes at her. She has grown at least an inch and her face is dusted with more freckles. Her eyes sparkle at seeing her father.

"Mummy's with the angels," she announces sadly. "You won't leave me again, will you Daddy."

"No. Of course not." He draws her onto his lap.

"Where were you? Where did you go?" Her warm tears drip into the crook of his neck.

But they are his own tears. He opens his eyes in the mist of the emerging dawn. Monday. A new day. A new week. Hell continues.

The dream was vivid. It has helped him to visualise her face again. Maybe it's a sign. *Keep fighting. Don't give up.*

The previous day, having plummeted so low, he has barely eaten, therefore devours the contents of his breakfast pack, secure in the knowledge no one would have messed with it, as all the items are individually packaged. Craving daylight, he decides to go out for some fresh air at exercise time.

As he waits in line, a screw approaches, holding a coveted pile of letters. The queue falls silent.

"Brown. Harrison. Buckton. Fairburn. Jackson."

Paul recognises the eloquent writing on the envelope. *Ring so-and-so. Meeting at such-and-such.* The letter has already been opened.

I can't imagine how dreadful it must be for you, Alana has written. *But please don't give up. The time will pass quicker than you think till you're back in court. Any jury worth its salt will acquit you. You must stay positive. All will turn out as it is meant to, trust me! You'll be able to put it all behind you and I will be right beside you like I was always meant to be.* He reads her closing section, with a touch of confusion. *The past can't be changed. What's done is done - let's look to the future.*

"I want to work today," he informs the officer directing all the prisoners after exercise. Subsequently, he kills the morning scrubbing industrial units in the kitchen. It is a mindless yet peaceful task, allowing him the freedom to mentally compose a letter to Emily that he can write later. It's something he should have done ages ago.

Dear Emily, please do not think I have forgotten you. I think about you all the time. I hope everything is OK and you are being a good girl for your

Grandma like you always are. I'm sure you'll be having fun at school and working hard.

I hope you had a lovely birthday. When I see you, which will be soon, I will take you somewhere special and we can make up for me missing your birthday. I will give you your present then.

I am well and looking forward to seeing you. When you receive this letter, maybe you can write a letter back to me. It would be good to hear about what you are doing and know you are well. I miss you millions.

Lots of love, Daddy x

He wants to write something that alludes to the night when it all happened – asking her to be thinking about what she remembers but the letter would be intercepted. He's stuck here and he's no choice other than to survive.

"I've set chess up mate. Come and take a thrashing."

Paul opens his mouth to protest but decides it'll pass an hour. He joins Stephen at their 'dining' table.

"How do you manage to stay upbeat?" Paul stares at Stephen who is pondering over where to move his first pawn.

"Visits, letters and being occupied. That's why I'm always reading. If I let myself think too much, I've had it. Especially after what I've done."

"It must be tough mate." Paul moves his pawn forward. "You haven't a bad bone in your body."

"I have to live with the knowledge that I've killed three people." Stephen's expression darkens. "Try having that on your conscience."

"It sounds like it was a moment of madness though. Anyone can make a mistake. The court'll take that into account at your trial, surely? They'll look at your background and all that?"

"I still took the lives of three people. I was off my box. What was I thinking - sitting behind a wheel in that state, I don't know? Living with that is a life sentence in itself." Stephen hovers a hand over a knight. "One day I'll be released but I'll always have to live with what I've done."

"It'll get easier."

"Will it?"

After writing the letter to Emily and laying down in bed, events of the fateful night start whirring around his mind. Although he's not going to admit to it, everything's become a blur and he can't think coherently. He can't remember exactly what happened. It's as though, as Nick suggested, he's blanked the memory. He closes his eyes. All he can see is Michelle lying on that kitchen floor so opens them again. Staring wide-eyed into the pitch-black cell is preferable.

Chapter Twenty One

Paul jumps to his feet at the words "Jackson. Table 34," relieved that his agonising wait has come to an end. He's been in the 'waiting room' for over an hour and is the third from last to be called. Relief becomes anxiety as he swaps the waiting room for the ambient visiting room and locks eyes with his mother-in-law. She doesn't move as he approaches her table.

"Hi Susan. I'd give you a hug, but we're not allowed any contact."

"I know," she says, stiffly. "I read the visitors sheet."

Paul looks towards the drinks queue. "Where's our kid? I thought you were coming together?"

"He wasn't allowed in."

"He's *here?* Where is he then?"

"Having to wait outside I'm afraid. The passport he brought as ID was out of date. Only just, but they still wouldn't let him in."

"But that's ridiculous. It had his picture on and all that, didn't it? How much out of date was it?"

"Only about two months. He had a right row with them. At one point they threatened to bar him completely. He's gutted at being refused."

"Me too. There's nothing I can do about it either."

"They spoke to him like rubbish. It shouldn't be allowed. Things are bad enough for us all. They could learn to have a bit of respect.

And there's the searching, the waiting, the dogs..."

"I know." Paul lowers his eyes, staring towards her sandals. "I'm sorry."

"What for?"

"Bringing you here." He looks her straight in the face. All he can see is Michelle. And pain. "And I'm sorry for -. I'm sorry."

"About Michelle? What happened Paul? What happened to my girl? What did you do?" Her voice is calm and full of sadness. Paul can't read whether she's blaming him.

She listens as he once again, imparts his version of events.

"But you were on holiday," she said. "You were fine when you all set off. Excited even. I waved you off, *remember?*"

Paul feels heavy. *What has he done?* He looks into Susan's watery eyes and knows he should *never* have married her daughter. For some idiotic reason, he had thought he could fix her.

"I had no idea things were that bad again," Susan continues, "you'd not even been married for a year. You were so happy on your wedding day." She looks like she's fighting back tears as she looks towards the drinks queue which has gone down a bit. "I will buy us a drink."

As Paul watches her join the queue, his thoughts drift back to the wedding day. Appearances had clearly been deceiving. He had been anything *but* happy. He sits, waiting for Susan to return whilst remembering how he had swung the car door open at the traffic lights.

"I'll walk from here," he had said to Nick, literally minutes before the service was due to begin.

"Eh, *why?*"

Paul slid out of the car before Nick could stop him. He bent down and said, "leave me alone for a few minutes. I need to clear my head."

The lights had changed to green and the cars behind were sounding their horns. Paul strode away from the car, cooled by the autumn breeze, which lulled him into a calmer state. It could be an ordinary day. Except he couldn't go in. He would have to call it off. He sank onto a bench, taunted by the happy church bells as he watched plants wobbling in pots beside him.

A few moments later, the bells ceased, and he could hear leaves whispering in the trees. The peaceful sound didn't do anything to relax his racing thoughts. He released a laboured breath, his solitude punctuated by the tapping of passing footsteps. He stared at the stone wall in front of him, beaten by years of wind and rain, darkened windows offering no clue as to what was going on behind them. The rhythmic beating of a pelican crossing ticked further seconds away and provided a stark reminder of normality continuing around him.

He rose from the bench. Without decision, Paul found he was walking in the direction of the imposing oak doorway. The breeze persisted, causing shadows to wave on the path and bushes to bow in the breeze. He felt sick. He had to do something.

But he had been a spineless idiot. Michelle's voice had reverberated around the stone walls of the church as she repeated her vows, peering into Paul's face the entire time, through her veil. She squinted in the sun's blaze from the window behind him. He managed a smile as he squeezed her hand.

"Now it's your turn Paul. Repeat after me." The vicar looked down at his sheet. "I, Paul Alan Jackson, take Michelle Marie Duffy ......"

The scent of lilies combined with the woody smell of the church was making him light-headed, as he glanced into the congregation. His gaze settled upon Alana. Something in her expression was willing him on. With what, he wasn't sure.

"Do you need me to say it again Paul?"

"No. I..." He stole a look at Michelle. This was all she wanted. Proof of his commitment. She looked stunning. Anxiety sparked from her eyes and her bouquet quivered within her grip.

"Paul?" Her voice was a murmur. "What's the matter? Tell me!"

He opened his mouth. The words wouldn't emerge. His eyes followed the length of Michelle's train to where Emily stood. She had counted the weeks down until the day she would be a flower girl at her parents' wedding. Clutching her flowers, she smiled as she pushed her hair out of her eyes. Something inside him gave way, like a burning ember, succumbing to the fire beneath.

Paul compliantly repeated his vows. The church echoed with silence between each line.

"I now pronounce you husband and wife. You may kiss the bride."

Turning to face Michelle, he caught sight of Alana saying something to Lee, she then stood and vanished along the aisle.

"Here you go. You looked miles away." Paul is jolted back into the visiting room as Susan parks a paper coffee cup and a Mars Bar in front of him. "You need to eat. You look bloody awful."

"Cheers." Paul manages to grin at her. As he sips his drink, he follows Susan's gaze towards the two children in the play area. "You haven't told me about Emily."

"I don't want to worry you."

"I need to know how she is."

"Not good, I'm afraid. She hasn't said a single word. She won't smile or even nod or shake her head. There's just no communication at all. I'd give anything to have her back how she was." Tears fill her eyes again. "She's been described by the specialist as *mute*. Some kind of post traumatic reaction. And I can't believe Michelle's gone." A tear spills down her cheek and Paul reaches for her hand.

"No contact," snaps a passing screw.

"Bloody hell." Susan withdraws her hand. "We need to get to the truth of what happened. And for you to be back at home."

"It means the world to me to hear you say that." Paul can't meet her eyes. He's frightened of what she might read in his.

"What I don't believe though," she's staring straight into his face. "Is that she did it to herself. No way."

"But the self-harming…"

"I know all about the self-harming. She did it in her teens, remember. All because I was too spineless to stand up to her brother and her father. I should have chucked her father out years before I did."

"I don't think she ever dealt with it properly. The way he was with her, I mean."

"It was the bullying too. She begged me not to go in to school, but I should have ignored her. The poor love would have crowds of girls waiting at the gates for her."

"I know. She told me about it."

"But I'm telling you - she wouldn't have had the nerve to shove a knife into herself – *not like that.*" Susan touches her own chest as she speaks. "Someone has done it to her. And I won't rest until I find out exactly what happened."

"It wasn't me Susan," Paul says quietly. He realises it's a matter of whether *he* stabbed her versus whether she did it to herself. And nobody thinks it's plausible she killed *herself.* He could be in trouble at his trial. He needs to speak to Emily. *On their own.*

"I can't bring my daughter back. But you need to be out there, looking after yours."

"I know," his voice is quiet.

"Your face is as white as a sheet. Are you getting any fresh air?"

"Not a lot."

"Five minutes remaining." A female is strutting up and down the central aisle like she owns the place. Several people gave her a dirty look.

"That went quick." The tiny bit of a lift Susan's presence has given Paul falls again. "It's a shame you can't stay longer."

"Well I think we've covered what needed to be said."

"I'm relieved you've come. Thank you."

"I'll keep on with Emily. She's bottling something up. It's more than just losing Michelle."

"Alright. Keep me posted, won't you. I'm really worried. And tell our kid I said hello. Tell him to sort his bloody passport out!"

Paul shakes his head at Susan as she looks like she's about to hug him.

"No sorry Susan. If I hug you, they will search me when I go back."

"I was searched on the way in. It wasn't *that* bad."

"Believe me," Paul grins. "It's a different kind of search."

Chapter Twenty Two

David rakes his fingers through his dwindling and greying hairline as he answers his phone.

"It's Nick, Paul's friend," announces an unfamiliar voice. "We said we'd let each other know if we heard anything."

"Has Paul been in touch? He's OK, isn't he?" Fear clutches at David as he imagines all kinds of scenarios. "Susan only saw him two days ago."

"He's hanging in there. We didn't have chance to talk for long - he wanted to ring you as well but there was a big queue for the phone. He asked me to ring you to say sorry that he didn't get to see you when you visited."

David thinks back to the sneering officer who noticed his passport was out of date. "Heartless jobs-worth. I kicked off with them in the end."

"You must have been totally peeved, having driven all that way."

"Well Susan was allowed in, so that was something."

"How's Emily doing? The kids keep asking about her."

"She's still not talking. *At all.*" David's chest is heavy at the mention of her. *God knows what she is going through.*

"Maybe we could get her together with my kids. They get on like a house on fire. Maybe she will talk to them."

"I'm not sure. She's not even talking to her friends at school and she sees them every day. Apparently lots of them are just leaving her be now."

"Do you reckon she saw anything?"

"Who knows? I bloody hope not." David glances towards his mantelpiece where Emily's first ever school photo smiles back at him. It's the only one he's got of his niece. "With a bit of luck, she'll have slept through the whole thing."

"Yeah. Let's hope so. It's awful enough she's lost her mum but…"

"I know." Nick goes on. "Paul has his *plea and directions* hearing next week. He thinks he might be able to go for bail."

"Yeah, I know. John, his solicitor has already asked me whether he can come here."

"You might end up with reporters around. It's been all over the papers."

"What do *you* think happened David? I'm just his friend. You're his brother. You know him better than I do."

"I don't know. He's not telling me much."

"I know she's dead, but she was an absolute cow to him." Nick's voice takes on an edge.

"I met him a couple of weeks prior to them going away and thought he was cagey." David says. "He wouldn't tell me much though. There's part of me that would understand if he'd snapped." *There. He's finally said the words out loud.*

"I know." Nick's voice has hardened now. "She controlled him. She was trying to isolate him. I could see it a mile off. Especially towards the end."

"I don't like to think he snapped but it *is* possible." David lowers his voice. "This conversation needs to stay between us Nick. If we think it's conceivable, he's no chance. What's the court going to think?"

"I know. I hope he gets off with it. Grounds of diminished responsibility or whatever. I'll never forget sitting in that visiting room, and I will have been seeing the *best side* of the prison too. "I don't know how he's standing it in there. It was bad enough visiting. I don't think I could keep doing that for a few years."

"It'll be more than a few if he's convicted of this." David can't imagine it. *His brother. Convicted murderer!*

"Do you think? We need to make sure the courts know what he was up against."

David glances again at Emily's photo. "There's a possibility Emily knows something that could change everything. It's bloody worrying."

"If what we're thinking is true, maybe it's just as well she can't or *won't* talk."

David springs into practical mode. "I think we need to be putting our heads together with his solicitor and seeing if we can say anything which'll help him."

"I'm going to be called as a witness, so he'll be wanting a meeting anyway. You could come along too, if you want. How do I say, under oath, that I don't think he snapped?"

"I don't know. Cross that bridge when you come to it. He has nothing to be ashamed about anyway." David's voice trembles now. It's all too much. I don't know how he put up with living like he has. I bet what we know only just scratches the surface."

"We'll meet for a pint mate. I'll fill you in on the bits I know about."

"I'll have to go." David jumps as his phone beeps. "Someone else is trying to get through. Keep in touch, won't you…"

"Hello?"

"David, this is Alana. I found your number in Paul's address book at work."

"Oh yeah." David brings her to mind from the wedding. All legs and blonde hair. The scourge of Michelle's life and little wonder … "You're Paul's secretary, right?"

"That's right. Have you heard from him?" David thinks her voice sounds as appealing as his memory of her. He reproaches himself for this momentary understanding of how Paul could be more justified for wanting Michelle out of the way.

"I tried to visit him a couple of days ago, but they wouldn't let me in." Anger prickles him again at the reminder of this. "Dreadful place. Not to be recommended. Hasn't your boss seen him? His solicitor, John?"

"Yes, but I want to see him. I wondered if he'd said anything to you. I'm surprised he hasn't posted a visiting order to me. Has he sent one to anyone else?"

"No idea, I'm afraid. But I'll tell him if I speak to him. He rings from time to time."

"I wish he'd ring *me*. Give him my love."

David is taken aback. Why is his *secretary* sending love? Maybe a figure of speech. He tries to remember whether she is married. There's a desperation about her voice. "Can you ask him to ring me? I can't believe he hasn't been in touch."

"He's getting his head around things. But of course I'll ask him. As well as the prison nightmare, we've to remember he's grieving for Michelle."

"I don't think he will be." Her voice becomes brittle. "It will be relief more than grief that he doesn't have to suffer any more!"

"Are you going to his hearing?" David changes the subject. "*Plea and directions*, it's called. It's next week. He'll be glad of the support."

"Yes, definitely. He's going to need all our strength."

"I know. Why they wouldn't bail him, I'll never know. As if a bloke like Paul could be deemed a *danger to women!*"

"Michelle was a danger to herself!" remarks Alana. "I never imagined Paul would be blamed."

David thinks this is another peculiar remark.

"What do you think happened?" She continues. "You must know

him better than most people, being his brother and all that?"

"He didn't tell me a great deal."

"He confided in me a lot. She was awful to him."

"Well you probably know more about it than me then," says David, sadly. "All I know is it's like a bad dream. Our kid's as soft as a poodle." As they end the conversation, he promises again to prompt Paul to ring her.

"Give Emily a huge kiss and cuddle from me if you see her."

"Oh," he waves at the postman, walking up his garden path. "I didn't realise you knew her so well."

Chapter Twenty Three

After an endless morning, Paul is jolted from his thoughts by a voice behind him.

"Jackson, you've visitors. Leave what you're doing and come this way."

"But it's not Saturday."

"Legals. I've put them in an interview room. They're waiting. Hurry up!"

Paul is led out of the workshop where he has been putting breakfast packs together, then through the association area, towards a room big enough to hold a table and four chairs. He is greeted by John, his solicitor, and the man who he presumes is to be his barrister. It is good to lock eyes with people who are on his side.

"Simon Booth QC. How do you do?"

"Good to meet you." Paul shakes the hand of the man wearing braces and exceedingly shiny shoes.

"How are you doing?" John reaches for and clasps Paul's hand, not matching the power of Simon's grip.

"Up and down. Bad days and not-so-bad days." Paul lowers himself into the chair opposite them. "I'm alright, I guess. I'm desperate to see my daughter, especially after what's happened."

"All in good time. You don't want her visiting you in prison, do you?" Simon's southern accent has a pleasant edge and Paul finds himself warming to him although he's a little irked by his lack of understanding about needing to see Emily.

He does sense, however, that this barrister will put his all into defending him. He silently thanks John for going one up and hiring a member of Queen's Counsel.

"I've filled Simon in on your case." John opens the file on the table. "There's a few points we need to go over."

Simon opens his briefcase. "Yes. Obviously, I needed to meet you prior to your plea and directions hearing at the crown court to hear your version of events." Paul recalls his own briefcase. Then he had been *'someone,'* instead of the *'nobody'* he is now.

"I know how difficult this must be for you, Paul," Simon shuffles through papers. "I concur with John that you shouldn't be on remand. Whatever has gone on leading to Michelle's death, a remand sentence wasn't the way. The judge who heard your case when it was passed to Crown for a mention, has a bit of a leaning towards the female of the species. He has four daughters. I'm informed he's come across some revolting cases involving male abusers throughout his career."

"Oh great!" Paul wishes he didn't know.

"However, he's known to be a little ruthless no matter what case he's hearing. In the scheme of things, you should have been granted conditional bail. Another judge may well have granted it. But here we are."

"Will I have the same judge at my trial?" There would be no point attending court.

Simon scanned down a sheet of paper "Judge Lakin. Hmm. I've had a few dealings with him. Nothing out of the ordinary. Firm but fair."

"What evidence do they have against me?" Paul tries to read the page upside-down.

"That's it." Simon's gaze flicks up from his papers. "The evidence is patchy. We should be able to achieve an acquittal. Obviously, you alerted the emergency services to your wife's injuries, there's witness statements from neighbouring holiday homes verifying a row was taking place, your prints are on the murder weapon..."

"I was chopping salad with it."

"Yes I know. There's the fibres and blood splatters that have been analysed, but these have been inconclusive. It seems it was a bit of a contaminated site, being that lots of people have stayed there prior to you. Hairs and fibres unrelated to your family have been recovered but there have been no matches on the police database. There's nothing *concrete* to suggest you killed her. There's one or two witnesses that are going to be called by the prosecution to speak of how you allegedly treated Michelle rather poorly throughout your marriage."

"Who are they?" Paul knows he kept their problems under wraps. But who knows what Michelle could have gone around saying? "I went through hell with my wife. No one knows the half of it."

"We'll come to that in a moment." He runs his finger down a sheet of paper. "It looks like they've called Michelle's mother, I think – I will double check that though. They've had a couple of attempts at speaking with your daughter, which would have been shown via video-link, but I understand there's been an issue with her not speaking since what happened?"

"Yes. There's some specialists working with her, but I've not seen her since I've been in here."

"You know she could visit you, if you wanted her to."

"She's been through enough."

"Also, for the prosecution, there's one of your neighbours at home and one of Michelle's work colleagues."

"One of her work colleagues!" Rage prickles the back of Paul's neck. "But I don't know any of them. And I don't know what any of the neighbours could say. And as for her *mother*, she visited me not long ago. I thought she believed me."

"If she can add weight to the prosecution, that'll be why she's been called. I imagine the aim of the prosecution will be to portray you as an aggressor, someone who regularly behaved abusively towards his wife, before exacting the final blow in a moment of rage, and the witnesses have been called up to verify that."

"But that isn't true."

"And that's what we'll be arguing against."

"How?"

"Did your wife have any enemies? Anyone else who could have made their way to your holiday home?"

"No. She was good at upsetting people, but not to that extent."

"Did many people know of the problems you were having as a couple?"

"They knew bits and pieces, but I didn't talk about what was going on, I guess I was ashamed. It's not exactly 'manly,' to be slapped and screamed at by your wife, is it?"

"Give me an example." Simon peers at him. "Obviously I've read all the statements and interview transcripts, but I want to hear it from you. A typical evening. What were you up against?"

Paul ponders, there are many examples. "I'll tell you about a night out we had about eighteen months ago, not long after we were engaged. We hadn't celebrated properly so my brother David was babysitting Emily whilst we went out for a meal. Michelle was on antibiotics and had only had one drink. She still managed to work herself up though, she had it in her head I fancied the waitress. She always thought I fancied other women. Especially my secretary."

As he sits remembering, he can picture her opposite him. Ten minutes had elapsed without her saying a word. *It was coming.*

"You bring me out for a meal," she pointed towards the waitress as she walked away, "then you spend all night making eyes at that woman."

"The only time I've glanced in her direction was when I was ordering food." Paul squeezed some mustard onto his plate. His face burned as he noticed the couple at the next table trying not to stare.

"Bet you wish you were taking her home instead of me?" Michelle banged her fork down, pouting. "You treat me like shit."

"Michelle." As he thrust the knife into his steak, he prayed she would somehow snap out of it. "I don't know what's wrong with you. We're supposed to be celebrating our engagement for God's sake."

"I'm sorry. I can't help it." She reached across the table and touched his arm. "It's only because I love you." Then she drew her arm back. "You have to admit though Paul, you don't help matters."

"What do you mean?" *Now what!*

"Bloody Alana. That's what I mean. I wish you'd move to a new firm."

"I'm sick of talking about this. If you can't allow us to enjoy our so-called engagement celebration Michelle, then I'm off home."

"He's all yours!" She said to the waitress when she returned to ask whether everything was OK. She flung her new engagement ring into her uneaten meal, then flounced out of the restaurant. The waitress scurried away, without another word.

Paul left his food and went after her, eventually finding her in the car park, sat on a wall. He was seriously pissed off. She had ruined yet another evening.

"Did she give you her number then?"

"I think you need to see someone Michelle." He marched towards her. "A counsellor or someone. You're going to wreck things."

"I saw how you were with her." She hopped down from the wall. "It hurts Paul. It really does."

He unlocked the car door. "I'm engaged to *you*, aren't I? Though God knows why! You're behaving like a spoilt bloody brat!"

"You're only with me 'cos of Emily." Michelle slid into the passenger seat.

"You're talking rubbish. As usual." He turned up the radio. *He might as well go off with Alana or someone else if he was going to be accused of it all the time.*

"You need to remember who holds the cards here." She thumped at the stereo's off button. "I call the shots with Emily and I can make sure you don't see her."

"What are you on about?" He turned onto the main road. "Have you been drinking whilst I was looking for you?"

"Not a drop. But if you've any ideas about other women, you need to remember what you've got to lose."

"How dare you bring Emily into this?" His voice was rising but he couldn't help it anymore. He tried to stay focused on the road. "You're crazy."

"So that was our engagement celebration." Paul feels sheepish. "She was bad when she'd been drinking but could be just as awful when she hadn't."

"Why did you stay with her?" Simon's voice is gentle.

"If I'm honest, mainly because of Emily." His soul slumps as he says her name out loud. "I couldn't have risked losing her and leaving her with a mother who was controlling, violent and unpredictable. I never knew what mood she was going to be in. Despite all that though, she was my wife and there was another side, a decent, loving side to her. Things were magical between us when we first got together. And she had been through a hell of a lot." Tears spear the back of Paul's eyes. Feeling close to the edge has become his way of life. He cannot recollect what happiness is.

"Why didn't you say anything? To us, I mean." John speaks now. "We knew things weren't great for you at home, but not that bad."

"I spoke to Alana a little. But to be honest, I thought things would ease off." Paul feels pathetic. "And I was ashamed, *wouldn't you be*? I should have been able to sort it. I'm such a bloody wimp."

"You're not." Simon looks at him. "You've nothing to be ashamed of. But our pressing job is proving *Michelle* stabbed *herself.*" He pulls another sheet from his file. "We also have the CCTV report. Your holiday cottage wasn't covered by CCTV, but the club's cameras show you both coming and going throughout the day."

"Did it show me going in and out when I went in the evening? Before I found Michelle, I mean.

Simon scans it. There's a still of you going in. But not coming out. They've got rotating cameras by the look of it." He looks thoughtful as he shuffles through some of his other papers. "One ace up our sleeve is Michelle's consultant from when she was younger, we have him as a witness. He'll verify the self-harming history."

"But that's scratching at her arms. This is shoving a knife into her own chest," Paul closes his eyes as the image from that awful night floods back into his mind. Suddenly her eyes are staring back into his.

"It's all self-harm, and looking at these reports, the damage she was doing to her arms and legs was far worse than merely *scratching* them." Simon continues.

"The police were trying to make me say it was a 'heat of the moment' thing – a row that escalated."

"That's precisely what the prosecution will do as well." Simon drives the heel of his hand onto the table. "But Paul, listen. They've nothing forensic. Absolutely nothing. You were the first on the scene and your prints were on the knife and all over the cottage but that doesn't prove or disprove anything." He shrugs his shoulders. "There's no eyewitness accounts either, other than of a row. But we have witnesses to confirm our side of things. We can verify what was happening for you at home." Clicking the lid of his briefcase shut, he exudes an air of what Paul hopes is triumph. *God! If he can get him off this ...*

"So that will all happen at the trial," Simon continues. "But in the meantime, we've got the plea and directions hearing, where you'll put your plea in and we'll try and get you bailed until the date of your trial."

"Do you think you'll be able to get bail?"

"On a charge like this, it's highly doubtful. But I'll argue the circumstances with your daughter. I'll do everything I can."

Chapter Twenty Four

The court clambers to its feet. Paul is released from the dock officer he has been cuffed to whilst being escorted from the cells below the crown court. Waiting for his turn has reduced him to a cluster of nerves. To be up into the dock at last, is welcome.

"All rise."

Searching the public gallery; he is encouraged by the presence of Alana, Michael, Susan, Nick, Jacqui and David. The temptation to acknowledge them nearly overcomes him, but he resists, knowing this could be deemed disrespectful by the judge and may make the difference between him gaining bail, or not. Maybe, the fact he has support will go in his favour. Alana, however, waves and smiles at him. He hopes the judge hasn't noticed. This might be the day he sees his daughter.

The public gallery is packed with onlookers. His case has encouraged media interest as well as the attention of domestic abuse campaigners. He looks over at them, imagining their thoughts. They've probably decided he's a wife-beating, sadistic murderer that terrorised and controlled his household.

Already they have dissected his entire life and though he has not yet faced trial, there is speculation about whether the death of his parents in his teens might have unhinged him, or if he has simply exercised his long-standing psychopathic tendencies. He's tried not to take any notice of what he has read in the paper, but it is hard. He can only hope the judge takes a more objective approach.

"You may sit down. NOT YOU!"

Paul springs back upright as the clerk regards him. "For the benefit of the court, held by his honour, Judge Lakin QC, please state your full name."

"Paul Alan Jackson." The eyes of the entire court room are upon him as his voice shakes.

"Your usual address?"

"42 Bracken Bank, Osbaldwick, York." An image of his home fleetingly flashes into his mind.

"And your occupation?"

Paul hesitates, he doesn't have an occupation anymore. Prison has turned him into an absolute 'nobody.' "Legal executive."

"Paul Alan Jackson, you are charged that on Monday 11th June, at Summerfield Holiday Park, Filey, you murdered your wife, Michelle Marie Jackson."

Buried grief unexpectedly surfaces at the sound of her name. He shuffles beneath the eyes upon him. The hatred of those in the gallery that already believe him to be guilty is raining down on him. *What do they know?*

"This charge has been reclassified from attempted murder to murder?" queries the judge, aside, studying a page before him.

"Yes, your honour. It has. Mrs Jackson passed away four days after the incident took place." The clerk continues, speaking in an authoritative voice, as he turns his attention back to Paul. "Paul Jackson. How do you plead to this charge? Guilty or not guilty?"

Paul clears his throat and waits for eye contact with the judge. "Not guilty." This time, his voice barely wavers. He then turns and faces the public gallery with his head held high.

Several pens scratch on notepads.

Simon gets to his feet. "May I address the court?" He waits for a nod from the judge before continuing. "Your honour. When Mr Jackson was first brought to court, bail was refused on the grounds he could interfere with witnesses to the allegation." He speaks slowly, perhaps realising the importance of every word. "As you are aware, Mrs Jackson has passed away. Therefore, that scenario is no longer relevant.

Mr Jackson would be willing to reside at his family home, surrender his passport, and report regularly at his local police station." He glances towards Paul. "I would ask you to consider the fact he hasn't had as much as a traffic offence in his lifetime. In addition, his conduct throughout his time on remand has been exemplary."

"From the papers before me, it appears that police attendance has been requested on three separate occasions for this family," the judge flicks through the pages on his desk. "Can you clarify this please?"

"No charges were ever brought against my client," Simon replies. "In fact, on one of the occasions, you see that it was actually him who had been attacked and needed treatment."

"Very well."

"I would ask the court to grant bail, in order that Mr Jackson can return to his daughter until the time when his case returns for trial. You may be aware that she is suffering some psychological problems as a result of what has happened. There is nothing to be gained from keeping her apart from her father any longer."

A gangly woman, dressed similarly to Simon, springs up from the prosecution bench. "Your honour, may I speak?"

"Go ahead."

The room is silent apart from a rustle as everyone turns their attention towards her.

"The prosecution in this case refutes this request," she begins. "It is upheld that a man, suspected and charged with the murder of his wife, the mother of his child, poses a threat to society, especially to women." Pausing, she looks towards the public gallery.

"It is recommended Paul Jackson continues to be held in custody until such time that he is cleared of all wrongdoing. This would maximise safety to the public, as well as safeguarding the reputation of the court. Also, it would ensure the defendant has no opportunity to interfere with the testimony of his daughter." She sits down.

Simon speaks again. "Your honour. I am aware of the severity of the charge. What the court is not aware of yet is the misery my client endured whilst trapped within his marriage. He has suffered enough as a victim *himself* and I would therefore reiterate my request for bail."

"There will be plenty of opportunity to argue these points during the trial." Judge Lakin stands. "I am going take some moments to deliberate." He then disappears through a curtain behind his bench.

"You may sit." The usher nods towards Paul whose entire body gives way onto the chair. The ensuing minutes are the longest of his life as he steals a look towards his few allies. Nick offers a thumbs up. Paul attempts to smile back. Several moments later, the collective movement of the court turns to the front bench, signalling the return of the judge.

"All rise."

Paul can't breathe. As he tries to avert his gaze from his feet, he cannot look up. *Please let me out. Please!*

"Paul Alan Jackson. You are charged with the murder of your wife. To this charge you have pleaded not guilty. I am sure you and everyone in this room will agree, the charge of murder is about as serious as can be. The safety and wellbeing of the public is of paramount importance.

It is for this reason, I have no choice but to order your retention in custody until such time that you are found not guilty by this court, if indeed you are. The comments made by your barrister are noted and I would recommend they form part of your defence. In view of the situation, I would ask the trial to be expedited in order that we can identify and ascertain the facts of what has occurred. I therefore recommend we reconvene within four weeks. Can we proceed to set a trial date?"

All the adrenaline drains from Paul. Not wishing to see anybody's expressions, he fixes his gaze to the floor.

A voice sounds from somewhere at the front. "How about Monday 9th September, your honour? It is envisaged a week would need to be allocated for the trial."

All is in slow motion. Another month! The splaying sun mocks him through the skinny skylights of the courtroom. *You're going back. You're going back!* He can't go back; he is running out of fight.

Nick has his hand on David's shoulder and Alana is hugging Susan. Alana is looking at him, over Susan's shoulder, her expression indeterminate.

"Can arrangements be made to assemble a jury? Monday the 9th September it is then.

Chapter Twenty Five

There had been a funny atmosphere most of the morning. Paul could sense something brewing.

"I need to speak to you," Michelle eventually said, half-asking-half-demanding. "It's important."

"What about?" Paul's lunch grumbled within him as he speculated over what was about to confront him. It could be anything.

"Not in front of *Emily*."

Emily's face crumpled at her mother's dismissal. She flounced from the room without looking at either of them.

Paul dutifully followed his wife as she took a seat at the kitchen table and fiddled with a place mat. Her gaze rested at Paul's feet as he leaned against the kitchen counter. After what felt like an eternity, she looked at him.

"What is it?" It had to be about Alana.

"There's no easy way to say this." A maddening pause ensued. *God, what was coming? It was like living in a soap opera.* "I've slept with someone else."

"*What?*" His voice was low but it was as though his heart had been ripped out of his chest. "What did you say?"

"I wasn't going to tell you but now I've thought about it, you have a right to know."

"*When?*" His body was rigid. The tension was pulsing through his neck. She was making it up. She had to be. Perhaps she was more deranged than he had given her credit for.

"Erm. Once or twice. I'm sorry."

"*Sorry!!* You must to be joking." Maybe this would explain her behaviour of late. She had been a right bitch.

"Who with?" he felt sick.

A ghost of a smile played upon her lips, making Paul wonder if she was somehow enjoying this admission. However, she was prone to smile nervously whenever she was involved in an awkward or sombre situation. She didn't answer.

The kitchen counter was propping *him* up now. It was a surreal sensation, as though he was viewing the conversation, rather than being a participant within it.

The image of his wife writhing around with another man tortured him. "Did you use anything?"

"What sort of a question is that?"

Paul's jaw was clenched so tightly, it was making his head ache. "No."

"You've put yourself at risk of pregnancy and God knows what. And me as well." Storming across to the sink, he filled a glass with water and guzzled it straight down.

"How can I be putting *you* at risk? We haven't had sex for ages."

"And you wonder why?" A tidal wave of pain washed over him. "How could you do this to me?"

"You don't want to know me Paul."

"You're my wife. *My* wife, the tart." His voice remained low, in an effort to keep Emily unaware. "We're supposed to be a family." He slammed his glass onto the draining board. "You know what? You're not worth it. He's welcome to you."

Uncrossing her legs, she swivelled around in her chair to face him as he paced around the kitchen. "I had to tell you. I couldn't live with it anymore."

"What? And I'm supposed to forgive you. Are you kidding?" He slammed his hand against the wall. It was sinking in. And she was telling the truth. At least, he thought she was. He didn't know how they could come back from this.

"Look, I know it won't be easy but…"

"It won't be possible." His voice rose. "How in God's name could you do this to me?" He slammed his fist on the worktop. "After all we've been through. I can't believe it."

Michelle got up and came towards him.

"Get away from me. Don't touch me!"

"It's your fault." Her eyes were menacing now. "You're hardly *husband of the year*." She jabbed her finger into his chest. "You don't do it for me anymore."

His body sprang into action. If he didn't move out of her way, he was going to lose it. "I can't bear to be anywhere near you! You make me ill." He was going to explode either with nausea or anger.

Without looking at her, he marched out of the kitchen and ascended the stairs. Carla stuck her head out of Emily's doorway, clearly having taken refuge. "It's alright girl."

"You leave this house and you're not coming back," Michelle screeched behind him, gripping the bannister. "I'll change the locks. I'll find a solicitor. And I'll make sure you never see your daughter again."

"You can't do that." He yanked clothes from the ironing pile in the airing cupboard.

"Try me." She sank down on the bottom step of the staircase. "If you think you're leaving, you can say your goodbyes right now."

Paul swung around. "She's coming with me."

"You must be joking." Michelle leapt to her feet.

"Try and stop me taking her. Just try." Striding into their bedroom, he hauled the suitcase from the top of the wardrobe.

"I'll call the police." Taking hold of the banister, she mounted the stairs, two at a time. "I'll say you're kidnapping her."

"Do it."

Randomly wrenching clothes out of drawers and cupboards, he tried to ignore her pleas for forgiveness, until incensed by his indifference; she grasped one of his wrists.

"Get off me," he wrenched his arm away and made towards Emily's room. "Go downstairs and put your coat and shoes on."

"Why. Where are we going?" She looked at him with bewildered eyes.

"I don't know yet. Go and put the TV on and I'll shout you when it's time to go." He snatched several items from her drawers and wardrobe, then headed into the bathroom to grab toothbrushes and toiletries.

"Paul, please!" Michelle was framed in the bathroom door. "We can sort this out. I'm sorry. I really am!"

"I want nothing more to do with you." He pushed past her, back into the bedroom where he continued slinging items into the suitcase.

"I love you. I'm sorry." As fast as he threw things into the suitcase, Michelle was tugging them back out. "I made it all up."

"Do you know something Michelle?" His frenetic attempts at packing halted. "I feel sorry for you."

"Then help me!" She shuffled closer to him. "I need you. I can't do it on my own."

"Ask your new man to help." Paul slammed the wardrobe door.

"I made him up. I wanted to hurt you. You must believe me. Please!" She hurled herself at him, wrapping her arms around his middle. "I'll do anything you want," she sobbed. "Please don't leave me! I wanted to make you jealous."

He prised himself out of her grip and grabbed for the suitcase. "Let me go! I mean it."

He left her bawling, face down into the bed. At least she had not become violent again. Robot-like, he collected Emily from the living room and steered her towards the car, ignoring protestations she would miss *Dora the Explorer*.

Drive Paul, he muttered to himself, shaking.

"Why were you shouting Daddy? I was scared."

They couldn't keep doing this to her. It was up to him to sort it. He was unaware of how long he drove. He didn't know where he was. He'd gone onto autopilot. *He probably shouldn't be driving.* But the concentration required for driving had stabilised his mind a little. However, he was nearing the motorway so needed to pull over whilst he considered what the hell he was going to do for the best.

Emily slumbered beside him, blissfully unaware of the circumstances. Paul was accepting he would have to find the strength to leave Michelle and fight for Emily.

It would be down to his version of events against Michelle's. It was possible, no it was probable, he would end up losing his daughter like Michelle had threatened. Courts nearly always came down on the side of the mother.

Angrily, he plucked his phone from his pocket. It had not stopped ringing since he had stormed from the house. He pressed the off button. Then leaning over the steering wheel, he rested his head on his arms and fought the urge to weep. For the home he wanted to give his daughter, for the life he wanted to give himself and for the wife he didn't have. They had adored each other in the beginning. Where had it all gone?

Chapter Twenty Six

He eventually found himself outside Nick's house. Emily went in pursuit of Jack and Imogen.

Nick beckoned Paul in and thrust a beer into his hand. "You look like shit mate. Is it Michelle?"

"Yep. She's been sleeping with someone else."

"*Really?* You're joking! Who?"

"Don't know. It doesn't matter." Paul accepted the bottle opener from Nick and wrenched the lid off his.

"For how long?"

"Once is enough, isn't it? How would you react if it was Jacqui?"

"She would never do that."

"I would have said the same about Michelle. She doesn't trust me, so she goes and does it herself. Crazy."

"She's capable of anything. You must have been off your box marrying her."

"She's a lot of things but I would never have thought she was a cheat."

"I would. Did she tell you herself or did you find out?"

"She told me."

"I bet you wanted to kill her."

"That's why I'm here. But as I was on my way out, she said she'd made it up."

154

"She's warped! I've always said it. Are you alright mate?"

"I guess I'm going to have to be."

The beers Paul consumed enabled him to fall into a woozy sleep on Nick's sofa. But it was to be short lived. Groggily, he awoke soon after, draped in a blanket. The house basked in darkened silence, but Paul's mind would not stop whirring. For what was an eternity, he lay, plagued by images of Michelle with another man. No matter how hard he tried to chase them away, they refused to leave him. He yearned for the steamroller to reverse from his chest and grant him some reprieve. Its pain was excruciating. In his mind, her face taunted him; first smiling lovingly at him, but then sneering, and then contorted with rage. Due to his agitation, sleep would not find him, but he was too exhausted to move: a prisoner of his own thoughts. He could never have imagined it would hurt this much.

Eventually, he would have to return home; there was no escaping from reality. Although there were people who would put him up in the short term; he could not encroach on anybody's hospitality for more than a night or two. Trapped and imprisoned within a toxic marriage, it was akin to being trapped in a spider's web. There were no answers.

"What do you want?" Paul opened one eye as he heard Nick speaking in a hiss at the front door. "Do one Michelle. You're not welcome."

"You can't stop me speaking to my own husband." *It was her.*

"After what you've done. You've a nerve coming around here."

"It's fine Nick." Paul's voice was a croak. "Let her in. I'll speak to her."

Within a split second, he heard the creaking of the living room door and could sense her presence in the room. "Paul, I need to talk to you."

"I'm awake." Not wanting to look at her, he didn't open his eyes.

"I'll leave you to it." Nick spoke from the doorway. "I'll be in the kitchen. And I don't want any trouble."

"God, he hates me, *doesn't he?*"

The weight of another body bearing down on the cushion beside him was oddly consoling after a night of loneliness.

"I'll do anything to put things right," she said.

In the light of the emerging day, he squinted at her. "If you loved me, you would not have gone anywhere near another man." He probably reeked of stale beer. He had not brushed his teeth, so he directed his face away from her as he continued. "I could never be unfaithful to you. Never." Alana flashed into his mind. *Hypocrite. Who was he kidding?*

"I wasn't. I was testing you."

"*Testing me?* How the hell do you work that one out?"

"To see how you'd react. I didn't think it through, did I?" Her hand gently touched his arm. "I wanted to test whether you love me."

"I don't believe you." The intensity of their marriage was crucifying. *Why did it have to be like this?* Why couldn't they discuss humdrum issues? What to cook for tea, Emily's homework, *anything* but the angst all the time. "I think you *have* slept with someone. But it's backfired on you and now you're trying to wriggle out of it." *What did she take him for?*

"I swear on Emily's life I did *not* have sex with another man." She crossed herself as she proclaimed this.

Paul dragged himself up against the cushions. "You know I detest you doing that!" His mother had been superstitious and had convinced him that to swear on a person's life was tempting something.

"But it's the only way you'll believe me."

"It's not just that, Michelle." He swung his legs around, so he was sitting beside her. "You're drinking far too much."

CHAPTER TWENTY SIX

"It's because I'm not happy Paul. If you were around a bit more…"

"You're controlling. You don't trust me. *And* you spat at me. What the hell's happened to you?"

"I know. I'm sorry." Her hand crept into his. "I'm begging you to forgive me. I want to make things better."

"I think you need some help Michelle."

"Of course I need some help. But you're never around."

"I mean *professional* help. With your anger and jealousy."

"I don't. I need *your* help."

"Michelle. It's only a few nights since you hit me. I can't live like this. If you don't ask for some help, I want out."

Chapter Twenty Seven

Tommo' chalks his cue. "When is it? Your trial, I mean? It's coming up, isn't it? I saw summat in the paper."

Paul has become familiar with Tommo over his three-month duration. He is one of the few inmates he associates with. Although in for ABH, he has always been amenable.

"Tomorrow. I want to move with it. The sooner I see the back of this place, the better."

"You're confident then?" Tommo slams a shot on the green. "You got a decent brief? You'll need one, to be outta *here*."

"I suppose so. I'm brickin' it if I'm honest." Paul fires at the red but sends the white hurtling off the table. "Shit."

"You'll be right. Specially if you've a brief with half a brain." Tommo reinstates the white ball at the top of the table.

"I should never have been here in the first place." Paul watches as Tommo bangs the blue into the middle pocket. "Good shot mate."

"Me neither." Grinning at Paul, he positions himself for the next shot. "To be honest mate, I hope you're released. You're not the usual type who finishes up in here. But don't raise your hopes. They can be bastards, them judges. All depends on whether they've had *any* the previous night."

"Course he won't be released." Barry sidles up to them. "People don't get banged up for what he's done without serving a stretch!"

"Who asked you, fucking scroat!" Tommo squares up to Barry who is evidently in for something serious. His cell sign stipulates thirty years.

"I'm only saying." Barry steps away from Tommo. "The tosser slashed his missus, didn't he? His sort shouldn't be roamin' the streets."

"You don't know…" Paul starts to say but Tommo already has Barry by the throat.

"Gerroff him, you bullying bastard." Another man of weaselly stature comes up behind Tommo and belts him across the back with a pool cue. Barry, noticing Tommo is off guard, takes the chance to seize the other cue and whack him in the face. Blood gushes from his lip.

Paul is rooted to the spot, wanting to help Tommo, but knowing he can't or he risks everything. He feels like more of a wimp than ever.

Within seconds, a siren wails around their landing and eight or so screws emerge from nowhere, using their combined force to bring the three men involved, colliding to the ground. Tommo takes some restraining. Resembling a pit bull, he thrashes viciously, trying to return to the 'ring.'

Eventually, the three are dragged off to the segregation wing. The remaining inmates endure early bang up, as is the case whenever anything occurs during association.

"It could take a while to start properly." John's voice echoes in the under-court cell. "The jury selection business can take forever."

"At least we're here and it's happening." Paul's belly growls. He should have eaten something. He felt too sick before they set off.

"Has Simon been down to see you?" John glances at the door. "I'm not sure if he's arrived in chambers yet."

"Yes. Not long before you. He was talking about plea bargaining." Paul's eyes roll at the memory. "It's worried me to be honest."

"Go on. What did he say?"

"Apparently," Paul shuffles on the concrete slab. "if I plead guilty to a lesser charge, such as voluntary manslaughter, I'll receive a lighter sentence."

"That's partly because the costs would be significantly reduced. There'd be no need for a jury either. They like that. But it's your call. I'll support whatever you decide."

"I'm not pleading guilty to anything. He warned me it's a gamble out there. Although the odds are more in my favour with the defence we have, the whole thing could easily go the other way."

"Well he's right, in a sense," John speaks slowly. "I suppose it does all hinge on the jury, who don't know you. Only what they're told. If they *do* find you guilty, you're looking at a fair stretch." He looks away.

"I'll take my chances." Paul yawns. He's not slept well. Guilt has been eating at him and it's more than the fact that Tommo is doing time in isolation after defending him. He's been plagued by flashbacks from the night of the stabbing. He's not sure whether he was awake or dreaming them and can't decide whether they're real or imagined.

John checks his watch. "I'm going to have to head back up. I'll see you up there, and Paul?"

"What." Paul tugs his jacket tighter around his shoulders.

"Good luck mate." He squeezes his shoulder as he stands up. "It's going to be a long few days but I've every faith. It won't be long 'til you're free with a bit of luck. No matter what's happened, we'll sort it."

"God, I hope so." Paul closes his eyes.

"See you soon mate." John raps on the cell door to be let out.

Paul nods. He's a bit spaced out this morning. His old life might have been lived by someone else, he is so far removed from it.

Everyone takes to their feet as Judge Lakin sweeps in, his well-heeled shoes clipping across the parquet floor. The defence and prosecution benches and the public gallery, containing Paul's supporters and the news reporters is packed. There are lots of faces he doesn't recognise, possibly the domestic abuse activists and womens' rights campaigners who already have his neck in a noose by all accounts. The judge nods, gratuitously. "Good morning."

Paul's attention is drawn to the back, where fifteen prospective jurors wait. John has told him twelve will sit. They are about to be selected and sworn in.

"You may be seated," says the usher. People descend to their seats. As Paul begins to sit, the usher shakes his head, and gestures an upwards motion with his palms.

Oh bloody hell, thinks Paul. *Great start.* He scans the public gallery for Nick, still worrying about his lack of belief in him, but then remembers Nick is to be called as a defence witness and is therefore not allowed into the court room. Alana waves at him.

"Paul Alan Jackson," states the court clerk, clutching some cards, "the names you are about to hear called, are the names of the jurors who are to try you. If you wish to object to any of them, you must do so as they come to the book to be sworn, and your objection will be heard."

Paul nods, squinting against the sunlight that penetrates the roof. His collar scratches his neck and he is already sweating, despite the air conditioning.

"Afdiq Ahmed," calls the clerk, reading from a card. The court remains hushed. The Asian man, around the same age as Paul, shuffles from his position at the back of the court towards the jury box.

"Helen Wentworth." A mousy woman scuttles beside him, head bowed. She looks like she would rather be anywhere but here. Paul doesn't like the look of her. She'll think he did it.

161

"Elliot Carmichael," A portly middle-aged man makes three. He looks straight at Paul as he takes his seat.

"Louise Chadderton." Paul stares at her and hesitantly raises his hand. He's not sure about this one and he's not taking any chances. He tries to place her.

"Yes? What is it?" The judge surveys him with an air of impatience.

He continues his scrutiny of the juror. *Yes. He is sure it's her.* "She … this woman worked with my wife. With Michelle. I'm sure of it."

"Is this true?"

A flush spreads up Louise Chadderton's neck, like climbing ivy, as she realises all eyes are on her. "It was a few years ago but yes, we worked together. I would have said something but I didn't make the connection. She must have used her maiden name for work, you see."

"We shall have to dismiss you from this case." The judge nods towards her. "Please leave the court by the public gallery and await further instruction."

The four are joined by another eight, none of them objectionable. The two excess jury members are sent out to join Louise Chadderton.

"You may be seated." The usher gestures to Paul at last.

The clerk stands in front of the selected jury box. Paul regards them all warily. His life is literally in their hands. Whatever opinion they form, that is it for him. They can all go back to their cosy homes.

"Helen Wentworth, please take this copy of the New Testament in your right hand, hold this card in your left and read from it."

Her voice is faint. "I swear by almighty God that I will faithfully try the defendant and give a true verdict according to the evidence." Looking towards Paul, she hands the bible back to the clerk.

Paul listens peripherally as one-by-one, the assembled jury swear their oaths, most of them Christian, one Muslim, one Jewish, two atheists; seven men, five women. He cannot decide whether it is a good thing there are more men than women. The youngest woman,

Victoria, appears around twenty-five and the oldest man, Robert, is somewhere in his late fifties.

There is a momentary shuffle in seats, then all eyes rest on the judge who clears his throat.

"Members of the jury. My name is Judge Lakin. Firstly, let me thank you for being here today, to assist with the case of Paul Alan Jackson, who is thirty-seven years of age. He stands today, accused of the murder of his wife, Michelle Marie Jackson, who was thirty-six at the time of her death." He looks down at some papers before continuing.

"The incident took place as the couple holidayed with their then six-year-old daughter, on Monday 11th June earlier this year. Mr Jackson has pleaded not guilty to the charge of murder at an earlier hearing.

"Members of the jury, over the next few days, you will hear the evidence of the prosecution in this matter. Assuming the case is not dismissed at this point, you will then hear the evidence of the defence. The case will only be dismissed if the evidence presented by the prosecution is deemed to be flawed or unstable." Pausing for a moment, he appears to be allowing time for his words to infiltrate the minds of his audience. Hope rises in Paul as he prays this dismissal occurs.

"It will be up to you to listen to each shred of evidence and witness statement, making notes on what you hear in preparation for your deliberations at the end of the trial.

When all witnesses have been cross examined, it will be your responsibility, based on what you have heard, to come to a decision as to whether Paul Jackson is guilty or not guilty of murdering his wife. You will also be offered the opportunity to find him guilty or not guilty of involuntary manslaughter. When you are asked to retire, you will be given further guidance on this." He turns to the clerk. "Can the names be listed of the witnesses in this trial please?"

"Yes certainly, your honour. For the prosecution, the following witnesses will be called: Detective Constable Joseph Calvert from North Yorkshire Police, Mr James Falen, Senior Surgeon at York District Hospital, Dr Mark Reynolds, Mrs Barbara Fawcett, neighbour of the accused and the deceased, Sergeant Neil Dodsworth of North Yorkshire Police, Mrs Susan Duffy, mother of the deceased and Mrs Monica Redmond, former work colleague of the deceased."

The clerk swaps the page he is reading from with another page from his desk. "I shall now list the witnesses for the defence: Nick Hambleton, friend of the Jackson family, Nurse Matthew Fraser from York District Hospital, Mrs Stratton, Deputy Head at Osbaldwick Primary School, Police Constable Stuart Rayner of North Yorkshire Police, Dr James Sowden of the North Yorkshire Primary Mental Health Trust, Barry Aitkin, Specialist Forensic Biologist, and finally, Paul Jackson, the defendant."

"My name is Margaret Yeoman QC." She stands from her seat at the prosecution bench. In her robes and wig, she is more like an old-school primary teacher than a barrister. Her sausage-like finger shoves her thick rimmed glasses back up her nose. "I act for the prosecution." She addresses the jurors. "I am about to present to you the events which have led the Crown Prosecution Service to the place we are at now.

Michelle Marie Jackson was a thirty-six-year-old woman. A young wife and mother, she had her entire life ahead of her. As is the case in many marriages, this particular couple were no strangers to marital problems and the usual ups and downs."

What does she know? Paul's insides gnarl around each other.

"Mrs Jackson wanted to hold her family together. You will shortly hear how Mr Jackson wanted to drive a wedge between them. You are about to hear the lengths he pursued to estrange himself from his wife. Many men may contemplate counselling or trial separations in difficult circumstances. However, Mr Jackson, on what should have been a happy family holiday, is accused of murdering her." She stops momentarily to glance at her notes.

"Members of the jury, I ask you to consider as you hear the evidence, whether the killing was occasioned in a sudden act of rage, perhaps as the result of an argument, or whether it was one of premeditated murder.

You will also hear the defendant's version of events, depicting *himself* as a victim in this situation. But you should not lose sight of a little girl, who has recently spent her seventh birthday without her mother or father. Her name is Emily. She was in the vicinity of events on the night of Monday June 11th, and has been so traumatised that she has not spoken since."

Yes, Paul thinks to himself. She may well be the one who really knows what happened. The court is silent, apart from the scrape of pencils of the jurors.

Stephen flicks playing cards between them. "Chin up mate. This time, next week, you could be back with your little girl."

"God I hope so. It could honestly go either way," Paul feels heavy. "I can't get my hopes up."

"Well there's not a lot you can do but wait and see."

"I know." Paul sighs half-heartedly, at his cards. Really, he can't be arsed with cards. "It'll be your appeal soon too."

"Yeah, but I haven't a hope of being released yet. Not after what I did."

"That remorse will reduce your sentence though."

"I know. Could still be hefty for three counts of manslaughter. Plus, all the families will be there. Wanting my head on a stick, no doubt."

"Let's play cards mate." Paul says. "I need to give my brain a rest."

Chapter Twenty Eight

Margaret Yeoman looks expectantly towards the judge. "You may begin." Sitting back in his seat, he crosses his arms.

"The prosecution would like to call their first witness, Detective Constable Joseph Calvert from North Yorkshire Police."

He has a stern expression as he is shepherded into the witness stand. "Take this bible in your right hand and repeat after me the words on the card, *I swear by Almighty God that I will tell the truth, the whole truth and nothing but the truth.*"

Facing the jury, DC Calvert reads from the card, then settles his focus upon Margaret.

"DC Calvert, you were one of the first officers at the scene, on the evening of Monday 11th June, at Summerfield Holiday Park."

"That is correct." His face is cherry-red. It is either nerves or the after-effect of alcohol.

"Can you describe the scene when you arrived at the Jackson's holiday cottage?"

"Certainly." He drops his hands onto the wooden ledge below him. "The paramedics had arrived ahead of us and were already working on Mrs Jackson. Mr Jackson was looking on. Everyone was in the kitchen, apart from the daughter, that is. We didn't learn of her presence straight away."

"Can you describe how Mr Jackson *presented*?"

"As you'd expect, shocked, scared, covered in his wife's blood."

"What did he say to you?"

"That he'd found her like that. That she must have stabbed *herself*. He claimed to have been in the pub the whole time."

"And did you check this information?"

"We did. He was there for a time that evening, although the CCTV coverage has not picked up his time of leaving."

"Did you believe, at the time, that Mr Jackson had no part to play in his wife's injuries?"

"Not at all. This disbelief increased when I came across reports of an earlier row between the couple, which had been heard by neighbouring holidaymakers."

"Was a weapon recovered?"

"Yes. It was still lodged in the chest of Mrs Jackson."

Margaret picks up a bag containing the knife. "The jury have a photograph of this. Is this the same weapon?"

He doesn't flinch. "Yes."

"What made you decide to place Mr Jackson under arrest?" Her robes rustle as she walks away from the witness box.

"Mr Jackson made the three nines call after claiming to have found his injured wife. As I said, he was covered in blood and in a distressed state. He was the only suspect."

"Have there been any other suspects since?"

"No. All other forensic analysis has been inconclusive and hasn't matched with anything on the DNA database."

"How many years have you served in the police?"

His chest swells. "Going on twenty-three."

"Mr Jackson explains his wife's injuries as self-harming. Have you seen many incidences of self-harming, such as this, in your career so far?"

"I would like to contest this question," Simon calls. "Psychiatrists, not police personnel, usually intervene in incidences of self-harming."

"Sustained," says the judge. "Although there's many cases of the police getting involved."

"OK. I'll rephrase my question," Margaret continues. "Have you attended many stabbings where the victim has fatally stabbed *themselves?*"

He pauses. "I can think of one or two occasions. But usually the person who has stabbed themselves has injured others first, often within their family. Possibly, upon realising the gravity and consequences of their actions, they then turn the knife to themselves. I would imagine the adrenaline has a part to play. I can't imagine, if she was there alone that…"

"Again, I object to this line of questioning." Simon's voice rings out across the quiet court room. "The witness is merely speculating."

"Sustained." Judge Lakin nods.

"In your experience as a senior police officer," Margaret clasps her hands in front of her chest, "do you believe Michelle Jackson could have inflicted this horrific injury upon herself?"

"No," he shakes his head. "I don't."

"No further questions."

It is Simon's turn to question him. "Your honour." He is unrecognisable in his wig and robes. "My name is Simon Booth, Queen's Counsel. I act in this case for the defendant, Paul Jackson." He turns to the witness box.

"DC Calvert, can you affirm Mrs Jackson's state of mind *before* this incident happened?"

"Of course not! How could I? As you said yourself, I'm no psychiatrist. Nor was I there prior to the incident."

"Quite. Can you confirm the first time you met Mrs Jackson was on the night we are ascertaining the facts around?"

"Yes."

"How are you able to say then, with any conviction, that a person capable of stabbing themselves would only be inclined if they had killed somebody else *first?*"

"In my years of police service, I have attended many cases of suicide. People have hung themselves, taken a drugs overdose or rigged up a hosepipe. Usually, methods are chosen that are as painless and peaceful as possible."

"Usually. So, in view of your *experience,* you're saying painful methods are *never* selected? People *never* decide to end it all, by methods such as leaping from a cliff or hurling themselves in front of a train or perhaps by fatally stabbing themselves?"

"No. I'm just saying…"

"No further questions."

Paul is mildly jubilant. If the rest of the witnesses follow suit, it will not be long until he is back with his daughter. He still has a long way to go though.

"The prosecution would like to call the next witness, Mr James Falen, Senior Surgeon at York District Hospital."

A silver-haired man approaches the witness box and repeats his oath in a velvety voice. The familiar sadness tugs at Paul as he realises this man was probably one of the last people to see Michelle alive.

Margaret addresses him. "Mr Falen, you worked on Mrs Jackson when she was admitted to hospital on the night of Monday 11th June."

"That's correct; she was brought in at about 11:50 pm. It had been necessary for the ambulance crew to stabilise her first. They had radioed ahead, requesting a surgeon be ready for her. I was on call that night."

"Can you describe her condition after she arrived at the hospital?

Was she able to converse? Had she spoken to any members of the ambulance crew?"

"No. She was unconscious throughout her admission and had lost a dangerous amount of blood. My colleagues took her straight into theatre to transfuse her whilst we worked on the injury."

"The jury have a photograph of the injury." There are several repulsed expressions as their attention is drawn to it. "Can you tell us about it?"

Paul senses the strength of their distaste and is certain it is directed towards him.

"Yes, it would have been inflicted by a single plunge of a four-inch by one-inch blade; its point of laceration at the centre of her sternum." As he speaks, he gestures towards his chest. "It had caused an internal laceration to one of the major blood vessels surrounding her heart, and of equal severity, it had caused a puncture to a lung, therefore her breathing and heart rate were overtly rapid." Speaking quickly, he runs out of breath himself.

"After surgery, Mrs Jackson was placed on advanced life support to ensure her other organs didn't shut down. We knew she only had a slim chance when she was taken up to ICU. I'm amazed she hung on for another four days after surgery. After an injury like that, the odds aren't good."

Paul listens, desolately. *If only he had been there, willing her to pull through. He hopes she didn't die on her own.*

"Did *you* think she may have inflicted the injury upon herself?"

"I heard mention of it, but it isn't likely. The blade had entered her chest deeply, with some considerable force behind it. It's more plausible she had been injured by someone else." Pausing, he glances back at the photograph as he refers to it. "The wound lacerations inside appeared inconsistent with one thrust and looked as though the blade had been pushed in further whilst inside her. I would be surprised if she'd been able to do that herself, given the agony she would have been suffering."

Margaret smiles. "Thank you. No further questions."

The judge speaks into the ear of the usher.

"We will adjourn for lunch," the usher calls. "The court will reconvene at 2pm.

For a moment no one moves. Then the courts' occupants collectively stretch and yawn in their places before dispersing.

Paul aches to talk with someone about how things are progressing. Alana waves again then turns to speak to David. He is returned to the dank cell, where he is presented with a limp ham sandwich and a cup of tea.

Chapter Twenty Nine

The judge looks at Simon. "Does the defence barrister require the opportunity to cross examine Mr Falen?"

"I have one or two questions," replies Simon with an air of authority, as he stands. "Mr Falen. We have established you and your staff received and worked on Michelle Jackson prior to pronouncing her dead four days later. Is that correct?"

"Yes."

"And you will have had the opportunity to study the results of the post mortem examination and the coroner's report?"

"Yes."

"How are you able to state *conclusively* that she would not have caused the injury to herself?"

"I said it was *unlikely*."

"But not impossible?"

"Of course not."

"That will be all. Thank you. Before we go on with the next witness," Simon continues. "I would like to draw attention to the coroner's report, exhibit 9b, which forms part of the bundle of evidence." There's a rustle of paper around the room as Simon pauses. "You will see from it that the cause of death was conclusively stated. Mrs Jackson had died as a result of lacerations and a lung puncture injury. There was no need for an inquest to be held."

As Simon previously suggested, so far all the evidence against him is circumstantial. They need more than this. Again, his gaze sweeps over the jury as he silently pleads with them to set him free.

"I would like to call on Mrs Barbara Fawcett." says Margaret.

Silly woman from across the road. What the hell will she say? She can't add any weight to the prosecution's case. He watches as she holds the bible aloft.

"Mrs Fawcett," begins Margaret, giving her a smile. "How long have you been a neighbour of the Jacksons?"

"Oh, about a year. They moved into our cul-de-sac over the summer, last year."

"How close do you live to them?"

"My house directly faces theirs."

"Can you describe the distance between your homes?"

"Yes. There's my house, which has a short drive running up to it, there's the road, then there's their drive leading to their house." With her hands, she attempts to demonstrate the distances as she explains. "I have a clear view of their house."

"And how well would you say you know the family?"

"Michelle, I knew well. She was at home a couple of days each week. She liked to be around to take and collect Emily from school on those days. She was a wonderful mother. I had a lot of respect for her. I don't know how she managed to juggle it all."

"How often did you talk?"

"Several times a week. I'm retired so I'm at home. Often, I'm out in the garden. Michelle seemed to enjoy our chats. Now and again I invited her in for coffee."

"Did she ever talk about her husband?"

"Oh yes. All the time. It was obvious she adored him. Her world revolved around him, and the little girl, of course." Her smile fades as she discusses Paul. "He was hardly ever at home. I was sorry for her. Like I said, she was a busy, working mum and deserved someone who would be around to help support her."

"How well did you know her husband, Paul Jackson?"

"He was aloof." Mrs Fawcett keeps her eyes fastened on Margaret as she speaks. She doesn't look at Paul once. "As though he didn't approve of her having anything to do with me. I think he was afraid of what she might say about him."

"What do you mean, Mrs Fawcett?"

"Well it was obvious, wasn't it?" As she spoke, she wrung her hands like a dirty dishcloth. "You hear about it all the time, don't you? Controlling men. Cowering wives. Women, watching clocks, waiting for husbands to return from the pub, never knowing what mood they're likely to be in or when they'll be back. No woman should be living like that." A mutter rose up from the public gallery.

"Did she confide in you often?"

"Sometimes. I knew she wasn't happy. She'd convinced herself he was going to leave her. She might have appeared confident in her everyday dealings but deep down she was very insecure, and it's no wonder."

"Living so close, did you ever witness them arguing?"

"Often. I felt sorry for Emily, poor little mite. Especially towards the end. Both her and Michelle looked miserable." Mrs Fawcett momentarily closed her eyes as if disturbed by the memory. "I could tell it was a matter of time before something had to give. I never dreamt it would be anything like this. I thought they might split up but not..."

"You state you heard them argue. What did you hear? How did you know they were arguing?"

"Mr Jackson, shouting. He was forever shouting. The poor woman was probably terrified out of her wits. He frightened me and I was all the way across the road. I've never heard a man shout like it."

CHAPTER TWENTY NINE

"Thank you, Mrs Fawcett. That will be all."

Liar! Paul bellows inside his head. *What in God's name is this woman doing in the witness box. They had barely known her! Attention seeking liar.*

Margaret sits down.

"Your testimony," Simon asks, standing quickly, "is based on assumptions that Michelle and Emily *appeared,* how did you put it? *Miserable?*"

"Yes. But there's more to it than that."

"Maybe you can enlighten us." Simon's voice oozes authority but has a mocking edge. "How many times did you witness Paul Jackson *controlling* Michelle Jackson?"

"I didn't actually *see* it. I could, you know, *tell* what was going on." She's sounding less sure of herself now, Paul thinks.

"I see. How many times did you hear Mr Jackson *shout* at his wife?" Simon moves closer to the witness box.

"A few times. The police were *always* outside their house."

Simon shuffles through several of the papers in his hands. "My notes say something different, Mrs Fawcett. The police were not *always* outside their house. Maybe twice? But moving on from that, did you ever witness Mr Jackson being violent towards his wife?"

"No." Barbara Fawcett's voice has faded to the point of being inaudible.

"Can you repeat that so the entire court can hear you please?" He steps back from her. "Did you *ever* witness Mr Jackson being violent towards his wife?"

"No," her voice trembles.

"I have no more questions for this witness." Even though she's been brought down, Paul's fury is at melting point. He doesn't want to imagine what he will say to her the next time their paths cross.

Paul recognises the next witness as the officer who came to their house after Michelle had battered herself with the telephone. It had been his morning at the gym which had caused all the trouble on that occasion.

I swear by Almighty God that I will tell the truth, the whole truth and nothing but the truth. He turns expectantly towards Margaret.

"Sergeant Dodsworth, you were summonsed on a three nines call, to attend a domestic incident at 42 Bracken Bank, Osbaldwick on the afternoon of Sunday 16th March of this year. Is that correct?"

"It is." His helmet balances precariously on the ledge in front of him.

"For the benefit of the jury, can you describe the circumstances you found upon arrival at the Jackson's house.

"Certainly. Our response was to an emergency situation. Mrs Jackson had requested help. Mr Jackson was alleged to have assaulted her."

Simon jumps from his seat. "This evidence is 'hearsay,' no charges were ever brought."

"Overruled," says Judge Lakin. "The officer is merely outlining his version of events."

"As I was saying," Sergeant Dodsworth continues. "Mrs Jackson had endured substantial facial injuries, for which we advised medical attention. She claimed she and her husband had rowed and consequently, he had lost his temper with her. There was no one else at the property apart from their daughter."

"Who answered the door when you arrived?" Margaret paces in front of the witness box as she speaks.

"Mr Jackson. He was calm, as though he was expecting us."

"So you arrested him because of the allegations?" Margaret tips her head slightly, watching for jury reaction.

"Yes, *and* because of her injuries, we would not have let him remain at the house. We always act on suspected situations of domestic abuse.

Our force has a zero-tolerance policy whenever it occurs. Given the fact a young girl was present and had possibly witnessed the attack, we were more concerned."

"Thank you Sergeant Dodsworth. I have no further questions at this time."

Simon shoots to his feet. "Can you tell me what charges were instigated against my client as the result of the arrest on this particular occasion?"

"I don't believe there were any at this time. It is often the case that wives..."

"*No charges brought.* Because Mr Jackson hadn't done anything to his wife, had he?" He steadies his voice for the next question. "For the benefit of the jury, can you please confirm Paul Jackson was released *without any charges whatsoever?*"

"He was, but only because his wife changed her story, to say she'd caused her own injuries. It happens all the time. We subsequently advised her that if a similar incident was to occur, there would be no opportunity to retract her claims. Mr Jackson would be prosecuted with or without her backing." His voice lowers then, as though he is divulging a secret. "We would have normally made a referral to the domestic violence unit but as it was Mr Jackson's first arrest, we were unable to involve them."

"Sorry?" Simon sounds victorious. "Did you state this was indeed the *first* occasion Mr Paul Jackson had *ever* been arrested?"

"That is correct."

"Can you clarify that other than on the night of his wife's death, the aforementioned incident was indeed the *only* time Mr Paul Jackson has ever been arrested in his life?"

"I would have to double check our records," he replies hesitantly. "But yes, I believe that to be the case."

"That will be all."

Paul listens in dismay as Judge Lakin announces they will adjourn for the day. He had expected they would hear from at least all the prosecution witnesses that day. There is still one to go. Here we go then, he thinks. *Back to the hell hole.*

Chapter Thirty

A hush has descended on the courtroom. *"Has the jury reached a verdict upon which they are unanimously agreed?"*

"Your honour. We have."

"On the charge of murder, do you find the defendant, Paul Jackson, guilty or not guilty?"

"We find him..." There is an expectant pause as the court looks tentatively at the spokesperson who appears to be basking in his own glory. He is relishing his momentary power like an 'X-Factor' host.

"Guilty," he declares, finally.

"No!" shrieks Alana from the public gallery.

"I'm not guilty. I didn't kill my wife!" cries Paul.

"Silence in court!" Judge Lakin shouts.

"But I'm innocent! I'm totally innocent! You can't do this to me!"

"You will refrain from shouting out, or this will be reflected in your sentence," bellows Judge Lakin. *"You will be returned to the prison where you have been held on remand whilst you await sentencing."* He turns to the clerk. *"Can we allocate a date for this?"*

"Your honour," she flicks through some pages. *"The next available sentencing date is not until February."*

"No! No! Please don't make me go back there! I can't do it! I'd rather you shot me." Twenty years or whatever they are going to give him, hangs ahead like a noose. *"Please! Don't make me go back!"* Two dock officers are

battling to pin him down in order to cuff him as he flails about. "Take your hands off me!" His attempts at kicking out at one of them are responded to by a deafening siren, which reverberates around the court, to signal additional help is required in his restraint.

Forcing himself into consciousness, he realises with relief, that the alarm is wailing within the wing.

"Cell C7," cries an urgent voice above the commotion. "In here quick. He's losing a lot of blood."

"Stay away from me! I don't want to be here anymore. Leave me alone."

"Give me the blade." A woman speaks this time. "Come on. We can sort this out."

A vision of Michelle emerges in Paul's mind. She crouches, tears sliding down her face, the blade directed towards her chest. He tries to squeeze the image from his head and not replay what happens next.

"We must have you looked at, but we can't come near you with the blade in your hand. Place it on the floor."

"Why did you have to find me?" The man sounds broken. It's echoing from the landing above. "I want to die. Why did you have to find me? I fucking hate the lot of you."

"You're needed in here!" Another man shouts urgently. "Yes, he's still has the blade. Make sure you're wearing gloves."

"Turn that fucking thing off," hollers someone from down the landing.

"Yeah," agrees another. "If he wants to top himself, let him get on with it."

Finally, the alarm is silenced. Paul has no idea of the time. All he knows is… there is no sign of dawn. Normally, he senses it at around 6:30. Yawning, he turns over, not wishing to lay awake for the remainder of the night. He has already counted every hour and is willing them by, needing to return to the courtroom.

Whilst staring into the darkness, he has revisited each word of the previous day, scouring each one for any slivers of hope which may lead to his acquittal.

It is feasible the remaining witnesses can be heard in the coming day or two. Perhaps he will only have to spend another two or three nights in here. But first he must face the evidence of his mother-in-law. From what he's read in her statement, she's arguing more over the fact that Michelle *could not and would not* have stabbed herself. Which is as good as saying he must have done it really.

Other than when she visited him in prison, the last time he had seen her was when she had been waving them away on holiday. God that had been a right trek.

The first leg of their journey had elapsed peacefully.

"Will it be much longer?" Emily had groaned from the back seat. "I'm bored."

"We're not even half way there yet!" Michelle smiled round at her. "We'll stop soon and grab a bit of lunch."

"Can we go swimming when we get there?" Emily chattered. "And go to the beach and to the park?"

"We'll have time to do it all, don't you worry. We're there for nearly a week." Paul stretched across the gearstick and squeezed Michelle's arm. He had liked seeing Michelle helping Emily choose and pack clothes for the holiday.

"That dress is gorgeous," he had heard Michelle say. "You look pretty in that colour. That's why Mummy chose it for you."

"Will you plait my hair Mummy?" Emily had thrust a hair bobble at her.

"Come here then."

Paul had sat on the bed with them, watching Emily sit as her mother had tugged at her hair.

"Are you packing your swimming cossie, Mummy?"

"Of course I am." She clipped two slides into her daughter's hair. "There's water slides *and* an outdoor pool."

Emily sighed as she twirled her plaits around her fingers. "I think we're all going to have a great holiday."

Paul winked at her through the mirror. "McDonald's or KFC? We'll have to sit outside though as we've got Carla with us."

"McDonald's!" she shrieked. "And can I have an ice-cream?"

"Why d'you keep gawping at that woman? Don't think I haven't noticed!" Michelle prodded Paul in the arm across the table.

"What woman?"

"Her!" Michelle gestured towards an attractive woman eating alone, two tables away.

"I'm not." *Oh no!* Paul's insides knotted around themselves.

"I've seen her checking you out as well, you'll be pleased to know." Paul squirmed in his seat. Michelle was making no attempt to lower her voice.

"Michelle, the only woman I'd ever look at is *you*." Raising his burger towards his lips, he decided his appetite was waning and dropped it back into its wrapper.

"You're patronising me." She slammed her drink onto the table.

"God, I can't win, can I?" He slid his phone from his pocket. Right on cue, it beeped.

"Who's that?" Michelle's hand swooped for it but was not quick enough.

"It's only David. He hopes we have a nice break."

"Let me see." Her hand swiped at the phone again.

"No." Folding his bony fingers around it, he put it in his pocket. "It's time you trusted me."

"If you'd nothing to hide, you'd let me see it!" Her chair scraped against the concrete as she flung it back. "I'm off to wait in the car."

He decided to leave her for ten minutes before heading to the car park of the motorway service station. There was no sign of Michelle at the car.

"Let's wait here for a few minutes. She's probably at the loo or something." They perched side-by-side at a picnic table.

Emily shivered in her short-sleeved sun dress. "I'm cold." Carla lay across Emily's feet.

The wind of the exposed motorway was whipping up around them. "We'll sit in the car. Mummy knows where it is."

For ten minutes, they waited in the silence. Carla gave a whimper and stretched herself out. A car pulled up beside them. Out got a man and a woman, a girl and a boy; a family. The girl and boy were fighting. They playfully punched each other but giggled as they did. The dad slung his arm around the mum's shoulders.

"It'll be OK." Paul leaned back and squeezed Emily's hand. She was probably thinking the same thing whilst observing the happy family beside them. His eyes locked with hers. "We'll have a brilliant holiday. Maybe I'll allow you to drag me on a few rides. If we ever arrive," he added.

"Where's Mummy?" There was an impatient edge to her voice.

"I'll ring her." Paul raised his phone to his ear. "It's switched off. We're going to have to wait. Here, I've put a game on the phone you can play."

They sat a little longer. "It's been half an hour." Paul glanced at the clock, trying to keep his exasperation under wraps. "We're going to have to have another look for her Emily." Fury was gnawing at him but he could not permit himself to be devoured by it. There was enough anger already. Trust Michelle to put a dampener on the start of their holiday. He couldn't believe it.

"What if we never find her? Will we have to wait here *forever?*"

Chapter Thirty One

Emily scampered around the cottage. "I'm having the bedroom with two beds! Then Carla can sleep with me! Can we go swimming?"

"Not now." Michelle dumped a laden box on the kitchen counter. "We were late arriving, remember."

"Don't blame me," Paul flung himself on the sofa, unable to look at his wife. "You were the one who cleared off." If it had been up to him, they would have gone back home.

"Let's concentrate on enjoying ourselves." Michelle shoved tins and jars in one of the cupboards. "What do you say? I'm sorry. You know what I'm like sometimes."

"OK." Something shifted inside him and he realised he could not be bothered with any more arguing. He stretched out on the sofa. "I'm as stiff as a board after all that driving."

"I say we go and have a look around the site." Michelle closed the cupboard door. "We could pick up a takeaway while we're at it. Saves cooking."

Emily strolled in between them as they wandered around the holiday park, holding a hand of each parent. Now and again, she would lift her feet from the floor to be swung.

"That's enough," laughed Michelle. "You're hurting my arm."

"Not as much as this hound is hurting my arm!" It was as though Carla was taking Paul for a walk, keen to explore the unfamiliar surroundings and food aromas.

"How about leaving the dog in the cottage so we can go for a drink?" Michelle suggested.

"OK. You go and buy them. Mine's a pint." He wrapped Carla's lead more securely around his hand. "I'll walk her back."

"I'll come with *you* Mummy."

Paul enjoyed having a few minutes to himself as he walked back to the cottage. Maybe being away *would* do them good. His phone beeped. *Thank God that hadn't happened in front of Michelle!* It might have set her off again. *Alana.* His insides 'jolted' slightly and he wondered whether it was a nervous reaction to Michelle or something evoked by Alana. Whatever it was, he'd have to piece it together. *Hope you arrived safely.* He would reply to her later but choose his words carefully. It was a fine line.

A squirt of aftershave, a comb through his hair and he was ready to join Michelle and Emily. This *could* be a good holiday and he would keep his phone on silent from now on.

Paul picked his way through the crowd to where Michelle sat, absently staring towards the partying children on the dance floor.

"Why don't you join in Emily?" Paul coaxed as he sat down next to his wife.

Shaking her head, she gripped her lemonade glass. "I don't know anyone."

Michelle tried to nudge Emily from the chair. "Do as Daddy says – go and make some friends."

Emily shook her head vehemently, the lights from the disco reflecting onto her face.

Sighing, Michelle took a swig from her glass.

"We can't stay too long," Paul shouted, checking his watch. "I don't want to leave Carla on her own in the cottage. She might chew something."

"What?" The *Bob the Builder* music was drowning them out.

They sat for a while, sipping their drinks and feigning enjoyment at the multitude of oversized bears and TV characters that kept popping up alongside the children on the dance floor.

"It's days like this when I wonder why I ever had kids!" Michelle said, as the air filled with smoke from the smoke machine. "What I wouldn't give for a nice meal in a civilised child-free restaurant."

"Don't be daft." But Paul could sense an undercurrent of truth in her comment. She had talked of having another but he was making excuses for now. If they were to, maybe having a boy would be good for her and redress the balance. However, his sensible side ruled this out for the time being. He sat, lost in thought, his hand cupped over Michelle's.

"Don't think I can't see you!" Michelle snapped.

"What!" His anxiety rose like trapped wind.

"You know what!" She slammed her glass down.

"I haven't a clue what you're on about!" Paul looked around. Could he not sit having a pint without this shit? *What was she on about?*

"Eyeing *her* up. I'm sick of it." Reaching down beside her, she tugged her handbag onto her shoulder. "How dare you sit with me whilst eyeing up other women?" She then flounced off.

Paul hung his head as a mixture of sympathetic and accusing stares were bestowed upon him. The expressions of sympathy were generally male, the accusing looks were female ones. *He must have done something awful to upset his wife like that!* He had no idea which woman he was supposed to have been 'eyeing up.'

With her mother gone, Paul thought Emily was more relaxed; she bopped around in her chair as she surveyed the enjoyment taking place on the dance floor. Paul sipped his pint, trying again not to notice the togetherness of surrounding families. Yet he was unable to prevent himself from unfavourably comparing his own to them.

"Ugh! I'm never drinking again!" Michelle grunted the next morning as she staggered towards the bathroom.

It had been after midnight when she had returned. Paul had been astonished she had located the cottage in the dark, given the state she was in. He had forced some pizza down her and put her to bed. It had gone unnoticed he had spent the night in the cottage's living room, unable to face climbing into bed with her.

That scenario had been increasing lately. Once, he had been unable to sleep properly without his arms and legs wrapped around her; now he wanted distance between them.

"Where did you go?" He called when he heard her in the kitchen.

"Just some bar. I don't know the name." She filled a glass with water then joined him in the living room.

"Michelle. What was all that about last night?"

"I thought you were looking at someone."

"Well I wasn't. And you spoilt what should have been a good evening." It had been shite. He would have cheerfully driven home if it wasn't for Emily.

"I'm sorry."

"Really?" He looked at her.

"Really. I'll sort it. I promise. I don't want to lose you. I know I can be a cow."

"Michelle. You're going to *have* to sort it. You're doing my head in. I think we should go out for the day." Paul threw several of the windows open, hoping to evict the stench of stale alcohol. "Some fresh air will do us all good, especially you." If only he could keep her

188

out of a pub, he thought.

"I'm not sure I could face it," she muttered, resting her head on a cushion. "Maybe you should go without me."

"Go and have a shower." He tossed her a towel. "I'll do you some tea and toast whilst you're in there. I promise you'll feel better then."

Obediently, she scuttled off whilst Paul flicked through the tourist literature left in the cottage. The sun blared through the windows. Emily was playing tennis with a girl she had befriended from a neighbouring cottage. That was a relief. At least Emily was not stuck, bored, waiting for her parents to pull themselves together.

"I've found somewhere we can go," he announced to Michelle as she emerged from the bedroom, rubbing at her wet hair with a towel.

"Oh yeah?" Michelle observed as he methodically stacked slices of bread on top of one another whilst buttering them. "What're you doing?"

"A bit of a picnic. We might as well go out for the day."

"I suppose. Where are we off then?"

"I've found a leaflet for a wildlife and butterfly park." He waved it in the air. "We can take Carla. It says well-behaved dogs are allowed as long as they're kept on a lead."

"Sounds fine." She nibbled at her toast. "Do you promise you forgive me?"

"Yes. Let's just forget it and have a good day."

"As long as you know I *am* sorry. I don't know what gets into me sometimes – I think it's all the past stuff."

"Emily'll love it." Paul decided to change the subject, not wanting to venture down that road. "There's go-carting, an adventure playground and a picnic area. It doesn't look too bad." He wrapped the sandwiches in foil.

"Right," she sniffed. "Give me ten minutes to put my face on."

Chapter Thirty Two

Emily giggled from the back seat. "Look at Carla," "She's guarding our lunch."

Michelle smiled as she turned to see Carla with her head resting on the sandwich box.

"You're going to have to stop again Paul," she said suddenly.

Paul glanced quickly in the mirror as he screeched the car up at the side of the road. Both he and Emily looked in the opposite direction, as Michelle leapt out of the car and retched at the roadside for the third time.

"I'm never drinking again," she groaned as she slid back into the car.

"I've heard that one a few times." Paul checked his side mirror as he smiled at her.

She fastened her seat belt, wincing it tightened around her stomach. "I don't know whether I should go back to the cottage."

"We're nearly there." Reaching for her, he rubbed her hand that rested on her seat belt buckle. "The journey's probably making you worse. We'll buy you a bottle of water when we arrive. You're probably dehydrated." He hoped she couldn't detect the forced sympathy through gritted teeth.

"Quite the expert on hangovers, aren't you?" She rubbed her middle.

"I used to be." He'd had a few whilst she'd been pregnant. He had gone out a little too much, he knew that. She'd been unbearably insecure and had driven him insane. She was bad enough anyway but adding hormones to the mix ...

By lunchtime, she was feeling more like herself again. To Paul's relief, she had stopped moaning. They had explored the butterfly gardens and she had waited with Carla whilst he had taken Emily go-carting. She said she couldn't face it in her fragile condition. "We're not going to stay here all day, are we?" She asked after they had returned to her.

Paul was annoyed. He should have known better than to relax. She never suggested *anything.* She was a pain in the backside.

"I like it here Mummy." Emily spooned yogurt into her mouth as though she had not eaten for days. "Besides, I haven't had a go in the playground yet."

"Why don't you two go on a boat ride," Paul said, wrapping the remainder of the sandwiches. "I'll stay with Carla and take photos of you both."

"No. You're all right." She took a swig of her water. "That's the last thing I want to do! There *must* be somewhere better we could go."

Paul thought she sounded like Emily when she was in full on whining mode. "We'll let Emily have half an hour on the playground then we'll go somewhere else. Maybe to the shops? Buy some souvenirs or something?"

"*Souvenirs!*" Laughing, she stood up. "You're turning into your father."

He snapped the cool box lid on, feeling his face harden. "You never knew my father." He hated it when she mentioned his parents. It was like she used his grief to mock him.

Carla was a nightmare whilst they looked in shops. If Paul or Michelle waited with her whilst the other disappeared into a shop, she would bark or howl. Michelle smacked her back end upon emerging from a bookshop. Carla lay down, ears flat against her head.

"Don't bloody hit her!" Paul spat the words at his wife, a mist of fury shrouding him. "She's only trying to keep us together. It's her instinct."

"God you think more of the bloody dog than you do of me." A couple of passers-by gawped at them. Paul was past caring.

"Don't you ignore me!" she yanked at his arm as he walked ahead of her. "Why are you ignoring me?" She grabbed the back of his jacket.

Pausing to face her, his jaw throbbed with anger. "You ruin *everything*, don't you?" His tone was low and calm, as though chastising a child. "What the hell is the matter with you?" Emily stood several feet away, watching.

Michelle swung her bag upwards. The thud of the books she had bought was heard in his ears as the pain pounded within his cheek.

"She must have caught him with his pants down!" Someone sniggered as they ventured past them. Michelle stormed off. Paul sank onto a bench, gripping Carla's lead. His face burned as he sensed everyone looking at them.

"Daddy, you're bleeding." Emily touched his face. "What's made Mummy so cross?" Emily looked to be holding tears back and at that moment, he could have cried with her. Man or not.

"You alright mate?" A man of a similar age approached them. His partner frowned, clearly not happy with his involvement. "It must have been summat bad to deserve that from your missus!"

"Not a right lot." He looked down at the floor. "I'm OK. I'd better go after her."

"I'd leave her be if I was in your shoes."

"Be thankful you're not."

"Come on." His companion pulled at his arm. "This is none of our business."

"Hope you sort it mate," he called back over his shoulder, as he was dragged away. Paul watched for a moment, wondering what might have happened if roles had been reversed. If he'd been the one to welly Michelle with a carrier bag full of books. He was certain he would have been lynched by passers-by.

He hauled himself up and reached for Emily's hand. "We'd better go and find your mother."

"Can I have some sweets first Daddy? And we could buy some for Mummy to make her smile again."

It was nearly an hour before they found her in a beer garden, enjoying the attention she was receiving from another table. It looked like it was occupied by a stag party. Paul watched for several minutes.

"Are we going to sit with Mummy?"

Michelle must have spotted her family watching her from the roadside. She stopped talking to the men and stared into her drink.

"That your bloke?" Paul heard one of them say as he, Emily and Carla ascended the steps and approached her table.

"Yes," she muttered, rummaging in her bag.

"You said you were single." The man looked at Paul, his voice trailing off.

Paul glanced at her ring finger. She must have slipped off her rings. He'd never known her to have done that. Maybe she did it all the time. Unbelievable.

"I lied."

"I'm sorry mate." His facial expression backed up his words. "I wouldn't have been chatting her up if I'd known she was taken, honest. You wanna watch her. Arranging to meet me later, she was."

"Thanks for letting me know," Paul replied, clasping Emily's hand. "I'm not blaming you."

Michelle knocked a glass to the floor as she rose to her feet. Shards of glass splintered out in all directions. Paul jerked Carla out of the way whilst he and Emily leapt back. Michelle stomped off again.

"I hope you're going to clear that glass up!" echoed a hostile voice from inside the pub.

"We need to go after your mother." He ignored the voice as he noticed another member from the stag party staring at him.

"Has your missus done that to you as well?"

"No." Paul raised his finger to his fat lip. "It's a long story." He backed away from the group. "I'll leave you to it."

As he ventured in the direction of Michelle's departure, the words of the party rang in his ears. "It's not too late to back out you know." There was a collective chortle of laughter.

"I know," he heard someone reply. "That little display was enough to put *anyone* off marriage."

Why am I going looking for her? Paul thought to himself. *Man up man!* Instead, he led Emily back to the car and drove, on autopilot, back to the holiday park. She had all the money anyway. She could find her own way back, that is if she didn't stay out all night on the pull.

Paul was calmer by the time she eventually returned. A beer had helped. "Have you eaten?" He searched her face for signs of trouble. "I've saved you some pasta." He hated himself. Keen to appease her, he'd saved her some tea. *What an idiot!*

"I've had fish and chips." Clicking the door behind her, she sat beside him. "Is Emily in bed?"

His heartbeat quickening, he forced himself not to move away from her. "Yep. She has been for a while. Where have *you* been?"

"You left me, remember?"

"What was I supposed to do? What were you playing at Michelle?"

"I don't know. I'm sorry. I really am." She squeezed a tear out.

"It's not good enough. You made a *right* show of me."

"I'm sorry. I can't say it any more. I can't turn the clock back."

He stared absently at the TV. "I know you can't. But you keep carrying on like this."

"I'll stop it. I promise. I'll sort it out."

"How?" He looked at her.

"I'll organise some help." She touched his hand. "I don't want to lose you."

God help me, Paul thought. She was making his head spin again. One minute she was whacking him in the mouth with a pile of books, the next, she was begging forgiveness. No wonder he was always mixed up and pissed off. "Where have you been? Even with catching the bus, you should have been back ages ago."

"I've been watching a show in the club. I've missed you, you know. I was lonely." She sidled closer to him again. "I am sorry." Peering at her, Paul thought he saw genuine remorse.

"Right. Let's somehow try and put it behind us." Paul forced himself to drape his arm around her. "Fancy a cuppa?"

"I fancy something else." She looked shyly at him, resting her hand on his thigh. "We need to get some practice in if we're going to start thinking about baby number two."

Paul wasn't going there with that discussion, but silently willed his libido to return. He was only in his thirties. A couple of years earlier, he'd have been stood up like a lamppost at the mere mention of a sex session. Now she was literally having to persuade him. He gathered enthusiasm into his voice, not daring to refuse her this time. He squeezed her hand that was resting on his thigh. "Let's lock up then you can show me how sorry you are." He rose from the sofa, winking at her.

Chapter Thirty Three

Lee watches Alana as she pours herself a coffee. It is no longer with desire though. "Bit tarted up for court, aren't you?" He doesn't trust anything about her anymore; everything she says and does seems to be directed at one thing - Paul Jackson.

Pointing her toes into her stilettos, she then slides onto one of the breakfast bar stools with her coffee. She looks as though she's ready for a night out. Lee recalls when she used to make that sort of effort for him. It's like she's given up. Nothing has been the same since they were given the verdict on the baby situation. *Firing blanks ... Jaffa.* He's heard it all. Not just from Alana either. Michelle had given him both barrels too when she'd turned up, five months before, throwing her accusations around.

He'd thrown open the door in response to her frantic banging on it.

"What the hell…"

"I'm looking for Paul," she had said, breathlessly. Evidently, she had been running.

"Here? Why?"

"Don't you know what's going on?" She sank onto the porch wall.

"What do you mean?" Lee hoped she wasn't going to say what he feared.

"Paul and *Alana.*" She was plainly in agony at having to place the names side by side.

"You're talking bollocks." Though maybe she knew something he didn't. Lee was listening.

"I'm not talking bollocks, but funny you should say that." She stood up again.

"What are you talking about?"

"Well *you* can't give her a kid. Maybe she thinks *my* husband can." She folded her arms and stared at him.

"How do you know that." Heat rose in his face and anger pulsed in the back of his neck. *What had Alana been saying?*

"It seems she's been confiding in *my* husband. About you firing blanks."

"Do you have to be so awful about it? Quite a bitch, aren't you? Alana's right."

"You haven't answered my question. I'm looking for Paul."

"You'll not have any help from me." And she wouldn't. He couldn't believe what she'd said to him. *Firing blanks.* He could have smacked her. And Alana.

"They're carrying on with each other. Can't you see it?"

Obviously, this scenario had crossed Lee's mind loads of times. And right now, things couldn't be much worse for them. He wanted to say to Alana, *Leave me. Go and find someone who can give you a baby.* But he wasn't ready to throw his marriage away yet. "I don't think so," he said to Michelle.

"But you agree there's a chance. Aren't you bothered? Or are you too ashamed of being a jaffa?"

Lee's face burned as he stepped towards her. "What did you call me?"

Michelle grinned. "You heard."

"Get lost." He clenched his fists by his sides. "Piss off from my house before I knock you out. You'll get what's coming to you."

"What do *you* need to be in court for? I don't know how you can bring yourself to be there." Folding his arms, he studies Alana as she smooths down the page of the newspaper she is reading. On the outside, she's beautiful. It's a shame about what's on the inside of her. "Shouldn't you be at the office, helping Michael to keep everything going?"

"He's in court as well. He's sitting with me in the public gallery." Alana meets her husband's eyes with an air of defiance. "We've closed up the office for the week."

"You're a hard-faced cow." Lee leans over her to pour his own coffee. "I don't know how you can look at him."

Taking a sip from her coffee, she leaves a crimson lipstick stain on the cup. "I don't want to discuss this now. At the end of the day, it's down to who the jury believes, not you."

"I just want you to stop behaving like his groupie. I don't know how you can bear to sit there." The thought of it makes Lee sick.

"I'm supporting him. Just like he would support me if things were different."

"I don't know how much longer we can go on like this Alana." He watches as she pins her long blonde hair into a bun in front of the hallway mirror.

"Leave it Lee." Her mouth is set in a hard line.

Lee peers at the face that used to smile at him. It now belongs to a stranger. Once upon a time, she would have kissed him goodbye, but those days are a lifetime ago.

Chapter Thirty Four

Margaret assembles her gown around her bulky shoulders. "Mrs Duffy," she begins. "Firstly, let me express my sincerest condolences for the tragic loss of your daughter."

"Thank you." Susan sniffs as she tosses back her shoulder-length hair.

"May I call you Susan?"

"Yes." She looks uncomfortable in her stiff blouse and jacket.

"Right Susan. I'll begin by asking you about your daughter's relationship with your son-in-law, Paul Jackson, back at the start of their courtship?"

"They were inseparable." Susan fiddles with her neck chain as she speaks. "Paul was all she ever talked about. It drove me insane at the time, in a nice way of course; it was always *Paul this-Paul that.*" Her mouth bears traces of a smile as she continues. "They were so in love. Really happy. Within two weeks, Michelle moved in with him. I thought it was too soon and told her, but they were besotted with each other. Then a year or so later, they moved into a flat that they'd chosen together. I was pleased for them. They'd waited days to hear if their offer had been accepted. They then went out for the evening to celebrate.

Yes, thinks Paul, bitterly. But what you don't know is she became drunk out of her brains, and slapped me, after becoming convinced I fancied some girl behind the bar.

It was the first hint of her violent tendencies but after several days of her tearful apologies, he forgave her and chalked it up to her state of inebriation. The making up had been amazing though – they had been in bed all day. And that's how their relationship became. Awful rows but incredible reconciliations. The drama between them intensified. Paul thought that perhaps this is how things were when two people were truly in love. He hated Michelle's jealousy and temper. But she was beautiful, clever and sexy. She became like a drug to him.

The smile drains from Margaret's face as she continues. "When would you say it started to go wrong?"

"Things altered when Michelle became pregnant with Emily. Their happiness appeared to melt away. I suppose it happens to lots of couples." She gesticulates wildly with her arms as she speaks. She always does when nervous. "Though I don't think they ever returned to how they were, even after Emily was born. Michelle clung to me whilst she was pregnant, which was unusual for her." Susan looks pensive at the memory. "She felt like Paul had abandoned her, she said he didn't want to be around her anymore."

"Did *you* think that was the case?"

"No." Susan shakes her head. "I think a lot of it was inside her head, though I'm not saying he couldn't have reassured her more. The weight was falling from her. Her face was gaunt, and she suffered with panic attacks." She looks thoughtful. "What should have been the happiest months of her life were the darkest. Paul became detached and distant. Michelle couldn't cope with what she thought was his rejection." Susan looks straight at him. For a moment, it is like seeing the ghost of Michelle. Disappointment is etched across her face.

Paul stares across the room at his mother-in-law, still not believing she is speaking for the prosecution. But, as she's already said, she doesn't believe Michelle killed *herself*.

"I knew it was a lot for Paul to deal with," Susan continues, still fiddling with her chain. "I thought things might improve after the birth."

"But they didn't?"

Susan shrugs her shoulders. "Paul was besotted with Emily. I can't fault him as a father – I think she was holding him and Michelle together. I know he was doing his best."

"Go on."

"Michelle had a touch of *baby blues*. Paul didn't know how to deal with her, that was a large part of it. I did what I could – well you do, don't you?"

Paul had been grateful for her help and had, himself, been concerned about Michelle. He had never stopped trying to reassure and care for her.

"I'd go around when he wasn't there." Susan is projecting her voice now, seemingly more comfortable in the witness box. "Help her with the baby. Make sure she was eating. Help her with the housework."

"What do you think Paul was doing when he wasn't at home?"

"Working, well some of the time. To be honest, after Emily was born, he *was* at home less. And I know Michelle was worried about Paul's work colleague."

Shut up now Susan. Paul can't believe it. *She's on one.* Her mouth is running away with itself.

Susan glances up towards Alana in the public gallery, leaving no doubt as to which woman she is referring. "Michelle thought one of his friendships could be bordering on something else. I did try and talk her out of it."

"But they married recently, didn't they – Paul and Michelle?"

Margaret's voice has a sympathetic edge.

"That's right." Her mouth is fixed in a stiff line. "The wedding gave Michelle something else to focus on for a time. Her attention was more on that than worrying about what Paul might be up to."

"What about the wedding day?"

Susan glances up at Paul now. Maybe she knows she's saying too much. Maybe she doesn't care. "He was late for the ceremony. I was beginning to think he was going to call it off. I don't think she'd have been able to cope if he had. He seemed to wobble at the altar and looked, for a moment, like he was going to change his mind."

"But clearly it happened. How were things after the wedding?"

"It didn't really change anything. They both went to work and cared for Emily. But I got a sense they were arguing quite a lot. Michelle seemed to be losing all her confidence. Her opinion of herself was poor."

"Did you ever try talking to Paul?"

"Not really. I wish I had. It can't have been easy for him. Any of it. I did what I could for them. Especially with them having little Emily to take care of."

"I'm sure you did."

"There hasn't been much mention of Michelle's father," Margaret says. "Apart from speculation. Can you tell us more about *their* relationship?"

"It wasn't good." Susan lowers her eyes and seems to shrink in stature. "Her childhood was spent listening to his unfavourable comparisons with her brother. Michelle would do anything for her father's attention. He seemed indifferent, no matter what she did."

"Did that continue as she grew older?"

"She didn't see eye to eye with him *or* her brother. He left me eventually for someone else and my son went with him. He was nineteen by then anyway. They didn't say goodbye to Michelle. They just went."

"How did she take it?"

"Personally. And she blamed me. *I blame me.* I stayed with him too long. She watched him speak to me badly and thought it was acceptable. Then she had boyfriend after boyfriend who spoke to *her* badly too."

"It sounds like it was a difficult time but it's good to hear a bit of background as to why she might have made subsequent life choices."

"Yes," agrees Susan. "She did tend to go after men who were like her father and brother – I did think Paul was different though. In the end, I saw things I didn't like but I don't believe him capable of cold-bloodied killing. There has to be some other explanation."

"One final question." Margaret speaks softly. "Given your opinion that Paul *maybe* wasn't the perpetrator of this crime, do you think your daughter could have killed *herself* in the way that has been suggested by the defence?"

"No." Susan looks straight towards the jury. "Never. But if it wasn't her and it wasn't *him, who was it?*"

"Mrs Duffy," Simon speaks in a gruff voice. "Before I begin, I too, would like to express my sadness for your loss."

"Thank you."

"It must be an awful time both for you and your granddaughter who I understand you are caring for."

"Yes."

"You are obviously a devoted mother, one who has endeavoured to support her daughter at many times when you knew her to be in need."

"Yes. Of course."

Simon adjusts his tie. "Does this include the episodes throughout her late teens and early twenties, when she repeatedly self-harmed?"

Susan looks uncomfortable. "That was a long time ago."

Simon continues. "Can you confirm you knew about your daughter, at that time, self-imposing lacerations to her arms, legs, stomach and buttocks, to release some of the mental anguish she was enduring?"

"Yes, but I didn't know how often it was."

Despite the grim nature of it all, Paul feels slightly lifted. *Trump card played.*

"Do you think, Mrs Duffy, that a woman able to inflict such sustained self-injury, is equally capable of causing herself the fatal injury, you are suggesting someone else has perpetrated?"

"I'm not saying it was Paul, but it was *someone.*"

"Answer the question Mrs Duffy. Given your daughter's history of self-harming, was she equally capable of causing her own fatal injury?"

Margaret stands up. "That is not for my witness to decide."

"Sustained." Judge Lakin collaborates.

"Did Michelle have any enemies that you knew of?"

"No."

"That will be all."

Chapter Thirty Five

T he final prosecution witness steps up. Paul feels utter relief that it is the last person that is going to speak *negatively* about him. This is, however, coupled with trepidation of not knowing anything about her or what she might say. She is roughly the same age as Michelle, with stringy, ginger hair and a wan complexion. As she takes her position in the witness box, she glances around the court room without meeting anyone's eye.

"You are Monica Anne Redmond," asserts Margaret after Monica has sworn her oath in a shaky voice. "Is that correct?"

She nods earnestly. "Yes."

"Am I accurate in stating you are employed at St Margaret's Catholic High School, as an office clerk?"

"Yes."

"The same school where Michelle Jackson was employed as a part time school bursar, for nearly two years?"

"That's right." Monica tucks some hair behind an ear. "We worked at the same school. She was my friend."

"Did you chat about things other than work?"

"Yes, all the time."

"Did Michelle tell you anything about her home life?"

"I know she felt a little left out from her husband and daughter sometimes, and worried constantly Emily preferred her father to her."

Good answer! Paul wonders if the prosecution witnesses might be more instrumental in securing his acquittal than the defence. They were all adding weight to the argument about Michelle's state of mind. To his horror, Paul realises he's smiling. He quickly straightens his face and hopes no one has seen him.

"Why do you suppose she felt, as you put it, *left out?*"

"Michelle used to say she was the parent who had to discipline Emily," Monica says, moving closer to the microphone on the ledge of the box. "Whereas her dad spent all the 'enjoyable' time with her. Kind of like a 'good-cop, bad-cop' situation."

She doesn't look bright enough to have that kind of insight, Paul thinks, bitterly. Someone has told her to say that.

"Did she also discuss her relationship with her *husband* with you, or did she just talk about her daughter?"

"All the time. It troubled her. She was convinced he was having an affair and constantly worried he was planning to leave her for someone else. I'd tell her not to be daft. After all, she was gorgeous. Men'd kill to have a wife who looked like her."

I can't believe she said that – that'll make the papers tomorrow, along with his mother in law's testimony, Paul thinks to himself. Monica flushes to the roots of her red hair. A titter of disapproval echoes around the courtroom.

"Did she confide in you any further than that?"

"Just that they were rowing all the time. I could always tell when she'd had a bad night. She would come into work with puffy eyes."

"Did she ever mention any violence?" Margaret glances towards where the defence are seated, evidently pre-empting a reaction.

She got one. "That's a leading question!"

"Overruled." Judge Lakin cuts in. "The question is perfectly relevant."

"She sometimes had marks on her. They could have been finger marks."

Simon leaps up again. "They *could* have been finger marks! Surely that's not credible evidence."

"Sustained," agreed the judge.

"After the police thing, her face was a right mess." Monica gestures to her own face, demonstrating where Michelle had borne her injuries. "She knew she could stay at my house if ever she needed to. I mean, no woman should be forced to live like that, being scared and hurt by their husband."

Stupid woman. Paul thinks to himself. I was more scared of *Michelle.*

"Usually, she wore trousers and long sleeves," Monica continued, "even on scorching hot days. I often wondered if she was trying to hide something. If only I'd have known things were so dire for her."

What a performance. Paul wishes he could say something. She looks as though she is going to cry.

"I'd have done something. Really, I would. I miss her."

All is still in the room apart from the continual tapping of the court reporter on her laptop as she logs the testimony.

"Thank you," Margaret smiles. "I know speaking about this hasn't been easy for you, but you've been helpful."

"Perhaps," suggests Simon in a booming voice as he approaches Monica. "Michelle Jackson wore long sleeves and trousers to cover the scars of the injuries she'd inflicted in her youth. Now you're aware of her self-harming history, can you see how that might be more logical?"

"I suppose so," Monica agrees. "But she could have been hiding bruises caused by her husband." Cautiously, she catches Paul's eye.

"But you're forming assumptions. You'd never seen any bruises or been told about any bruises."

Monica drops her gaze. "No."

"No further questions."

"I think," Judge Lakin repositions his wig, "we should take a brief recess. Shall we say fifteen minutes?" The question is put to the clerk who nods.

Everybody darts gratefully in the direction of the exit. Paul remains seated, drained as he notices John ascending the steps into the dock.

"I'd like a few words with my client."

The dock officer steps to the side. "Go on."

"How are you doing?" John squeezes Paul's shoulder.

"OK, I guess," he stretches. "Knackered."

"We're doing fine, you know." John glances towards the public gallery which is now empty. "Simon's doing an excellent job of discrediting the lot of them. I'm confident. Aren't you?"

"I'm still worried the jury will side with the prosecution. Their barrister knows what she's doing too." Paul and John look across the court room to where Margaret is deep in conversation with someone.

"The bottom line is, it's down to who the jury believe. And the defence witnesses haven't been up yet, remember. Still - it might not come to that. Personally, I think the judge has called a recess as he's considering the dismissal of the case."

"What!" Paul, sits upright, adrenaline coursing through him. "What makes you think that?"

"It occasionally happens if the prosecution has a weak case, and I think they have. Simon agrees. I had a brief word with him before I came up to see you. He's going to make an application. He's gone to put an argument together."

"That's brilliant! Do you really think he could be about to dismiss it? And free me?"

"Don't build your hopes up yet. Anyway Paul, you sit tight, we'll be on again in a few minutes. I'm going to grab a coffee."

"I wish I could join you." Paul's shoulders droop. His backside is numb with the endless hours perched upon the solid seat. It is dubiously grubby compared to the other seats in the courtroom. His head throbs with tension and his tongue is like a dehydrated slug inside his mouth. It is nothing a gasp of fresh air and a cup of coffee can't fix. But he is not to be afforded those privileges. Not yet anyway. Maybe soon. Perhaps in a few hours' time, he will be back with his little girl.

Chapter Thirty Six

Paul watches as everyone files back into the courtroom, whilst making mental calculations of how long it might all take. Six more witnesses; including himself.

Paul notices that the jury haven't come back.

"I would like to make an application, Your honour," Simon begins, "for this case to be dismissed. In my opinion, the evidence presented against my client has been weak. All that has been put forward by the prosecution is either hearsay or explainable. I am of the belief that there is no case against Paul Jackson to answer."

A hush descends. *This is it.*

After a few minutes, the clerk of the court coughs in readiness to speak. "Has the judge had the opportunity to deliberate as to whether the case should proceed with the evidence of the defence?"

Paul closes his eyes, hardly daring to believe it might be about to be hurled out of court, enabling him to saunter into the luminous sunshine, tantalising him through the ceiling of the courtroom. The face of his daughter swims into his mind.

"I have considered whether the case can be dismissed at this stage." Judge Lakin speaks slowly. "And I have decided to hear the evidence of the defence in this matter, to come to an accurate verdict. So if we might reassemble the jury?"

Paul's hopes plunge with a resounding thud.

Simon takes a gulp of water, as the jury file back in. After a few moments, he looks towards them. "Ladies and gentlemen, you will now hear the case for the defence. You will learn of the impossible circumstances in which Paul Jackson had to live throughout his relationship with Michelle Jackson. How he had to spend his life walking on eggshells, so as not to evoke his wife's jealous anger which had the propensity to erupt in violence. How he fought to maintain peace in the face of extreme adversity.

Paul was a devoted father *and* husband, who vowed to stand by his wife through bad times and good.

On the night in question, her state of mind was impaired to the extent that Paul was temporarily forced to escape from her whilst she calmed down. He did so in the knowledge that his daughter was safely asleep, in her bed.

Members of the jury, in my view; your job in this case, is not to deliberate as to whether this was a *spur-of-the-moment murder*, or *pre-empted murder*, as has been suggested by the barrister for the prosecution.

Your job is to decide, based upon the facts you hear, whether Paul Jackson actually killed his wife. The evidence which will now be presented, I'm sure, will clearly show you that he didn't.

"The defence would like to call their first witness to the stand," proclaims the usher. "Mrs Caroline Stratton, Deputy Head Teacher at Osbaldwick Primary School, York."

Paul flushes at the realisation that David is about to discover what became of the generous wedding present he gave them. The incident was the catalyst for Emily's school becoming concerned about her welfare.

He and Michelle had enjoyed a pleasant morning; they had cooked breakfast and cleaned the house from top to bottom. Glimmers of her former self radiated; she giggled as he crawled inside the duvet cover as they changed the bed. There was a feigned mocking of his attempts at ironing before she took over from him, and a joint pinning down of the dog to brush her, then he vacuumed the carpets.

"I'll be pinning *you* down later," he'd said to her. "Housework always makes me horny."

"Maybe you should do it more often then." She slid her hand under his t-shirt and tweaked his nipple.

Rain was slashing the window panes but home, for once, was a secure, sheltered sanctuary.

"I'm off shopping." Michelle announced, yanking some carrier bags from the hallway cupboard. "I'll pick up something nice for tea."

"How about a couple of salmon fillets? And we could watch a film. We could make a night of it." Paul wound the wire on the vacuum cleaner. "I'll take Carla and Emily for a walk while you're out."

The constant whirring inside him had subsided and he was as close to happy as he dared to be.

As he paced along the park with Carla, his steps became lighter. Emily bounced in puddles behind him, twirling her umbrella. Gazing into the clouds, he was certain the sun was trying to break through.

They arrived back home with ratted hair and flushed cheeks. The scent of drying laundry reached out to tempt them in as they discarded sodden coats in the porch.

"I think hot chocolate is in order." Attempts to tug off Emily's wellies, resulted in Paul dragging her across the floor of the hallway. Streaks of water followed her. Then Carla shook the rain from herself over them both.

CHAPTER THIRTY SIX

Emily giggled. "Only if I can have your marshmallows as well."

"No chance!"

They sat laughing at each other's chocolate moustaches, as they dried out in front of the fire. But suddenly, the door slammed with such vigour that they both jumped.

Emily looked worried. "What was that?"

"It's OK love. I'll help Mummy put the shopping away. You drink your chocolate." He strode into the hallway. "Where's the shopping then?" Michelle's hands were empty.

She stood in front of him, looking thunder.

"I didn't bother." She flung her handbag onto the floor. "I bumped into your fancy piece at the supermarket."

"Fancy piece!" Paul massaged his temples. "What are you on about?"

"You know precisely who I'm on about." Michelle glared at him as she yanked her coat off. "Alana. Ignorant bitch completely blanked me. Looked at me as if I was something she'd stepped in."

"No, you're wrong." He walked towards her and held his hand out to take her coat. "Perhaps she didn't see you."

"You're defending *her* now." She flung the coat at him. "How touching. What the hell have you been telling her about me?"

"Nothing. I wouldn't. We've had this conversation already." Gathering up her coat where it had fallen at his feet, he hooked it onto a peg. "You know that."

"I don't believe you. I think you're carrying on with her."

Wearily, he dragged his fingers through his damp hair. "I thought we were past all this. You've been OK with me all week. Look let's forget this conversation. Let's not spoil things. We'll *all* go shopping." He picked up her discarded handbag and held it out to her. He would be having words with Alana.

"You don't love me anymore." Michelle surveyed him with an icy stare, as they drove back from the supermarket.

"Of course I do." God, shut up! Fury threatened to erupt from somewhere inside him. He'd have probably shouted at her had it not been for Emily behind him.

"But you don't fancy me do you, not like Alana. I understand." She folded her arms and pouted. "She's very 'Barbie-doll-ish,' isn't she?"

"Leave it Michelle." Paul jammed a CD into the stereo.

"You *do* fancy Alana." She pressed the eject button. "I knew it!"

"Of course not!" Her constant accusations were not helping him to concentrate on the road.

Michelle was winding herself up. "We're not gonna last much longer, are we? I might as well find someone else. Someone who wants me!"

"Michelle," he cried out. "Stop it!" He couldn't deal with this for much longer.

She pulled down the passenger sun visor. "Look at me. I'm not surprised you hate me. Ugly."

"You're beautiful. Please stop it Michelle."

"Yes, you're beautiful Mummy." A small voice sounded from behind them.

"You don't mean that." Her angry eyes surveyed Emily through the mirror.

"That's enough." Paul thumped the steering wheel. "Leave her out of this!"

"You're a dick!" In one swift movement she reached over the gearstick and yanked the steering wheel. The car swerved onto the kerb as Paul slammed his foot onto the brake. An image of his parents flashed into his mind. This was how his father would have slammed *his* foot onto the brake, eighteen years earlier. He was dizzy for several moments, as he fought to regain composure.

"What're you doing? Are you trying to kill us all?" Paul gasped as he spoke, feeling utter relief that no one had been walking along that stretch of footpath. Emily sobbed in the back seat, her arms wrapped tightly around her bear.

As they walked down their garden path a short time later, Paul whispered in Emily's ear.

"Daddy needs to talk to Mummy. I want you to put a programme on upstairs until I say it's good to come down." Her knowing nod tugged sharply in his belly.

Michelle raced ahead of them and let herself into the house. Clearly on a mission, she strode straight into the living room.

As Emily and Paul dashed in behind her, they realised she was battering the TV with the doorstop. It was as if she had already planned her attack.

"Daddy!"

"Upstairs! Quickly! Now!" He raced into the living room, where for a moment he remained rooted to the spot as his wife attacked their TV. He wouldn't have thought she was strong or angry enough to inflict this amount of damage. The present from his brother had masqueraded proudly over their living room since their wedding day. It was his pride and joy. In fact, it was the whole family's pride and joy.

"Enough!" As he bolted towards her, she stopped attacking the screen with the doorstop but rammed her foot against it instead, as she screamed out in temper. "What's got into you?" Grabbing her from behind, he held her firmly with her arms at her sides, until the anger drained from her body, to be replaced by a violent trembling. God, he was out of his depth here.

"I'm sorry! I'm sorry! I can't take it anymore." Her feet were hardly touching the floor as she leaned against him with the entire weight of her body.

"You can't take *what?*" There was no way he was letting her go - there was every chance she could fly at him and she still had the doorstop in her hand.

"You don't love me. Emily doesn't love me." Tears were sliding down her face with the force of a waterfall. "I can't take it anymore!"

Emily appeared, surveying the TV. Michelle had not managed to smash through its robust screen but the numerous dents and shadows covering the display made it obvious it would only be fit for the tip.

Tears filled her eyes. "I'll be the only girl at school without a TV. It's not fair!" Carla followed behind Emily innately, as she stamped back up the stairs, probably guessing it was the safest place to be.

Paul dragged the mangled TV into the back garden. It would have tormented him if it had remained in the house where he could see it. It was going to break his heart to cart it to the tip.

"Daddy'll sort a new one." He pushed Emily's hair out of her eyes as he tucked her into bed. Somehow he would have to raise the money. His brother would be devastated if he was to learn what had become of his gift to them. He hoped he could keep this one quiet.

Emily turned away from him. This was horrendous. It was going too far. He felt ashamed, spineless and sick in equal measure.

Chapter Thirty Seven

M iss Sanders had called him at work. "Mr Jackson. I need
you to come into school for a word about Emily."

"Is she OK? Do I need to come now?" The familiar
anxiety jerked at his insides. Emily had barely spoken to him since
the TV incident. It was obvious the situation was affecting her deeply
and Paul was clueless how to handle it.

A nagging voice inside him was saying *go! Leave. Take Emily and fight
for her!* Yet in other moments he felt compelled to stay, magnetised
by the house he loved, the family he had yearned for, and the wife he
felt was his responsibility. Yet he hated her too and he was scared one
day he would retaliate. From being a strong and decisive person with
self-belief, his energy and strength had drained to a level where he
no longer recognised himself.

"Lunchtime will be fine." Miss Sander's voice jolted him back to his
latest predicament. "I'd like you to come on your own if you don't
mind. I'll explain when I see you. Try not to worry." To his relief, he
heard kindness in her voice. "Emily's OK. We just need to talk to you."

As he replaced the receiver, his head dropped into his hands. An
explanation was not necessary. He knew what was coming.

It was a surreal experience, waiting outside the school office. The
scent of rubbery plimsoll combined with custard, transported him

back to his own school days. The scraping of chairs and far-away chattering laughter brought Emily's anguished face into his mind. They should be ensuring she enjoyed a carefree childhood, like he had until he had lost his parents. *Why were they doing this to her?*

"Thanks for coming at such short notice. We know you must be busy." Miss Sanders stretched out her hand. Paul followed her towards a door which she held ajar for him. "This is the Deputy Head, Mrs Stratton." Signalling to a chair, she gestured for him to sit down opposite them.

"Pleased to meet you, Mr Jackson." The second woman rose to her feet to shake his hand. "I'm one of the child protection officers. I've been taking a bit of an interest in Emily lately. We've been noticing a few changes."

"Child protection officer?" Paul's words caught in his throat.

"Yes. Don't look so worried. We're here to help, not to accuse. Clearly you're having a tough time of things."

Paul hardly dared meet their gaze. "What's Emily been saying?"

They both sat back. "Perhaps you could tell us what you *think* she might have been saying. That might be the best starting point."

Paul gulped. *What might she have said? Well, it could be anything. They had been through so much lately.* This was the stuff nightmares were made of; being sat in front of her teachers like this.

"My wife and I." He cleared his throat. "We've been having a few problems. We're trying to sort things out though."

"Emily told us about the episode over the weekend." Miss Sanders spoke slowly as she tapped her pen against her notebook. "About what happened to the TV."

"She told you … everything?" Paul slowly brought his eyes up to meet Mrs Stratton's.

"Yes. She knows she can talk to us. And children often do. Disclose things, I mean. We're glad she thinks it's a safe environment in which she can speak to us."

"You mean unlike at home?" His defensiveness was probably not doing him any favours, but he was out of his depth. He clasped his hands in his lap.

"No. That's not what we're saying. Not at all. But she's clearly troubled." Miss Sanders paused as though she was searching for the right words. "Her schoolwork's suffering and she's become withdrawn. She keeps talking about mummy and daddy always shouting."

"We're not shouting at *her*." Paul sat forward in his chair.

"We know." Miss Sanders reached out and touched his arm.

He studied the pattern on the carpet. "We're going through a bad patch." Shame was burning into his heart like a hot skewer.

"There's help out there you know. You don't have to deal with this on your own. We could put you in touch with…"

"We're fine," he shuffled in his seat. "We don't need help." His eyes remained fixed on the floor.

Mrs Stratton put her hand on his arm this time. "You can access support, for yourself. If you need to." The gentle way in which she looked at him made Paul believe she knew more than she was letting on. His eyes were hot with shame and misery.

"We're not telling you what to do, of course. Only you can make that decision."

"Thanks. But I'll sort it. And I'm glad Emily can talk to you," he added faintly. *Was he?* "I'll talk to my wife. Now I know how we are affecting our daughter. I promise. We'll sort it out."

"I want you to take this." Mrs Sanders took a card from the inside of her notebook and pressed it into his hand. There are numbers on it you can ring. It's all confidential. Many of them are geared up towards helping women but there's no reason why men shouldn't be able to access them as well…"

"There's no need, honestly." His face was blazing as he tucked the card into his jacket pocket. "I can handle it. I'll make sure Emily doesn't hear anything in future."

Michelle had sat quietly as he spoke to her later. Emily was sound asleep when he had checked.

"If we're not careful they'll bring social workers in." Paul sat beside his wife. "I'm worried Michelle. I can't cope with all that. We're her parents. It's up to us to make sure she's happy."

"So you're saying I'm a crap mother?" She folded her arms.

"No. I'm saying we need to stop arguing in front of her. It's worrying her and affecting her schoolwork. And it was bloody embarrassing being dragged in there."

"And you're blaming me." She took a swig of her odorous red wine. Its vinegary undertones were penetrating the entire room.

"Bloody hell!" Paul was aware he was rolling his eyes. "Why do you have to be so defensive? I'm only trying to talk to you about it."

"What I can't understand," her face clouded over some more, "is why *you* were called into school. On your own as well. They could have spoken to me at home time."

He cleared his throat. "It's, it's because of the TV."

"What do you mean?" She banged her glass onto the table beside her.

"*They know about the TV?*" They both glanced towards the gaping space it had inhabited.

"You told them!" she spat the words out. "You're joking right! I'm sick of you talking about me."

"I didn't tell them!" He tried to keep his voice steady. "I didn't need to." *Oh God, he had set her off again!*

"It was *you* who made me do it!" She drove her finger into his arm. It's *your* fault." She stopped. "You mean *Emily* told them." Fury seemed to be seeping from her every pore.

"Yes. That's how much we're upsetting her." Amidst her anger, he searched her face for a glimmer of remorse.

"You mean *you're* upsetting her." She dug her fists into the sofa.

"I didn't smash the TV Michelle." He sprang up and walked towards the window. "It's not my behaviour that's having such an awful effect on Emily."

"She's all you bloody care about."

"Course I do. She's my daughter. I want her to be happy."

"That's what *you* think." Michelle spoke in a low voice.

"What did you say?" Paul swung around, praying he had misheard.

"Nothing." A smirk danced upon her wine-stained lips.

"You said *that's what you think?* What did you mean by that?" His voice raised slightly and his breathing shallowed.

"She's not yours." Her gaze held his as she became strengthened by the power she was yielding. She had literally winded him.

"Don't talk rubbish." But something in his heart flipped.

She took another glug of wine. "You're not her father. It was easier to let you think you were at the time."

"You're talking crap again. I know you are." He drew a footstool towards himself and straddled it, as he continued to face his wife. "Admit it. You're trying to hurt me. I was there every step of the way. I was the first person to hold her when she was born." He was keeping his voice steady but inside he was bubbling like an unspent volcano.

"But you weren't there at her conception."

"You're one nasty piece of work Michelle." His whole body shook as he spoke and his head was throbbing with anxiety.

"We'll request a DNA test." Michelle finished the remainder of the wine left in her glass. "I'll prove it."

"Then whose is she?" Paul decided to play along for a moment. "If she's not mine, that is?"

Michelle leaned over the arm of the sofa and grabbed the wine bottle by the neck. "Do you think I'm going to tell you that?"

"Michelle, she's my little girl. For God's sake, don't do this to me!" Paul was staring at her school photograph as he spoke. Desperately, he searched for a characteristic in her image that matched his. The hair colour could not be relied upon because all three of them had the same glossy, dark hair.

Everyone had always said she had his eyes though. Paul studied them now. They were shaped similarly, slightly slanted, the same shade of blue. Michelle had often remarked it was unfair for a man to be blessed with such long eyelashes.

"She *is mine*." His tone contained an air of defiance as he rose back to his feet. "Your evil little plan has failed. I don't believe a word you come out with." The voice of his father emerged in his ears. *Stay strong lad. Stick up for yer sen!*

"She keeps going on about it." Paul dropped his head into his hands as he spoke to Alana the next day. They were eating lunch in a café opposite the office. John had been with them but had been called away.

"She reckons she told 'the real father' at the time but he didn't want to know." Paul glanced at her. "She says she decided to let me believe I was Emily's Dad. She'd been scared apparently that she would be left on her own if she'd come clean at the time."

"Paul, I want you to hear me out." Alana spoke slowly, reaching across the table and placing her hand on his arm. He probably should have pulled it away but he didn't. The hum of normality and clattering crockery echoed all around them. "Emily is one hundred per cent your daughter. She is the double of you."

"Do you think so?" He pushed his omelette around his plate with his fork. The aroma of oily eggs was making him feel sick. No longer able to take pleasure in anything, he didn't even enjoy eating.

"I know so." She drew her hand back. "You can't let Michelle poison your mind like this. I'm shocked she's sunk this low to be honest."

"She's a bloody convincing liar, I'll give her that." He put his cutlery on top of his omelette. "When she was telling me all this, her face didn't flicker."

"Right, listen to me." Alana pushed her plate away. "The way Emily throws her head back when she laughs, that's you. Her puzzled expression when she's deep in thought, that's you. Her height. Her lovely, dark hair. Her smile. The way she waves her hands around when she's speaking. And her eyes …"

Paul felt his face burn as he watched Alana. "OK, you're embarrassing me!"

Her gaze locked into his, and she held it for a little longer than was comfortable. "You should take Emily and start over. With me."

Chapter Thirty Eight

Two of the younger jurors are whispering. The usher frowns at them.

"Mrs Stratton," Simon adjusts the cuff on his gown. "As well as being the deputy head at Osbaldwick Primary School in York, you are also employed as the child protection officer. Is that correct?"

"Yes. The head teacher and I jointly share the responsibility." Her voice is gentle, it reminds Paul of the sympathy extended to him during their meeting.

"What does that role entail exactly?"

"Well," she hesitates. "A child might make a disclosure to their class teacher or one of the teaching assistants. Or occasionally to a member of the lunchtime staff. Whoever receives the information has a contractual obligation to write down, word-for-word, exactly what has been divulged, and in what context, before passing it to me or the head, as an urgent priority."

"Then, based on the information, we decide on the best course of action. That could be to ask the parents in for a discussion, or it could be to notify all staff a child has contact with, that they are to be monitored. In some cases, however, a referral to Social Care is necessary."

"Can you tell the court what happened in the case of Emily Jackson?"

"Emily is in year two of our school. Which means we've had

three years with her. She is a chatty, well-behaved little girl with good attendance and not-so-good punctuality!" She smiles at this recollection.

"Did you have many dealings with her parents?" Simon asks.

"Not especially. I'm aware they both worked, therefore am not surprised they didn't volunteer for such things as PTA events. Like many parents, one or both were there when it mattered; parents evenings, sports days and Christmas productions."

"When was there an indication of any sort of problem?"

"Not until Emily reached year two in September of last year. She returned after the long holidays quieter and withdrawn. As time went on, Miss Sanders, that's her class teacher, overheard her saying to her friend that she couldn't invite her for tea because Mummy and Daddy were always shouting." Mrs Stratton glanced towards Paul. "She said her house wasn't a happy place. That's when we were first alerted. We monitored her after that."

"Did she speak to her teacher directly?"

"She came in upset one day, saying Daddy had been taken away by the police but they had brought him back. She worried they might come back for him but *keep* him next time."

Paul's shoulders sag. He should have left with Emily. None of this would have happened and Michelle would still be alive.

"Did Miss Sanders press her on this?"

Paul notices many members of the jury are scribbling onto their pads.

"As teachers, we're trained not to ask leading questions. She did, however, ask her what she meant. She said Mummy was always cross with Daddy, and she never smiled anymore."

"Was that the only time she talked to her teacher?"

"No. Miss Sanders made it clear to Emily, if she ever wanted to talk to a listening ear, then she would make a quiet bubble, for the two of them, where she could tell her anything troubling her. She called it *bubble time*. She makes a circle with her hands as if making a bubble herself.

"Within days, Emily appeared at school one morning asking for some bubble time."

"What did she say?"

"Her parents had been angry after a shopping trip. She said they'd been shouting in the car." Mrs Stratton looks troubled at the memory.

"She described how her daddy had nearly crashed and she had been scared. But what had upset her most was that her mother had smashed the family's TV. Emily had been tearful as she explained it would probably cost too many pennies to buy a new one."

"Did she definitely say it was her *mother* who had smashed the TV?" Simon looks from her across to the jurors again.

"She did. Which was when we decided to bring in Mr Jackson, on his own, to discuss the situation." She gestured up to where he sat in the dock. "We thought that to invite *both* her parents in, would exacerbate an already delicate set of circumstances."

"And?"

"Well, he came in quickly. We noticed he avoided eye contact completely as my colleague and I spoke to him. In fact, his eyes were mostly fixed on the floor throughout the entire conversation. And he was guarded in his answers."

"At the time, why did you think he was, as you said, *guarded*?"

"I have no evidence, only the impression that he seemed depressed and anxious. We could tell there was something going on. I've seen mothers act in this way when things are the other way around." She swapped her hands from side to side as if to demonstrate her point. "He admitted there were problems and said he was trying to sort them out. He was vague about things and uncomfortable, as if he couldn't leave fast enough. He did promise he would talk with Mrs Jackson though."

"Did you take it any further after that?"

"No, we decided to keep a close eye on Emily and a written record of anything untoward."

"And was there anything else?"

"No. Nothing specific."

"Have you tried to discuss the night her mother became injured with her? Or did she try to talk about it with you?"

Paul's shoulders are rigid with tension and he is aching from the stress of the trial. *Has Emily said anything to her teacher?* This could be crucial.

"No." Mrs Stratton looks pensive. "She's gone from being a little girl who we would have to remind to be quiet when she was sat on the carpet, to not speaking at all. We can't quite believe it"

Simon glances at his notes. "I understand there's work in progress to address this?"

"Yes. There's a child psychologist involved. But she's not making a great deal of progress. Emily is not saying anything."

"We've seen the psychologist's report," Simon says softly, "and there's nothing within it that can shine any light in respect of the case we are dealing with. There is a copy of this report in the evidence bundle." He nods towards Judge Lakin and the jurors, then turns back to Mrs Stratton. "Have you anything else you'd like to add?"

"We will keep trying. As a school, I mean, to return her to the little chatterbox she used to be. We keep reminding her of bubble time and she's a wonderful little artist. Sometimes emotion or memory comes out that way."

"Quite. Thank you. No further questions."

"I have two questions for this witness," states Margaret as she gets to her feet. "Firstly, did Emily say she had actually *seen* her mother destroying the family's TV?"

"No. She did not. She just said she *knew* it was her."

"And did she talk about them *both* being angry and shouting or just one of them?"

Mrs Stratton glances towards Paul again. "Erm both, I think, but…"

"Thank you. That will be all."

Chapter Thirty Nine

Paul watches as Nick ascends the three steps into the witness box and swears his oath.

"Mr Hambleton," Simon begins. "You are a family friend of the Jacksons?"

"That is correct."

"How long have you known them?"

"I've only known Michelle since she got together with Paul, but I've known Paul for over twenty years. We were at college together. We'd have been sixteen when we met."

A memory flashes into Paul's mind of their collar length hair, drainpipe jeans and the world at their feet.

"It wasn't long after Paul had lost his parents in a car accident. I'd lost my dad to cancer the previous year. Perhaps this was what made us such close mates."

"Did you spend time with the Jacksons as a couple, or only with Paul?"

"My friendship is with Paul so I generally saw him on his own. But my wife and I," he nods towards Jacqui in the public gallery, "spent time with them as a couple as well."

"How would you describe their relationship?" Simon twists his own wedding ring.

"They were happy at first. But then, aren't most couples?"

Paul thinks Nick seems comfortable in the witness stand. "But it was pretty full on. I thought Michelle was intense. She didn't want to share Paul. With *anyone.*"

"What gave you that impression?"

Paul instantaneously recalls a time when Jacqui had suggested they all take the kids on a camping trip. *I don't think so,* Michelle had protested. *We'd prefer to make our own holiday arrangements.* He can recall her voice throughout nights out that they'd had all been on. *Paul, I want to go home!*

Nick continues, "Michelle was always reluctant to make arrangements that involved her and Paul spending time with us; she preferred to have him completely to herself. She was jealous if there were a few of us out and hated him talking to other women. Even ones that were there with their partners. She tolerated us." Nick fiddles with his cufflinks as he speaks. "Towards the end though, he'd lost touch with a lot of them. To keep the peace at home, he had to let some friendships slide."

"Did Paul confide in *you* about his marriage?"

"Sometimes, although details had to be dragged out of him. He seemed trapped. I stressed a bit about him sometimes. My wife would vouch for that!" He looks back up at Jacqui. "Paul became someone different from the easy-going man I'd always known. He seemed on edge and put a lot of energy into keeping things amicable at home."

"In what way?"

"He could never spend time away. Even when he had Emily in tow, Michelle would constantly ring him. I know she was threatened by relationships he had with *anyone*, male or female. Oh, and he was always broke," Nick adds. "I would guess she controlled all the money.

It was the final few months when I would say things were at their worst."

"Go on." Simon takes several steps away from the witness box, as if to give the jury a better view.

"There was the time he ended up in hospital." Nick takes a deep breath. "Michelle had launched a plant pot at his head. After she'd wrecked the house. He should have had her done for it but I know he was too ashamed. Because she's a woman, she got away with it. The system's all wrong. If she'd been a man…" He looks across at the media presence then back at Simon. "I blamed myself when that happened, after all, it was me who had dragged him to the pub."

"Imogen! Jack!" Paul recalls how Emily had shrieked with delight as she raced towards her friends.

"Right that's them off our hands," grinned Nick, pushing a pint of beer towards Paul. "I think we can chill out for a bit. Nice day for it." He slid back in his chair. "How's it all going with you?"

"Hanging in there mate. Not too good." He took a sip of his beer. "I'm expecting some results on Monday."

"Results?" Nick looked uneasy. "You're alright, aren't you?"

"Yeah, not me." Paul looked over to where the children were playing on the climbing frame, out of earshot. He'd already planned he was going to tell Nick. He was going crazy with it. "DNA results."

"DNA results!" Nick bellowed, then lowered his voice. "Who for?"

"Michelle keeps telling me Emily's not mine." Paul tried to avoid Nick's eyes. His life was like a soap opera. "It's doing my head in."

"Hell." Nick let out a low whistle. "After all that with the 'other man' situation too. Just when you think someone can't stoop any lower."

"I know. I don't think I believe her. It's just, well, she won't stop going on about it." His fingers cleared the condensation from his glass in a downwards motion as he spoke. "The thought of it being true is making me ill. It's not that I'd love Emily any less, it's well, Michelle keeps threatening that she can take her away from me. Stop me seeing her. She'll make out I've no rights and no say over Emily and all that kind of thing."

Nick lifted his sunglasses, so they rested on his head and rubbed his eyes. "I can't imagine what you're going through."

"Anyway," Paul continued. "I had to put my mind at rest. So I know either way. At least then I know what I'm dealing with. I've used one of those mail order kits."

"They cost a fortune, don't they? How does it work?"

"A swab from me; and one from Emily; I took it before she cleaned her teeth the other day. Said it was for the dentist. Thankfully, she didn't ask any questions."

"Will it be accurate?"

"Apparently. I'm having the result sent into work."

"Wise move. At least Michelle can't do any more damage, that way. Make sure you let me know *as soon* as you find out." He wagged a finger at his friend. "I'm sure it'll show up as *you* being her dad. I'll be gob smacked if it goes the other way. She's the image of you!"

"That's what Alana says."

"You talk a lot about Alana. There's nothing going on is there?"

"Nah. I've enough on my plate!"

"She's bang tidy though. No one would blame you. Especially living with what you've got to live with."

"Well I'm not. She's a friend – that's it."

"What will you do if Emily's not yours?"

It was a question Paul could hardly bring himself to contemplate.

"Dunno." He shook his head. "Whatever happens, I'll cope."

"How you're still with that woman is beyond me." Nick took a gulp from his pint. "Me, I'd have been long gone."

"It's not as simple as that," Paul said quietly, peering into his glass.

CHAPTER THIRTY NINE

"Unless you're in my situation, you can't understand. Nobody can."

"Try me. I want to know what's keeping you there."

"If I was to leave, I'd not only lose my wife. I'd lose my daughter, home, possessions, everything." He 'counted' the items on his fingers as he reeled them off. "Michelle controls the lot. Whoever said it's a man's world is having a laugh."

"I don't know how you live like it. What are you going to do?"

"You don't know the half of it." They looked across to where Emily was playing, happily oblivious to it all.

"There's always a sofa at ours, you know." They'd had the same conversation on many occasions.

"Thanks mate. It's not that I don't appreciate it," he said. "But I'm her husband." He drummed his fingers against his glass. "If only she'd see the doctor for some anti-depressants or something. If she'd trust me." He momentarily closed his eyes.

"There might come a point when you've to face you can't fix it. You can't..."

They looked at the phone which screeched menacingly between them on the table. Nick viewed it with distaste. "Turn it off. I'm nipping to the bar."

Paul laughed, with feigned bravery.

"It's awful, you always having to pay for stuff," Paul groaned as Nick returned from the bar with another pint for them both and the menu for bar meals between his teeth.

"It's fine mate." He put the glasses down and passed Paul the menu. "You can return the favour when you've escaped. You will one day, you know."

"Maybe," Paul pretended to be absorbed in the menu.

"He was lucky you were there for him." Simon's voice brings Paul back into the crowded, yet silent courtroom.

"He wouldn't talk about it. He'd clam up. It was as though he thought he should be handling things differently but didn't know how to. He was scared of her, I think. Of her moods and her unpredictability."

"Do you know of any other violent incidents?"

"Like I said, he was ashamed. He would have kept them to himself."

"It sounds like it was a deeply troubled marriage."

"It wasn't his fault. He's an average bloke wanting a quiet life."

"Thank you. That will be all." Simon checks his watch.

Margaret stands. "You described yourself as…" She looks down at some notes. "A friend of the family?"

"Yes."

"Yet I haven't heard any words that imply any sort of friendship towards Michelle?"

"As I said, I knew Paul a lot longer. It was him who needed the support."

"But as we've heard from Michelle's mother, friend and neighbour …" Margaret points towards them in turn, "…Michelle, in fact, was in dire need of support. You were only ever interested in hearing one side of things."

"Because I knew what was going on."

"Like you've said yourself, you did not *know* what was going on. Paul, as you've alleged, was too ashamed to discuss his home life. You made assumptions. How could you possibly *know* what went on in their household?"

"I knew enough. I knew how withdrawn he'd become, the weight he'd lost, and the fact that he never had any money on him although he had a good full-time job." Nick sounds as though he is battling to keep annoyance out of his tone. "I heard her screaming down the phone at him when he was with me as well."

"As might many women when endlessly abandoned with their child at home. Especially whilst their husbands are out, gallivanting. And you encouraged this. Perhaps your own wife doesn't mind but..."

"Irrelevant." Simon called out.

"Agreed." Said Judge Lakin. "Stick to the Jackson's marriage."

"You're bound to defend him," Margaret continued. "I'm unsure as to why you've been called as a witness."

"Because I offered him an escape." Nick's voice rises. "She hated me. I hated her. I wouldn't blame him if he'd snapped to be honest."

Paul stares at his friend, dumbfounded. He resists the urge to shout at him across the courtroom. He's done for.

"No further questions," Margaret smiles.

Chapter Forty

Paul watches as Nurse Matthew Fraser walks to the witness stand. He was woozy when he last saw him and he would never have recognised him again, had he not been introduced to the court. His introduction to him had been because of the afternoon he spent in the beer garden with Nick and the kids.

He had walked home from the pub with Emily. She had picked some flowers to take back to Michelle. Paul hoped they would pacify her, knowing she would not be happy at him for having had a few beers and lunch without her. She'd been with her mother but that wouldn't make any difference. As he approached the house, his lunch curdled within him as he contemplated her mood.

"I'm back," he called, throwing open the door. The sun streamed into the gloomy hallway and an 'earthy' smell sprang back at them. Carla, her ears flat against her head, had attempted to conceal herself beneath the staircase, in between the vacuum cleaner and the ironing board.

"Emily, take Carla upstairs." Emily shot over to her and then upstairs. Paul picked his way through the soil and broken pot scattered across the floor. Its point of contact was evident; there was a huge dent in the plasterwork. The house was heavy with silence. *Where was she?*

Melancholy grabbed his chest, and squeezed hard, as he noticed a photo, looking as though it had been stamped on. An image of him and Michelle, clad in their wedding clothes smiled up at him from behind shards of broken glass. He jumped as the living room door was opened.

"What have you done?" Paul looked at Michelle.

"It's your fault."

"How? I wasn't here." Digging his hands into his pockets, he tried to keep his voice low.

"Exactly. *You're never here. And* you switched your phone off, as usual." Her voice was dead. She stood with one hand on her hip.

"I met Nick and the kids whilst you were at your mums." Paul bent down and picked up the larger pieces of broken pot.

"Talking about me, no doubt."

"You think you're so important, don't you? Do you think I've nothing else to talk about in my life apart from you? Perhaps now and again I need to escape from here and from you? *From all this!*" Paul stood up and placed the pieces he had collected on the table.

"Why've you even come back?" Michelle spat the words at Paul.

"I live here."

"For now, you do. Push me any further and I'll make sure you end up with nothing. There's not a court anywhere, that would give you the house, *or* Emily."

"You underestimate me." He took a dustpan and brush from under the stairs. "*And* you forget where I work Michelle."

"Emily's not yours," she spoke in a loud voice. "You're *not* her father!"

"Shut up," he hissed. "I'm starting to hate you. One day you'll get what's coming to you. And I'll know next week about Emily. I've had a test…"

A blow to the side of his head silenced him. Her rage echoed in his ears as he dropped to the floor. She'd managed to clock him despite her smaller frame compared to his. Soil and pot surrounded him. The hallway swirled around. On his hands and knees, he tried to balance. A sickly, woozy sensation stole over him as he noticed blood dripping from his head onto the black and white tiles they had painstakingly chosen. With all the strength he could muster, he reached into his jacket pocket and dialled Nine. Nine. Nine.

"Police please." Paul sensed her coming up behind him but he was unable to prevent her from grabbing the phone from his hand and throwing it at the wall. *Thank God he'd connected to the police though.* He'd have been in trouble otherwise. He put a hand to his wound. "Will you bring me a towel please? And a glass of water. I don't feel good."

The door slammed as she retreated into the kitchen.

Paul slid into a laying position, the coldness of the tiles slightly helping the dizziness to subside. He closed his eyes to quell the spinning and was aware of Emily at his side and the dog licking his head.

The doorbell was being rung continually. He squinted in the haze, relieved to notice a pair of eyes observing him through the letterbox. Then Michelle's footsteps clattered past him.

"I don't know who's called you, but you're not needed." Her voice was steady as she spoke to the police in the porch way. "Everything's fine here."

"If that's the case, can you tell me why there's a gentleman laid on your floor with a head injury?"

The door was pushed open and the owner of the eyes crouched down beside Paul. "Is there anyone else in the house?" he asked gently.

"My daughter. And the dog." Paul weakly pointed upwards to where Emily and the dog were, having now run upstairs and concealed themselves behind the upstairs bannister.

"He *fell*," muttered Michelle.

"Is this true?" Paul assumed the words were being directed towards him. He feebly pointed towards the plant, still with its roots intact, that had struck him. Once upon a time he would have covered for her. But not anymore.

"We're going to need another unit here." One of the officers spoke into his radio. "And an ambulance. Domestic incident. Man, with head injuries. There's a young girl present. We're going to take the woman in for questioning."

"*You're going to arrest me?*" Her voice was a squeak.

"You can't expect to clonk your fella around the head and carry on enjoying the afternoon sun." He unclipped a set of handcuffs from his belt. "Name?" he demanded.

"Michelle Jackson."

"Michelle Jackson. I am arresting you on suspicion of causing actual bodily harm. You do not have to say anything, but it may harm your defence if you do not mention when questioned, something which you may later rely on in court. Anything you do say may be given in evidence."

"You don't need to put those on me surely." She gasped in response to the rattle of the handcuffs.

"Is there anyone who can have your little girl?" The policeman looked at Michelle.

"David," murmured Paul, from the floor. "My brother."

"Do you have a number for him?" Michelle hesitated, then perhaps realising there was no alternative, she reeled off David's address.

Still handcuffed, she was escorted down their drive to the waiting police car. This would give them all something to talk about, Paul thought as he listened to the approach of a siren.

"Right mate. I want you to keep still. We're going to look at your head. Hopefully you'll be back home before you know it." Two paramedics; a man and a woman crouched at either side of him.

"I'm OK, honestly. I'm a bit better, I think." Paul tried to sit up. "I don't need to go to hospital."

"You're concussed, and it looks like you're going to need stitches." One of the paramedics guided him back into a laying position. "We're going to lift you up onto the stretcher. Don't worry about your house. Or your daughter. The police are going to take care of her."

"You'll take her to my brother's?" he weakly called up to the female officer who was sat beside Emily at the top of the stairs. Carla squatted beside them, her head in Emily's lap.

"Is that OK with you?" The woman had an arm around Emily's shoulders.

She nodded in response, not taking her eyes off Paul.

"Come on then poppet." She hauled Emily to her feet. "Do you want to take your doggy with you?"

"I want to go with my daddy." She had hold of Carla's collar. "Can I?"

"But you'd be bored at the hospital. And you can't take your dog there. Dogs aren't allowed in hospitals." She patted Carla's head. "As soon as your daddy has been patched up, you can come back here and look after him."

"OK then." The officer held her hand as she trailed down the steps. "I'll see you soon Daddy." Paul sensed a teary kiss on the side of his cheek. "I'll look after Carla and the ambulance people will look after you."

"We need to take an X-ray. It's important, Paul, that you try to keep your eyes open." The nurse leaned over and peered into his face. "You can't go to sleep. Not with concussion."

"That's easier said than done when you're laid on a trolley in a warm waiting room!" Paul rubbed at his eyes, trying to keep them from closing. "And that light's bright."

"There's two people in front of you." The nurse shone a torch into his eyes. "It won't be much longer. Is there anyone you want us to ring?"

"My work colleague Alana," Paul said immediately. "Alana Noakes. I don't know her number, my phone, well, it's … I know her address. I can't imagine I'll be able to go to work tomorrow. I need to let her know."

"The lady on the front desk will look it up." The nurse scribbled onto the back of his notepad.

"Thanks."

"How did this happen?" The X-ray technician was moving bits of machinery around him. He felt strangely cosseted as he lay, with things whirring and flashing around his head.

"Oh, a bit of a fall." He flinched at his own words. He had never been any good at lying.

"Had you been drinking?"

"One or two." His cheeks burned.

"You're definitely going to need stitches. I'll pass the X-ray pictures back up to triage as soon as the doctor's seen them." She ripped the Velcro open that was holding his protective radiation vest in place. "You could be in for a bit of a wait though."

"It's fine. My head's throbbing, I don't feel like doing anything else apart from lying still!" Paul put his hand up to his head and realised the wound was still bleeding.

He closed his eyes as he was wheeled out of the darkness into a lighter, more airy waiting area. The disinfectant smell merged with illness reminded him of the time they had attended casualty when Emily had reacted to her injections as a toddler.

"Remember not to go to sleep Paul," said a nurse.

"Do you think I could have some painkillers?" Paul tried to open his eyes.

"Oh my God! Look at the state of you!" Loud footsteps came dashing over to his trolley.

He grimaced in pain as he tried to turn his head towards the source of the familiar voice.

"Alana, you soon got here!"

"Is this your wife?" The nurse smiled at her.

"No, my friend." He stretched his arm out towards her. "She'll be telling me off for spoiling her Sunday. You didn't need to come here. I only wanted to send you a message about not coming to work tomorrow. I've no phone at the moment."

"Don't be ridiculous! I wanted to come." Alana grabbed Paul's hand whilst staring at his head. "What's happened? Please don't tell me this is down to Michelle."

Paul turned away, not up to facing another lecture on how he should leave his wife. He wanted to pull his hand away, it felt strange.

"How did it happen? Was Emily there?"

"David's looking after her. At least I hope he is. You'll have to check for me. The police were taking her there."

"*The police?* Oh my God! What happened?"

"I went out for a few pints, and a bite to eat with Nick. I stayed out for longer than I should and turned my phone…"

"That doesn't give her the right to do *this* to you!" Several people stared at them.

"Keep your voice down! My head's killing!"

"Sorry."

"I don't know what Emily saw." Paul tried to shield his eyes from the overhead fluorescent light with his hand. "But she saw me like this. And that's bad enough."

"What did she hit you with?"

"A plant pot. Shows what a hard head I have!" Paul smiled, then immediately winced at the pain it caused him. "It smashed the pot to smithereens!"

Alana didn't smile. "I don't know what to say."

"That's a first."

"This is serious Paul." Alana let go of his hand, stepped away from the trolley and tugged a stool towards her to sit beside him. "Where is she now?"

"The police took her. She was arrested." A twinge of guilt clutched at him.

"Well that's something at least. I hope you're not planning to forgive her."

"I don't know," he sighed wearily.

"You know I'd help you look for somewhere else to live."

Paul sighed. "I can't deal with all that right now."

Simon looks at his notes, then at Nurse Fraser. "You looked after Paul Jackson during the night of Sunday May 6th after he had sustained a head injury at his home?"

"That's right. It was decided he'd be kept in overnight, for observation. It'd been a particularly nasty injury with some swelling." Matthew Fraser indicates the site of the injury on his own head. "It had required eight stitches."

Paul inadvertently raises his hand to rub at the site of his healing scar. He has been told that eventually it will fade away to nothing. If only other scenarios were so straightforward.

"Did Paul tell you how he'd come to receive the injury?" Simon continues.

"Not directly. I understand his wife had admitted it to the police in interview though. And one of my colleagues heard Paul talking about the incident with his visitor whilst he lay on the trolley, waiting to be admitted."

"I myself, took a phone call from the police the next morning before

I went off duty. They said they were letting Mrs Jackson go because Paul wouldn't press charges. I was disappointed at the time, but I understood." He looked up at Paul. "It takes courage for *anyone*, man or woman, to progress a complaint about their spouse through the courts. I talked to him about it whilst I was checking his blood pressure. I told him he wouldn't be given a choice in the future.

To be frank though, I personally cannot see why she wasn't prosecuted, with or without Paul's say-so. I said this to the police on the phone." He pauses for a moment, then adds, "If it had happened the other way around, I'm sure it would have been different. If it had been *him* who'd done it to *her*, I mean."

Paul can remember him clearly now. He is a small yet stocky man with a gentle voice and on the night it all happened, he made Paul feel less ashamed.

"Is domestic abuse something you come across frequently in your line of work?"

"I've recently attended some training. Usually men are the perpe-trators, but they are coming forward as victims of it more now."

"Why do you think this is?" Simon tips his head to one side as he waits for a response.

"Your honour," Margaret calls as she rises to her feet, "the evidence being put forward by the witness would be expected from a psychol-ogist, not a nurse."

"I disagree," says Judge Lakin. "Mr Fraser is a front-line nurse and his views are perfectly valid, as you just heard, he has specialist training in this area - please continue."

"I'm not sure why this is." Nurse Fraser clears his throat. "Maybe it's to do with women drinking more alcohol. Or the fact that nowadays, women are often more financially independent. Overall, as I learned in my training, all domestic abuse is to do with power and control no matter who it is. From what I've heard so far, it sounds as though Mrs

Jackson had incredibly low self-esteem. I know this to be common in perpetrators of domestic abuse, whether they are male or female. One thing I've come across in my job though, is that men are far less likely to speak out about it. They somehow see themselves as weak, and a failure if they do."

"In your opinion, did Paul tick the boxes of being this type of domestic abuse victim?"

"You mean someone who would be afraid to speak out?"

Simon nods.

"Definitely. I could sense how embarrassed he was. He accepted the helpline numbers I offered him, although I had an inkling he would never use them. As healthcare professionals, we're limited to what we can and can't do and what we can say. For instance, we can't be seen to be offering opinion. I wanted to advise him that these sorts of situations usually deteriorate rather than improve." He shrugged. "But obviously, I had to keep quiet."

"Thank you, Nurse Fraser. I have no further questions."

"Frankly, I'm surprised you've been called as a witness," Margaret says as she stands. "I would say your testimony is based on general knowledge about domestic abuse, not precise information on the case. We are trying to decide whether Paul Jackson is guilty or not guilty of the murder of Michelle Jackson." Her voice becomes icier. "In fact, I could have looked up most of what you have said on the internet."

Nurse Fraser remains silent.

Sarcastic cow, Paul thinks to himself.

"Your honour," her gown swishes as she turns to the front bench. "I have no questions for this witness. None, whatsoever."

"One further question, your honour," Simon gets back up.

"Go on," says Judge Lakin.

Simon and Nurse Fraser face each other. "As my colleague has stated, you clearly have a sound knowledge in the matter of domestic abuse."

"Yes."

"Obviously the situation we are discussing here is of a *reverse* domestic abuse scenario, one of a male victim, rather than the societal *norm* of the female." He sweeps his gaze over the courtroom. "I would like you to clearly state, yes or no, whether in your professional opinion based on what you saw of Paul on the night he was in your care, whether *he* was *the* victim of domestic abuse in *this* relationship."

"Yes. Most definitely," Nurse Fraser replies.

"No further questions."

"We'll break for lunch for one hour, fifteen minutes," orders Judge Lakin. "Please arrive back punctually at two fifteen."

"Court dismissed," echoes the usher.

Chapter Forty One

Alana strides towards the exit. "I need some air." She says to no one in particular.

She's dreading going home later. Her marriage has been under sufferance for a while anyway but all this – well, it is blowing them completely apart. *See what happens*, she tells herself. *Stay calm.* If Paul is acquitted then, who knows? Either way, she isn't going to stay with Lee. Sometimes you must go after what you want. No matter what, *or who* is in the way.

At times, she has been gob smacked with how Michelle treated Paul. He is different to Lee; sensitive and fun-loving instead of angry and jealous. She has often mused that Michelle and Lee would be better suited. They certainly wouldn't have spoilt a pair. But Michelle burst into Paul's life, filling a void that Alana herself should have filled. She can recall her anger at the news that he was going to attempt a holiday with her.

"We've decided to have a week away." Paul had appeared in the reception area at work. "Try and put things behind us."

Alana stopped typing. "A holiday. After all that's happened? Are you mad?"

Bloody hell! It was always two steps forward, three steps back.

He grinned. "Possibly. Though it's probably what we all need." He leafed through the papers in his pigeon hole. "It might do us some good."

"Well I'm shocked you've forgiven her so easily." Alana swung her chair around to face him. "I mean, look at the state of your head." She tried to keep the fury out of her voice. She couldn't bear the prospect of not seeing him for a week. Or two. Whilst he played at happy families. With her.

"I know. It's not exactly colour coordinated is it?" He touched his head. "I mean, who'd use bright blue stitches?"

"That's not what I meant." Alana wanted to shout at him. "What if she does something like this again? And if you're miles away from home, there'll be none of us around to support you."

"I don't think she will." He continued shuffling through his papers. "She was locked up nearly all night. It gave her a lot of time to think. I don't believe she would risk being banged up again. She *is* sorry."

"I'm sure she is." Alana pursed her lips as she stacked files. "For now. Until the next time." What was it going to take for him to leave her? She wanted to shake some sense into him.

"Ah that's the one." He grabbed a brown envelope.

"Is that the-?" She leaned forward in her chair.

He nodded. "I daren't open it. What if it says I'm not her dad?"

"It won't say that." Although it flashed through her mind that the wrong result might prevent them from going on holiday. She raised her arm towards him. "Do you want me to open it for you?"

He passed her the envelope.

She took a post knife from a drawer and sliced it open at the edge. She glanced at Paul, ever so slightly relishing this moment of 'power' over him.

"Right." She cleared her throat and smoothed the page out in front of her. "There's a load of numbers and percentages and things. I can't make head nor tail of that lot. Anyway, the important bit. Listen while

I read it out." She glanced at Paul who looked terrified. *"Conclusion: The probability of Mr Paul Jackson being the biological father of Emily Jackson is..."*

"What? Come on Alana – you're worse than an episode of Come Dancing!"

"99.9999%. Therefore, it is practically proven Mr Paul Jackson is the biological father of Emily Jackson."

"Pass it here." Paul took the page and scanned it as a big smile spread across his face.

"What did I tell you? That should put your mind at rest."

"I do feel better." He sank onto a seat, tension seemingly seeping from him like air from a punctured tyre.

"Are you going to say anything to Michelle?" The telephone rang. Alana pressed a button that would activate the answering machine to pick up the call.

"Probably not." Paul stuffed the letter into the envelope. "Unless she mentions it again. We're getting on better so I don't want to rock the boat."

"Well," Alana said. "I hope it stays that way for you. You don't deserve to be bullied." She didn't hope that at all. Really, she hoped it grew worse and he would leave her.

"You make me sound like a right wimp."

"I'm sorry. I don't mean to. Being married is hard enough, without extra grief. Life passes too quickly for it to be spent with someone who makes you unhappy."

"Are you OK?" She thought he looked concerned and that warmed her. She kept wondering how much longer they could go on like this, tiptoeing around how they really felt about each other.

"Yeah fine." She jostled herself back to reality. Really she would have liked to have disclosed her own home life misery and how she was wasting time away with Lee when she should be with Paul. "Just wondering how the office will survive without you. When are you going anyway?"

"This weekend. Only to the East coast. Someone who Michelle works with is renting us her cottage. It's on a nice park with a pool and a club and everything."

"How long are you going to be off for?" She'd be counting the days. She hated herself for being like this. She was becoming a little obsessed with him. She could never get him out of her mind.

"Only a week." Paul slid the letter into his briefcase.

Alana follows John through the revolving door of the court building, exchanging the headache-inducing strip lights for the dreary early-afternoon drizzle. She drinks in the fresh air.

There are around ten reporters wielding cameras and television equipment coming towards them. It's like a scene from a news channel.

"Are they all here because of Paul?" Alana mutters as a bulb flashes in her face. She's glad she brushed her hair and reapplied her lipstick.

"How well do you know Paul Jackson?" a woman calls to her.

"We're not saying anything at the moment." John, thankfully more accustomed to this scenario, steps in front of Alana. Cameras are flashing all around them.

"I am acting for Mr Jackson in his trial at this court," John announces as several microphones are thrust in front of him. "At this stage we are unable to comment on the case. The trial is proceeding, and the outcome will be announced in due course. We'll be able to comment more fully then."

"I hope they throw away the key!" yells a woman from the back of the crowd. She clutches a plaque sporting the words *Justice for Abused Women*.

"How can *you* be here, supporting him after what he's done to his wife?" shouts another woman.

"It wasn't him." Alana retorts. Shit! She shouldn't be saying anything! John's going to go mad. Plus, she's drawing attention to herself.

"What makes you so sure?" A microphone is shoved in front of her face, but she brushes it aside.

"Do you think he killed her?" She backs away from another microphone as the words are shouted at her.

"No comment."

They push their way through the crowd of reporters and supporters, ignoring pleas for information. They will be answered soon enough. The realisation makes her jittery. With ringing ears, she follows the others into a wine bar. She can't think straight and a glass of something is what she needs. Then a hand yanks her back from the entrance.

"What are you doing here?" she snaps at her husband.

"I think we need to talk, don't you?"

Chapter Forty Two

"We'll hear from two more witnesses today," says Judge Lakin. "We'll have the final one and the closing comments tomorrow. "Mr Booth, would you like to call your next witness to the stand?"

There is a collective stretch and silent yawn in the courtroom. Simon shuffles through some papers.

Simon stands. "I would like to call Police Constable Stuart Rayner of North Yorkshire Police to the stand."

The usher leads a middle-aged man with a stern expression into the witness box. He swears his oath then looks expectantly at Simon.

"You attended at the Jackson's home following an incident which took place on Saturday May 19th. Can you tell the court who made the call to you?"

PC Rayner's tall frame towers out of the witness box. "It was a silent three nines call," he replies, placing his helmet on the ledge of the witness box. "It connected through then was cut off. It was Mr Jackson, in need of some help." He clasps his hands next to his helmet. "It had been made from a mobile phone before being disconnected. The number was registered to 42 Bracken Bank, Osbaldwick, therefore we were in a position to be able to trace the call and respond."

"Who answered the door on your arrival?"

"Mrs Jackson. She didn't come to the door straight away. I had already seen Mr Jackson on the floor through the letterbox before she answered. When she came, she insisted no help was required. We had to push our way in."

"Why was Mr Jackson on the floor?"

"He had a head wound which we subsequently found had been caused by a blow from a plant pot. This was smashed, along with a mobile phone, in the hallway."

"How did you know Mrs Jackson had attacked her husband?"

"She was the only other adult in the house, to our knowledge. Neither she nor Mr Jackson gave any information that suggested otherwise. We were concerned when we discovered the presence of their daughter. I personally delivered her, with her dog, to the brother of Mr Jackson."

"Did Mrs Jackson admit to the assault?"

"She did but claimed at first, that she had acted in self-defence. She was shocked at being arrested. However, once in custody she was compliant and full of remorse. We were unable to pursue the complaint without Mr Jackson's say-so and he had informed staff at the hospital that he wanted the matter discontinued."

"Would you have been more inclined to prosecute, without his blessing, should circumstances have been turned around?"

"Could you please be more specific?" Judge Lakin's voice rings into the pause.

"Yes." Simon appears to think for a moment. "Would you have treated the attack more seriously, had it been a man hitting his wife around the head with a plant pot, in front of their young child?"

"Yes, if I'm to be honest." PC Rayner looks uncomfortable. "We'd have had him in front of a magistrate the next day. With or without the partner's blessing."

Simon nods. "No further questions."

"PC Rayner. Did you say to my learned friend that Mrs Jackson said during interview that she was acting in self-defence?" asks Margaret.

"Yes. We invited her to counter complain but she did not want to. There were no sign of any marks or injury on her and she was very calm," he replies. "We took note of her initial reluctance to let us in, in order that her husband could be treated. If she had been in any way fearful of him, I'm sure she would have invited our intervention as soon as we arrived at her door."

"How can you be sure Mrs Jackson did not act against her husband in self-defence?"

"I suppose I can't be certain." He shrugs slightly. "We weren't there, were we?"

"That will be all, your honour," Margaret smiles towards Judge Lakin.

Paul notices her line of questioning to the defence witnesses is brief, as though she is attempting to make points that will fix in the minds of the jurors.

Dr John Sowden, Senior Psychiatrist for the North Yorkshire Mental Health Team, ascends the steps, swipes the Bible from the stand into the air, and confidently repeats his oath. He then observes Simon, with a business-like air.

"Can you confirm to the court, the times at which you have treated Michelle Jackson?"

"Certainly." He hands the Bible back to the usher. "She was known to us throughout the period of her being about fourteen-years-of-age to eighteen. She then came back, following referral from her GP when she was twenty." He glances down at his notes as he speaks. "She improved once she had followed a course of psychotherapy but then was re-referred to our team following the birth of her daughter."

"Did you treat her personally?"

"I did. I grew to know her well. Her main problem was of self-harming. That was her 'release;' her way of dealing with what was troubling her."

"When you say self-harming, can you be more specific?"

"Certainly." He runs a finger down his notes. "She was first referred to our service at the age of fourteen after being admitted to A&E following an overdose of paracetamol."

"Were you able to ascertain whether this was a serious attempt at taking her own life? Or, as it is often described, a cry for help?"

"I don't see this question's relevance," interrupts Margaret. "We are deliberating something that took place nearly two decades ago – she was a teenager."

"Overruled," Judge Lakin nods across to Dr Sowden. "Please continue."

Paul feels heavy as he recalls the silvery lines on her arms. It was a period of her life she hadn't liked to talk about and now, here it was, laid bare for all the world to see. Nevertheless, it is hopefully what will save him and reunite him with his daughter.

"Michelle admitted in therapy her actions had been, as you put it, a cry for help. It stemmed from boyfriend troubles, not uncommon at the age she was at. I was also concerned about the lacerations that appeared on her forearm which was a prolonged attempt at releasing her own deep-rooted self-hatred." He taps the front of his forearm as he speaks.

"She didn't try to conceal these from you?"

"Only at first. As is consistent with this type of self-harming, she was overwhelmingly compelled to carry out the self-mutilation and she described the sense of relief the cutting provided. As time went on, I learned of the extent of her extremely poor self-image. She didn't care about the scarring she was causing, as she said she was ugly and unloved anyway."

Paul thinks back to when he had first seen her scars. Her shame had been as deeply ingrained as the cuts themselves. He had wondered why she always wanted to make love in the dark; why she would steer his hands away from her scarred skin. It had only been when she had forgotten once to lock the door as she showered, that he had seen them. He had kissed the top of her head as she explained about her previous illness. He had promised her she would never know despair like that again. But she had. And she had *died* in despair. And it was his fault.

"What was causing her to do this to herself – the main catalyst?" Simon's voice breaks into Paul's thoughts.

"Whilst I'm not casting aspersions, I would say the sudden abandonment of her father after her parent's divorce was a huge factor. Michelle had spent her entire childhood, placing him on a pedestal, but for reasons perhaps only known to him, he'd always been dismissive of her. She also spoke of being bullied, both at school and by her elder brother – I think in both cases it was pretty severe bullying. She didn't have a close bond with anybody; in fact, she seemed alone in the world at that time. Her mother was engrossed in her own troubles."

Paul glances at Susan. Tears are streaming down her face. Emily is not the only casualty of all this.

"But she must have improved for you to be able to discharge her from therapy by the time she was eighteen."

"She had." He smiles as he refers to his notes again. "She had a boyfriend by that time, had left school and things had settled down at home. She had begun an accountancy course at college. Her self-harming episodes were still taking place, but to a considerably lesser extent. However, I realised at the time she may represent to us if events took a turn for the worse."

"And they did?"

"Yes. She was re-referred by the hospital in her mid-twenties. A boyfriend, again, had been at the root of another suicide attempt. He had a flat on the eleventh floor of a high-rise block. Unfortunately, he had chosen that location to end their relationship. It had taken a team of specially trained officers over an hour, to talk her down from the window ledge."

Shit! Paul thinks to himself. She's never mentioned that one.

"Was she still cutting herself as well?"

"It began again around that time. It was exacerbated also by the fact that her father's new wife had given birth to a little girl. Social media was in its infancy then, but Michelle had gone to pieces after seeing pictures of her father and the half-sister she never expected to be allowed to meet all over Facebook. We upped the interventions, settling on an anti-depressant approach combined with psychotherapy. We were seeing her weekly, sometimes more. She divulged she was running out of space to cut. Her arms were a mass of faded lines by this time. I understand she was cutting at the tops of her legs and on her stomach and breasts."

Paul watches the jury. They all appear to be listening intently. Several scribble on their notepads. He feels a sense of calm. This is his defence.

"She spoke of a release of self-hatred and pent up anger taking place as the blood flowed out of her wounds. Like many self-harmers, to cut herself was something she was in control of, at a time when control was lacking elsewhere in her life."

"But again, this episode of self-harm was a transient one?"

"That is correct. We were astounded with the sudden change after she began a relationship with Mr Jackson."

"In what way?"

Paul notices that many people are glancing towards him and shifts uncomfortably on the hard plastic seat.

"Overnight she stopped cutting herself. She wanted to stop the anti-depressant tablets too, obviously that was something she was strongly advised against. She discharged herself from our service, saying she was fine and had her boyfriend to look after her."

"She sounds like a person who needed a partner to stabilise her."

"Yes. I believe having a boyfriend increased her sense of self-worth. When things were going well, anyway. It seemingly 'validated' her."

"I am now," Simon pauses, perhaps searching for the correct words, "going to move forwards to the incident we are here to decide about. Whether or not Michelle stabbed *herself*. We know from the witnesses we have heard from so far that the couple's relationship was under great strain and Michelle was incredibly unhappy.

Margaret stands. "Your honour, it is my opinion that my learned friend here is leading the witness."

"He's acting for the defence," responds Judge Lakin. Paul's hopes rise a little. This is going well.

"Knowing Michelle in the professional capacity in which you did, can you say whether, in your opinion, she would have been capable of fatally stabbing herself in the chest on the night of Monday June 11th?" Simon glances at Margaret, possibly expecting another objection.

"Well," he lifts his chin into the air and exhales loudly. "She was certainly no stranger to a knife." Each point is made by 'counting' on his fingers as he speaks. "Her moods and well-being are controlled by the quality of her intimate relationships. Her marriage was obviously in trouble."

"Could the witness please answer the question?" Judge Lakin drums his fingers on the desktop.

"Definitely. I'd say it was possible she killed herself."

Paul closes his eyes.

Chapter Forty Three

Paul has been awake for ages, rehearsing his answers over and over.

"Jackson. It's time for you to make a move. Prison van'll be here soon."

Stephen stirs, and Paul sits up. He's been going over what Simon will ask him. They have been through it all, question by question. There is an unmovable knot inside him at the thought of being questioned by Margaret.

"Tell the truth," John has reassured him when he has expressed his anxiety. Look her in the eye and be as brief as you can. That's all you can do."

"What if she tries to trip me up?"

"That's her job, unfortunately. All you can do is relax and put your faith in the jury. I've Googled them all and we've no women's activists or anything."

Paul dresses quickly, taking care with his tie. It is a huge relief to shed his prison clothes and put on shirt and trousers again. It helps him to feel more 'normal,' although they now hang from him. A belt is necessary for his trousers, but it is pointless to ask for one. *It poses a suicide risk.* He shaves, then slicks back his hair with wet hands. It is badly in need of a trim and flops straight back into his eyes. He should have opted for the standard prison number two all over but he can't bear to look like the rest of them.

"Are you sorted?"

He takes one last look at his reflection before directing his attention to the officer who waits at the door of the cell. "Here's your breakfast pack. You've got about ten minutes."

"This might be the last time you wake up in here mate." Stephen claps him on the back on his way into the loo. That's all Paul needs, listening to him taking a dump whilst he eats. Like he doesn't feel bad enough. He stares into space, whilst trying to force his breakfast down. His insides churn with each spoonful yet he knows he needs every ounce of energy to survive the day. This is the big one. It is possible by the end of this day, he might know his fate. He hardly dares to believe that he might be reunited with Emily in a matter of hours.

"How are you feeling?" Stephen calls from behind the wall.

"Sick," replies Paul.

"Well I hope I don't ever see you again." The toilet flushes. "In the best possible way, of course."

Still nauseous with nerves, he is grateful for the forward-facing seating position in his cubicle within the prison van. He tries to take his mind back again to 'the night' but as always, only finds a darkened blur. He probably needs therapy, not cross examination, to sort it all out.

He watches fields and trees speed by as the journey progresses. Scenery he has always taken for granted but never will again. If he is to be set free, he will never take anything for granted. He aches to be amongst normality, to have his freedom back and to be able to walk in the park, with Carla and Emily beside him. He wants his life back, although it will never be the same.

Paul notices many members of the jury nod and smile at each other upon being seated this morning. This must be the norm after several days of being thrown together. Hopefully their unity will be carried forth into the verdict. He needs to ask John what will happen if they don't agree. He can't go through this again.

Everyone else takes their positions. Paul notes, with an element of misplaced humour, people in the public gallery, even the media, have resumed the same seating positions as in previous days.

"You're up soon. Are you ready for it?"

Paul rises from his seat in response to John who he spots ascending the steps towards him.

"Ready as I'll ever be."

"This is what we've been waiting for. Remember what we've discussed."

"Will do." He sniffs.

"You'll be fine." John slaps Paul's shoulder and makes his way back down.

"All rise."

The reassembled court stands whilst Judge Lakin re-takes his position. The usher stands up.

"You may all sit."

It feels like they have been there for two months. David gives Paul a brief thumbs up. Alana, beside him, looks lost in thought. The usual quiet seeps through the courtroom as the clerk clears his throat and addresses Simon.

"Would the defence barrister like to call the next witness to the stand?"

"Thank you. I would like to call on Barry Aitkin, Specialist Forensic Biologist."

A weathered man, with thin grey hair and a large moustache steps up and swears his oath.

"Mr Aitkin, you attended the scene which had been preserved for your inspection at Springfield Holiday Park on Sunday June 10th?"

"That is correct."

"There is a copy of your report within the bundle of evidence as well as a series of photographs which I would like to draw the attention of the court to."

"Yes."

"Can you confirm whether, in your opinion, the blood stains found on the clothing removed from the defendant could have been caused by him personally inflicting the wounding blow with the weapon we have seen exhibited?"

"No. As I've said in my report, I would have expected there to be evidence of upward splattering on the defendant's clothing and skin or even secondary spattering if he had been in the vicinity of an attack however, there was nothing to suggest that. There is no denying that his clothing and skin were heavily stained with Mrs Jackson's blood, but that could have been as a result of him assisting in the aftermath of whatever happened."

"So, to clarify, you are saying that the forensic evidence of blood splattering, suggests that Mr Jackson did not stab his wife?"

"Yes. That is what I am saying?"

"Thank you."

Simon sits, smiling and Margaret stands.

"Mr Aitkin. You have admitted that Mr Jackson was heavily stained in the blood of his wife, Michelle Jackson?"

"That is correct."

"Then I fail to see, how you can say with such a degree of certainty that he couldn't have inflicted the injury on her. How do you know that he didn't jump out of the way for example?"

"That would be impossible." Despite the circumstances, the hint of a smile seems to cross his lips. "Mark my words, blood spurts out of a person faster than someone else can move."

"But you cannot affirm with any degree of certainty that Mr Jackson might not have got changed or washed prior to the arrival of the emergency services."

"Believe me, the SOCOs would have found any discarded pieces of clothing or traces of blood in a sink. They are extremely thorough."

"I am not disputing that. But perhaps our defendant could have been just as thorough when covering his tracks."

Simon stands. "Your honour. Surely we are not going to allow the prosecution barrister to argue with the evidence of an expert witness?"

"Sustained."

Paul is feeling less nervous now. Margaret has been clutching at straws.

"No further questions," she says.

"Paul Alan Jackson, please stand and take the Bible in front of you, into your right hand and repeat the words from the card into the microphone."

"I swear by almighty God that I shall tell the truth, the whole truth and nothing but the truth."

"Thank you. Please remain standing."

"Paul," Simon begins. "We've heard several witness accounts of incidents between you and your wife in the latter part of your relationship. Can you, in your own words, describe what married life was like for you?"

"Yes." He glances around the courtroom, not quite trusting the sound of his own voice. "Michelle was a beautiful, loving woman who gave me a great gift; our daughter." He falters as he speaks towards the microphone, recoiling as he hears it echo back at him through the surrounding speakers. He's always hated the sound of his voice when it's amplified or recorded. He notices David and Alana whispering to each other. What are they whispering about? It throws him a little off track. He fights to focus. "Erm … Michelle was always intense, about me and her, I mean. In the beginning, though, I found it flattering, to be truthful."

A sudden memory catches him unawares of how she had always wanted to hold his hand, even when he was driving. Whenever he needed to change gear or turn a corner, he would have to keep letting her hand go. He had always liked that. Well, up until the last year anyway. They had been immersed in each other, once. That was partly what had kept them together. He had always been trying to recapture that initial magic they'd had. At the time, he had never felt anything like it.

"For the benefit of the court," Simon steps closer to Paul. "Can you say what you mean by *intense*?"

"Yes. Before we had Emily, she wanted to spend every moment with me. She hated us being apart and preferred us to do things on our own; she often said we didn't need anyone else. She used to try and persuade me to ring in sick at work, so we didn't have to be separated."

For a moment he recalls how she had loved dancing and could dance all evening whereas he would be on and off the floor for a rest; till she beckoned him back over every time he flopped onto a chair.

He can visualise her face during the slow songs at the end of the night. In their happier days, he used to refer to this period of the evening as the erection section. He had fancied her back then. Watched by the wallflowers as she called them, they would be inseparable on the dance floor. God, what's he playing at? He's not in the dock to reminisce about the old days. He literally must fight for his life.

"How did that change as time moved on?" Simon cuts into his thoughts.

Paul hesitates. "Maybe if I'd been a little firmer right away and insisted we did some stuff on our own, things wouldn't have become so bad. Whilst she was expecting Emily, she became clingy. Afterwards it grew. She was possessive and jealous and didn't trust me, although I'd never personally given her cause for this. I wondered, like her mum had, whether she had post-natal depression."

"Have you ever had an extra marital relationship?"

"Absolutely not." Though he knew this question was coming, it still annoys him.

"Can you say why your wife didn't trust you?"

"It stemmed back to when she was younger. She'd been abandoned by her father at an age when she needed him. She'd been let down by previous boyfriends as well. Knowing all this made me better equipped to tolerate her insecurity. I hoped, as time went on, she'd realise she could trust me."

"How did getting married nearly a year ago change things?"

"If anything, Michelle became more controlling. Our finances, my e-mails, my post, even my telephone calls." Paul tries to discreetly wipe his sweaty palms onto his trousers. "I wasn't my own person anymore. It wore me down, to be honest."

"So how did you deal with the situation?"

"I'd try to reassure her. All the time. But sometimes that just sent her into a rage. I once went with her to the doctors. She needed anti-depressants or counselling or something to improve her self-esteem." He brings his hands up and clasps them in front of him.

"You mentioned rage. How did that manifest itself?"

"I've always been embarrassed to talk about it. You'd think, a tall, well-built bloke like myself, well I used to be well-built until all this." He laughs, nervously. "Well, you'd think I would have been able to stop her from scratching or slapping me."

"How often was that sort of thing happening?"

"It was becoming more regular. It was as though she couldn't express herself verbally; she had to fly at me or throw something at me."

"Did you ever tell anyone about what was going on?"

"Of course not! I'm a bloke. I don't think anyone would have believed me! Or they'd have thought I'd gone soft!"

Someone had once said that. "Call yourself a bloke!" a voice had sneered outside a club one evening. Michelle had been drunk and had gone berserk when she had seen him speaking to an old female college acquaintance. Her slaps had done the talking, undeterred by the gathering onlookers. No one had tried to intervene.

"Let's move forward to the night of Monday June 11th. Please describe in your own words exactly what happened. Your honour, you have the statement which will collaborate with Mr Jackson's testimony."

This is it. Paul has been through this time and time before in his head. "I'd spent the morning with Emily at the beach. We'd tried to include Michelle, but she hadn't wanted to come. However, we'd come back and had a drink with her early in the afternoon. Emily was bored so I'd taken her off to the amusements. Michelle hadn't wanted to come. By the time we returned from the seafront, she was having a sleep. I decided to leave her be and got on with the meal we'd planned. I'd bought a few bits and pieces whilst I was out with Emily."

"Michelle. Are you here?" He remembers how he had tentatively pushed open the cottage door. "Ssssh," he had said to Emily, after looking in the bedroom. "Mummy's asleep. Go and play outside."

Whilst he stabbed at baking potatoes, Emily tore around with Carla and her ball. Paul then relaxed on the steps of the cottage, listening to seagulls and Emily's laughter whilst sipping a beer.

The sound instantly took him back to camping holidays he'd enjoyed as a kid. He and David would hurtle around whilst his dad presided over the barbecue. Yet it was his mother who did most of the work, shopping, slicing, seasoning, marinating and par-cooking; but she always allowed his dad to take the glory. He'd been lucky with his upbringing and wanted the same for Emily. His parents would have adored Emily and probably made all the difference with Michelle too. If only they'd lived.

"Why didn't you wake me?" Michelle's voice behind him made him jump. "How long have you been back? Don't you want to spend any time with me today?"

"Which question shall I answer first?" Paul laughed as he swivelled his body around on the cottage steps.

"White or red?" she called from the kitchen. His heart plummeted as he heard the rattle of the fridge door being opened.

He quickly went inside. "Michelle, why don't you eat something instead? You'll feel better for it tomorrow. I'm gonna put the steak on soon."

"I'm only having one glass. Stop acting like you're my father. We're on holiday." She held a glass towards him.

"Alright, I'll have one with you." The vinegary red wine made him shudder as he took a sip. He'd never been a fan of wine.

"Isn't it pretty Mummy; the sky's gone pink." Emily said later.

Michelle was still drinking. The sun was slipping behind the hills.

"Mmm," agreed Michelle.

Paul put his arm around her shivering shoulders. The simplicity of observing a sunset with his daughter and wife would always stay with him.

"I think you should be off to bed." Michelle drew Emily in for a hug. "You look tired out. You've had a busy day."

Emily stretched as she stood up. "Will you tuck me in Daddy?"

"I'll be there in a few minutes." His eyes were fixed on the sunset and he tried not to focus on the fact that Michelle had not been part of Emily's 'busy' day.

"And will you tuck me in Mummy?" Emily said with a yawn.

"Shortly." Michelle had finished the bottle of wine and was opening another.

"Are we going to eat something soon?" Paul looked at her. "The potatoes should be done now."

"Soon. After we've settled Emily. And you've given me a good seeing to." She was slurring her words.

"Not when you're tipsy already. You need to eat."

"You're turning me down?" Her eyes flashed angrily at him. "Again?"

"I'll be back in a minute." He brushed past her. "I'll check on Emily." *Call yourself a man*, flashed into his mind again. Most men were open all hours when it came to sex. He used to be. But the prospect of his drunk wife didn't turn him on one bit.

Emily lay in the slim bed with her hair fanned out on her pillow. "Night Daddy," she muttered, clutching her bear. "Is Mummy coming too?"

"She'll be along soon." He patted Carla who was sprawled out on the adjacent bed. His heart sank as he heard the tinkle of a bottle connecting with a glass and the glugging of more wine being tipped out. He felt like wrenching it from her and tipping it down the sink.

"Right that's it," he asserted as he strode back into the kitchen. "I'm not taking no for an answer! You're going to eat something."

He piled salad onto the chopping board. Cucumber. Tomatoes. Lettuce. He launched himself into slicing up tomatoes.

Michelle propped herself upon the counter. He could sense the force of her condescending gaze.

"I don't do it for you anymore, do I?"

"Not when you're drunk." It was true.

"What the hell's wrong with you?" She banged her hand on the worktop. "You can't even look at me! Have you got someone else?"

"Michelle. Enough. Leave it out. We're supposed to be on holiday." He threw lettuce leaves into the colander. "You're ruining it."

"I think Alana's the reason you don't want anything to do with me!" Michelle stormed towards him. "You can't keep one woman satisfied, let alone two!"

"Stop it Michelle." He took a step back which was about as far as he could go in the tiny kitchen.

"I think it's about time you were honest with me."

"Michelle, for God's sake." He tried to turn back to face the chopping board.

But she'd grabbed his shoulder and her wine-laced fumes were in his face. "A little late for that, don't you think? Is that why you don't want sex with me anymore? 'Cos of Alana?"

"I don't want sex with you anymore because of you!"

"You bastard!"

"And then what happened?" Simon rests his hands on the bench.

"In that split second, rightly or wrongly..." Paul's voice wobbles. "I took off. I needed to escape. She was winding herself up and the drink wasn't helping. I thought some space between us might diffuse things."

CHAPTER FORTY THREE

"And then what happened?" Simon asks.

"I walked around for about ten minutes. Then I went to the club and had a pint. I thought I had given her long enough to calm down. Nothing could have prepared me for …" He stops, the remainder of his sentence hanging in the air.

"In your own words, Paul, please tell the court what happened when you returned to the cottage."

"Michelle was just laid there." The courtroom is a sea of faces. He's not looking at anyone. He can see her again. He's back reliving it. "There was blood all over the place. She'd stabbed herself with the knife I'd left out."

"What makes you say she'd stabbed herself?" Simon asks. This is it. The crux of it all. Yet still a shadowy blur to him.

"Because I'd let her sink that low, then I'd left her on her own. It was *my* fault!" His voice cracks. "I left the knife there for God's sake! She'd a history of self-harming and I walked out, leaving her drunk and angry, with a knife in front of her!"

"Did you see her stab herself?"

"No."

"Did you stab your wife Paul?"

"No, I did not. I would never have harmed a hair on her head. Despite everything." He's surprised to notice tears dripping from the edge of his jaw onto his trousers. He did not realise he was crying.

"What happened next?"

"I was in shock, panicking. I checked her pulse. She was alive. I didn't think she'd die. She was so young. She had her whole life in front of her." Paul wipes at his eyes. "And I'd left Emily in the cottage with her!"

"I have no further questions, your honour." Simon turns towards Judge Lakin. "Can I request a short recess before my client is cross-examined by the prosecution?"

"Five minutes," agrees the judge. "In view of the short timescale though, the court must remain seated."

A whisper echoes. John makes his way towards Paul.

"You're doing well." He squeezes his shoulder. "Just the final push now!"

"I didn't mean to start bawling!" He tries to smile. "Do you think it'll have done any good?"

"It's not a bad thing. It shows the jury what you've been through. Hang in there mate. It's nearly over."

Chapter Forty Four

Margaret stands. "Mr Jackson, are you alright?"

"Yes, thank you."

"Good. We will begin then. "How many hours a day did you leave your wife on her own?"

"I had to go to work," Paul replies. "Besides she worked a few hours each day as well."

"But you never exactly rushed home after work, did you?"

"Sometimes I had to work late, or I'd maybe have something to do on the way home…"

"Like a visit to the pub?"

"Occasionally." Paul stares at her.

"I would suggest it was more than occasional. In fact," Margaret's voice rises up a gear, "I'd suggest you left the house as often as you could."

"That's not true. I didn't go out much."

"Mr Jackson." Her mouth is set in a thin line. "You were demonstrating conduct such as that of a single man. Coming and going as you pleased. It's no wonder your wife was suffering."

Paul tries not to be beaten back by her. "I did my best to reassure her. And I took Emily off as often as I could, to give her a break and some time on her own."

"But that's not what was needed! Your little *daddy and daughter* unit was making her more unhappy. Could you not see how isolated she felt?"

"We tried to include her," he states, miserably. "She wasn't interested."

Her voice quietens. "I can imagine though, that it must have been difficult for you at times."

"It was." He is baffled at her sudden softening of attitude. *What is she up to?*

"You must have been demoralised at her exertion over your financial affairs?"

"It was awkward sometimes, but I had got used to it."

"But it wasn't just your finances was it?" Margaret steps away from him. "She was going through your phone as well?"

"Yes."

"How did that make you feel?"

"Awful. I'd never done anything for her not to trust me."

"I can imagine it must have made you angry. I understand from your statement that she put herself in charge of your e-mails and post as well?"

"Yes." Paul holds eye contact with Margaret.

"You must have felt awfully emasculated?"

"Sometimes." He shrugs. "But I wanted to keep the peace."

"I expect you'd have done anything, to be in control of your own life."

"Yes. But I hoped things would improve in time."

"But they didn't, did they? Things were becoming worse. You must have been anxious about the effect on your daughter."

"I tried taking Michelle to the doctor."

Margaret doesn't acknowledge this, she just continues. "And then, you go to the trouble of taking time out for a family holiday. And that's ruined with drinking and jealous behaviour."

"We'd only been there two days."

"You must have been frustrated."

"A little."

"And angry."

"At times."

"If it had just been you and Emily there, things would be different." Margaret's tone was gentler. "Or if you'd gone with people whose company you enjoy and seek out. You knew that. If only your wife was out of the picture."

"I never considered that. At all." *Reverse psychology.*

"Any man would snap given the pressure you were under."

"I didn't snap. It wasn't easy."

"But Paul, your wife was on and on at you. You were powerless to change anything. She'd been drinking and you'd have wanted to shut her up. Anybody would have. People can only take so much. No wonder you…"

"No!"

"No one is saying you planned anything. Maybe it was self-defence … we've all heard how she treated you!"

"I didn't kill her!" This woman is doing his head in.

"Your prints were on the knife and her blood was all over your clothes, not to mention the broken glass everywhere and the fact that you'd been heard rowing."

"The blood on Paul's clothes," Simon cuts in, "was proven to have occurred because of him comforting Michelle afterwards. We have heard from an expert in the matter. I object to this goading line of questioning."

"I've nearly done," Margaret retorts. "And I'm merely assembling the facts."

"I didn't kill my wife." Hot tears are leaking from Paul's eyes.

"No further questions."

All attention is on Paul as he fights to gain self-control. He looks down at his feet and wills the whole thing to be over. If only he could protest his innocence with entire conviction. The memory, he has read, often blanks out trauma. Maybe this is what has happened.

"We shall break for lunch," Judge Lakin addresses the court after a few moments. In this time, I, along with my colleagues for the defence and prosecution, will finalise our closing comments. These will be heard when we recommence proceedings at 2pm. The jury will then be given the opportunity to retire and consider their verdict."

"All rise."
Everyone springs up, like a collection of jack-in-a-boxes.

Chapter Forty Five

Margaret loosens her collar as she speaks. "Ladies and gentlemen of the jury. You will shortly be asked to decide on the verdict in this case. As you consider the testimonies you have heard, please do not lose sight of Michelle Jackson, who does not have the chance to testify for herself." She pauses for a moment.

"The witnesses in the prosecution have acted as her voice. We have heard about a devoted wife and mother, albeit lonely, a woman plagued by insecurity. Her work colleague speaks of her regret at not being able to assist in what was, seemingly, a situation of domestic abuse." Margaret gestures towards Monica.

"This situation has been collaborated by the police, who have been required to attend on Michelle's behalf, and by a neighbour who was compelled to overhear lengthy arguments between the couple.

Members of the jury, it is your responsibility today, to decide whether Mr Jackson killed his wife in a *premeditated* attempt to gain back the unchallenged life of a single man. Perhaps there was another woman involved. Or perhaps not. We do not know whether this was the case.

Or you may decide he killed in a sudden fit of temper." Margaret pauses again, sweeps her gaze over the jury members, her expression indicating that is the option she is campaigning for. "Of course, as a couple, they were under a tremendous amount of pressure and everyone has a breaking point.

However, you may decide there was blame on both sides and that Mr Jackson killed his wife in an act of *diminished responsibility*. The judge, in his final direction to you, will offer further guidance on this.

Finally, I would like to remind you of another factor, central to this case. A vulnerable child forced to endure and witness events in her brief years; that no person should be subjected to in an entire lifetime. A little girl who has had her mother taken from her. As you are considering your verdict, remember she too, deserves justice."

Paul tries to read some of the expressions of the jurors. No one is giving anything away.

He watches as Margaret snaps her notebook shut and looks expectantly at Simon.

"Ladies and gentlemen. Whilst I agree it is of the upmost tragedy that Michelle Jackson cannot be here to defend herself today; the choice you must make is not one of *how* her husband supposedly killed her, but whether she died at his hands, or at her own." His hands move in parallel in the air from one side of his body to the other, depicting the supposed finality of these two options.

C'mon Simon, Paul urges silently. *Do your stuff.*

"We have heard from several witnesses over the course of this trial, some who are friends or family of the couple, and some who tried to assist them in various ways, as they battled against the destructive force of their marriage. One thing, however, is clear. Michelle Jackson, a confirmed self-harmer, was in great pain emotionally and mentally at the time of her death. Fuelled by drink and the ever-present fear of abandonment, she believed, at that moment, that she had nothing to live for.

Paul Jackson is a man who worked hard for his family. There were efforts by him to gain medical help for Michelle and he repeatedly cajoled her about her excessive alcohol intake, in fact he did all he could to keep things calm at home.

Finally, he attempted to take her away from the usual routine, on holiday to spend some quality time as a couple and as a family.

I urge you, in your deliberations, to see this heart-breaking situation for what it is. A suicide. An appalling waste of a young life.

In my mind, Paul Jackson's only mistake was not realising how low his wife had sunk.

He himself, was a victim. As you have heard, men are not only the perpetrators of domestic abuse. In this case, both he, and his daughter were suffering at the hands of Michelle. I only hope that the press interest in this case, serves to raise the profile of this issue. I further hope it persuades other male victims who are enduring the same misery, to speak out.

There are many kinds of domestic abuse, as you all probably know, and, in my mind, Paul Jackson has endured most of them to some degree; physical, emotional, verbal, financial and sexual.

I will conclude with this important point. The lack of forensic evidence against Paul Jackson. Yes, his DNA was all over the crime scene and yes, the blood of his wife was all over him. That has been explained, and there is no denying that he was there. What *is* missing is forensic evidence that confirms he perpetrated the act of violence against his wife. The only evidence that points to that is circumstantial. He sweeps his eyes over each member of the jury. "I would therefore urge you to find Paul Jackson not guilty of murder or manslaughter!"

"Thank you both." Judge Lakin glances towards the clock, then down at his notes. "Members of the jury," he says after a few moments. "It is time for you to retire and consider the evidence you have heard since the start of this trial.

You will have to decide unanimously, beyond reasonable doubt, whether Paul Jackson is guilty or not guilty of fatally stabbing his wife, Michelle Jackson.

If you decide Paul Jackson did, indeed, deliver the fatal wound to his wife, you then have to decide on the context in which the attack was instigated." He pauses for a moment to allow the jurors, who are scribbling furiously on their notepads, to catch up with him.

"You may be of the opinion he planned to kill his wife, before carrying out the act." Here, his speech slows. "This decision would carry a severe penalty and therefore should not be reached lightly. You would find the defendant guilty of murder."

Paul shrinks into himself at this prospect. It is too horrendous to envisage. Yet he can hear the word *guilty* resounding inside his mind. Although he can scarcely admit it, he has already prepared himself for this outcome. His head is fuzzy and there is a pain behind one of his eyes.

"You may decide he did fatally stab his wife, but the act was not one of premeditation." He pauses again. "You may here conclude, as the prosecution have already suggested, that Paul Jackson reached the limits of his endurance within a hopelessly unhappy marriage and lashed out against his wife in a fit of temper. If you reach this decision, you will find him guilty of voluntary manslaughter. This, while serious, carries a lesser penalty than the aforementioned indictment of murder." The judge stops again for several moments. Paul is hit by the overwhelming threat of a panic attack.

"Or you could find Paul Jackson guilty of involuntary manslaughter. You would have to agree on the opinion that the defendant was mentally out of control and unable to realise the consequences of his actions. We have heard of the alleged strain he was under. You must decide whether his mental functions were impaired enough to carry out the act for which he is standing trial."

Paul clenches his fists in his lap, his fingernails digging into his palms whilst he worries the judge is trying to lead the jury toward this verdict.

"Your other option is to find the defendant not guilty of any indictment. This is not a decision that should be reached easily either. You must remember a young mother is dead. If she was unlawfully killed, it is your job to ensure she, and her daughter, receive justice. If you collaboratively find Paul Jackson not guilty, you would have to believe Michelle Jackson, as the defence allege, killed herself, regardless of whether or not she set out to.

As we heard from Mr Falen, the surgeon earlier, the death resulted from lacerations to the chest caused by the knife. We know the cause of death. There was no one else near this incident, nor were there any witnesses to it, therefore the Coroner was forced to reach an inconclusive verdict. We also have a lack of forensic evidence against Paul Jackson, as we've heard from the defence barrister. From the forensic report you have in your possession, you can see Paul Jackson's finger prints on the murder weapon, as well as his clothing being covered in his wife's blood, but it is acknowledged he had been using the knife to chop food and the blood staining was caused as he comforted his injured wife.

It is your job to bring this situation to a conclusion. You have, as I am sure you will be aware, an important role, each one of you. You must discuss each option thoroughly and take as much time as you need for your deliberations.

In closing, I will reiterate the four options: the indictment of murder, the indictment of voluntary manslaughter, the indictment of involuntary manslaughter or not guilty of any indictment."

That is it. Four choices. Paul needs some respite from the stifling room. His shortness of breath has given way to rising sickness.

"Is one of you willing to put yourself forward as the spokesperson for when you return with your verdict?"

The members look around at each other, then one or two arms begin to be hesitantly raised.

"You," he asserts, pointing at Helen Wentworth, who has not raised her arm. Her already tiny form shrivels under the scrutiny. "I will now ask you to retire and consider your verdict in this matter. You will speak to no one outside the jury about this case."

They obediently file out of the room. His life is literally in their hands. The court stands as the judge disappears through a curtained exit. David gives a thumbs up to Paul who smiles weakly back. The dock officers are approaching, ready to lead him back to the underground cell to await the departure of the return prison van, unless the jury comes to a verdict in super quick time. Paul can't do anything other than hope now.

Chapter Forty Six

Paul's belongings sit in two clear polythene *Her Majesty's* prison bags at his feet, as he chews an apple in his cell. They travel back and forth to court with him each day, in case he is released. He hopes he is not tempting fate by doing this. It is not as though he will be keeping any of it, it will all be binned. It is tainted with the stench of prison. Disinfectant, damp and despair. There is no way he will want to set eyes on these things again if he is acquitted. The possibility is something he hardly dares to imagine. He takes in the barren walls of the cell for what he prays is the last time. Never having put any pictures up, the area around his bed is as stark as he found it. To personalise it would have been an acceptance of his circumstances.

"It must be like groundhog day each morning for you." Stephen grins at him as he comes out of the toilet. "I'll keep my fingers crossed for you mate."

"Thanks. I hope to God I won't come back today, but really I think it'll be after the weekend before anything happens."

"You're a decent bloke," Stephen picks up an apple. "You shouldn't be in here. Not like me. Look at what I've done..."

"Anyone can make a mistake. You aren't your actions. Anyone can have a moment of..."

"C'mon Jackson, no time for tearful goodbyes." Paul looks up to see Officer Smith jangling his keys at the door. "Van's waiting."

"What about the stuff I had removed from me when I was re-manded?" He asks the officer who is processing his transfer to court. "If I'm released, I'm going to need my keys and wallet."

"The personal effects you were arrested with are going backwards and forwards in the court van, Jackson. You'll be given them if you're released."

Paul walks towards the fingerprint scanner to register himself out.

As the van makes its way down the motorway, Paul dares to believe, this might be his final journey as an incarcerated man. *If the worst happens, you'll have a strong case for appeal.* John's words reverberate in his head. They have been doing that all night. Paul knows John has been trying to prepare him for the worst to happen. He couldn't stand it. He will crack up if he must go back. He's been punished enough. What for, he still can't be certain.

"Did you manage any sleep last night?" John grins as the cell door clangs behind him. "I didn't."

"Not a lot," Paul tries to smile back. "I'm bloody shitting myself, to be fair."

"Everyone's here for you, you know." He sits down on the slab beside Paul. "But obviously, it all rests on the jury. Personally, I think our case was far stronger than that of the prosecution; as does Simon. I think it's the lack of concrete forensics that'll see you acquitted. Like Simon and even the judge have said, all the evidence is circumstantial. But as you know yourself, these things can go either way. And they must all agree."

"What if they don't? What if say, only seven or eight of them think I didn't do it?"

"Then it goes back to the judge to decide. He could go with the majority or the prosecution could apply for a retrial."

"No! I couldn't go through all this again."

John pats Paul's shoulder. "I'm sure it won't come to that." He stands and knocks on the cell door. "I'm going to head back up, I want to see whether the jury have reconvened. Hopefully they won't keep us dangling much longer."

Paul tries to pre-empt his fate from the faces of the jury as they stride in procession back into the jury stand. One or two look at him, in a friendly way, maybe, *did they*? He cannot be sure. There are one or two frowns. His gut is churning like a cement mixer. That'll go down well if he throws up in the dock. "Can I have some water?" he says to the dock officer as he gulps in the warm air.

If he is found guilty, he is not sure he will be able to hack it, no matter how much he has tried to convince himself that he would be able to cope. Dizziness steals over him. He does the panic attack thing and tries to steady himself by breathing in-through-his-nose; out-through-his-mouth; in-through-his-nose; out-through-his-mouth, which reminds him again of Michelle. Why couldn't she have been normal? Why did it all have to turn out like this? His fingers grip the sides of his grimy chair, not wanting to speculate as to what some of the staining might be. He hopes he isn't going to be asked to stand up. Not whilst he feels like this.

"Members of the jury, have you reached a verdict upon which you are unanimously decided?" Judge Lakin addresses the spokeswoman.

"Your honour, we have been unable to." The small woman stands, looking nervously around the room.

A groan of shock ripples. The tension that has gripped Paul slides out of him like water down a plughole. This means some of them believe him to be guilty. He wants to know what the proportion each way is.

"If I grant you more time, are you likely to use that time to reach a unanimous decision?"

"I think so," she replies. "I think we need an hour or two more."

Paul has a dark sensation battering the inside of his chest. He's going to be sent back to prison. Emily will be grown up when he sees her again. No way is she ever stepping foot into that place.

"In that case," continues Judge Lakin. "I will ask you to return to your room and try to reach a majority verdict. If you need to ask any questions to reach that, you can request an open court at any time. You will of course, continue to adhere to court protocol and not discuss the case outside your group."

Chapter Forty Seven

Susan needs to be on her own. Whichever way the verdict goes, she cannot bear to be there.

She attends to the grave at least once a week. In life, she knows she has not done enough for Michelle. She constantly berates herself for the mistakes she has made, one in particular, and she knows she will have to live forever with the guilt.

On the night of the incident, Michelle had sobbed down the phone, begging her mother to drive across to where they were staying.

"Please Mum," she had cried. "I need you. You keep my head straight."

"Not drinking wine would keep your head straight, dear."

"Why do you always have to judge me? Why can't you be here for me?"

"Because you're there and I'm not going to drive for nearly three hours to play referee between you and your husband. Sort it out yourselves."

"He doesn't love me Mum. Neither do you."

For a moment, Susan was unsure if she could say the next sentence. Then she decided that it needed to be said.

"He won't love you if you're constantly drunk and blaming him for everything. Bang your heads together - start putting Emily first."

"Like you put me first, you mean!" She had then ended the call. Once upon a time before the age of mobile phones, she would have slammed the phone down.

At times, Michelle had irritated her with the never-ending angst and depression. She could never pull herself together and always blamed someone else. But there were the times she had ignored her, when all her daughter had needed was a listening ear. Susan had cut her short or not even answered the phone at times. The least she can do now is sit with Michelle and keep her company. As well as ensure her grave is kept tended and colourful.

Today she has brought pink carnations. Long-lasting flowers that will brighten and cheer her grave for at least a couple of weeks. Michelle had always adored flowers. Susan would have bought her a bunch each day, for the rest of her life, if she was able to have her back again and undo everything that has happened.

She stops short as she reaches her destination, acknowledging the enormous bouquet of wilting tulips and lilies that holds firm against the breeze with a couple of heavy stones, still in the florists' wrapping upon the granite pebbles. They were Michelle's absolute favourite flowers. She had carried them in her wedding bouquet. Susan steps then leans forward to read the card, it simply says *sorry*.

She wipes furiously at the tears that plunge down her face. Who is sorry? Why haven't they written their name? Why are they sorry?

What she has heard this week in court has made her realise that lots of people in Michelle and Paul's life knew about their problems. They have all stood back, wanting to keep out of it, just like she has. However, she hadn't suspected things were quite so horrendous. *Poor Emily.* Susan has not managed to help Michelle as often as she should, but she can certainly be there for her granddaughter now. When she's ready to talk about it, Susan will always be ready to listen this time.

She owes that to all of them.

"Come on sweetie pie," she cajoles her granddaughter as they approach the car. "We'll be late for your swimming lesson if we don't hurry up. She looks at Emily's pinched face and dark eyes, wishing for the millionth time her sparkle would return. "How was school today?"
Silence.
"Have you fastened your seatbelt? What did you learn about?"
Her silence breaks Susan's heart. Emily still won't speak. It's like she's in her own little world and from what she can gather, the child psychologist isn't making any progress either. The present work is the drawing of pictures, but all Emily ever wants to draw is pictures of houses. Maybe that's saying something? Maybe not.
"I'm going to sit over there and watch you Emily." She squeezes her granddaughter's hand as she leads her into the changing area. "Then we'll have our tea at Jumping Jacks. What do you think?"
Silence.

Chapter Forty Eight

For Paul, it has been a torturous day. The last two hours have been the worst. His throat burns, and he can taste the bile from when he was sick in the cell. He has decided he will not be able to go on if they find him guilty. He will find a way of doing himself in. He is at a point where he can hardly think straight.

"Has the jury now reached a verdict to which the majority are agreed?" The judge asks.

"Your Honour, we have." Her voice sounds small compared to the commanding boom of the judge. All is suddenly in slow motion for Paul. This is it.

"A verdict for which at least ten members of the jury are agreed? Please answer yes or no."

"Yes, we have."

"Good. Then I will read out each indictment and I would like you to answer either guilty or not guilty. Do you understand?"

"Yes, your Honour."

"To the charge of murder, do you find the defendant, Paul Jackson, guilty or not guilty?"

His head is buried in his hands. He is not usually a religious man but at this moment, he offers a prayer. For a moment he thinks he might be sick again.

The spokeswoman hesitates. It is as though she is relishing her momentary power over her audience. She has probably never commanded this sort of attention. "Not guilty," she eventually declares. A small whoosh of excitement rises in the public gallery. Paul wants to punch the air in celebration. For a split second anyway. He hasn't got murder but he's not clear yet.

"To the charge of manslaughter," Judge Lakin's voice barks out again. "Do you find the defendant, Paul Jackson, guilty or not guilty?"

He can still go down. Not for as long but even so, he knows he will receive a hefty stretch. He will miss Emily growing up. He would...

"Not guilty."

Paul jerks his head upright. A buzz this time emits from the public gallery.

A few moments pass. They take forever until Judge Lakin clears his throat. "Paul Jackson," he looks straight at him, meeting his eyes. "You have been found not guilty of all charges. You are free to leave this court."

Paul hauls his shaking body up from the seat. He is stunned. He is free! It's over! They've acquitted him! The whole horrendous nightmare is over! "Where do I go?" Paul asks the dock officer.

"You can go that way if you like." He gestures towards the steps that John has frequently run up and down throughout the course of the trial.

He is greeted in the centre of the room by a fuddle of hugs and handshakes. Though ecstatic at being freed, his acquittal is bittersweet. Nothing can ever undo what has been done.

"Be warned," says John as they approach the court exit. "There's going to be a lot of reporters waiting in the street. We'll have to make a statement. I'll deal with it."

With his keys, mobile phone and wallet back in his possession for the first time since his arrest, Paul is a *valid* person. "I'm hungry," he says to Jacqui and Alana who border him either side. Alana has linked arms with him which is uncomfortable. "For the first time in months, I could eat a horse. It's a good feeling. I'll have a quick something to eat then I need to get to Emily."

"You look like you could do with a decent meal in you," observes Jacqui. "We'll give this statement, and then we'll go somewhere special."

"A greasy spoon would be an improvement on my recent dining experiences!" He thinks back to the prison servery and its tampered offerings with revulsion. For a moment, he is queasy again. It will be a long time, if ever, until he can erase the memories of that place.

Alana lets go of his arm in readiness for the exit through the revolving door. He's pleased. There is something about her grip on his arm that is possessive. His attention switches to the sea of reporters camped outside the court doors. Paul feels panicked. "There must be about fifty people out there!" They spill along the cobbled street and surge like a wave, separating him from John as they emerge outside. He wrestles with the urge to rush back in.

"How do you feel Paul?" A woman holds a microphone in his direction.

"Great thanks," he shouts back as flashlights go off all around him, disorienting him. It is like something he would watch on the TV.

"Do you think you'll sue for wrongful imprisonment?" shouts someone else.

"What has life inside been like for you?" a man yells right in front of him.

"Where's your daughter? Are you going to her now?"

"Do *you* think your wife killed herself?"

"If you didn't kill her, who did?"

Paul looks across to where John is conversing with a cameraman. Paul dutifully makes his way over as John beckons him.

"I'm going to say a few words to this BBC reporter." John grabs his arm to pull him in beside him. "You stay next to me, so they can take some pictures, and then we'll leave. Don't worry. I'll do all the talking. Once they've been given what they want, they will leave you be."

"OK. Thanks. I wouldn't have a clue." There are a million luminous dots clouding his vision from the camera flashes. There is no way he would be capable of giving a coherent, newsworthy statement himself, therefore he is grateful to John.

"My client, Paul Jackson, has been through a traumatic experience." John begins to address an array of furry microphones as a moment of quiet descends on the flurry of activity. "He was a victim within a volatile relationship, then cast as the villain of it.

He has been pushed to the limits of all endurance; emotionally, mentally and financially. Then, to have subsequently spent three months unjustly imprisoned is dreadful. The jury's findings coincide with the earlier verdict from the coroner's court. No conclusions have been reached of how Michelle Jackson died. With no direct witnesses and no concrete forensic evidence against my client, the cause of her death has turned out to be inconclusive.

Maybe some good can arise from Paul's story. Hopefully his acquittal will set a precedent in this type of case. Maybe it will encourage more men to speak out when they're trapped in similar situations. Currently, the 'system' in this country, mainly recognises women as being at risk from domestic abuse; a system that has failed my client.

He needs to be left alone whilst he focuses on bringing his daughter home to rebuild their lives. I hope the media will afford him some time and space to mourn his wife's death properly. That is all we wish to say currently."

They stride away from the flashing bulbs. Paul has a jauntiness to his step for the first time in a while. He never has to see that place again. He can put it all behind him.

Chapter Forty Nine

Alana imagines Lee's face, shrivelled with anger, at the other end of the phone. "He's been acquitted," she tells him. "We're in the pub. Why don't you come over? It looks bad that you're not taking an interest and can't wish him well."

"No, you're all right thanks," Lee sounds snappy. "I'm not in the mood."

"I hardly think you've cause for any kind of celebration." Lee's voice oozes sarcasm.

She glances up to check no one is listening. "Lee. It's over. Let it go now."

"Yeah, well for you maybe."

"Lee. For God's sake…" Then she realises she is talking to a disconnected line. She smiles at Paul who looks at her, momentarily distracted from his conversation with Jacqui.

"Everything alright?"

"Same as ever." She slides into the chair beside him, remembering Paul is now free and single. This cheers her. "How's your pint?"

"Bloody wonderful. Though I'd better not have any more!" Laughing, he places his glass on the table. "I'm not used to the stuff, am I? Let's order some food then I must get over to Susan's."

"What are you thinking?" As they anticipate the arrival of the food order, Alana notices Paul staring into space. She hopes he is thinking the same as her.

"I feel awkward," his voice cracks. "I'm here enjoying a beer and looking forward to food and she's, well she's … rotting in the ground."

"I know." Alana touches his arm, enjoying the proximity of his taut bicep beneath her fingertips. "But you've been punished enough. You can't persecute yourself anymore."

"But no one else is being punished, are they?" Nick chips in. "There's just the assumption Michelle did it to herself. He turns to John. "Does that mean they will never look for anyone else?"

"I wouldn't have thought so." John looks puzzled for a moment. "I guess there will never be any firm evidence to verify it was suicide but that is probably what will always be insinuated."

"It's on the local news already," exclaims Jacqui, holding up her phone. "I can't believe the interest."

"It's down to the domestic abuse element," John says. "There's a lot in the papers about female sufferers." He puts his menu down. "You don't hear about it being the other way around. I'm pleased. That it's gaining attention, I mean. It'll pave the way for others. If anything good can come out of this. If it can help one person." He slams his hand onto the table as he makes his final point. "No one, man or woman, should be hiding in shame, behind closed doors."

"That's exactly what I've said, all along." Alana can't disguise her joy at the outcome. "I'm pleased to have you back Paul. You should never have been in there."

"When I've finished this, I need to see Emily."

Alana places her wine glass next to Paul's pint. "I'll come with you. It would be good to see how she's doing."

"If you don't mind," Alana deflates with what he is probably about to say. "I'd rather get David to take me and see her on my own. It's been months. I reckon I'll have some explaining to do. At least she'll be back in her own bed tonight." His face lights up as he talks about her.

Alana would have loved to have been part of this. And she isn't relishing the thought of returning home. *It'll all keep,* she thinks to herself.

Chapter Fifty

Emily has grown by at least an inch. Her hair is in pigtails and she has two gaps in her teeth. Paul has missed that. Missed teasing that boys have kissed them out. Missed pretending to be the tooth fairy. There will be plenty more teeth though.

"Hello poppet." He holds his arms out.

She doesn't move. She sits glued to Hannah Montana or whatever it is.

"I'm never going anywhere, ever again," He blinks back tears as he stares at her. "You don't know how happy I am to see you!"

Paul hears a whimper from the kitchen. "Carla!" Susan lets go of her lead and his dog bolts towards him. "She definitely remembers me! You haven't forgotten me, have you girl?" Carla runs in circles around them, periodically leaping at Paul to smell and lick him.

"Right. Let's take this lot to the car." He rises from his crouch. "We're going home. Do you want to come with us Susan? Help Emily settle in?"

"No. I'll leave the two of you alone. I'll give you a call in the morning."

Emily's stares out of the window all the way back. Paul sits in the back with her, asking her about school but she doesn't reply. She has a vacant look about her as though she's not even hearing what is being said. Carla, strapped in the boot, is going berserk with excitement.

298

"Do you think it's all over?" David asks from the driver seat.

"I hope so. Why shouldn't it be?" Paul leans forward and lowers his voice.

"It's just they haven't arrested anyone else. Will they still be looking?"

"John doesn't think so. I think they're satisfied to make assumptions. Let's change the subject, shall we?" Paul is exhausted. This gives way to anxiety as they approach the final few turnings towards home. The neighbourhood is evening-quiet and in darkness. They pass by the village church where he and Michelle were married; the hut where Emily attends Brownies, Emily's school, then, all too soon, they turn up Bracken Bank.

"Do you want me to come in?" David pulls up outside the house.

"No. I'll be fine." He unclips his seatbelt then Emily's. "I think we need to do this on our own. Paul leans forwards in the back seat, surveying the exterior of the innocent looking, semi-detached house - the home he and Michelle had longed for. The memory of how they had literally skipped down the street from the estate agents after their offer had been accepted, slides into his mind.

Even that recollection is tarnished by the subsequent ruination of their celebratory night out. He tries to shake his memories away, unable to endure them. "I'll give you a call tomorrow."

Paul plods up the garden path. Emily trails behind him. He notices the medley of weeds, wild flowers and overgrown plants then is compelled to turn around, in response to Mrs Fawcett's eyes burning into his back. A mischievous urge materialises, making him wave at her.

Turning back to his house, he notices all the windows are curtained; keeping prying eyes out but holding painful memories steadfast within. They come at him like a high-speed train as he unlocks the door.

"You alright sweetheart?" he says to Emily. "Do you want to turn the TV on in the lounge – the little one from upstairs should still be in there. I will get you a drink. It might have to be water though. We will need to go shopping."

He walks to the lounge door. Carla stays firmly attached to Paul's side.

Gathering the pile of post, he sinks into the thick green carpet at the foot of the stairs, inhaling the scent that lingers of his former life.

He flinches at the holes that shatter the hallway plasterwork and the yawning spaces on the walls where happy pictures once hung. His gaze falls upon the pile of post. Mrs Michelle Jackson. A pay slip. Mr and Mrs Jackson. A bank statement. Then a card, addressed only to him. *With deepest sympathy.*

With wobbly hands, he grips the card, tears blurring his vision. He squeezes his eyelids shut, quelling them before Emily sees. He will deal with the post later.

Amidst the mustiness, he can pick out a whiff of wine, leather and a plug-in air freshener. As he rises higher on the stairs, he senses Michelle's perfume. It is overwhelmingly home; unbearably so. He wanders in and out of rooms. All is peculiar, yet familiar. Their bed with the checked duvet cover, clothes that litter the carpet from when Michelle was packing to go on holiday, hair tangled in Michelle's hairbrush.

A trace of soap scum lingers in the bath tub. Michelle was the last person to have a bath in here on the morning before they went away. Her mug is next to the bath. *'I Love My Mum!'* it declares. Remains of coffee are congealed and mould covers its base. He used to constantly go on at her but leaving cups upstairs and not rinsing the bath out.

You self-centred pillock! Always thinking about yourself! What about me? Terrified, he looks around, imagining he has heard her voice.

Then the sound of her crying.

"Emily. Carla. Come on. Let's go out for a bit."

They appear and dutifully follow as he snatches up his keys and strides out of the house, locking the door after them. Thankfully, David has driven his car back from the holiday park so there is no need to confront that place again. Miraculously, the Ford Focus starts first click so he turns up the heater. The car too, smells unused and unlived in. It emits a hint of Michelle's perfume. She is everywhere, in each nook and cranny of his being. He grabs his phone from his pocket.

"David. Do you mind if we crash at yours tonight after all? I can't face being in the house."

He turns the car around in their cul-de-sac. We're going to stay with Uncle David. Just for tonight."

Emily stares out of the window.

"We've no shopping in Emily. We will go back tomorrow. Promise." He's starting to feel frustrated that his daughter won't reply. He's desperate to speak with her. "We've loads of catching up to do. Lots of things to talk about." He smiles at her through his rear-view mirror, hoping for a reaction.

This is seriously weird. From being a complete chatterbox, she really isn't saying a single word.

"Grandma says you don't talk anymore. Is that because you're sad about Mummy?"

"Of course, you are." Paul responds into the space his words leave. "I promise it'll soon be easier." They pull up outside his brother's house. "I'm back now and you can talk to me about anything you want."

When you do, Paul thinks to himself, who knows what is going to come out. What have they done to her?

301

Chapter Fifty One

Alana tuts as Lee tosses the evening newspaper at her before retreating to his armchair.

"Page one," he announces. "He's front page news. And so are you, though not in a way I care to see." He looks at her in a way that makes her uncomfortable.

Alana ignores him and looks at the smiling picture of herself clutching Paul's arm. It's nearly dark outside, mirroring the misery that has descended over her since this afternoon. She had hoped she would see more of Paul than she has and is wrestling with jealousy towards Emily. Paul had only wanted to return to *her*. Alana might as well be invisible. She used to feel close to him when they worked together, things seem to have changed.

The nights are drawing in. As are her feelings of estrangement from her husband. What lurks beneath his bad-tempered exterior, she no longer knows. It depresses her immensely. Paul is free, but she is not. Her marriage is on borrowed time, and so, if she stays with Lee, is she.

They have been a couple since they were fourteen, having defied the odds to keep their relationship going for this long. They were warned they would become different people. That their marriage would not weather the years. If she'd never met Paul, the odds were still stacked against her and Lee. They had both emerged from problem backgrounds; both sets of parents had not warmed to either of them whilst they were dating. All sorts of things had gone wrong with the wedding. From things not fitting to important people not being there, all topped off with the DJ not turning up in the evening.

Then there was the biggie, the 'baby thing.' She shakes the newspaper out across her lap.

HUSBAND CLEARED OF STAB MURDER CHARGE

A man accused of stabbing his wife to death after an argument, has been found not guilty of her murder.

Paul Alan Jackson held his head in his hands and appeared to weep as the jury cleared him after nearly four hours of deliberations.

The thirty-seven year old legal executive has spent three months on remand after being accused of killing his thirty-six year old wife, Michelle Marie Jackson, following a row which occurred in their holiday cottage at Summerfield Holiday Park, Filey.

Walking free from York Crown Court, via his solicitor, Mr Jackson told reporters he felt 'great,' and his priority now, was to bring his seven-year-old daughter home and rebuild their lives. He has asked that the media give him space to grieve for his wife. Speculation has arisen that she may have taken her own life, whilst in the throes of depression. Her history of self-harming was disclosed during the trial.

Mr Jackson's solicitor, John Gibbs, branded his three-month incarceration as 'dreadful,' stating his client had been pushed to the 'limits of all endurance' within his marriage.

He added that Mr Jackson had been failed by a system that mainly recognises women as being at risk from domestic violence. He conveyed his hope that Mr Jackson's case would set a precedent for other male sufferers of domestic abuse.

"Good morning, Gibbs, Brown and Jackson?"

"John, it's Alana," she announces the next morning.

"Alana, what's up? Are you ill? You don't sound your normal chirpy self this morning."

"I can't go into it, but I need a couple of weeks off. I'll take it as annual leave."

"Oh. Right. Are you sure you're OK? You sound dreadful. Anything I can help with?"

"I'll fill you in later, I promise. I must go." Placing her mobile phone on the bedside table, she sinks back against the headboard. Her eyes wander to the walk-in wardrobe, where Lee has left the doors open after emptying his half of the rail. Looking up to the high shelf, she can see he has used all their holiday cases. Drawers are ajar and emptied. His bathroom shelf is bare. The paperwork she has moaned about him littering the house with. All traces of him; bagged or boxed.

He will be back later for anything that remains. She is to pack it up for him. He will return at a time she is not there. He does not want to see her again.

It is a surprise to Alana that she feels this low. Her muddled mind tries to analyse it. She stares at his side of the bed, the sheets creased from where he slept on them two nights ago. At least whilst he was with her, she had a certain amount of control over him.

If Paul wasn't so focused on bloody Emily, Alana wouldn't be this depressed. Finally she moves, swings her legs over the side of the mattress and begins tugging the sheets from it. Then, with a surge of energy, she spends the morning hurtling around the house, bagging things up for the charity shop, slinging things into the bin, cleaning, eradicating, distancing. Then she lays, exhausted, on the kitchen floor, like an abandoned dog, wondering what the hell she is going to do next.

Chapter Fifty Two

For a moment when Paul wakes up, he thinks he is in his cell. Sitting upright, he peers around. Sunshine seeps around the edges of the curtains like an eclipsed moon, making him want to rejoice. For a moment he enjoys the hum of birds singing.

Then the familiar jerk of guilt, which is there whenever he permits himself any happiness. *Michelle is lying in the ground.*

Pulling on his trousers, he stretches, before padding into David's kitchen to make coffee. As he breathes its welcome smell, he tries to replace his heaviness with optimism. To drink a proper cup of coffee is like a new experience and he knows he will never take anything for granted again.

He tiptoes upstairs and puts his head around the door of the guest room, smiling at the Emily-shaped huddle under the duvet. He's sure that he can get her back to normal before long. Carla opens her eyes and pricks her ears up when she notices him but doesn't move. Then he taps on his brother's door. "David. I'm going to nip out for an hour. Emily's still sleeping. Is that alright?"

"Hmm. Yep. See you in a bit."

He parks up outside the barber's shop in readiness for the eight thirty opening. Paul flicks through the newspaper as he waits. His vindication has made page four of one of the nationals. His thin face stares back at him, making him realise he needs to straighten himself out. His first step will be to put the house on the market. He and Emily need a new start to have any hope of eventually putting things behind them. But first – a haircut.

Paul nods in gratitude as the barber holds the mirror behind his head. Save for a few grey hairs, he looks more like his former self. He strides out into the September air, hungrily gulping it down, like his freedom. He buys another newspaper and heads towards a café. He wants to scour every bit of printed information about his case. He worries they'll decide they made a mistake and call a retrial.

"You want to sit *outside?*" asks the waitress in the café, as he orders himself a latte and a bacon roll. "Rather you than me. It's chilly this morning!"

Paul warms his hands around his cup, then takes his suddenly vibrating phone from his pocket.

"Morning Susan. How are you?"

"The house is empty without Emily, but I'll adjust. I wanted to check up on her. It must feel strange. Being back at home, I mean."

It is oddly comforting hearing his mother-in-law's voice over the phone. "She's sleeping. Or at least she was an hour ago. We ended up going to our David's last night, so I've nipped out for a haircut." A passing bus drowns him out for a moment. He sticks a finger in his ear. "I can't believe how she is. It's like having a different girl."

"I know. Hopefully her being back with you might change that."

"Well I'll keep you posted and obviously I'll keep sending her to the specialist appointments."

"Thanks. She's possibly the only person who can shed any light over what happened to her mother. I know the court is making out like Michelle killed herself, but I'll never accept that Paul. Never."

Paul sighs as he pushes the froth on his coffee around with a spoon. *Not this again.* He's been acquitted. They've returned an inconclusive verdict. Insinuated suicide. "Susan. I think if Emily had heard or seen anything that might help the inquiry, she'd have talked by now.

"Well I won't rest till I know the truth. She obviously has some sort of post-traumatic stress thing."

"I'll give you a ring over the next day or two and fix up a time to visit." As he puts the phone onto the table, he notices a florist at the other side of the road, reminding him of what he needs to do next.

Michelle Marie Jackson. Daughter. Mother. Friend. There is no mention of *wife. At peace now.* He traces his finger over the lettering and steps back to take in her grave. The two perspex vases are filled with red carnations.

There is a large bouquet, in the same wrapping as his, with a card which says 'sorry.' He snatches it up to inspect it. *Sorry?* Who is sorry? A myriad of possibilities cascade through his mind. Everyone is *sorry* she's dead. Is it someone sorry about the verdict? A so-called campaigner? Or something deeper? He studies the card for a moment, then rips it up.

He notices a solar lamp has been speared into the ground. Susan is probably the only person apart from him that knows Michelle was afraid of the dark. They always had to keep the landing light on overnight with the door ajar.

"Michelle, it's me, Paul." He waits as though expecting a response. "They let me go. I should never have been there. And you shouldn't be here." He wonders if there's anyone around, listening. The only sound is the rustle of autumnal leaves and the occasional squawk of birds. "I've picked Emily up. She's not herself but I'll get her right." The face of his wife bursts into his mind. It is a happy face. It reminds him of what should have been.

"Why?" He whispers. His cheeks sting as cool air chills the tears leaking from his eyes. "We could have made you better. You shouldn't be here." A sob catches in his throat as he sinks in front of her gravestone. He drops the bouquet of roses to the ground.

Emily twirls her pig tail around in her fingers whilst spooning cereal into her mouth with her other hand.

Paul smiles at her across the table. "I went to have a haircut. Do I look a bit tidier Emily?"

His brother stacks the dishwasher. "You look older than me now. What are you both up to today?"

"My plans involve a park, an ice-cream, a dog and an Emily." He leans over and ruffles her hair.

"Come here Emily. Let me roll up your sleeves whilst you're eating that." He gestures for her to sit with him at the picnic table with her newly acquired ice-cream.

"We need to talk about Mummy." He studies her face.

Sadness creeps into her eyes but he decides to carry on.

"She wouldn't want you to be sad for long Emily. She would want you to be your chattery, noisy self again. She'll be watching you grow up from heaven."

Still nothing. This one-way conversation feels impossible. There's little reaction from her. Paul is consumed with guilt. She's a shadow of the little girl she was.

Chapter Fifty Three

Emily is glued to the portable TV as the doorbell rings. "That must be Grandma, she said she might call around." He still needs to replace the TV Michelle smashed. "You can turn that off now." He folds the newspaper up. He has been looking at houses to rent.

Emily glances out of the bay window.

Paul is stopped short by the panic in her face. "What's the matter Emily?"

She stands in front of the lounge door, obstructing him. *Who is it? What's got into her?* He peers through the window. "It's OK Emily. It's only Alana, who did you think it was?" Moving her out of the way, he heads towards the front door.

Emily hides behind Paul's legs as he opens it.

"What's up?" Alana glances back down the drive and steps forward. She looks worried.

"I'm not sure to be honest. Anyway. What can I do for you?" He opens the door ajar to invite her in.

"Shut the door, quick. Lee and I have split up. But he's just been back for some things. We've had another row and he might have followed me here."

"I'd rather not be involved..." Paul is taken aback as Alana shuts the door with a bang and slides the chain across. Emily is retreating towards the kitchen with an expression he has never seen. *What on earth...* "Why don't you sit down Alana. I'm going to have to sort this daughter of mine out."

"Hello you." Paul senses the softness of Alana's jumper as she brushes past him, towards Emily. "What's the matter?"

Emily slides down the wall and crouches at the bottom.

"Emily. Get up." Grasping her arm, Paul hoists her to her feet and kneels in front of her. "I'm sorry Alana." His eyes don't leave his daughter's face. "She's not been the same since... well, you know."

"It's alright. She needs help though. She can't be spoiling things."

"What do you mean, *spoiling things?*"

"For us. For the future."

Paul hears a gushing noise and a trickling before he notices a pool of liquid seeping around Emily's feet quickly soaking his knees. "Emily!" He wrinkles his nose against the smell of urine and stands up. "You haven't done that for years!"

"You'd better go and change," Alana nudges her away from the wall, an expression of disgust on her face. "We need to talk without kids listening. Go on."

"Go home." Emily's teeth are chattering. "I don't want you here."

She spoke! Paul is torn between feeling delight at hearing her voice and fearful at what's unfolding.

"Come here Emily." Paul steps forward.

"I saw," Emily whispers. "I saw you all in a fight."

Paul faces Alana and steers Emily to his side.

"She needs shutting up again." Alana's voice has an edge to it now. "As does Lee. I'm not scared of shutting either of them up. Permanently."

"Emily go upstairs." Paul extricates her from his leg. "Now." He must calm this down. "We'll talk about what you saw shortly."

Alana takes a step towards them.

"Alana, back off. You're scaring her."

He notices she is staring at his golf bag at the foot of the staircase. They all jump. Someone is knocking and kicking at the door.

"Open up." It's Lee.

"What?" Paul nudges Emily towards the stairs. "Emily. Go to your room! Now!"

"Go away Lee!" Alana's voice is a growl. "Fucking go away. Paul tries to reconcile this with the efficient, breezy voice that answers the phone at work.

"No! Daddy!" Emily screams as Alana lunges at her around the side of Paul.

"Emily. Do as you're told." He pulls her towards the stairs. "Why are you trying to get to my daughter?" He spins around to face Alana. A prickling sensation is creeping up his spine. Their faces are close enough to kiss. He can smell her sour breath. He swallows hard.

"She's going to land us all in it. Or he is. *My fucking husband.* We're finished anyway. Me and him. It doesn't have to be like this for us. We can leave now. Just me and you."

Paul slumps to the foot of the stairs, sobbing uncontrollably as the memories suddenly rush back. "I'm so sorry." He feels like he's going to puke. He can't breathe. "It was a moment of insanity. I snapped. I've ruined so many lives."

"Michelle was making your life a misery. You know she was. You did the right thing. And so did I. We can be together now." She tries to kiss him.

He leans back. His chest is so tight.

"All we have to do is get away from here."

"It's over," Paul sobs. "I'm going to have to face it. Own up."

"You do what you want. I'm not letting you take me down too. No way. I'm out of here"

The letterbox rattles again. "Emily. Are you alright? The police are coming. Go to your bedroom."

Paul looks from the door to Alana who has moved back from him and is now eyeing Emily who is only inches away from her.

Alana wrenches one of Paul's golf clubs from its bag and steps forward. There's a whoosh of air as the weapon is hoisted overhead then the crack of bone against letterbox metal.

"Aaargh! You fucking bitch! You've broken my finger!"

"Daddy!" Emily's sobs are desperate. "I know what happened. I saw you hurt Mummy. I don't want you to go away again. I want *her* to go away." Crouched on the third stair, she slithers higher as Alana steps towards the stairs, brandishing the golf club above her head. Its glint reflects in the filtering sunlight onto the hallway wall. "Daddy!"

"Stay away from my daughter." He yells as Emily yowls in pain, Alana has struck a blow across her back. As she raises it above her head to strike again, her eyes are calm and staring. Paul lunges towards her. However, there's a thud as the club strikes him on the forehead. Dazed, he grapples with her as she raises it again. He throws himself onto the stairs to prevent it crashing onto Emily for a second time. Blood is trickling down the side of his face. He staggers back as the golf club connects with him again.

Emily has managed to flee to the top of the stairs, her face contorted with pain. Paul grips Alana's leg as she tries to push past him towards Emily. He's losing his grip as she thrashes around on the stairs. Too dizzy to stand up, he sinks his teeth into her leg, trying not to retch as he tastes her flesh between his teeth. Then blood. She screams and sinks her needle-like nails into the side of his face. There's a repeated banging at the door amidst the screaming and yelling. The door slams against the wall and there's a shower of plaster.

Lee springs towards the stairs and steps over Paul. In one deft move he has gripped Alana's wrists above her head and Paul manages to force his weight down on her feet. She continues to flay around, like a beached fish. "Fucking get off me," she wheezes, repeatedly.

"I've called the police," he says again. "I couldn't live with the knowing anymore."

Alana spits into Lee's face. He releases her wrists and instead grips her throat with one hand, squeezing.

Alana becomes limp in his grasp and makes a gurgling sound.

"No Lee. Ease off. It's over. Things are bad enough." Paul's muscles are shaking with the stress of holding her legs.

Lee relaxes his grip. Two of the fingers on his other hand are black and his face is beetroot red.

"The police are here." Emily springs back from the landing window in response to the howl of the sirens.

Chapter Fifty Four

There is a long beep, signalling recording has begun. The whiff of body odour and stale chewing gum is making Alana nauseous. She takes a sip of tepid water from the plastic cup and tries to swallow.

DC Calvert clears his throat. "Interview with Alana Noakes. Today is Sunday 28th September, the time is 11:23 am and this interview is being conducted at Fulford Police Station in York. I am Detective Constable Joseph Calvert of North Yorkshire Police; also present at this interview is..." he signals to his colleague.

"Detective Inspector Sarah Mexbrough of North Yorkshire Police."

"And..." Calvert looks at Alana. "If you could state your full name for the tape.

"Alana Elizabeth Noakes."

"Thank you. Representing Mrs Noakes is..." Calvert, moves his gaze to the solicitor.

"Yes, I'm Melissa Greenwood of Ford and Hemmingway Solicitors."

Alana is incensed at being assisted by a stranger. A duty solicitor at that. John has refused. Apparently, there would be a conflict of interests as he has already represented Paul on the same case. Alana is sure he could represent her if he chose to. She hates him right now.

"I'm going to go through your rights again Alana," continues Calvert. "As you know, you are under arrest. You do not have to say anything, but it may harm your defence if you do not mention when questioned, something which you may later rely on in court. Anything you do say may be given in evidence. Do you understand?"

"Yes. *She is exhausted, having spent the night on a lumpy mattress in a cell, tormented by the events of the previous evening. Lee will pay for this. He has ruined everything.*

"You have the right to have someone informed of your detention. So far you have declined to use that right. Is that correct?"

"Yes."

"You have the right to independent legal advice. You have chosen to exercise that right and you are free to pause the interview at any time should you wish to speak with your solicitor." Calvert gestures towards Melissa. "This can be done with or without us present. Do you understand, or do you need any of it explaining?"

"I understand." She drags her fingers through her hair. *God, she must look a sight. What she wouldn't give for a soak in the bath.*

"Right then. Let's begin." He looks at her with hard eyes. "Alana Noakes, you have been arrested because it is alleged that on Monday 11th June, you conspired to murder Michelle Marie Jackson at Summerfield Holiday Park in Filey. You will also be facing a charge of perverting the course of justice."

The tiny interview room maintains an eerie silence, apart from the continuous whirring of the recording machine.

"What response," asks Calvert, "do you wish to give to these allegations?"

Alana's bottom lip trembles and her eyes fill with tears. *Is there any point denying it?* If she complies and goes down the mental health route, she'll be treated with leniency. She's already lied to her solicitor but suddenly decides that there's no point any more. "It all went too far. It wasn't supposed to be this way."

The two officers exchange looks before DI Mexborough writes

something down. Melissa shifts in her chair. Alana wishes she'd spoken to her about how to handle admitting it. She half expects her to say something now, but she doesn't. Obviously not bothered. Bloody *duty* solicitor.

"Right Alana," continues Calvert. "I think you'd better start at the beginning. What were you doing in Filey?"

The train journey from York to Filey had only taken an hour. Alana was excited when she descended the train, knowing she was literally minutes away from Paul. It was Monday and she had rung in sick at work. She felt guilty but as she sipped her coffee on the promenade, her guilt slipped away with the outgoing tide.

Before looking for the bus stop, she had a stroll along the beach, wishing Paul was walking beside her. Having Googled Summerfield Holiday Park, she had discovered a bus that was on the hour. Looking at her watch, she realised the next one would be in twenty minutes.

As she walked along the sea front to pass the time, she pondered on the best course of action. She needed to see Paul on his own and come out with it. How they should be together; the only thing holding them back was their respective miserable marriages. When he clapped eyes on her, he would melt. He had said, only recently, Alana was an oasis of calm within his chaotic life. The last three days with Michelle would have probably been hell for him. She was here to offer him a life worth living. For as long as she could remember, she had been in love with him. It was only when he announced his holiday plans, the jealousy needled her to the point where she could no longer cope. The sooner the inevitable confrontations took place, the quicker they would all be able to go forward with their lives.

The shock would probably drive Michelle into a further bout of self-harm, but Alana was unmoved by this prospect. Without Paul around, Michelle would probably need to be admitted for psychiatric care. With a mother so unstable, Alana was doing the best thing for Emily too. She would bake with her, make her clothes, curl her hair and read her stories. She would be the mummy Emily deserved.

Having caught the next bus, Alana alighted at the holiday park entrance. Her stomach rumbled, a reminder it was past lunchtime. A knot of anxiety joined the hunger pangs as she contemplated the enormity of what she was planning. There was a pub serving food opposite the holiday park entrance. She realised that she could not risk bumping into Paul whilst he was with Michelle. Creeping in, she glanced around to check they were not there, before she settled in a secluded corner, concealing herself behind the menu and a vase of flowers. There were several other families dotted around the pub; it made Alana warm inside, knowing soon, it would be her, Paul and Emily sitting down to lunch as a family.

She ordered a salmon and cream cheese bagel and a cup of tea. She was tempted to order wine to steady her nerves but was aware of the necessity to maintain a clear head for when she spoke to Paul. She just had to find him now.

She strolled through the holiday park, hoping she looked like any other holiday-maker in her flowing green sundress and floppy hat, which she had tucked her hair into. With her eyes hidden behind sunglasses, she was hopeful she would not be recognised.

She headed towards the central point of the park, in time to see Paul's Ford Focus heading out of the car park towards the main road. She descended onto a nearby bench to take in the unfamiliar surroundings. Then she spotted Michelle wearing a short white dress and her dark hair knotted into a bun.

After ten minutes, Alana was sure Michelle was alone. She gazed mournfully into a wine glass, deep in contemplation with the dog stretched out beside her. The woman had it coming to her. Here she was, on holiday with her gorgeous husband and beautiful daughter, and instead of spending time with them, she preferred to sit boozing on her own. Resisting the urge to stride over and dig into her about it, Alana instead headed towards the 'To the beach' sign.

She hired a deckchair, bought an ice cream and settled herself down. A family enjoyed themselves beside her, building a sandcastle. The mother lay on a sun lounger with a book whilst the father helped his little girl. She was probably slightly younger than Emily with strawberry blonde hair and a smattering of freckles. She kept running off to find shells for her sandcastle and fill her bucket up with sea water for the moat.

"You do right letting your little girl to do all the leg work," Alana laughed at the father as she observed them.

"I know," he replied, smiling back at her. The mother glowered at her from behind her book. *Another Michelle!* Alana thought. Prefers to lie there with her book than take an interest in her husband and daughter. *Selfish cow!*

Alana enjoyed watching the sandcastle take shape. She was itching to assist in its construction and talk to the little girl, but she held herself back. There would be plenty of time for that sort of thing once Paul had done the necessary.

It was the cruellest twist of fate she had not been granted the gift of motherhood. Those who were, never appreciated it, whereas she, well she would have been a fantastic mother. It made her ache.

The tide was drawing in and people were packing up. Alana was astonished she had been sleeping for nearly two hours. She lay back in her chair, transfixed by the toppling waves as they inched closer.

She could have stayed longer, soothed by the sound of them rising and falling but needed to book into a bed and breakfast. Then find Paul.

Chapter Fifty Five

Alana swept an approving gaze over the quaint room which overlooked the sea. It was a stone's throw from the holiday park.

"Is it just for tonight?" asked the hotelier as she jangled the keys. Her cheeks were as bright as apples.

"I'm not sure." Her eyes fell appreciatively on the kettle and Shrewsbury biscuits. "Can I book it for tonight and keep you posted about tomorrow?"

"That's fine," she replied, stuffing her hands inside her gingham pinny. "As long as we stay as quiet as we are. I might have to push you for a firmer commitment if we start filling up. Is Mr, er Noakes joining you?"

"Possibly not tonight," Alana smiled, secretly. "But hopefully by tomorrow. He should be bringing our little girl."

"We can always make up a camp bed for her. "How old is she?"

"Six," replied Alana, feeling a thrill. She dumped her overnight bag on the bed. "And she won't be any trouble. She's a lovely little thing."

"Perfect," smiled the lady. "Breakfast is between seven and nine and the front door gets locked at eleven. There's a key on your room fob if you're out any later than that. Enjoy your stay."

"We will."

She needed to identify which cottage they were staying in. As soon as she declared her intentions, he would have the excuse he craved to finally break free from his bitch of a wife. There were several clusters of cottages but no sign of the Ford Focus. He must still be out with Emily. She jumped as her mobile phone rang. "Hello," she spoke quietly.

"Where the hell are you?" hissed her husband's voice. "Why aren't you at work?"

"Well hello to you too." She looked around her. "What do you want?"

"I want to know where you are Alana. Are you ill or something?"

"No, er yes. Look I'm fine. Everything's OK."

"What time are you coming home?"

"I don't know. Later. Since when did *you* become my keeper?" Shit! A seagull squawked overhead.

"Alana. Where are you? Was that a seagull?"

"Ten out of ten."

"Have you followed that waste of space on holiday?"

Shit, shit, shit. "He's not a waste of space."

"So you have?"

Alana sighed. "I needed a break for the day."

"You're my wife. You're chasing around after some other man and you expect me to sit back and do nothing."

"I'm not chasing anyone." Alana walked towards a bench at the side of the playground. "It's you that's chasing. Leave me alone Lee."

"Are you coming home tonight?"

"Look I don't know. I need some time alone."

"We need to talk. Tell me where you are. We have to sort this."

"No way. I want you to leave me alone."

"Tell me where you are. I know things haven't been good but – you're in Filey, aren't you?"

"How do you know?"

"You haven't deleted the train timetable page. It's still in the computer history."

Damn! "So what?"

Alana shivered, glad she had changed into jeans and a jumper back at the hotel. Her hair was tied up and she had applied a little make-up in preparation for seeing Paul. He would be shocked she had gone to the effort of following him on holiday. She could not wait to see the expression on his face.

But Lee's phone call had unnerved her. She decided that a glass of wine wasn't actually a bad idea after all. She managed to bluff her way into the club. "My husband's inside," she smiled sweetly at the bouncer. "He's got my pass in his wallet." She found herself a dark corner and tried to zone out the stuffed animal crap and wild children going on all around her. She needed to think straight. She hoped Lee wouldn't turn up. If he did, she was sure he would struggle to find her. But she'd keep looking over her shoulder, just in case.

By the time she summonsed enough courage to get moving with it all, over an hour had passed. A man had offered to buy her a drink, which she'd accepted but he'd quickly given up his efforts of trying to make conversation with her. She wasn't in the mood for small talk. Or for being chatted up. It was time to find out whether Paul was in the cottage now. Then she could decide on the next thing to do.

It was Paul's car Alana spotted first at the end of a row of cottages. There was only one cottage with all its lights on. She could just about make out the shape of someone moving around inside. She edged closer. There was no point in putting it off any longer.

Alana listened to Michelle shouting.

"Bet Alana's the reason you don't want anything to do with me!"

That comment pleased her – clearly she was still an issue between them. "You can't keep one woman satisfied, let alone two!"

"Stop it Michelle." She strained to hear what Paul, in a quieter voice, was saying in response.

"I think it's about time you were honest with me."

"Michelle, don't start again."

Alana's temper was rising as she witnessed first-hand what was probably a daily occurrence.

"Not now, not here, Emily's in there."

You poor bloke, thought Alana. *She really doesn't deserve you!*

"Bit late for that, don't you think? Is that why you don't want sex with me anymore?" Alana could hardly stand the sound of Michelle's grating voice. "Cos of her?"

"No. Because of you!"

Good, Alana thought. They're definitely not having sex anymore.

"You bastard!" The force of the expletive rang out into the serene June evening. If there was anyone around, they would have heard it.

Alana jumped as a door slammed. Crouching lower behind the bin, she listened as furious footsteps stormed away from the cottage.

She'll have gone to drown her sorrows like she always does, Alana thought to herself. At least I can go and talk to him now.

All was quiet for a while. Alana stayed behind the bin knowing this was her chance but not daring to take it. She decided to go for a little walk around first, get her head straight and pluck up the courage. Michelle would be gone a while if she was going back down to the bar.

Half an hour later Alana's leather sandals slapped against the steps to the cottage door as she ascended them. She listened for a few moments, heard nothing, so tapped on the door, then immediately panicked and resisted the urge to run away.

THE MAN BEHIND CLOSED DOORS

"Paul," she called softly. "Are you in there?"

"You!" shrieked Michelle as she swung the door open. "What the fuck are *you* doing here?"

"I-I thought you'd gone out," Alana stammered, her body rigid with shock. Oh shit!

Michelle yanked Alana inside the cottage by her wrist. "Go on then!" Fury sparked from her eyes. "I'm waiting for an explanation! And it better be good!"

"Look at the state of you!" Alana looked Michelle up and down calmly. This was the best way to handle it. Talk down to her. It couldn't be difficult. "You're a disgrace. No wonder Paul's cleared off. You're pissed out of your brains. All you care about is drink."

"That's not true," Michelle said quietly. Then her voice rose. "And what the fuck would it have to do with you?"

"He's my friend," Alana retorted, staring into Michelle's face, which was contorted with rage. Maybe this was how it was all supposed to happen. "And I care about him."

"I bet you do," Michelle replied, her lips curling furiously as she leaned against the kitchen counter and folded her arms, studying her opponent. "Alana, we're having a family holiday. I want to know what you're doing here!"

"I came to check he's OK." Alana's voice was even. In her temper, maybe Michelle would clear off and Alana could wait with Emily until Paul came back.

"OK?" Michelle shouted. "Who? My husband? Of course he's OK, you stupid cow! Why wouldn't he be?"

"Because you're a violent, bullying bitch, that's why!" Alana retorted, her voice rising. Checking herself, she lowered it again. "Don't think he hasn't spoken to me about what you're doing. He's that miserable with you, he's got to confide in someone!"

"He's been talking to you!" Momentarily, the rage appeared to drain out of Michelle.

"Of course," Alana said smugly. "We've become close."

"He's my husband!" Michelle's eyes glittered, with what Alana see, was jealousy. She stood straight and dropped her arms by her sides. Both hands curled into fists. "I've always known you couldn't be trusted."

"Don't you think you should keep your voice down?" Alana looked down the corridor of the cottage. "Isn't Emily asleep?"

"Don't you say my daughter's name!" Michelle shrieked, as she stepped closer to Alana. "She's nothing whatsoever to do with you!"

"I spend a lot of time with her actually," Alana smiled, coming further into the cottage and hoisting her handbag back up on her shoulder. She was on her guard; she knew at any moment, Michelle was likely to go for her. "We enjoy each other's company. You don't deserve her, the way you carry on!"

"Look here you." Michelle spoke in a more controlled voice. "Emily is my daughter and Paul is my husband. I don't know what business you think you have turning up here like this, but I would like you to leave. Now!"

"I'm going nowhere." Alana glanced backwards out of the open door. "Not until I've spoken to Paul."

"Why? What the fuck do you want with my husband?"

"You'll see." Alana smirked, noticing how worried Michelle looked. And she should. Alana was going to win him, whatever it took.

"You're already married, aren't you?" Michelle poured dregs from a wine bottle into a glass, her hands shaking. "Piss off back to your own husband and leave mine alone!"

"You're pathetic. Look at you with your bottle of wine. You're not fit to have Paul. How you treat him. And Emily for that matter. They would be happier with me!"

"With you!" Michelle slammed down the bottle. "Don't be

ridiculous. If you want a child, then bloody have one of your own!"

Alana felt the familiar cloud pressing on her.

"What's up with you?" Michelle sneered. "Lost for words suddenly? That's not like you!" She took a step closer to where Alana stood, waving her wine glass as she spoke. "Oh, of course. I've just remembered. Lee can't get you up the duff, can he?"

Alana could not think of a retort.

"You haven't got it in you, have you?" She took a swig of her wine and laughed raucously.

"Shut your nasty mouth?" Alana moved closer to Michelle, so their faces were almost touching. Venom was escalating in her. God help Michelle if she pushed her much further. "Good God, you stink, woman." She grimaced as she inhaled a faceful of stale alcohol. "No wonder Paul doesn't fancy you anymore!"

"At least I can give him babies." Her face hardened as she jabbed Alana in the shoulder. "What is it? Do you think I'm going to roll over and let you take my husband and daughter away from me? Go on..." she cocked her head towards the door. "Piss off from here and book yourself into a sterility clinic or something."

"You evil cow!" Alana hissed as she tried to slap Michelle but instead screamed as Michelle grabbed her between the legs, nipping as hard as she could.

"Barren bitch!"

"Take your dirty hands off me," she grunted, as she reached and grappled for the empty wine bottle. She was going to pay. The bottle slipped out of her grasp and crashed onto the floor, splinters flying in all directions. Michelle squeezed tighter.

"What the hell is going on?" Paul appeared in the cottage doorway. "What are you doing here?"

Alana was in agony from where her groin had been gripped. "She's an animal." She lurched towards Paul. "I'm leaving Lee. So you can leave her now."

Michelle slammed her palm upon the handle of a knife that had been discarded on a chopping board.

"And what are you going to do with that?" Alana laughed as Michelle stood facing Paul.

"Michelle. Are you nuts? Put the bloody knife down. We can sort this out."

Alana noticed the rapid rise and fall of Paul's chest as the blade of the knife reflected onto his chin. "Enough Michelle," Alana backed away from them. "You're going too far."

"I'll decide when I've gone too far." Then, turning her attention back to Paul, she said. "At least now I know I wasn't going mad. It's been her all along, hasn't it?"

"No. She's just a friend."

"No wonder you can't get a hard-on with me. Not when you're wishing you're with that slag." She waggled the little finger of her other hand, the knife still pointing towards his chest. "You're crap in bed anyway. Do you know how many times I've faked it?"

Alana watched as they stood, breathing into each other's faces and then gasped as Paul suddenly grabbed the handle of the knife and turned it around to point at Michelle.

"You've made my life hell for long enough. I can't take it anymore." He looked to be tightening his grip on the handle. He brought his elbow back as Michelle's scream perforated the air.

Alana leapt in between them, her shoes grinding the broken glass onto the tiles as the knife speared Michelle's chest. Alana took the full force of the huge spurt of blood. Gasping, Michelle staggered back, knocking a bin over and banging her head against an open cupboard before sliding down the cupboard onto the floor.

Alana was excited at what Paul had done and sickened in equal measure. Vomit filled her mouth and she swallowed it back down.

She'd never seen as much blood in her life. She grabbed a towel and crouched over Michelle until their eyes were level.

"Help me," Michelle croaked. Alana wrapped the towel around the handle of the knife before curling her fingers around it. She heard Michelle wheeze as she gritted her teeth and forced the knife further into her, hitting an obstruction and hearing the crack of bone. More blood spurted up at her. She twisted the knife as she unwound the cloth. Michelle lost consciousness. She stood, staring at her for a few moments.

"What have we done?"

Alana rose from her crouch taking care to sidestep the pooling blood.

"Oh my God. What the hell have we done?" Paul repeated.

Alana backed towards the cottage door. Then, with one last look at Michelle and Paul who stood, gripping the work surface, staring at his wife, she slid her sandals off, and strode away into the shadowy dusk, the towel in one hand and her sandals in the other.

Chapter Fifty Six

Calvert has appeared to listen intently to Alana's version of events. "Then what did you do?"

"I started running," admits Alana. "I wasn't going to hang about, was I? I knew the police could come at any moment."

"You decided to let Paul take all the blame?" Calvert frowns. "I thought you were in love with him."

"I was. I am." Alana, exhausted, drops her head into her hands. "I panicked! We didn't plan to kill Michelle. She pushed us both over the edge. I honestly didn't mean for Paul to take all the blame." She takes her face out of her hands, her hair moist with sweat and tears, clinging to the sides of her face like seaweed to a cliff. "I knew about her self-harming and thought that would be blamed."

"So," continues Calvert. "When you realised Paul had been arrested for the murder of Michelle, why didn't you come forward then?"

"It was him who stabbed her first. I just finished her off. Although to be honest, I thought he would be bailed. The more time that passed," Alana sobs, "the more scared I was to own up. Especially after she died. I never thought she would die."

"What do you think happens when someone is stabbed in the chest? Where did you go next? You must have been covered in blood."

Michelle's scream had resounded in Alana's ears even when she was too far away to hear. She thought she would probably hear it for the rest of her life. Running towards the woods that bordered the holiday park, she was certain that at any moment someone would come up behind her, then she was overpowered by the smell of Michelle's blood. Forced to stop, she leaned against a tree and vomited her insides out; the hot liquid spurted through her nose and splattered over her feet. Weeping, she continued running towards what looked like a clearing in the woods. She could hear the rush of the sea.

"Then what?" Calvert's voice jolts her back into the room.

This was something she had never wanted to relive. "I had a carrier bag in my pocket, so my jacket went in there with the towel, I tied it up and it went into the bin. Then I ran out into the sea to wash the blood off. It would be easier to return to the hotel, soaked to the skin and say I'd fallen in rather than be splattered in blood." Alana recalls the loneliness of that night and tears slide down her face. "I stayed on the beach and dried out for a while. I could hear the sirens – I didn't know if she was dead or not."

"What time did you return to the hotel?"

"I don't know. It was late. I managed to get to my room without being seen."

"Didn't you ever consider coming forward?"

Alana pauses. "My husband suspected I'd been there," she replies. "I wanted to confess but he stopped me." She is going to bring him down with her. As much as she can. "He seemed to think that leaving a bunch of flowers on Michelle's grave somehow exonerated us."

"He's being questioned too. Am I right in thinking you went home the next day and carried on as normal?"

"Yes." Alana speaks in a small voice. She looks at DI Mexborough who has been writing notes.

"We'll leave it there," announces Calvert. "The time is," he checks his watch, "twelve thirty seven pm. This interview is concluded. A long tone sounds from the recording machine as Calvert presses the stop button and ejects the two tapes.

Alana's watching him through her tears as he seals and initials them. "What's going to happen?"

"You'll be returned to your cell. We'll bring you back out when we've been authorised to charge you." He passes the tapes to his colleague. "You'll appear in court in the morning and will no doubt be remanded in custody until your trial." He looks towards Melissa. "Do you want a few minutes with your client before we lock her back in?"

Chapter Fifty Seven

Melissa stifles a yawn and stretches as the police personnel vacate their seats. "Yes, if you don't mind, thanks." It has been a long morning. She looks at Alana who again has her head in her hands. It's true what they say about beauty only being skin deep. She'd been taken aback by how pretty Alana was when first arriving at the station, despite being somewhat bedraggled. She can still hardly believe this demure woman in front of her was capable of such violence.

"Well that was a surprise." Melissa's voice sounds throaty after sitting in silence, listening for so long. "You told me you were innocent prior to the interview."

"I know. But I've told the truth now."

Melissa looks at the trembling woman. "You should have told the truth in the first place."

"I thought you were on my side." Alana's bottom lip wobbles.

"It's not about sides. I'm paid to represent you and I can only do that if you're straight with me." She glances down at the extensive ream of notes she has taken throughout the interview. "Is there anything else I should know?"

Alana shakes her head. "It's all out in the open. What do you think will happen?"

Melissa thinks for a moment. "It will go in your favour that you have finally admitted it. But what will go against you is the fact you have allowed so much time to elapse before telling the truth." She pauses. "I can't say to be honest. I would guess at about ten years, of which you'll probably serve five if you're lucky."

"Five years," Alana gasps, her shoulders shaking with sobs. "I can't do it. I'll crack up."

"You'd be surprised," Melissa says, coolly. "People can endure far more than they imagine."

Alana seems to momentarily brighten. "If I know Paul's waiting for me, I can cope with anything."

"I wouldn't count on it," mutters Melissa as she makes for the door of the interview room to signal she has finished her conversation with her client.

Epilogue

Wife Killers Finally Get Justice

The people responsible for the death of Michelle Marie Jackson were finally brought to justice earlier today.

It was in June last year that thirty-six-year-old Michelle was stabbed to death in the presence of her six-year-old daughter, at their holiday cottage in Filey. The incident happened following a row between the couple that had been overheard by neighbouring holidaymakers.

Paul Jackson, of Osbaldwick, York, had already served four months as a remand prisoner, having been previously charged with his wife's murder, of which he was acquitted.

Due to a lack of concrete evidence against him, the jury was unable to make a judgement which they could uphold beyond reasonable doubt. It was accepted at the time that Michelle may have inflicted the injury upon herself, following many years of self-harming.

The daughter of the couple has been suffering with post-traumatic stress disorder and as a result, hadn't spoken since the night of the attack. She broke her silence in September when brought face-to-face with Alana Elizabeth Noakes, Jackson's accomplice.

The court heard Jackson, 37, admit that he had snapped, after years of living in a domestic abuse situation with his wife. He had plunged a knife into her chest after a furious row between the three of them, where his wife had threatened him first with the knife. He had wept whilst saying he had been unable to take anymore.

Noakes admitted being infatuated with Jackson, having worked with him for many years. She confessed to administering the final blow with the knife, by pushing it further into the victim. Whilst it is acknowledged that the killing was probably not premeditated, Judge Cole, in his closing comments, highlighted how Michelle had been left to die by Noakes.

It was accepted that Jackson had also suffered a degree of post-traumatic stress disorder, causing him to blank out in relation to the details and memory of what he had done. The grounds of provocation were acknowledged in sentencing. Jackson was sentenced to five years in prison, for which he has already spent four months on remand. This means he will be eligible for parole in nearly two years' time.

Noakes was found guilty of voluntary manslaughter and for per-verting the course of justice, and sentenced to seven years which will commence in a secure hospital where her mental health can be worked with. "You are a danger to others," Judge Cole asserted in his final comments. "Your delusional thinking has ruined the lives of several people."

Noakes's husband, Lee Noakes, 39, was given a suspended sentence after being found guilty of perverting the course of justice. Judge Cole told him that "he lacked moral fibre and that his decision not to act sooner had made a terrible situation even worse."

The mother of the deceased, Susan Duffy was outside court today. She said, "I always knew my daughter would not have taken her own life in this way. I am devastated at what has happened and my only concern now is looking after my granddaughter, who I feel is the biggest victim in all this. I can't bring my daughter back but am relieved that at last, the people responsible are being punished for what they have done."

David Jackson, the defendant's brother, was also asked to give his reaction outside court. He said "My brother is not an evil man, he simply snapped with the stress of the conditions he was living in. He deserves sympathy and support, not a prison sentence. Had this case involved a woman, living within a domestic abuse situation instead of a man, the support and the outcome would probably have been very different. The system needs to change."

Reading Group Questions

1. Did the reference to 'behind closed doors' hold any significance for you? What has it come to mean in today's society?

2. According to statistics, 1.9 million adults aged 16 to 59 are victims of domestic abuse. Of these, 700,000 are male. Do you think this is a true reflection of today's society? Discuss whether and why you believe this figure is on the rise.

3. To what extent do you feel sympathetic towards Michelle?

4. How do the various forms of domestic abuse appear throughout the story?

5. Did the couple have a marriage worth saving? Is there anything that might have helped them?

6. The novel has occasionally used differing viewpoints for the duration of a chapter. How have you found this, as a reader?

7. What was the difference in tone and emotion when you compare the 'past' backstory to the unfolding 'present' story? How have they been linked together?

8. Who are the 'victims' and 'villains' in the novel? Where are the grey areas?

9. What are your thoughts in relation to 'blacking out' and 'becoming mute' in terms of memory retrieval?

10. How might the outcome have differed if Alana didn't exist?

11. How does your own emotion connect you to the story?

12. Discuss the relationship between Michelle and her daughter, Emily.

13. What do you think will become of Paul next?

14. To what extent do you agree or disagree with David's comments in the epilogue?

15. How can the effects of the trauma Emily has suffered be minimised as she grows older? What will she need?

16. How does society deal with the subject of self-harming? What do you think are the reasons behind it starting and continuing?

17. What could have happened within this story which could have brought about a happier ending?

Afterword

I'd like to thank my wonderful husband, Michael, for all his help and the faith he has in my writing. He acts as first reader for my early drafts and is an amazing support.

I am so grateful to my book cover designer, Darran Holmes, who understood exactly how I wanted my cover to look, and to photographer, Sue Coates, who took my 'author photo.'

Thanks to Martyn Bedford, the inspirational tutor who helped me shape this novel which I worked on throughout my MA in Creative Writing at Leeds Trinity University. Shortly after I graduated, 'The Man Behind Closed Doors,' was shortlisted for an international debut novelist prize, *The Luke Bitmead Prize*, which was hugely encouraging.

A special acknowledgement must go to my two beta readers, Jack Donovan and Jane Wing for early feedback on the story and to Steve Whitaker, (Journalist for the Yorkshire Times) for the wonderful and detailed critique he took the huge amount of time to give me. Thanks also to my friends and family for continuing to support and believe in me.

The experiences I've known in my own past relationships have shaped me as a person and indirectly offered much of the emotion and material for my writing. At the time, it was difficult, but now I am grateful for the empathy and personal growth it offered

Lastly, and importantly, to you, the reader. Thank you for taking the time to read this. I hope you enjoyed it.

Before You Go

I hope you have enjoyed this book. I would be hugely grateful if you could take the time to leave a review by returning to the retailer. By doing this, you are making an enormous difference to my career as an independent author.

You might also be interested in joining my 'keep in touch' list (on www.autonomypress.co.uk) so I can keep you posted of my news and forthcoming publications. When you join, you will receive a free copy of my short story collection, *How to get Away with Murder.*

This was my second novel. My next novel, 'Left Hanging' is now available. I have offered the opening chapter at the end of this book to whet your appetite.

If you haven't already read my first novel 'The last Cuckoo,' visit my Amazon page to find out more.

Thanks again for supporting my writing career. I hope you'll keep in touch!

Left Hanging - Chapter One

<u>Kerry</u>

"Ed. Put the BBC on. Listen to this!" I stare at the TV as I call to my husband who is in the next room. The front of Parkside, half a mile away, flashes onto the screen. The beautiful hotel we married in six years ago is cordoned off and is swarming with police. "They've found a man's body. He's hung himself apparently. Give it a rest, you two." I glance at the twins, fighting over a truck. "Gosh, he was only in his thirties. Gives me the creeps." I lower my voice. I'm talking to myself, as usual.

Ed isn't listening. He never is. There was a time when he'd have jumped up and come through when I called him. There was even a time when he'd have preferred to be sat in here with me. Most of the time he's in his own bloody world. I rise from the low sofa in the 'playroom,' past my squabbling five years olds and poke my head into the lounge. It's the only room in the house, apart from our bedroom, with any semblance of order – that's because the twins aren't allowed in. "Are you watching the news?"

Ed momentarily raises his quiet brown eyes from his computer. The early evening sunset floods through the bay window, illuminating the thinning hair at the top of his head. He used to get upset about this loss but he's learning to accept it.

"Why? Should I be?"

I really miss my husband. We've grown so far apart since the twins were born and the gulf widens all the time. I sit beside him and point the remote at the TV. "Oh, it's finished. That hotel we got married in. A man's hung himself there." I watch for a flicker of a reaction – that he's at least a tiny bit interested in something I'm telling him. "He was in one of the rooms." That should get his attention. He doesn't know what I know about his penchant for hotel rooms.

"Oh. Right." His voice is monotone and his gaze returns to the computer screen.

"Maybe we know him?"

"Maybe we know *who*?

"You never listen anymore Ed. *What is wrong with you?*"

"I'm sorry love. I need to get this finished." He reaches for the remote and clicks the TV off again. "I'll be with you soon love. Promise. I'll bath the boys and read them a story if you like. Give you half an hour to yourself."

"I want time with *you*, Ed. Why don't we ask your mum to come and sit with the boys after they've gone to bed?" I brighten at the thought, already mentally planning my outfit. "We've not eaten yet. We could go to that new restaurant we drove past last week. We've not had a night out together for ages."

"Sorry love. I'm wacked."

Whilst he's upstairs bathing the boys, I set about clearing their carnage. We bought our beautiful home whilst I was pregnant with them and I'd never felt happier. But from being somewhere relaxing and wonderful, home has become a place of work. I have progressed from being a newly-wed, then a radiant new mother, into a nag and a referee. Something has to give. I wish Ed had agreed with my suggestion of going out. I am still going try and make our evening special though.

We're becoming like house mates. Apart from once a week -

missionary position, usually on a Saturday. Life still goes on around us but it feels as though we don't join in anymore. As the earlier news report showed, life is short; we can *never* know what's around the corner.

"They're ready for you." Ed stretches his arms above his head and yawns as he walks into the kitchen towards the fridge. "I think that's earned me a beer. Smells good in here. What are you making?"

"It's the herby veg in the oven that you can smell and I've got us both a nice steak to go with it." I stand behind him at the fridge, putting my arms around his waist and kissing the back of his neck. It's as far as I can reach.

"Mummy!"

"I think you're wanted." He laughs as he swings around to face me. "I'll check the veg and get some pepper sauce on the go. I'm starving."

"Open a bottle of red too." I walk towards the door. It's good that he's having a little drink. Maybe it will relax him a little.

The twins are in their own rooms now and they're sleeping a bit better than they were when they shared. However, George is still catapulting around his room when I go in.

"Sleep time buster."

"But I'm not tired Mummy."

"You will be when you lie down. You need all your energy for swimming tomorrow."

I finally concede by allowing him to lie in his bed with his nightlight on and a book. I kiss his cheek then go in to see Alex. He's nearly asleep with his arms around his sheep. "Night-night sweetie pie." I kiss the top of his head, then head for the bathroom.

I hate the bathroom mirror. The lighting is so unflattering. *God I look a mess today!* No wonder Ed hardly looks at me anymore. I drag a comb through my mop, regretting for the zillionth time, having it cut shorter, then pull my make-up bag from the shelf for some urgent rectification. Next I swap my jeans for a skirt from the top of the ironing pile. I hurry downstairs in case Ed's got side-tracked from watching the dinner.

I'm pleased to find he's still on it. He's got the steaks in the pan and two large glasses of red are waiting on the table. I take a large sip from one then set about finding some candles.

"*Candles!*" What do we want candles for?" He laughs as I light them. "Are we planning a power cut?"

"Because we're not *just* husband and wife." I give him what I hope is a disparaging look. "The boys are in bed and we're having a lovely Saturday evening together."

He turns back to the steaks without saying anything. He hasn't noticed my skirt, my makeup or anything. He never does. He used to compliment me all the time.

"I wonder who the man is." I stab at my steak, disappointed it's a bit overdone. I won't say anything though.

"What man?"

"The one they found at our hotel."

"Kerry! Do we have to talk about that whilst we're eating?"

"S'pose not." I take another sip of wine. He's right. It's not really the time or the place to discuss someone who's topped themselves. I look at my husband in the candlelight. He's never known how handsome he is with his angular features and long eye lashes framing his eyes. The boys have got his eyes too, which I'm glad about. Mine are piggy and deep set. My self-confidence is diminishing all the time. I guess it comes from having a husband who doesn't notice me anymore.

"Stop staring at me," he laughs, drinking his wine too. "You're making me nervous."

"I love you." I put my fork down and reach for his hand.

"You too. Now let me eat my dinner." He pulls his hand away and picks his knife up."

He always used to say *I love you too.* Now it's just *you too.* And he *never* says it first.

The rest of the meal is spent talking about the boys. Then he snaps the big light on. "I'll load the dishwasher. You chill for a bit."

"Can't we chill together?" *God, he's become hard work.* "The dishwasher can wait, can't it?"

"Might as well get it done."

"I'll go and park my arse on the sofa then. Wait for you."

I click the TV on as I pass it. The local news is on again and they're repeating the story about the man at our hotel. I don't normally take much notice of the news but this time I do as they've added CCTV of him entering the hotel through revolving doors. It's quite grainy and the image hasn't been captured face on.

"I don't think I'll be late to bed tonight." Ed flops beside me on the sofa. "Shall we put a film on?"

"Can't we spend some time *together?*" I snuggle into him.

"We are doing. Choose your film. Anything you like." He clicks the TV onto Netflix then hands the remote to me.

I settle on *Passenger.* It's got everything. Romance for me and sci-fi for him. We went to see it at the cinema together. It was in its last week so we had the whole cinema to ourselves. We'd even sat in the back row. Maybe the film will draw us a bit closer. Ed's become so distant. I just want him back.

I'm pleased when he puts his arm around me as we watch the film. I sip at my second glass of wine, feeling a little more content with the warmth and the weight of his arm. Thirty minutes in, his breathing slows and I realise I'm watching the film alone.

"Ed." I shake him before he becomes too far gone. "Ed. Come on. Let's go to bed."

"Um. Yes. OK love." He stretches and gets to his feet. "You go up. I'll turn off and lock up."

I'm sick of him calling me *'love'* all the time. It makes me feel a hundred years old. Taking the remainder of the wine with me, I head up the first flight of stairs to check on the boys. I switch off George's night light and slide the book from under his arm. I lightly kiss his forehead. Alex has kicked his duvet off so I cover him back up and kiss him too. I climb the next flight of steps to our room, the other room of the house that's usually a child-free zone. That is unless we end up with one or both boys in our bed.

It's my favourite room in the house. All cream and silver with a chandelier above the bed and mirrored wardrobes – I wanted a 'boudoir' feel to it. I pull my sexiest nightie from the drawer beside my bed. It's the red, slinky number Ed bought me before I became pregnant. It's a bit snug on me now so I keep my stomach sucked in. I've started the gym again – I desperately want to drop a dress size. Maybe Ed will fancy me again.

His expression is hard to read when he walks into our bedroom. "What are you wearing that for?"

"You know. I thought ..."

"Sorry love. I'm knackered." He sits on the edge of the bed and starts unbuttoning his shirt.

"But it's Saturday." I sink onto the bed, reaching over to touch his shoulder. "What's happening to us Ed?"

"Nothing love. You saw me downstairs. I can hardly keep my eyes open."

"You need to start being at home more." I tug my nightie back over my head, hoping that the sight of me naked in the mirrored wardrobes might just do *something* for him. He doesn't look up but peels his socks off instead. "Through the week, I mean. You're never here. It's no wonder you're always tired."

"There's always tomorrow morning."

I'm stalling before putting my PJ's on, wanting him to look at me.

"What for?"

"You know."

"I'll just lock the boys in their rooms, shall I?"

Ed sighs and pads across the bedroom to the en-suite, closing the door behind him. I sigh too and swing my legs into bed. This has to change. I will make sure it does. No matter what it takes, I will draw him back to me. Make him want me again.

Available at Amazon

About the Author

The domestic thrillers I write shine a light into the darkness that can exist within marital and family relationships. I have been no stranger to turbulent times myself, and this has provided some of the raw material for my novels. I have a sign on my wall saying 'careful or you'll end up in my novel' and this is definitely true!

I am a born 'n' bred Yorkshirewoman, and a mum of two grown up sons.I can offer living proof that life begins at the age of forty, as this is when I decided to escape my unhappy marriage. Recently I have married again and found been able to find my own 'happy ever after.'

This is not something you will find in my novels though! I think that we thriller writers are amongst the nicest people you could meet because we pour all our darkness into our books – it's the romance writers you've got to watch...

I plan to release four novels per year and if you'd like to be kept in the loop about new books and special offers, you can join my 'keep in touch list' by visiting www.autonomypress.co.uk. You will also receive a free collection of short stories, 'How to get Away with Murder.'

You can connect with me on:

- https://www.mariafrankland.co.uk
- https://twitter.com/writermaria_f
- https://www.facebook.com/writermariafrank
- https://www.autonomypress.co.uk

Also by Maria Frankland

Thanks so much for your interest in my work! All my books are available on Amazon.

The Last Cuckoo
A compelling story that shows how home can be the darkest and most dangerous place to be

Anna Hardaker is following you ...

This seemingly innocent Tweet fills Jamie Hardaker with confusion and fear. After all, his mother Anna has been dead for nearly three weeks.

What follows is an orchestrated Twitter campaign to lead those Anna loved, and didn't love so much, to the truth behind her "accidental" death.

Don't Call Me Mum

A gripping page-turner of family anguish and a mother's solitary fight against the system

Tom is hyperactive, with severe behavioural issues. In infancy, he screams all night. As a toddler he is destructive and fearless. At school, he is disruptive and lacking in concentration. As he grows, so does the havoc, reaching a crescendo in his teenage years.

In her quest for support, Sarah consults every specialist available to her, to be met with blame and indifference. This memoir, which tells the story of a mother and son ostracised, challenges the 'I blame the parents' view. It is a 'must-read' for any parent who struggles and feels alone.

Left Hanging
Within a marriage can be the sweetest, or the darkest place to be

Ed and Kerry Huntington-Barnes have an idyllic life, with their five-year-old twins, successful careers, a luxurious house and an affluent lifestyle. Yet the secrets they're harbouring force their separation.

Kerry is fighting her own demons, amongst which is the knowledge that she is the wrong gender for her husband to ever truly love her.

Parallel to this it the death of a local man, Russell Lawson, which affects both Ed and Kerry in different ways. Will his widow Davina, and the other shadows that surround their separation and Russell's death, destroy their lives, and their sons' lives even further?

This is a story that portrays the darkness that can exist inside marriage and the hatred that can linger amongst families that are supposed to love each other.

The Yorkshire Dipper

How many lives will be lost before something is done?

The River Alder bodes a notorious threat. The local police are over-stretched and under-resourced.

With each life that is pulled into the river's depths, journalist Lauren Holmes becomes more suspicious and more determined to bring the truth to the surface.

Her police sergeant fiancé is well-placed to help her. Yet he is committed to maintaining police reputation and is happy to accept each death recorded as 'drunken misadventure.'

Can Lauren get to the bottom of the deaths without risking her own 'accident?'

Out 3.2.21 - Available for pre-order now

Made in the USA
Coppell, TX
21 September 2020